Luminaries and Legionaries

Rose Gravestone

DKS Publishing LLC

To the girlies who feel too deep and love too hard…

I created a duo of an empath and obsessed anti-hero just for you.

Author's Note

Hello, lovely reader! Welcome to Luminaries and Legionaries, book one in the sensual and twisty Greywood Legionaries series.

Please be advised that this book contains some dark and triggering content. If any of the following triggers bother you, this book probably won't be for you.

- Dub-con.

- Mentions and depictions of child abuse (flashbacks to abuse).

- Alpha-hole, domineering hero.

Dorian is a character with questionable morals and a skewed perspective on the world. Only proceed if you enjoy your MMC's morally grey.

Contents

Chapter One
Mira Greene

I 've always enjoyed going on night hikes in forests. It's appealing for a wide variety of reasons. First, there are no people around to stress me out. Second, the clear Vermont sky offers the most beautiful, picturesque view of the stars. On especially clear nights, I can even see the faint halo of the Milky Way glittering above me. Finally, the most fascinating forest creatures come out at night--creatures that inspire fear in most people, and with good reason. Yet, they have never once harmed me, despite their predisposition to do so.

After all, I'm human; most animals that have been hunted to the point of near extinction in these parts should either hate humans enough to attack them or run from us all together.

Despite all odds, I find myself sitting on the forest floor, my back leaned against an age-old oak tree. Three adorable wolf pups clamber over my lap, yipping and pawing at each other. The patriarch and alpha of the pack lazes beside me, head lying on his front paws. He emits a low, contented rumble as I stroke his rich black fur. The mother of the pups trots around me, playfully tussling with other members of the pack, her reddish-brown fur gleaming under the moon's silvery glow.

I've been told often, repeatedly, and by very reliable sources that I should *not* go out to seek the company of wild animals. The thing is, I never *have* to seek them out. They're the ones who come to me.

Maybe it's because I'm planning on becoming a vet; maybe it's because I've always been an irritatingly sensitive soul. Perhaps it's attributed to the positive energy I once had before it was beaten out of me. Whatever the case is, I can't go out into the wild *without* finding myself confronted by creatures of nature.

"I'll have to go soon," I tell the alpha. "I have my early-morning classes tomorrow. Please don't eat a hole through my shirt this time." While the alpha has never once harmed or bitten me, even when I was certain he would, he has no problem destroying my clothes in an effort to get me to remain with his pack. I think he might regard me as a member of it.

The alpha's head lifts from the ground and he turns around to give me a narrow-eyed look, letting out a growl of warning. It's as if he's saying, "*stay right the fuck where you are, and don't you dare stop petting me.*"

First time he gave me this look, I nearly shit myself, thinking that he'd decided I was prey. Four months later, I understand that he simply doesn't want me to go.

"I come back every week," I remind him. "Twice a week, usually. I always bring treats that I home-bake. That's gotta give me some brownie points, right?"

He licks his front muzzle and stands, turning around to face me. When I'm standing, the alpha comes up to my waist; seated, he towers above me in a way that would be intimidating to anyone with a modicum of sanity.

The same reliable sources who tell me to stay the hell away from wild animals have also told me that they're quite certain I have little sanity, which I happen to agree with. The alpha butts his head against the backpack lying beside me, silently requesting more food.

I try not to bring too much to spoil the pack, since I don't want these wolves to *rely* on me for their meals. They need to preserve their instinct to hunt. But, considering the deer carcass I found about a mile away, I know that these fellows *do* know how to hunt. They also happen to enjoy the peanut butter treats I bake for them.

"One more," I tell him, unzipping my backpack. "Then I really do need to go." It's nearly midnight, and it'll take me the better part of an hour to drive back to my school's campus.

As soon as I withdraw the plastic container filled with treats from my bag, the pups start yapping, whining, and diving for it. One of the pups nips my shoulder, making me wince. The alpha releases a bone-chilling growl, picks up the pup who bit me by the scruff, and tosses him aside. The pup promptly rolls onto his back, showing his belly with a whine, effectively submitting to his patriarch. The alpha releases another low growl, eyeing the rest of his kids with his ears pinned, warning them not to get rowdy.

I don't know what I did to get this wolf to be so protective over me, but he is. He's smacked down his pack members more than once when they started being rough with me. He nearly killed a younger wolf when she drew my blood with a play-scratch that didn't feel very playful.

"Thank you," I tell him, withdrawing a cookie and setting it on the ground in front of me. The wolf's ears perk right up as he leans down to sniff the treat and gobbles it up.

I feed the two pups that now lie over my legs next; I chuck a third cookie at the final pup, who gets back on all fours to accept the offering.

Naturally, the six other wolves in the pack come barreling toward me at the scent of food. I toss the remaining four cookies in the distance, smiling as the wolves butt each other out of the way and start scrapping over the treats.

I sling the empty container into my bag, stand, and stretch my arms over my head. The alpha promptly bites down on the loose material of my shirt, giving me a look that warns me to stay exactly where I am. He doesn't flatten his ears or growl in earnest; instead, he releases a frustrated whine.

"I know," I tell him. "I'd like to stay here too, but we've discussed this before. I need to get back to *my* home while you stay in yours. How am I going to become a vet so I can *truly* help you if I start missing classes?"

The alpha releases another whine and gives a sharp tug on my shirt. A ripping sound follows, and I sigh. "I'm running out of shirts, my friend. You're racking up quite the bill." I bury my hands in his coarse fur, giving his neck a scratch. "Come, now. You know how it goes. If you want, you can walk me down the mountain. Sound fair?"

The alpha chuffs and steps back. He lets out a low noise that gets the attention of the rest of his pack. They yip, bark, and whine in response before returning to fighting over the cookies.

With a final low rumble, the alpha turns around and trots to his pups. He starts to groom them and paw at them. Apparently, today will not be one of the days he walks me down the mountain. That's fine by me—last time he did, he actually tried to get in the passenger seat of my car.

Rubbing at the little nip on my shoulder, I sigh and roll my eyes, thanking whatever higher power exists that I'm up to date on my rabies shots. None of these wolves are infected, but as a magnet for wild animals, it pays to be safe.

When I'm far enough away from the wolf pack, I grab my phone out of my bag and power it on, checking my messages. Cara, my close friend and roommate, sent me two texts about an hour ago. There's another from Valerie, my other roommate and good friend, which was sent at about 10 p.m. Both girls texted me some variant of *let us know that you're not dead when you're back to civilization.*

Cara knows about the wolf pack that's half-adopted me, and she delights in frequently reminding me that I'm insane for spending time with them. Valerie is also aware, though I don't think she cares much—she's more reclusive than I am. I shoot texts to both women, letting them know I'm making my way back to dorms. They're probably asleep by now, but they still expect me to text back.

Pocketing my phone, I tense when I hear something in the distance. Not too far away, a rustling of leaves is coupled with labored breaths, piercing the silence. It's not the wolves; they wouldn't stalk me, they'd outright barrel after me. And those exhalations... they don't sound *animal*, but *human*.

I palm the switchblade tucked into my belt and pull the mini bear-spray off the keychain that hangs from my backpack. I never go on night hikes unarmed, thought I've never had to actually *use* the weapons I bring. The knife has only ever cut stems of pretty flowers I want to bring back with me, and the bear spray hasn't even been tested.

"Deeper," a low, masculine voice in the distance murmurs. "You gotta go deeper than that if you want to get the job done."

Jesus Christ. There must be a couple who decided to come to the forest and fuck. That explains the panted breaths and weird commentary. I'm not keen to stick around like a peeping tom, so I hurry forward, trying to keep my stride as quiet as possible.

That's when my foot catches on a rock, and I go tumbling head over foot, getting scraped up by sticks and pebbles before crashing with a loud thud and yelped, "*Shit.*"

So much for being inconspicuous. I push myself to my hands and knees, letting out a low groan of irritation at the pain radiating through my shoulder. I'm going to have one hell of a bruise tomorrow. I already feel it forming.

"What the fuck was that?" the very same voice who was telling someone to go deeper questions. "Did you hear that? There's someone out here."

Another male voice responds, his words too faint for me to discern. The back of my neck prickles with an oncoming sense of danger, giving a chilling warning that something deeply sinister is unfolding.

I didn't accidentally bypass a couple having sex. No, something darker is going on here. Any time my neck gets this prickling pins-and-needles sensation, it's always preceded me stumbling head-first into danger.

The first time was when I was only six.

The last time was when I left my stepfather's house and got the fuck away from that monster.

I have no interest in landing myself in more trouble, which is precisely why I push to my feet and start hurrying down the mountain. These woods are familiar to me; I've navigated them countless times, so I don't need a trail to guide me. The moon, stars, and my instincts are enough.

The tingling on my neck swiftly morphs to a burn as I hear heavy footfalls following me. Someone, *more than one person,* is chasing me. My hear trate speeds up, sweat gathers on my brow, and every finely honed instinct I possess tells me that I need to get the hell out of here *immediately.*

The footsteps grow progressively closer, and my breaths quickly turn into pants—I am *not* a runner. I attempted to join track and field in high school and didn't make it past tryouts.

"Hey! Stop!" A male voice calls, *far* too close for comfort.

Instead of listening to him, I try to speed up, but it's futile. A moment later, a hand grabs my arm, and I find myself being ripped backwards with such force my shoulder pops out of its socket. Shooting pain eats through my arm, chest, and even *back* as my body tells me in every way possible that something's horribly wrong. I bite my lip against the noise of pain that tries to crawl up my throat as I'm promptly tossed to the ground, jarring my shoulder. A *gigantic* male form hovers over me. My backpack tumbles a few feet away, out of reach.

Tree-trunk thighs straddle my waist as the man descends. Firm hands pin my arms to my side, and this time, a small whimper does escape me, a product of pain and the *tremendous* fear that curdles my stomach. I stare, wide-eyed, up into two bright eyes, a peculiar shade of green. Verdant, I think. A flashlight is shined in my face, not by the man straddling me, but by someone else. I squint and turn away from the sudden, blinding light.

"What. *The fuck*. Are you doing here?" the man above me growls.

"Nothing!" I squeak.

A forearm lands on my throat. No pressure is applied, but the threat is very, *very* clear: if I say the wrong thing, this guy will choke me. Then... *then*, he might bury me along with whoever else he was digging a hole for.

When he told someone to go deeper, it wasn't sex talk. As well as I know my own name, I know two facts about the man pinning me to the cold forest ground. First of all, he's a killer. Second of all, I just stumbled on him disposing of a body.

I often wish I didn't have the intuition I do. It used to break my heart to realize just how many bad people there are in this world. Now, it all feels like more of the same. I've accepted that there are no truly good people left—or perhaps they never existed.

Now I've been caught by someone who isn't just a bad person, but a bad person who might kill me. I squeeze my eyes shut, turning my head to the side.

"Hey," green-eyes snaps. The word isn't friendly; it's threatening. "Fucking *look* at me."

Breath shuddering out of me, I force myself to comply. I slowly pry my eyes open and look into the face of the man who might be the harbinger of my death.

Several things strike me at once. He's beautiful; the sort of otherworldly masculine beauty that shouldn't exist, especially not on an individual like this one. The flashlight casts a glow on the side of his face, and it illuminates features that are unreasonably stunning, especially for a killer. Dark sable hair, disheveled from his little run. *Glowing* verdant eyes that glimmer in the night. Angular chin with a small cleft; cheekbones that could cut diamond.

I never thought death would wear such a pretty face. I suppose it's not the worst thing I could see before I go.

I crane my neck sideways to look at whatever dick is standing nearby and shining a flashlight in my face. Verdant Eyes removes his forearm from my neck, only to take my chin in an iron grip and force me to face him. "Don't look at him," he says warningly. "Look at me, and kindly explain what in the actual *fuck* you're doing here tonight. *Who sent you?*"

Sent me? If there was any doubt that he was up to something criminal, his words dispel it. "Nobody sent me," I say in as calm a voice as I can manage, which comes out surprisingly steady. "I come here a few times a week for a night hike to clear my mind. There's a wolf pack I visit nearby."

The words spill forth in a frantic bid to convince them that I saw nothing and know nothing. The former is true. The latter isn't, but I don't feel like explaining my uncanny intuition or my unsettling knack for knowing things about people that I wish I didn't. There's no way to articulate it, and I don't want to make this guy feel threatened.

"Bullshit," Flashlight Guy says. "You tucked tail and ran—pretty fucking poorly, I might add. You've got a knife on your belt. Why the *fuck* would you need a knife for a night hike? No, somebody sent you to spy on us. *Who?*"

"Check my texts," I squeak. "They'll confirm what I've said. I didn't see anything, I swear. I heard someone say *go deeper* and assumed people were up here to fuck, which is why I was hasty to get away."

Verdant Eyes tilts his head to the side as he appraises me. "I know you," he says after a long beat.

"No you don't," I say hurriedly.

That makes him release a dark chuckle. "Yes, I do. Mira. Mira Greene, right? I've seen you around Greywood."

Fuck, fuck, fuck. I *do* go to Greywood University, but I don't recall ever seeing *this* male around. Then again, I tend not to pay attention to faces; a skill I learned when I started getting overwhelmed as a child. Looking into faces serves as a direct line to seeing a person's true nature, and I am *sick* of learning things I wish I didn't.

"I ran into you at the library once," he goes on. "I helped you get a book from a high shelf."

"What?" I breathe. I don't *ever* remember seeing this guy before.

My befuddlement appears to irritate him. "You don't remember? I asked you for your number."

Flashlight Guy releases a snort of disbelief. "You did *what?* Asked a *girl* for her phone number?"

"Shut up," Verdant Eyes snaps at Flashlight Guy. Back to me: "You said you have texts to prove you're here for a hike?"

"Doesn't matter if she's here for a hike," Flashlight Guy says. "Even if she wasn't sent by anyone, she saw something. If she didn't see something, she heard something. That's a loose end."

I have a dreadful feeling that these guys are not the sort to let loose ends walk away. "What I heard was someone saying *go deeper*," I say, trying to keep the tremor from my voice. "I'm not a fan of watching public sex, so I tucked tail. As far as I'm concerned, the two of you could've been fucking under the cover of darkness. I heard nothing important. Please let me go—I guarantee I won't say anything."

"Maybe you *didn't* hear or see anything," Flashlight Guy says, "but then we chased you. You're currently pinned down on cold soil. You could report that. If you report that, it could cause someone to take a closer look at us. They won't find anything, of course, but I'd prefer not to be under investigation. Investigations are headaches, and I don't react nicely to potential headaches."

"I am *not* going to report you," I say firmly. "What I want is to go home so I can get up in time for my 9 a.m. class. I already stayed way too late with the wolf pack."

"Okay," Verdant Eyes says. "Everyone calm the fuck down. Mira, I'm going to back up enough for you to grab your phone. Is it in your back pocket?"

Maybe I'll still get out of this alive. Flashlight Guy doesn't seem to want to let me go, but Verdant Eyes is slightly more reasonable, even though I've shirked him by not remembering him. If he asked me for my phone number, he probably liked me; if he likes me, he might hesitate to see me as a loose end. I usually have no problem gauging someone's emotional state—in fact, I can't seem to *stop*—but right now, my fear is overwhelming my ability to get a good sense for him.

"Mira?" he prompts, arching an eyebrow.

I clear my throat. "It's in my back right pocket, and I can't move my right arm. I'll need to sit up to grab it."

His brows furrow. "What's wrong with your right arm?"

"I think my shoulder's dislocated. Not sure yet, but it hurts a lot."

Flashlight Guy scoffs. "Bullshit. If it was dislocated, you'd be crying and screaming in pain."

I contemplate informing him that I have experienced *far* worse pain than a mere dislocation, so a shoulder out of its socket is very manageable, but decide against it. He won't care, and I don't feel like talking about my past. "Okay."

"She could lunge at your throat with a knife," Flashlight Guy comments. "She has one on her belt."

Verdant eyes runs his hands along my belt, swiftly unclipping my knife and tossing it toward Flashlight Guy. "I'll pull back. You'll sit up and grab your phone. Don't make any sudden moves. Agreed?"

I nod. "Yeah, agreed."

He does exactly as he said he would, leaning back. I prop my left hand on the ground to push myself up, grimacing at the pain shooting down my right arm, then awkwardly reach for my phone with my left hand and wriggle my ass until I've managed to retrieve it. Before I can enter the password, Verdant Eyes snatches it from my hands. "Password?" he asks—*demands.*

I frown. "Can I put it in?"

"No. It wasn't a question. You are treading on *extremely* thin ice, Mira. I'd highly recommend you cooperate."

I swallow my pride and tell him the six digit code. He spends several long minutes tapping around my phone, probably going through my texts, social media messages, and who knows what else. Meanwhile, I try to move my right arm around without much success—it's *defi-*

nitely dislocated. I do *not* feel like paying the medical bill to get it fixed, so I'll need to ask Valerie to help me relocate it. She's a pre-med major, so she'll probably be able to help.

That is, if *I make it home tonight.*

"She's telling the truth," Verdant Eyes says. "There are texts with her friends confirming her story." He looks back at me. "The fuck were you doing with a wolf pack?"

I lift my functional shoulder in an awkward shrug. "Animals like me."

He gazes at me for a beat. "Huh. Okay. I'm going to talk to my friend for a few minutes. You're going to stay right where you are and keep quiet."

I swallow. "Are you going to kill me?"

"What makes you think that?" Flashlight Guy asks suspiciously. "If you didn't see anything, that is."

"I inferred," I respond. "Your line of questioning has been very particular."

"You're unnervingly calm," Verdant Eyes observes.

"I'm really not," I assure him. "This just isn't my first life or death scenario. I've learned to dissociate."

Flashlight Guy releases a disbelieving grunt.

Verdant Eyes frowns, staring at me in silence.

After several beats, he comes to a stand, grabbing my backpack and swinging it over his shoulder. Pointing at me, he instructs, "Stay. You move, we'll assume you're a threat. Got it?"

I smile grimly. "Trust me, I'm not going anywhere."

Chapter Two
Dorian Acheron

"**S**he's going to be a problem," Connor says the moment we've stepped out of Mira's earshot.

I drop her backpack on the ground and hold up her phone. "I scanned it. Nothing in recently deleted messages or calls indicate that she's been sent by someone."

"She could have a burner," Connor points out. "She could be here on a rival's orders. Our operation is relatively new. The boss will not like that we've already fucked up."

"We didn't fuck up," I correct him. "This is a wrong place wrong time scenario. Besides, do you really think Sergei fucking Novikov would be happy if he found out we killed a girl who might or might not have seen something?"

"If she's a threat, yes," Connor responds, folding his arms. "You're protective of her. You know her?"

I glance over my shoulder at Mira, who looks a little lost as she sits on the ground. *Platinum hair reminiscent of a Targaryen; piercing, clear grey eyes; tiny form with enticing, delicious curves and creamy, unblemished skin.* I saw her in the library precisely two months ago. Earbuds nestled in her ears, she was standing on tiptoes, reaching for a book. It was her hair that got my attention—I couldn't stop imagining what it'd look like coiled around my fist or fanned out on my pillow. *Then* I saw her eyes, and I had to have her. Except... she barely seemed to notice me. When I helped her with her book, it seemed like she was gazing right through me. I thought she was on drugs for a second, but there weren't any signs of that. No dilated pupils, no disoriented movements. She was stone cold sober.

She intrigued me, so I dug into her a bit. She's nineteen years old and already on track to graduate next year as an animal science major. Mira enrolled in Greywood with a year of college credits already under her belt and completed a summer semester last year, propelling her further ahead. The girl seems addicted to school.

She doesn't appear to have any friends aside from her dorm roommates and rarely explores Greywood apart from visits to the library and campus café. I've watched her a few times on campus; unless she's with one of her roommates, she always has her headphones in, and often seems lost in her own world. Daydreaming, maybe. For some reason, I haven't been able to fucking *stop* watching her. There's something... *compelling* about her, for lack of a better word.

"Know of her," I say. "I've dug into her before; she's not involved with any of our rivals. She's innocent, Connor."

"How much are you willing to bet on her?" Connor questions. "Because if we let her go and she talks, that'll mean problems. None of us like problems, and our boss fucking *hates* problems."

I give Connor a hard look. "You're acting like we've never done ops together. If you'll recall, I am the first to advocate for tying up loose ends. She is not a loose end, she's an innocent."

"An innocent you want to fuck," Connor observes. "Have you?"

"No."

"Shame." He casts her a lingering look, tilting his head to the side. "Very pretty."

"Don't," I say harshly. "Do not. I've got dibs."

He arches an eyebrow at me. "Oh? I thought you hadn't made a move."

Because I haven't been able to find a way to get close to her. I knew when I first saw her that I'd have Mira. I simply haven't had the opportunity to ease my way into her life. Something about the idea of Connor hurting her rubs me the very, *very* wrong way. Our legion will do a lot of fucked up shit, but we will *not* hurt innocents. Even our boss made that abundantly clear to us.

"Not yet," I grunt.

Connor sighs. "We gotta figure out what to do with her. Seamus is almost done with disposal. He'll be here soon, and he'll ask what the plan is. We need to have it figured out by then. I want to go home. It's been a long night."

I work my jaw. "We can call Sergei and ask for instructions. He'll be expecting our call, anyways." He orders and supervises our missions from afar.

Connor's brows lift. "You want to run this all the way to the top of the flagpole?"

"Better than killing her."

"You've killed women before," Connor says, brows drawn. "What's the problem here? You really want to fuck her that bad?"

"I killed women who were *menaces* before," I correct. "Not nineteen-year-old girls that keep to themselves. I told you; I've dug into her. I don't think she's going to be a problem. So, yeah, I'd rather call Sergei and ask for directions than end up reporting that there were *two* dead bodies to dispose of tonight."

Connor considers me for a long moment. A lot of people think I'm a sociopath, which is entirely inaccurate. I feel plenty of emotions and have empathy, I just don't let my feelings *control* me. And the people who think *I'm* bad have never run into Connor. Not only does he have the build of Thor, he is *actually* a sociopath. Killing a witness would be nothing to him—just a calculated move to keep our legion and operation safe.

To pass the time, I squat down and zip open Mira's backpack, checking through it. There's nothing remarkable to be found; an empty container that smells faintly like peanut butter, AirPods, a few notebooks.

"Fine," Connor says once I'm done. "Call him. We'll do what he says."

I pocket Mira's phone, pull my own out, and dial the infamous Bratva Pakhan himself. Not long ago, the Russian mob boss decided it was time to branch out from his home in the motherland and set down some roots in America. He has several businesses here, but no criminal dealings. He crossed paths with my unofficial legion on one of his state visits and was impressed with our skills, so he offered to sponsor us. Usually, I'd say fuck no to having a boss, but Sergei is an exception. He makes working in the criminal underground look like an art form; graceful, precise, lethal, *beautiful*.

Sergei picks up after three rings. "Status?"

"Mission complete. One complication."

A pause comes over the line. Connor walks up to me, leaning close so he can listen to both sides of the conversation.

I hear Sergei's muffled voice, presumably speaking to someone nearby. A moment later, he's back with me. "Give me the overview." His thick Russian accent seems more prominent than ever, making his order ring with command.

I tell him in clear, concise detail about our situation with Mira. She saw nothing. She heard what she thought was sex—*hilarious. If I was fucking, there'd be a lot more noise*—and ran. Connor and I went after her, detaining her. She was compliant with our requests and seems to sincerely want to forget about this.

Sergei's silent for two minutes after I finish, during which I feel my heart rate speed up. I might not know the girl personally, but I've learned plenty about her, and she does *not* deserve to die. Certainly not before I've had a thorough taste of her.

"I see," Sergei says. "What do you think is the best course of action?"

I know the words are a test. He wants to see what my response is and judge me off it. If I lie, he'll know; the man is like a walking lie detector. He'd be able to tell even over the phone.

"I don't want to get rid of an innocent," I say, then allow my logic to take over. I distance myself from the intrigue Mira inspires, and think over the situation with sheer calculation, shedding my veil of emotions so I can see the facts clearly. "Letting her go right off the bat won't be advisable, either. She's shaken and possibly hurt. She might tell someone about this after she's come back to her senses. Better to watch her for a while until we know."

Another pause ensues. "You have regard for her," Sergei says, sounding faintly surprised.

"No—"

"Not a question, soldier, I can hear it in your tone. Do *not* lie to me, *ever*." He pauses, letting his unspoken threat sink in like a blade into flesh. "Do you know her?"

Connor smirks; I glare at him.

"Not really, sir. We've run into each other before. She intrigued me, so I looked into her."

"Have you been intimate?" Sergei questions.

"No. She doesn't even remember me."

"What have you learned about her in your... *looking into her?*"

"Full name is Miranda Greene. She's nineteen years old. Animal science major, several semesters ahead on studies. Reclusive, doesn't have many friends, but enough people know her that her disappearance would raise eyebrows."

"Is she malleable? Will she listen to orders?"

"Don't know, sir."

"Find out. Keep her close for a period of one week. Put her in your house. Better yet, in *your* room. Work out whatever interest you have while ensuring she's trustworthy. Earlier, you said she might be hurt. What did you mean?"

"She said she had a dislocated shoulder."

"She said or she *does*?"

Connor leans close to say, "Grown men with a shoulder dislocation aren't able to keep down their yells of agony. There's a reason it's an effective torture method. If she was *that* hurt, she'd be bawling."

"You'd be surprised," Sergei responds coolly. "Shock does interesting things to people. Connor, a word?"

Connor takes my phone from me and walks away. Whatever Sergei says to him makes his features tighten. After two minutes, he says his goodbyes and hangs up.

"Verdict?" I ask.

"She's your charge. Watch her closely. Keep an eye on her, bug her, keep track of her communications. And figure out if you want to keep her."

Something in my chest tightens. Part of me leaps at the prospect of *keeping* her. The first image that floats through my mind is a particularly dirty one; Mira, collared and tied to my bed, waiting to take my cock like a good girl. Sobbing through an orgasm. Taking everything I'm fucking *aching* to give her.

Mira, in my bed for longer than a week.

The prospect is ludicrous. I don't know her beyond some surface level facts I've gathered. I shouldn't *want* to know her, yet I do. The monster within me reaches for her, and that fucker wants her for *keeps*.

"What do you mean?" I ask.

"I mean, Sergei noticed you sounded protective of her. If you want to keep her, that'll be the easiest route to ensure her loyalty. If you don't, find her pressure points and be ready to press hard on them. He'll want to know your choice at the end of the week." He shakes his head. "Fucking ridiculous. I should've shot her when—"

"Do *not*. Finish. That fucking sentence," I warn. "You only get so many passes for being unfeeling. You need to have a code."

"My code is no loose ends. And that right there," he points at me, "is why Sergei asked about you wanting to keep her. Figure it out. One way or the other, she's gotta stay silent."

Seamus chooses that moment to appear in the distance. He strolls up to us, his steps silent, a black duffle bag swung over his shoulder. He looks between me and Connor with arctic-blue eyes, then frowns.

"You gents care to let me in on what's going on?" he questions smoothly.

His British accent is suave as hell, something that drops panties and brings blushes to masses of girls wherever he goes. He looks and speaks like an aristocrat, but Seamus Archibald the Third is from a line of title-only nobility. His father has a gambling problem and is shirked by the upper class; his mother refuses to show her face in society out of shame. Seamus fled to the states for college to get away from them and found out that he's pretty handy with a rifle shortly thereafter.

"Yeah," I say. "We're going to have a guest for a bit."

I give Seamus the breakdown. He proves to be *far* more accepting of the situation than Connor. That's Seamus, though; he's content to go with the flow. Happy to seem like he's there to help, while in reality he's thinking about a dozen ways to separate your head from your body.

"Got it," he says amiably. "I'll be nice." He looks over to Connor, who's frowning.

"I'll stay out of it unless you fuck up," Connor concedes.

Which means that I'll have the opportunity I've been searching for to get close to little Mira, even though it's under the sort of circumstances that might have her despising me forever. If she despises me, I'll need to press on her pressure points. I'd prefer not to have to do that, so I suppose I'll now be undertaking the unenviable task of somehow getting her to like me. After I chased her down like an animal, pinned her to the forest ground, and hurt her. *Lovely.*

"You finish up?" I ask Seamus.

He nods. "Yup. All's done. Shall we see to our new guest?"

"Connor, head down to the car," I tell him. "You've already scared her. That won't help matters." With a grunt, Connor takes the duffle bag from Seamus, turns, and stalks off. Mira watches him go with wide eyes.

"Take it easy," I tell Seamus. "This'll be sensitive."

I affect a casual posture and expression as I stalk back over to Mira, trying to present myself as unthreatening. She watches me closely, as if I'm a lion preparing to pounce.

"Hallo, love," Seamus greets, stopping beside me. "You look positively dreadful. What happened to your shirt? It looks like a piece of it was torn off by a wild animal."

"Hello, Brit. My shirt *was* torn by a wild animal. Long story." She looks back at me. "Am I going to be staying here or going home alive?"

Seamus lets out a chuckle, while I shake my head. "Neither. Nobody's going to hurt you, but we would like to keep you around for a bit. You heard incriminating things, and it's important to be sure that you won't tell anyone about tonight."

"I won't," she promises. "I'm exceptionally good at keeping things to myself."

There's a weight behind her words that makes my brows furrow. Almost as if she already has experience keeping her mouth shut. *Interesting.*

"Then you won't be our guest for long," I say. "Just for a week or so."

"I have absolutely no reason to trust what you're saying," she observes. "How do I know you won't hurt or kill me if I upset you?"

Excellent question, spoken in a surprisingly calm tone. "You'll be under my protection. Nobody will hurt you. You'll see that for yourself." I crouch down in front of her, my eyes drawn to a small tear in her shirt that kind of looks like teeth marks. There's a bit of blood right near her collar bone. "What happened there?" I tip my chin at the spot.

She glances down. "One of the wolf pups got nippy. The alpha put him in his place. They're still learning at that age."

At first, I thought her wolf story was bullshit; then I read her texts, and now I see the evidence before me. "You really come out here to spend time with wolves?"

She nods. "Yeah. The pack kind of adopted me. I helped the mom of the little ones through a tough delivery, and they decided to keep me after that. I visit them a lot."

"You want to become a vet?"

"That's the goal."

I share a quizzical look with Seamus. There's something befuddling about her; she obviously thinks she's facing down death, yet she's not choosing her words carefully or stumbling. It sounds like we're acquaintances getting to know each other, not like I'm someone who ran her down like an animal.

"Okay," I say. "Let's get going."

"Do I have to go with you?"

"Yes." I give her a hard look that warns her not to fight or try to run. I don't *think* she will, but then, I don't really know her.

"Can I stand up, or will you kill me for that?"

Seamus releases a chuckle. A half smile steals across my lips. This one is really something. "You can get up."

I watch her push to her feet, rising to her impressively short height. She can't be very far above five feet; practically a dwarf compared to my 6'4.

"One of your arms is hanging considerably lower than the other," Seamus comments. "You alright, love?"

She glances down at her right arm. "I think it's dislocated. I was gonna have one of my roommates help force it back in place if I made it home tonight."

I realize that her arm really *is* dangling low and limp, but Connor was right when he said that dislocations are an excellent interrogation tactic. They're painful as fuck; I had one over the summer, and it robbed me of my breath. Mira's just staring at her arm with mild irritation. I start to wonder if she's in shock; the girl is taking all of this *far* too well. No tears, no begging. A little bit of panic earlier, but now just calm questions and answers, like she doesn't give a shit what'll happen to her.

She doesn't *seem* to be in shock, though. She's alert and keenly focused. A little distant, but not in the hazy, detached state I've seen others retreat to when genuinely overcome by shock. Maybe it's something else?

"Did you hit your head when I took you down?" I ask her.

She raises her eyebrows, giving me a long look. "Oh, no, I'm not in shock. I told you, I've been in life-or-death situations before. Like everything, I guess it's just something a person gets used to."

I tilt my head to the side. How did she know where my line of questioning was heading? *Who the fuck* is *this girl?* Who would just say that so... freely?

"Can you walk, love?" Seamus asks her, tipping her a wide smile.

She narrows her eyes for a second as she gazes at him. "Jesus, you're the *really* dangerous one here, aren't you?"

Seamus pauses, his suave smile dropping for an instant, showcasing a flicker of the killer beneath. "What?"

"Yeah, I can walk. It's my shoulder that's fucked, not my feet. My arm really does hurt, though. Can I maybe stop by my dorms tomorrow morning before class?" her eyebrows furrow. "Actually... can I even *go* to class? I've never been a captive before, so this is kind of new to me. If I reiterate that there is absolutely *no* way I'll tell anyone *anything* that went down tonight, can I go home?"

I smile at her. She's a little dizzy, but it's in an endearing way. "No."

She lets out a long breath. "Yeah, I kind of figured you'd say that. I'm assuming that if I try to run off, you'll send *him* after me," she says, tipping her chin at Seamus.

"Why would you think that?" I ask.

"Because he's the most dangerous."

Seamus slowly turns to look at me, no longer smiling. "You've vetted her? She seems to know an awful fuckin' lot, mate."

She does, indeed. My suspicion is starting to grow.

"I wasn't sent here by anyone, I promise. I'm literally just here to see my pack. Wrong place, wrong time."

Seamus takes a step forward, folding thick forearms over his broad chest. "Then what makes you think I'm the most dangerous one?"

She lifts her left shoulder. "I don't know. A feeling, I guess. I get them a lot. They usually aren't wrong."

"That's not gonna do it, love," Seamus says, taking another step. "What do you mean, a *feeling?*"

"You really want the whole breakdown of how my thoughts get from point A to point B?" she asks doubtfully. "It'll take a while. I usually have a hard time keeping track of them."

"Mira," I say lowly. "If you were sent by someone, now's the time to admit it. I can protect you, but only if you tell the truth."

"Jesus, I wasn't sent by anyone, okay?" She waves at Seamus. "It's the smile, the demeanor, the eyes. His senses are better honed than yours or Flashlight Guy's—he walks like a predator. He's obviously trained in some form of combat. He also has this easygoing air, and he can give a fake smile where even his *eyes* don't betray him, but his energy stays the same. Stalking, watching, lurking. Not in a pervert way; in a fucking *wolf* way. *That's* how I know he's the most danger-ous. Flashlight Dude wears his danger on his sleeve, not masking it. He doesn't have a moral compass. I don't think he has feelings. *You,*" she nods to me, "have a moral compass that you can reprogram, and you have feelings that you know how to ignore. Not push down like most people do, but genuinely *disregard*. That makes you more dangerous than Flashlight Dude, but not as dangerous as the Brit." She looks to the sky, letting out a long breath. "Are we done now? We good? Have I convinced you I wasn't *sent* by anyone? If you're going to kill me, please get it over with now. Don't string me along."

My lips part as I stare at her. She says she doesn't remember me, and I believe her. Yet, she managed to nail me within thirty seconds. She managed to get *Seamus* in thirty seconds. He takes a step back from her, retreating from a girl for possibly the first time in his life. He gazes at her with open shock, as do I.

"Oh shit, I just got myself killed, didn't I?" she asks. "I didn't mean any of it; I was totally bullshitting and pulling all of that out of my ass. The brit is the easy going, non-dangerous one—in fact, none of you are dangerous." She grimaces as she looks down at her arm. "Can I go home now?"

I try to unfuck my brain long enough to say, "No."

She nods sagely. "Yeah, okay. Can I have my phone back?" she nods at the backpack. "And my backpack?"

My eyebrows furrow. "Why?"

"I need music. Phone for my playlist, backpack for my headphones. Both of you are a lot to handle, like bundles of chaos and violence. It's overwhelming. I'm kind of starting to *want* you to kill me."

Seamus takes a step forward, nudging my shoulder with his. "I gathered you called dibs on her. What would it take to give me a go? This one's fucking *fascinating*."

"More than you have," I growl.

Meanwhile, Mira gives a slightly hysterical sounding cackle. "You can't afford me, Brit." He opens his mouth to dispute; she cuts him off. "I don't mean your wallet—you've got the look of wealth. I mean your *sanity*. I can barely hold my own sanity most of the time. None of you could handle my brand of crazy." Her throat clicks with a swallow. "So... about my phone?"

My eyes briefly flutter shut as I shake my head. "No phone." I clear my throat, inhale a deep breath, and relax. Try to ignore how attractive and confounding Mira is. "Okay, here's what's going to happen. First thing, you need your shoulder fixed. I don't want you in pain longer than necessary; the sooner it's back in place, the sooner it can heal."

"I can handle the pain," she assures me. "I would like use of my arm, though."

I incline my head. "Right." As much as I detest the idea of allowing Seamus to touch her, especially now that he's expressed interest in her, I don't know how to put a shoulder back in place. He does. "Seamus?"

He nods, also composing himself. "Yeah, I'll get it done. Come here, love, we'll get you all fixed up." He doesn't bother giving her the charming smile that often makes the sum total of the female population swoon. He gazes at Mira with a mixture of wariness and vibrant intrigue.

"You gonna kill me for getting your number?" she asks him.

Her question pulls a smile from him. "Nah, love. You're too pretty, too *innocent* to kill. Come on, we'll get it over with quick."

"Then, we'll go back to our place," I say, staring at Mira. "And figure out next steps."

Chapter Three
Mira

The Brit steps forward slowly, a predator on the prowl. I watch him *very* closely—I wasn't kidding when I said he's the most dangerous one here. His aura, his energy, his vibe—the intangible feeling that I get from people—never changes. It's flat, dissonant. It's his smile that *really* makes him frightening, though; I've never seen someone fake a smile that well.

"You need something to bite down on so you don't rip your cheek or tongue clean off?" he asks as he comes to a stop beside me. "It's gonna hurt, love."

I nod. "Yeah, I know. I've had dislocations before." *Not all of them were accidental; getting dragged around by your arm as a kid tends to fuck up your body.* "I'll be good. I won't scream."

Brit's brows lift in disbelief. I guess his doubt makes sense. Joint dislocations are phenomenally painful, but I learned many years ago how to keep quiet while getting my *broken bones* set. That's a different kind of pain, a literal bone-deep agony. Back then, I knew if I made a single peep, I'd get another broken bone.

"Okay, then. I did my duty by offering." He stares hard at me. "I'm not going to make it hurt any more than it has to, understand? It'll be over quick." He glances at Verdant Eyes. "You'll need to keep her still for me, Dorian."

Dorian. The name suits Verdant Eyes. It brings to mind Oscar Wilde's book, The Picture of Dorian Gray. I wonder what *this* Dorian would see if he stared at a picture of his soul. Something terrifying, to be sure.

Dorian walks up to me, flanking my left side. When he raises his hands, I flinch. It's an instinctual reaction that I can't keep down. His brows furrow, but he doesn't comment as he puts one rough, calloused palm on my arm, and the other on my waist. His hands are warm, his body's warm, and there's something enticing about his energy, like the notes of a siren song. I bet he is *most* skilled at luring in girls with his appearance and sexy vibe alone; he looks like he'd make a killing as a model. Or porn star. The big-dick energy emanating from him is overwhelming.

"Ready?" Brit asks.

I nod. When he takes my right arm, I try to hide my flinch, but don't succeed. I'm flighty right now, firmly in survival mode, so even though I'm doing a good job of keeping my fear from the surface, I'm not so good at masking my reaction. I inhale a deep breath and nod again at The Brit.

He takes my wrist in one hand and moves the other to grip me just below my shoulder. He bends my arm at the elbow and rotates it outwards. A new wash of pain overcomes me, and I squeeze my eyes shut, gritting my teeth and steeling myself.

"Looks like a partial dislocation," Brit says. "Means it'll heal nice and quick. Lucky girl." Abruptly, he shoves my arm up and back into its socket, and I hear a loud pop and *feel* it as my shoulder's forced back into place.

Shooting agony overtakes me, preventing me from thanking him. Primal tears prickle at my eyes, a noise bubbles up in my throat, but old instincts keep me from letting it out. I inhale and exhale several times, my breaths shaky, and count the seconds until the worst of my pain subsides. Slowly, it dulls into a deep-set ache—not as bad as it was before, but not pleasant, either. When I think I can use my voice without crying, I open my eyes and glance at the Brit. "It's better now, thanks. I did *not* feel like paying a hospital bill."

Brit stares at me with furrowed eyebrows. "You didn't make a single noise," he observes. "Your breaths got so shaky I thought you were going to pass out or scream, but you did neither."

"Yeah, I don't pass out much. Well, I am prone to heat exhaustion in the summers, but it's not too hot out now. Can you let go of me?" I glance between him and Dorian.

Brit releases me immediately, taking a step back and raising his hands to show he won't touch me again. Oddly enough, the gesture calms me. He might be the most dangerous one, but I have an inkling that he has his own honor code, and it's a strong one that's rooted in... *justice, maybe?* He strikes me as a vigilante. Flashlight Guy is a stone-cold killer. Dorian is a little trickier, because I think he might be a mix of both. He's smooth but coarse. He's got morals, but I think they can be rearranged to fit his narrative. And I'm willing to bet that there's very little he won't do, but the few limits he has never get crossed.

I look at Dorian. "Um, can you let go of me, too? You're intimidating."

Dorian doesn't. He's watching me with a deep consideration, brows furrowed as he sweeps his thumb over my arm. "Are you immune to pain or something?" he asks.

I release a low, somewhat sad laugh. "No." *Just used to it.* "That'd be pretty cool, though."

"Try to move your arm, love," the Brit says. "Make sure it's alright now."

I gingerly rotate my shoulder, wincing at the pinpricks that ignite. Then, I flex my hand, move my arm, do a range of motion tests, all of which prove that my arm is perfectly functional, albeit *very* sore.

"It's good now. Back in place. You *did* make it quick; I've had doctors do a shittier job." Once again, I look at Dorian. "You're still holding me."

"I am," he agrees. *You should get used to it*, his eyes say.

Uh...no thanks. There's something intriguing about him, but my survival instincts are finely honed. "Will it get me killed if I shake you off? Asking you politely isn't working."

"It won't get you killed, but dismissing me could get you pun-ished." I shrink back at the threat; Dorian smiles faintly. "Not like that, pretty girl. You won't be getting buried or swimming with the fishes—no time soon and not by our hands, anyways." When I tense, he adds, "Or by our orders. You can calm down."

"I can't," I disagree. "I need music for that. You won't give me my phone or backpack. Ergo, I'll still be freaking out in... how long did you say I'd be your *guest*?" I question. "A week? I guess I've gone in panicked states for longer, but it's been a while." I'm not looking forward to remaining in fight or flight for that long, but I'll manage.

"I said I wouldn't kill you," Dorian reminds me, gently squeezing my arm in reassurance. "I won't."

"Yeah, my brain heard you. I sort of believe you. I'm still freaked out and totally off balance."

He tilts his head to the side. "Do you always blurt out whatever you're thinking?"

"No. Usually I only blurt out about a third of what I'm thinking. The rest stays inside. Can you please let go of me?"

He slowly pulls away, then steps back.

"How'd you get here?" Dorian asks. "You have a car?"

"Yeah, a beat-up Honda. It's parked in one of the makeshift dirt parking lots about a quarter way up the mountain."

He frowns. "Why didn't you leave it in the public parking lot at the base?"

I shrug. "Less chance of running into people at my spot, even though there usually aren't people out here at night. I come on weekend afternoons when I have time, so I learned to avoid the public parking lot then. This mountain's one of the less-popular ones, but people still visit. It's beautiful." I frown. "Are you guys at the regular parking lot?"

He chuckles, shaking his head. "No, Mira, we're not. We also have a spot not far off."

I gaze at him. "How do you know my name again?"

"We ran into each other at the library."

I nod. "Yeah, I remember you saying that, but I don't usually give out my name. If I told you, I'd remember you."

He pauses for a beat. "You really don't remember me?"

I shake my head. "No. Did I have my headphones in when we met?"

He nods.

I snap my fingers. "That's why. I zone out when I have music on. The outside world gets blurry. You didn't answer my question."

He shrugs. "I asked around about you."

I can feel the shift in his energy as the lie rolls off his tongue. "No, you didn't."

His eyebrows inch up. "How do you know?"

"I felt it. Well, if you didn't ask around, I guess it'd be better if I *don't* know how you figured it out." I sigh. "It'd probably freak me out more. I'm already freaked out enough."

"Has anyone ever told you that you're fucking *fascinating*, love?" Brit questions, gazing at me with a deepening interest.

"Usually, they tell me that I'm insane." I can't exactly disagree, since I'm yet to meet anyone who can *feel* other people the way I do. Cara swears I'm an empath, but I don't like the supernatural connotation around that word. It's not like I see dead people or smell emotions, I just sort of... *sense* them.

"We're all a bit mad here," Brit says with a charming grin. This time, his energy shifts to something a little more positive, and I think it's the first time I've seen his smile be at least half-genuine tonight. Nothing on his face indicates the shift in his emotions; he looks as sincere as he did the other times, but now he feels sincere.

Very, very dangerous.

"Come on," Dorian says, swinging my backpack over his shoulder. "Let's get going. Stay close. We'll talk more in the car."

I inhale a deep breath, steeling myself. "Okay."

I follow behind him as he begins to walk down the mountain. While every inch of me *aches* to run away, I know I'll only get chased down again, and I *really* don't feel like going for another tumble. What I want is to curl up in my dorm room bed, blast my classical music playlist, and sleep this shitty night away. Instead, I'm walking into a completely unknown situation with no guarantees that I'll get out of it alive. I think that Dorian was telling the truth when he said he won't hurt me, my gut tells me he meant it, but he mentioned a punishment earlier. Really, I don't know *what* to think or believe right now.

The Brit walks behind me, and I feel his gaze burning a hole into the back of my head. I think he's trying to figure me out—both men are—and that confuses me. Most people don't care to figure me out. They catch a whiff of my brand of crazy and run in the opposite direction. I prefer it that way, since I'm not very good with people. I get along much better with animals.

Dorian slows a bit to walk beside me, wrapping a hand around my good arm. I stiffen immediately, a chill coursing through me at his touch.

"Easy, I just have a question," he says.

I swallow and give a nod. I wasn't kidding when I said he's intimidating; both his physique and aura seep menace, but there's control intermingled with it. Precision and calculation, which only ups his fear factor. He's tall and muscular enough to kill me with a single hand, but I don't think he will.

"Alright," I say slowly.

"Earlier, Connor said you were bullshitting when you mentioned your shoulder dislocation. You agreed."

So Connor is the name of the psychopathic giant. Good to know.

"I didn't agree, I just didn't *dis*agree," I correct.

Dorian nods. "Right. Why?"

I shrug, then grimace at the soreness in my right arm. Since it was only a partial dislocation, I hope it'll dissipate by morning. I can already feel the swelling drastically reducing. "He'd made up his mind that I was lying or exaggerating, and I've learned that trying to change someone's mind is a time-wasting endeavor. I didn't see the point. He wanted to kill me, anyways, so what would a dislocated shoulder matter?"

He contemplates this for several moments while we walk in silence. "You've also said it's not your first life or death situation. What did you mean?"

"Exactly that," I say. I don't feel like digging through the graveyard of my childhood, certainly not with a predator like Dorian watching me. For all I know, he'll use anything he learns to manipulate me.

He squints at me. "You gonna expand?"

"I'm clumsy," I respond, which is true. I'm especially clumsy when I zone out—the world sort of falls away. One time I found myself on the edge of a cliff during a hike, simply because I'd stopped paying attention to where I was going.

"You're not the only one who's good at vetting out lies, Mira."

I nod. "Yeah, I believe that. I guess it would be useful with the life you lead."

"And what life do you think I lead?"

I need to step carefully. "One that causes you to chase down someone who happens to be around when you're doing something in the middle of the night. One that has you wearing no less than three knives strapped to your body, and possibly a handgun in your boot—I could be wrong about that one, I can't tell for sure."

His thumb strokes over my arm, and I weirdly enjoy the sensation. I'll need to be careful around this guy for sure, otherwise I'll find myself in even hotter water than I've already landed in.

"I think I like you," Dorian says, sounding perplexed by the prospect.

"Please don't. I'd rather you *dis*liked me and wanted to get rid of me as soon as possible. Not in the permanent way, but in the *Jesus fuck this girl is so annoying I'm gonna let her go back to her dorm room* way."

"You're adorable," he says, looking at me like I'm a cute little woodland animal he wants to scoop up and keep.

"Not really."

"You are to me."

Something warm pulses in my chest at his response. I'm usually too zoned out from people to have emotional reactions to them, which is how I prefer it, but this guy has *all* my attention.

"Christ," the Brit says from behind us. "You need to ease the fuck up, Acheron. Otherwise you'll get yourself into a bloody mess."

Dorian doesn't say anything, but he does let go of my arm and returns to walking in front of me. I frown at the realization that I miss his warmth. Earlier tonight, he was contemplating killing me before he recognized me. He dislocated my shoulder and threatened me more than once. I need to remember that, and remember that I am still firmly in danger, so I should *not* be feeling anything fuzzy.

A few minutes later, we veer right and emerge into a dirt parking lot. There, an imposing black SUV with tinted windows sits, engine purring.

"I'll take shotgun," the Brit says. "You two can have the back."

Dorian doesn't respond, but he leads me to the rear and opens the back door for me. "In you go," he prompts when I hesitate.

"Is Connor going to kill me?"

"No. He has orders not to, and he doesn't disobey our boss's orders. You're good, Mira, I won't let anything happen to you."

I inhale a deep, steadying breath, but I can't stop my eyes from darting around. When I'm scared, I can be a pretty fast runner. Earlier was an exception—the darkness and uneven forest terrain worked against me. Now, I might be able to outrun Dorian, if I dart into the forest and disappear among the shadows.

But then what? He goes to Greywood. Given his illicit midnight activities and mention of his boss, he's clearly tied to a criminal organization, which means he'll probably have an easy time tracking me.

"Don't even think about it," Dorian advises. "You run, I'll chase, I'll *catch you*, and I *will* punish you. Get in the car, Mira."

Knowing better than to ignore his threat, I step into the car. Connor glances at me through the rearview mirror. His eyes are startlingly vacant, his energy unerringly blank. It's like he's empty of life.

"Any problems?" he asks Dorian.

"Nope. Seamus helped her put her shoulder back in place."

Brit's name is Seamus. It suits him.

The giant's eyebrows rise. "It was actually out of place?"

"Yup," Seamus confirms. "Not fully, or she'd be in a cast for a few weeks—just a partial dislocation."

Connor grunts. "I didn't hear any screams. You sure you fixed it?"

"She didn't make a bloody peep. Shit was weird," Seamus says.

It's strange to be talked about as if I'm not here, but I'm happy to have the reprieve. Something akin to respect flashes through Connor's gaze as he glances at me again. So, he *does* have feelings, just not very many of them. *Interesting.*

I remain silent as Connor pulls out of the dirt lot and onto the winding road that leads down and out of the canyon. My anxiety and fear continue prickling in my chest, but I try to keep my breathing steady. That becomes impossible when my mind decides to lead me down worst case scenario routes, complete with gory images.

Me without my head.

My bones getting buried in a grave.

Connor strangling the life out of me without a flash of emotions.

Seamus putting a bullet in my head.

Dorian slitting my neck...

"You're hyperventilating," Dorian says, putting a big hand on my thigh. *He's right.* My breaths sound unnaturally loud in the quiet of the car. I try to get them under control—and fail.

"I need—" I pause to try to breathe. "My music. *Please.*"

Dorian's lips purse. "You have a playlist on your phone?"

I nod frantically.

He unzips my backpack and pulls my AirPods out of their case, handing them to me. I splurged on them last year, wanting a nice headset with noise cancellation that didn't break every few months.

He grabs my phone from his pocket and unlocks it. *Guy memorized my password.*

"Spotify?"

I shake my head. "Apple music. Classical—" I pause as another image of blood spraying from my neck terrorizes me.

"I got it," he says. "Put in your headphones."

As soon as I do, Chopin floats from my earbuds. I focus all my attention on it, on the complex melody and harmony. Slowly, my breathing calms. My anxiety and fear abate, leaving behind a low warmth that comes from my thigh. I glance down to see Dorian's hand is back on it. I don't like his proprietary touch. More to the point, I don't like how comfortable and calming it is; nothing about this guy should bring me peace. I gently lift his hand and deposit it on his lap. He smirks at the gesture, shaking his head as if I've amused him. After giving me a long look, he pockets my phone and pulls out his own. I lay my forearm against the window and lean my chin on it, getting lost in images of myself playing piano until everything else melts away.

Chapter Four

The car eventually pulls up into a suburban neighborhood, which I'd guess is about a twenty-minute drive from Greywood. We pass several houses that increase in size and glamour. Eventually we go into a gated community. *Not community*, I realize after a moment. A gated fucking *mansion*, a home that I instinctively know belongs to these three.

The house looks like it came straight out of a gothic novel—grey brick exterior; three stories tall and wide; a freaking *tower* on both ends of it. I would not be surprised if it's stood here for well over a century and was once owned by some mega-rich dude with pervert tendencies. There's a mixture of vibes coming from the house itself; some are dark, some are light. I think that this house has seen many horrors, but it's also seen laughter, friendship, and tight-knit bonds.

The bond between the three guys in the car with me is tight. Seamus and Dorian are closest, and Connor... well, I think he sees the other two as his property. I'm reasonably sure he's deep on the antisocial spectrum, and the few people I've met like him aren't capable of friendship so much as possessiveness. They can see another person as an extension of themselves, they can form attachments, but they don't get sweet or cuddly sentiments.

Connor parks the car in a circular driveway that has a *fountain*. Obviously, these three are wealthy, though I don't know if any of them were born into wealth. I think they've managed to acquire it through whatever business had them digging in the forest at midnight.

Dorian taps my thigh, signaling for me to pull out my headphones. I've calmed down through the car ride, so I take the risk, popping one of my beloved AirPods out.

Dorian watches me, unspeaking. His stare is unwavering, unapologetic, and strikingly bold. He exudes confidence, and something about him suggests his self-assurance is earned through life experience. I hold his gaze despite the faint discomfort it stirs in me. "What now?"

A small smile lifts his lips. He's unreasonably handsome, and it seems wrong to see such beauty on a person who ran me down like I was wild game he was hunting. The devastatingly sexy upwards curve of his lips feels like a personal affront.

"Now, we go inside. We'll talk over a drink."

"I don't drink much," I respond. "Do we have to talk?"

"Yes. It'll be brief. You don't have to drink—I can get you a soda. We have pretty much everything stocked up." He takes both my AirPods and returns them to their case, slipping it back into my backpack. "Stay in the car."

He opens his door, grabs my backpack, and rounds the vehicle. Connor and Seamus exit the car in unison, leaving me alone in the luxurious interior. The three of them meet at the front of the hood and exchange hushed words, occasionally throwing glances in my direction. I wonder if I should tell them they could've spoken freely in the car while I had my headphones in. I've trained myself to mentally detach from people and their energies when I'm listening to my classical music playlist. It took a while, but I eventually learned to blur out the presence of others and entirely immerse myself in the melodies of specific songs. Sometimes it's the only way I can sleep.

Connor says something with furrowed brows before turning and walking into the house. Seamus and Dorian stay outside a bit longer, chatting. Seamus slaps Dorian on the shoulder, breezes his gaze over the car, then heads inside, as well. Dorian rounds the car and opens my door for me.

"Am I still safe from swimming with the fishes?" I ask. "Or being buried in a grave? Hey, if you kill me, can you bury me in a specific spot on the mountain? I'd like to be near my pack."

Dorian stares at me for a long moment before a small smile tips up his lips. He shakes his head with amusement. "Nobody's killing you. Let's go inside."

"Can I have my phone?"

"No. You can have it for school tomorrow."

"So I'm going to school tomorrow? That's relieving. I'd lose what little sanity I have left if I missed classes and got behind." I tilt my head. "It's surprising that you're giving me my phone *and* letting me go to school." I watch him closely, searching his eyes. They remain completely blank; he has a masterful poker face on, but his energy hums with calculation. "Oh, you're gonna bug it tonight. Okay."

"Do you always just... *know* things?" Dorian questions, taking my arm and gently pulling me out of the car.

I shake my head. "No. That'd be really useful, but no. I don't know a lot of things—it's not like I can foresee the future or anything. That would be nice, though. Then I wouldn't have gone up to the mountain tonight." I frown at the tear on my shirt, which reveals a bit of my waist. "Or torn my shirt. God, the alpha is such a jerk. I love him and he's protective of me, but he's also irritatingly possessive. I have to bribe him every time I try to leave. Last week, he walked me down and tried to *get in my car* with me."

"You have a thing for taming wild beasts?" Dorian asks, gazing at me.

"Not really. *They* have a thing for claiming *me*. I've seen the alpha run down a rabbit and snap its neck with a single bite, but if one of his wolves gets rough with me—even when it's playful—he puts them in their place. It's like I said, I think he sees me as a pack member. A weak one in need of protection."

"Are there any other forest friends you have?" Dorian questions, taking my arm and steering me toward the house. I go willingly, because I suspect running is futile.

"A skulk of foxes on another mountain."

"Tell me about them," Dorian requests.

I glance at him, startled. I'm used to people asking me to shut the fuck up, not encouraging me to go on. "Why?"

"I like hearing you talk. You have a soothing voice."

"Oh." I pause as he opens a grand wooden door that has a *lion* engraved on it. He leads me into a polished entryway, with a coat closet and a *hat rack* that has fedoras reminiscent of those worn by 1960's gangsters hanging on it, along with a few holsters and... *is that a bulletproof vest?* Weird.

Beyond the entryway, a maze of hallways branches off in various directions, the walls adorned with intricate moldings and softly illuminated by overhead lights. One to the left leads to a staircase of polished wood, its banister carved with delicate patterns that look like vines. Another hallway to the right is a path to what looks like the kitchen, which gleams with a beautiful marble center island. Straight ahead, the largest opening beckons toward a sitting room.

Dorian leads me straight into the lovely living room. The decorations are simplistic, with a color scheme of navy blue and black. A dark blue furniture set stands proudly before a huge flatscreen TV mounted on the right wall, with a simple black coffee table separating them. An awesome stone-and-marble fireplace holds court on a wall to the left of the entrance, surrounded by bookshelves on either side. The room has a high ceiling, and a bank of windows with tinted glass on the back wall, facing the side of the property. It's pretty in here—there's something refined and tasteful yet simultaneously unhinged about this house.

"The foxes," Dorian prompts, motioning for me to sit on the couch. He sets my backpack down beside it.

"Right," I say, sinking into the plush navy cushions. "I was hiking last winter when a white-furred vixen happened to dart across my path. She didn't stop to approach me right then, but she did stalk me for a little while as I walked. After I ate lunch, I offered her a crust of bread from my sandwich. She emerged from the banks of snow to accept it. It was an otherworldly experience. She blended with the snow so seamlessly—it was only her blue, *blue* eyes and dark pink nose that made her stand out." I smile as I reminisce. "We stared at each other for a while, she chittered at me, then trotted away. I went back a few days later and she found me again. That time I came armed with treats. She liked the fox-friendly cookies I baked for her and stuck around for a bit longer, even let me give her a stroke on her neck. I started visiting her regularly, and each time, she was more receptive to my touch. Two weeks later, she dumped the most adorable kit in my lap." My smile grows at the memory, one of my favorite moments with furry friends. "That threw me for a loop, since most animals are really protective of their young, but she just offered hers up to me. I figured that meant she trusted me way more than creatures of the wild should ever trust humans. Shortly after, five more kits came stumbling out of the woods and started falling over each other to climb on me. It was really cute. I visit the foxes less frequently than the wolves since they're less attached to me, just once or twice a month."

"Have the foxes adopted you?"

I shake my head. "No. They're not possessive of me like the wolves. They just feel safe around me, and I give them treats." I grimace. "It was pretty awkward when the vixen dumped a headless squirrel on my lap as a gift. I shuddered at that one, but still gave her a treat. The kits are nippier than the wolf pups, but the biggest kit is protective of me and warns the others to play nice, and the dominant foxes in the skulk have taken to me. They're really cute." I smile. "I want to visit them again soon." A long breath escapes me as I think about the gas bill that visiting all these animals racks up. *Murder.* "I spend most of my paychecks on gas and supplies for treats, which is tough, but totally worth it to hang out with my furry dudes. What are you doing?"

"Making a drink," Dorian replies, rifling through a minibar hidden in an antique cupboard by the bookcase. "What do you want? We've got most of the usual sodas."

Huh. We're really going to talk over a drink. "Sprite, please." I watch as Dorian fixes himself a drink from a mini fridge, then grabs me a sprite. He hands me the can, taking a seat on the couch beside me, close enough that his leg bumps mine. I shift to the side to get some distance, which he tracks with sharp eyes.

"Right." He takes a long pull of his drink. "You're intuitive—alarmingly intuitive. I'd like you to tell me what you think you stumbled on tonight."

"Absolutely nothing," I say firmly.

He arches a brow.

"Okay, two guys fucking who didn't want an audience and were willing to threaten me to not tell anyone about their sex."

He chuckles. "This isn't a test, Mira. What you say won't impact the length of your stay with us or how we treat you, but I need to understand what you do and don't know."

"Why?"

"It's important."

I nod. "Okay, but why?"

He sighs. "Answer the fucking question."

I twist my lips but comply. "You guys were burying something. Remains, I think. You're too smart and experienced to bury a full body—it'd be found eventually—but maybe bones? Even teeth? For all I know, *ashes*. Anyway, I was at the wrong place in the wrong time, so I got spooked at the noises you were making and ran. You and Connor chased; Seamus stayed behind to finish up. You caught me, hurt me—I'm pretty sure it was accidental—and the psychopath assumed I was a loose end to tie up. You talked him down, made a call—probably to your boss?—and got direct orders for Connor not to kill me. Maybe it was suggested you supervise me for a while?" I blow out a long breath. "I'm surprised Connor recognizes any authority figure. I'm surprised any of you do, for that matter. Your boss must be quite the person to have earned your loyalty." I clear my throat. "That's all I've got."

Dorian blinks slowly, brows furrowed. "That's *all* you've got?"

I'm assuming he's taken aback because I nailed everything spot-on. I wish I didn't; I wish that my intuition wasn't what it is, but it's a curse I got saddled with, so I try to make the most of it. It's pretty useful with animals—I have an easy time figuring out if they're hurt and where they're hurt. I expect that'll come in handy once I become a practicing vet.

"This house is cool. This room has good vibes. I don't want to go to the basement, though, the energy there's dark."

"I never told you about a basement."

"You didn't have to."

Dorian gives his head a shake. "You're going to take some getting used to."

"No, I'm temporary. You don't need to get used to me. You should get super irritated by me. My weirdness doesn't have an off switch." I do have an unfortunate habit of getting chatty when I'm anxious, though.

"I don't think it's weird, Mira," he says softly. "I don't think *you're* weird."

I swallow hard, thrown by his sincerity. "Then what do you think I am?"

"Remarkable."

Woah. That word has an unusual impact on me; it's like I've just taken a sledgehammer to the chest. It nearly knocks the wind out of me. I've been called a lot of things in my life, and a large sum of them were pretty cruel. Even kinder terms were still double-edged. Cara fondly refers to me as insane. Valerie tells me I'm off my fucking rocker regularly. I don't think anyone's called me remarkable before.

"That's weird," I finally say.

Dorian tilts his head to the side. "Is it?"

I nod. "Yeah. You should be freaked out like everyone else. You should want me off your case ASAP."

He leans forward. "That's what you're used to, isn't it? I guess we'll both have an adjustment. Seamus was right when he said we're all a bit mad here. Your brand of peculiarity might be new, but it's by no means the worst."

I nod. "At least I'm not a stone-cold killer who buries remains in the woods at midnight. Why are you still on about adjustment? I really don't see the need for us to get used to each other. I'm here as a precaution. You'll figure out my weak spots and be ready to use them against me, then let me go after a week. Do you want me to list my pressure points now so I can leave in the morning?"

He shakes his head. "No, I'll find out what I need to. There are multiple things I'd like to figure out about you, and it'll take me more than an evening to do it."

I frown. "Like what?"

"Like how you feel," he says.

I arch an eyebrow. "Presently? Pretty freaked out."

"I don't mean *now*, Mira. I mean how you'll feel when I'm inside you. On top of you. All around you."

Holy—fucking—shit.

Chapter Five

Mira's eyes widen so quickly, it looks like they might bulge out of her skull like a cartoon character. Her breath catches, pushing the subtle mounds of her breasts against the fabric of her shirt. I glance down at the tear exposing her belly, thinking about how easy it would be to grab the fabric and rip, splitting it all the way up. I wonder what color bra she's wearing, and what kind of noises she'd make when I taste her nipples. Moans? Whines? Whimpers? Words spoken in her smoky, raspy, sex-and-sin voice?

"Um…" she trails off, blinking rapidly. I don't think I've yet seen her rendered speechless. On second thought, I have, but it was when she was fearful for her life. I think she's still half-fearful that she won't make it out of this alive, but part of her also believes me when I tell her that I won't hurt or kill her, allow the others to, or give an order for someone else to.

I like the blush that rushes to her cheeks, staining them a pretty red. I like how her gaze lowers as if she's embarrassed. I think I might like everything about her—she's gorgeous, intriguing, fascinating, intuitive, and very clever. Brave, too, and bravery has always been a turn-on for me.

"I… am not going to have sex with you," she finally says, staring at the TV.

"You are," I disagree. "Eventually, you are. Preferably sooner rather than later. I can read people pretty fucking well, too, Mira. I *know* you're interested in me. But," I shrug, "you're also scared and un-nerved. We can wait for that to pass until desire is the most prominent thing you feel."

"I am *not* going to have sex with you," she repeats more firmly, lips thinning. She sets her sprite down on the coffee table and folds her hands in her lap, curling her fingers so tightly her knuckles turn white. She's less embarrassed and more *worried* now, which makes my brows furrow with contemplation.

I didn't dig into Mira very far when I did my research on her; I only know about her life at Greywood, nothing before or after.

"Look at me," I say, quietly. She exhales, then slowly cranes her neck to the side, meeting my gaze. Her body remains facing forward, her posture stiff. There's something panicked in her eyes that I *really* don't like. I'm not a rapist, I'm not someone who will *ever* get off on forcing women. I have my fair share of kinks and taboo enjoyments, but desire on *both* sides is a must for me, otherwise I don't have any interest.

Mira's gaze holds no desire now, only deep-seated wariness and flighty panic. She has the same look she did in the forest, when she was pinned beneath me. I can only think of two reasons for her nerves: one, she has no experience; two, she has a sour experience. Too many women have to suffer the latter in this day and age.

"Have you had sex before?" I question, sipping at my Moscow Mule.

Her brows furrow. "Yeah. I'm not a virgin. I've had sex a few times."

I incline my head. "Did someone... hurt you during it? Or force you?" Even the words leave a bitter taste on my tongue.

Her frown deepens as she regards me, then her expression smooths out. "No, I've never been forced or hurt during *that*." The way she says it makes me believe she has been hurt in other ways, which tracks. Her tolerance for pain can shame some of the toughest motherfuckers I know, and her calmness in the face of death, along with her indication that she's faced life-or-death scenarios before, is telling.

"Have you enjoyed your other times?" I go on.

She rolls her eyes. "Why are we talking about this? I'm not going to sleep with you. It doesn't feel appropriate for us to even be having this conversation."

She *will* sleep with me—as soon as tonight. More, she'll have sex with me, and she's gonna get fucked by me. I won't have to force, merely coax. I've sensed her desire and openness to me more than once tonight.

"Answer my question," I tell her.

"Why?"

I sigh. She has an almost childish way of asking *why* frequently, but I don't think it's because she's trying to be annoying; I think it's because she's trying to puzzle things out, make them click in her mind. She might be alarmingly intuitive, but I get the sense she's also perplexed by people.

"Because I want to know."

"Okay, but why?" she presses.

"Because we are going to fuck eventually, pretty girl. You might hate yourself for it, but you're into me. You want me. That isn't a question; it's a statement of fact. Again, you're not the only one good at reading people."

She tilts her head to the side as she considers me. Her body shifts to face me, shoulders turning in my direction. Another subtle sign of her interest.

"Huh," she says.

"Have you enjoyed sex in the past?" I ask again, prompting her.

She shrugs. "Not really. It wasn't bad or forceful or anything, it just didn't feel good emotionally, which meant it couldn't feel good physically. It was never about *me*, it was about a guy taking what he wanted with little regard for how I felt, and I didn't enjoy feeling like a warm hole for someone to get off in. I tried a few times with a few different people, curious to see what all the hype was about, and it never worked for me. Those times were moments I hated my intuition the most, because maybe if I *didn't* have such a good sense for people, I might've had a good time. I didn't, though, so I decided I just didn't like it and moved on." A faint smile pulls on her lips, but it's withdrawn and melancholy. "I see what desire does to this world. I feel how the wants of men muddles their minds. And when I truly think about it, I'm pretty glad that I have no part in it. It's freeing."

Ah. Mira thinks she's above the basest of instincts because she's never had a *man*—not boy—focus on her during the act. That will not be a problem with me. She'll be the center of my attention.

I live in a house with dominant guys. Connor is the type to spank a girl's ass until she's sobbing for mercy, then squeeze it while he's fucking her—sadist through and through. He needs to deliver pain to really get his blood rushing. Seamus, on the other hand, likes scenes of all kinds—tying a girl up any number of ways and playing with her however he feels like in the moment. It changes from person to person and scene to scene. He leaves his bedroom door open, enjoys other people watching him work, so I've witnessed him do a whole range of shit with girls. I think the thing that really gets *him* off is begging.

As for me... I certainly have particular tastes, and all of them center around the pleasure of my partner.

"That's not going to be a problem with us," I tell her.

"You're right, because we won't be having sex. I'm not interested in it."

I pick up one of her hands, turning it over in mine and uncurling her fists. She has tiny hands, fitting for her tiny self, but they're elegant—smooth palms, long fingers. Lots of old scratches and bite marks marring the skin, though.

"I think you will be interested in my brand of sex," I tell her. "Because it will be about you. In fact, my enjoyment hinges on the reactions of other people at the worst of times—with you, that'd be magnified tenfold. A hundredfold, maybe."

She watches me examine her hand, looking confused. "Why?"

I smile faintly. I'm starting to like her way of asking that question with an almost innocent curiosity and tone of befuddlement. I decide to lay it all out for her, tell her my desires, and see how she takes it.

"I like to control everything that happens in the bedroom," I say.

She rolls her eyes. "Typical."

Sensing her interest wane, I press on. "Not in a typical way. Some guys like a sadistic approach, other's tastes differ from person to person and scene to scene." *Exhibit A: Connor and Seamus.* "I have a pretty consistent baseline; I like to control a girl's pleasure. Decide when she gets an orgasm, how she gets it, how many times she gets it. That's the most interesting and enjoyable part for *me*, watching another person's body mold under my touch. Making it bend to my will." Her eyes widen as she meets my gaze, but they're no longer wide with fear or discomfort, they're wide with a mixture of confusion and intrigue. "I'd say I'm a bit sadistic when it comes to sex, *especially* punishment, but my trade isn't pain. It's pleasure." A faint smile tugs at my lips. "So many men are terribly unoriginal. Disappointingly so. A punishment is easy when you redden someone's ass, but pain tolerances build. That gets old. Forced orgasms? Not so much, that's an entirely different form of torture."

Mira's breath hitches again, and interest brightens her eyes, mixing with a good dose of apprehension. Her pupils dilate from a blend of arousal and fear. My cock stiffens, pressing against the zipper of my jeans until it's outright uncomfortable and aching for relief. I am *very* interested in tying Mira up and seeing how long it takes her to beg for reprieve, to cry her way through as many orgasms as I want to give her. I want to edge her until she can't take it, then force her to come until she sobs.

"You like the idea," I state.

Her blush deepens. She shakes her head again, but it's a lie. She *does* like the idea; she's also daunted by it.

"We can talk more about it later," I say after a beat, releasing her hand. It falls limply to her lap. "When you're interested in a demonstration, let me know, but try not to wait too long." I lean forward, reaching out to tuck a strand of hair behind her ear. "The longer I wait, the harder I'll go on you, the *hungrier* I'll be." I lean back. "For now, let's go to bed. When do you have classes in the morning?"

She swallows. "Nine a.m."

I nod. "Good, I have my first class around then, too. What classes do you have tomorrow?"

She rattles off a list of advanced credits in a breathy voice.

"So your last one is at 5 p.m.," I say with a nod. "Busy bee with a full day. You an overachiever?"

She shrugs. "I just like getting things done. I like advancing myself in life, and school's an excellent steppingstone. The more I do, the closer I get to my goal, and the better I feel. Besides, staying busy helps me ignore other people."

I incline my head. "Word to the wise, don't ignore me. Ever. If I get too hungry for your attention, I might turn feral, and I don't know if you can handle a feral version of me."

"Why do you like me?" she asks suddenly. "I don't get it. I'm as weird as it gets, and I'm not especially receptive to you. What's the draw?"

I consider that for a moment. "I've never met anyone like you, woman or man. You're fascinating; a package that's shiny, pretty, unique as it gets, and alarmingly intelligent. Brave, too, and quirky. It's a package that appeals to me."

She contemplates that. "Okay. Can I have my own room tonight?"

I smile. "No."

Her brows touch. "Why? You make me uncomfortable. I want to sleep."

"I'm going to keep you close so I can keep an eye on you," I explain.

She gazes at me, eyes glazing. I'm starting to learn that's an indicator of her doing whatever it is that gives her such an amazing ability to see *through* people and to their true intentions. I wasn't joking when I said she's remarkable, and my urges to unravel every bit of her and make her *mine* are only getting stronger.

"That's not the only reason why," she says decisively. "There's something else." Her cheeks flush again, and she looks away, turning her full attention to the wall.

"You're right," I agree softly, inching forward on the couch. She inches back, so I inch forward more. We play the advance-and-retreat game until she's pressed up against the arm, and I'm hovering over her, with barely any space separating our bodies. My gaze travels over her half-frightened, half-captivated expression, then settles on her parted lips. *How would they taste?* Delicious, I'm sure. "What's the other reason?" I ask her.

"I don't know," she says too quickly.

My lips curl into a slow smile. "You do," I disagree. "You know *exactly* why. Say it."

She shakes her head.

I put a hand on her thigh, causing her to jump and flinch backwards. That sort of reaction stems from experience; there was a time when I flinched at unexpected contact, too, and it was after some pretty dark shit went down in my life. I'm not certain yet, but I think Mira's been hurt before. Not sexually, but physically.

I almost let go of her and let the topic drop—*almost.* But then, I can't help myself. "Say it, Mira. Or would you like me to?"

"Please don't."

I stroke my thumb over the rip in her jeans, enjoying the smooth warmth of her skin. "I want you in my bed because I *want* you. It's little wonder that I want to fuck you, but that's not what I'm looking for tonight. I'm looking to see how *I* feel with you there. I'm looking forward to finding out what kind of sleeper you are—will you cuddle into me before or after you fall asleep, or at all? Do you curl up into a ball, lie flat on your back, or rest on your side? I'll admit, I'm also *very* curious to see what your hair will look like when it's fanned out on my pillow." I pause, gazing at her lips. "*I want to see it all.*"

She swallows thickly as she watches me. She squeezes her eyes shut and opens them, glancing down at the place where my hand rests on her knee. She picks it up and deposits it back on my lap, making me chuckle.

"There's an animal in this house," she says out of the blue. "Besides you and the other two insane guys, I mean. Can't tell if it's a cat or a dog, but I want to meet it. Is it yours?"

"You'll have to go to the basement for that," I tell her. She stiffens; I smile. "Not the part of the basement you're getting bad vibes from." I'm quite sure I know which room she doesn't want to go near, and there's a good reason for it. "The other side."

"I don't want to go down there," she says, frowning.

I shrug. "We have a half-feral cat. She just had her litter, and she's nesting in a cardboard box down there. I bought her at least a dozen different beds, but," another shrug, "she chose the box."

Mira's eyes brighten. "*Kittens?*"

Hiding a smile, I nod. I had a feeling that the mention of kittens would excite her.

"How old?"

"Almost a month."

She bites her bottom lip. "Can I sleep with them tonight?"

I feel my brows raise. "You'd stay in the basement? I thought you didn't want to go down there."

Her brows draw down. "Yeah, you're right. I should leave them where they are. Can I go down to see them, then sleep here tonight? On this couch?"

I like that I make her nervous. I don't get the sense she's afraid I'll force myself on her anymore—now she's intimidated by my little monologue of exactly *why* I want her in my bed. I *could* set her in the spare room right next to mine tonight, but I'm not going to. I don't want to. I'm going to have her under my sheets with me.

"Yes to going down and meeting the litter, no to staying on the couch. You'll be sleeping in my bed—we've already discussed this."

A cute little pout steals over her lips, and now I'm picturing kissing them again. Biting her bottom lip. Feeling them wrapped around my cock.

"Can I have my phone while I sleep?"

Our tech center is right next to the TV room downstairs, and it has the right equipment for me to get a bug and tracker into her phone. I'll know what she's doing on it, who she's texting, and where she is at all times. She's already guessed that I'll bug her, so I don't think she'll do anything sketchy on it, like send out an SOS to her roommates.

"Yeah. Let's go down to meet the litter. Then we can go to sleep, and I'll give you your phone."

"And headphones?"

I like the hopeful glimmer in her eye. "And headphones." I stand, taking her hand and lifting her off the couch. She looks down at our hands, her frown returning.

"Why are you holding my hand?"

"Because I like the way yours feels in mine." Strangely, I really do. I'm not usually a hand-holder; in fact, I'm not usually one to chase girls around. I've never had or wanted a girlfriend; I've never even kept a hookup in my contacts for longer than a few weeks. With Mira, though… I wouldn't mind keeping her around for a good, long while.

"Why?" she asks.

Adorable. I stroke my thumb over her hand as I walk her down the hallway and toward the wooden staircase that leads to the basement. There's a separate staircase that leads to a room where interrogations sometimes take place. My legion doesn't really like taking people back here for questioning—scrubbing evidence from our home is a hassle—but sometimes it's necessary.

"I like it because yours is tiny. *You're* tiny." At the top step, I pause, lowering my head until it hangs by her ear. "I'm very much looking forward to finding out just how easy it'll be to pick you up, pin you against a wall, or hold you down."

Her free hand reaches up to clutch my arm, even as her head shrinks back. *Mixed reactions.* She'll touch me even when I'm overwhelming her, which is a good sign. I *definitely* look forward to finding out how we'll fit sexually. I've had experiences with plenty of girls who *said* that they were into what I liked, that we shared kinks, but tapped out just as I was starting to have fun. The only time a partner has made it through a punishment is a girl who decided she didn't want a safe word. Watching her wince with every step she took afterward was immensely satisfying.

I think I'll like *anything* I do with Mira even more.

Chapter Six
Mira

I follow Dorian down into the Basement of Doom. He doesn't let go of my hand, and weirdly, I don't mind that so much. The point of contact is warm and ignites a feeling of safety in my belly. I know that's total bullshit; there's not a single thing about this situation that's safe. Dorian happens to be the biggest threat in my life right now, but I appreciate the sense of calm that washes over me, even if I know it's fake and unreliable. Since I can't have my music yet, I'll take what I can get.

I half-expect him to bring me to a place with cement walls stained with old blood, but instead we descend into a TV room. There's a comfortable-looking red velvet couch, accompanied by several stuffed chairs. Across from the couch is a *mega* TV that makes the one upstairs look like an old box from the 20th century. *This* one spans nearly the entire wall. Underneath it is a console table with a cable box, Xbox, and several remotes lined up neatly. *Too* neatly; they're set at perfect 90 degree angles, three inches away from each other. *Someone's got OCD.*

The bad vibes here aren't as intense as I expected, meaning that whatever place is giving off the horrid energy in this house is hidden somewhere nearby. I don't bother trying to discern where; I don't need any more scares tonight. My attention is shortly taken up by a cardboard Amazon box in the corner. Little mewls and tiny meows sound from inside it.

"Credence isn't very friendly," Dorian warns me. "The kittens are cuddly and don't mind being held, but their mom is pretty... what do the animal-enthusiasts call it? Spicy?"

I smile. "Yeah, spicy cats refer to the bitchy, hissy ones. Funny enough, my kindle app is filled up with *spicy* books, and none of them have anything to do with a cat's personality. Isn't it weird how modern-day adjectives have so many meanings?"

Dorian gives me a strange look filled with vague bemusement.

"Is Credence okay with people going up to her?" I ask him.

He nods. "Usually, so long as they don't touch—*what the fuck?*"

A blur of gorgeous black fur leaps out of the box. A beautiful cat with slitted green eyes and a glossy coat regally pads her way across the floor, ears perked up, tail twitching with interest. Her eyes remain fixed on me; I let go of Dorian's hand and smile, sinking to my knees on the ground. I slowly stretch my hand out as she approaches me, palm up, offering her my scent. Credence sniffs the air, blinks slowly, then promptly butts her head into my hand.

"Hey, sweetheart," I greet, scratching behind her ear. "Not so spicy, are we? You're *gorgeous,* has anyone told you that?"

"She *is* spicy," Dorian says, sounding perplexed. "Connor's threatened to turn her out or skin her more than once after she's clawed him. He still has scars from the last time he tried to pick her up by the scruff and toss her outside."

I nod. "Yeah, well, Connor seems like a prick. Is Credence nice to you? Is she your cat?"

"She was living here when we bought the house, so I took responsibility of her. Credence *tolerates* me," Dorian replies. "A few times a month she'll *allow* me to pet her, not walk right up to me and demand attention." I can feel his gaze on me. "Who *are* you?"

"Mira," I reply, chuckling when Credence braces her front paws on my knees and leans deeper into my pets. I switch my position to cross-legged on the ground. She steps back and circles me, rubbing her body along mine. Scent-marking me, probably.

"Are you human?" Dorian asks.

"As far as I know," I reply. "It's a terrible affliction. Humans suck. Most of them ignore their true nature and disregard empathy. I stick to my nature and have *way* too much empathy, which animals can sense. Ergo, they won't leave me alone. Not that I'd want them to." I smile when Credence curls up on my lap, rubbing her cheek over the tear in my jeans. She starts kneading my knee; I wince as her claws sink into my skin.

"Oh no, I think someone needs a nail-trim," I say.

Dorian squats down beside me, reaching his hand toward Credence. She recoils, yowls, and hisses at him in warning.

"Jesus," Dorian says. "This is *ridiculous*."

I blink at him. "I already told you I've been adopted by a wolf pack *and* there's a fox skulk that's taken to me. Both species are known for being extremely antisocial with humans." A frown furrows my eyebrows. "Speaking of, I'm surprised Credence doesn't mind that I stink of wolf. I should've changed before I came down here. Is it really surprising that your mean cat likes me?"

"I guess not," Dorian says. "Hearing it is one thing, seeing it is another." He braces his hand on my shoulder. Credence tracks the gesture, then promptly hisses and claws at Dorian, who withdraws his hand just in time.

I grin at Cadence. "Possessive already? Wonderful. Don't worry, my love, I'm all yours." I lean down to kiss her head. "God, you're so pretty. All that healthy black fur and those gorgeous green eyes. So, *so* pretty."

"She's not pretty, she's fucking *evil*," Dorian seethes. "Seriously, what the hell is happening right now?"

"Don't you need to bug my phone or something?" I ask him. "Wait, quick question, what should I tell my dorm roommates about my absence for the next week? They'll want an explanation."

"Tell them you're having an affair with a hot guy," Dorian dead-pans. "Should be believable enough."

"It won't be," I disagree. "They know I'd never shirk them for something as dumb as sex. That'll make them more suspicious."

"Are they trustworthy?"

"Yes. Not with everyone—Cara likes gossip—but they'd never share something I told them in confidence. We're loyal to each other, to the grave."

"I'll check up on that. If it tracks, you can tell them you saw something you shouldn't have and I'm keeping you close for a while to make sure you're not a threat. I'll talk to the other guys about it in the morning."

Surprised, I gaze at him with a frown. "You'll let me... tell them the truth? Aren't you worried they'll tell someone?"

"Not if they want to keep you safe, which is a point you'll stress to them," Dorian replies. "I'm not going to hurt you; no one here's going to hurt you. This is just a precaution. Make sure they know that saying anything would only put you in hot water, which you're already trying to clamber out of." He shrugs. "Sometimes a partial truth is better than a complete lie."

"Oh. Okay," I say dumbly, absently stroking Credence's belly.

"I'm gonna go into that room for a bit," Dorian says, nodding to a closed wooden door not far from the edge of the huge TV. "Stay here. If you leave or try to run, I'll know, and we'll have problems."

"I won't leave or run, there's a very cute cat in my lap," I tell him. "I'm just going to chill here. What time is it?"

Dorian pulls his phone out of his pocket, checking the screen. He winces. "2 a.m. I'll be quick, then we can go to bed."

I glance around the basement. "Can I sleep here? That couch looks comfortable."

"Nope," he responds. "Stay put, Mira." He turns and walks toward the door, opening it. I catch a glimpse of a desk with four computer monitors and a bunch of computer boxes. Looks like someone here's very technologically adept. He enters the room, leaving the door cracked so he can still see me. I return my attention to Credence, cooing as I stroke her.

After a few minutes of bathing in pets, the mewling of kittens grows louder. Credence meows at me, then pads back to her box. She leaps into it, and a moment later she jumps back out, holding a kitten by the scruff. I press my hands to my chest, melting at the sight. She carefully sets her kitten in front of me. The kit blinks up at me with big blue eyes, considering me for a moment, then awkwardly climbs onto my lap, meowing.

"Oh my goodness," I murmur. "I think I just fell in love with you." I stroke my hand over the kitten's fur as Credence goes back to the box and brings me another kitten. And then another, and another, again and again until I have eight kits climbing over themselves, kneading me, batting at my hair, and meowing adorably.

"Do they have names?" I call out to Dorian.

"Nope," he calls back.

I pout. "That's not cool. They're over a month old, they should have names."

"So give them names," comes a reply, only it doesn't originate from Dorian. I glance over my shoulder, eyes narrowing as I spot Seamus standing at the bottom of the stairs, leaning against the wall with a casual smile. "Hallo, love," he greets.

"Hello, Brit," I reply, echoing my own greeting from earlier tonight. Once again, a sense of danger strikes me in the chest. Seamus is too relaxed, too easy going, and his smile *reaches his eyes*, yet quiet menace rolls off him in palpable waves. I don't think he means me harm right now, but I suspect that could change in a heartbeat.

"You seem to be getting on with our furry friends," he observes.

"They are very cute," I agree. "I'm glad Credence likes me. I'm surprised you guys allow a kitten litter in your House of Horrors."

"House of Horrors, hmm?" Seamus says, stepping forward. He watches as Credence rolls to her belly in front of me and meows, requesting more attention. With her kittens hanging from my shirt, perched on my shoulders, and even climbing up my back, I pet the one on my lap with one hand while reaching forward to stroke her with the other.

"We're not monsters," Seamus says calmly, coming to a stop by the couch. He leans against the arm of it, watching me bathe in the attention of all these adorable felines.

I give him a knowing glance. "Aren't you?"

"I suppose it depends on who you ask," he replies lightly. "To those who stay on our good side, we certainly aren't. Those who oppose us? They'd probably be the first to call us monsters." He releases a breath of laughter. "The ones who are still alive, that is."

"Seamus, get the fuck out of here," Dorian calls from the tech room.

I feel my lips thin at the subtle threat. "I'm not going to oppose you—any of you. I don't even want to *be* here."

"I know you won't go against us," Seamus agrees. "You're a good girl, aren't you, love?"

I feel like there's a double-meaning behind his words. "I guess," I mutter. "I'm certainly not a *stupid* girl, and I'm not keen on getting killed."

"Seamus, get the *fuck* out," Dorian repeats, harsher. "I've got this under control."

"I know you do," Seamus replies, still staring at me. "But I think I'll stay a while." I direct my gaze at the cats, uncomfortable with his presence. I don't think he'll hurt me, but I do think he might want something from me. Earlier, he asked if Dorian would be willing to share me. I don't intend to sleep with Dorian, and I *certainly* have no interest in sleeping with Seamus. He's too... feral.

"Where is she sleeping tonight?" Seamus calls out.

"My room," Dorian replies.

Seamus smiles at me. "If you get bored of him, you're very welcome in *my* room, Mira."

"No, thank you," I say, shaking my head. "I'm not interested."

"Hmm," Seamus hums. "*I'm* interested, though. *Fascinated*, which is quite unusual. Not much fascinates me, but you do."

I lift a shoulder, swiftly catching the kit that tumbles from my neck with a hand. I set her on my lap. "Find someone else to be fascinated with."

"How's your shoulder?" he asks, glancing at my right arm.

I blink, having forgotten about it. The pain has already waned until it's barely noticeable—just a low pulse when I shift too abruptly.

"It's fine. Thank you for putting it back in place."

"You're very welcome." He grins. "I'm good with my hands."

Dorian emerges from the tech room, my phone clutched in his hand. He pockets it and turns a cutting gaze on Seamus.

"Back off," he warns lowly. "You've got a revolving door of hookups, focus on them."

Seamus tilts his head. "So do you." He glances at me. "Do let me know if you change your mind, love. I'd be happy to give you the ride of a lifetime." He taps the couch twice and winks at me before trotting back up the stairs.

I sigh, shaking my head. "Can I go home *now*?"

"Nope. Say goodnight to the kittens, we're heading to bed."

It's a process to extricate myself from Credence and her kittens. I give them all kisses and cuddles, then pause to examine one of them. A black kit with a patch of white fur over one eye doesn't appear to be doing so well. Her breaths are shallow wheezes; there's colored discharge clogging her nose, and the membranes in her face are a bit swollen. She's the runt of the litter, and she's struggling.

"This one needs to go to a vet," I announce to Dorian. "She's sick. Upper respiratory infection, I think. Kittens are super susceptible to them."

Dorian's eyebrows lift as he gazes at me. "Oh?"

I nod. "Yeah. I've seen this before, I'm ninety percent sure that's what it is. Babygirl needs antibiotics and special formula to help her get back on track."

The kitten meows her outrage at being examined so closely; Credence leaps up and grabs her by the scruff, taking her back to the box. I smile vaguely at how utterly adorable they are, even though concern for the runt is dampening my mood.

"Where have you seen it before?" Dorian questions, watching me with lowered brows.

I frown right back at him. "You don't believe me? People don't usually question my affinity for animals or experience with sick ones."

He shakes his head. "No, I believe you, I'm just curious to know where you've seen it before. Have you worked with vets?"

"*Work* with vets, present-tense," I tell him. "I have a job at a local animal shelter. The pay is shit and most of it goes to my wolf pack, fox skulk, and groceries, but the experience is fantastic. One of the vets there is kind of a mentor to me; she lets me shadow her during examinations and surgeries. She's offered to write me a recommendation letter when I apply to vet school, which will be super useful." I gaze back at the box with Credence and her kittens. "Can we take them with us to wherever your room is?"

Dorian shakes his head, smiling faintly. "No, leave them be here. You can check on them in the morning."

I bite my bottom lip as I look at him. "I'd like to clarify that I do not want to spend the night with you. I'd really prefer to have my own room, or even take the couch down here."

Dorian's smile widens. "Noted. Now get your ass over here and let's go to bed."

Dorian's bedroom is on the second floor of the house, and it's a study in minimalism. A king-sized, four-poster bed lies against the far wall, with dark grey covers pulled over it. Off to one side is a bathroom and a walk-in closet. On the opposite wall is a bank of windows that faces the courtyard of the house. There are no pictures or knickknacks.

"You want to shower?" Dorian asks me once he's closed the door and locked it with a key.

"Yeah. I should get the smell of wolves and cats off me. Credence thoroughly scent-marked me."

Dorian nods. "I can give you one of my shirts to replace yours."

"And shorts?" I ask hopefully. I'd rather not be half-naked around Dorian. Despite my fear, the man is potent as hell, and I don't want to lose control of myself.

His lips twist. "I have old basketball shorts with drawstrings."

"Okay. I need to go back to my dorm room in the morning to grab my school supplies. And pack a bag, I guess, if you really are planning on keeping me here the entire week."

"I can accommodate that. I'll take you there before classes—will your roommates be home?"

I nod. "Yes, they will. Speaking of, I've been thinking about what I should tell them. I know they'd keep quiet if I told them the truth, but I don't want to burden them with that." I look at the floor. "People shouldn't be forced to carry certain secrets with them. It's a heavy weight to bear. Instead, I could tell them something else. Maybe that I was being chased around by someone you know of or was in some sort of danger, and you offered to protect me. Since I don't want to bring the threat to them, I'm staying in your gothic, super secure McMansion."

Dorian ponders that for several moments. "Have a lot of secrets you're carrying around, do you?"

I smile grimly. "Yep. And the weight is crushing on a good day, deadly on a bad one. But I can handle it—I've carried a lot inside for a very, very long time. Cara and Valerie are different. They've both been through some shit and I don't want to add to it."

"Huh," Dorian says slowly. "Okay, yeah. That's fine by me. I'll still run it by the other guys in the morning. He disappears into the closet, then reappears with a big white shirt and huge blue shorts. He hands me the clothes. "Go shower. Take your time, feel free to use my products."

I glance at his pockets. "Can I have my phone?"

He pulls it out and hands it to me. I turn and head to the bathroom, closing and locking the door behind me. I set my clothes on the granite counter between two white-basin sinks with stainless steel faucets, and turn on the glass-enclosed shower. While it warms, I investigate my phone, trying to discern if anything's wrong with it now that it's bugged. I really don't like the idea of someone tracking me or seeing everything I do on it, but I suppose it could be beneficial. Dorian won't be as suspicious if he can see that I'm keeping my lips sealed physically and digitally.

I shoot off a text to Cara and Valerie while mulling over what I'll tell them tomorrow. Someone followed me in the forest and I stumbled upon Dorian at the base of the mountain, who was out with his crew for a night hike because they're fucking weirdos. He scared off whoever was chasing me. When I mentioned I didn't want to bring trouble back home with me, he offered to let me stay with him for a while. I'll paint a picture of him being a good guy. Hopefully, it'll work.

I'm quick in the shower, using Dorian's products to scrub my hair and body thoroughly. Once I'm done, I wrap myself in a towel and use some of his toothpaste on my finger to brush my teeth before getting dressed. I have to cinch the waistband of the shorts phenomenally tight for them to stay up. The shirt is like a dress, falling to my knees, but I consider the extra clothing a blessing. I'm not comfortable sleeping in Dorian's bed, especially not after he's made his interest and intent to sleep with me clear, but I don't see a way around it. I also can't deny that I was titillated when he was telling me about his kinks. I don't *want* to be attracted to him, but I am, which means I'll need to tread carefully.

When I step out of the bathroom, Dorian goes in to take his shower. I don't bother trying to escape or leave the room; he locked the door, and I don't want to make things worse for myself by rousing suspicion. My backpack's set at the foot of the bed—he must've brought it up while I was showering. I grab my headphones from it and pop them into my ears, turning on the forest-noises that I sometimes fall asleep to.

Dorian emerges from the bathroom, wearing only a towel wrapped around his hips. I glance up from my phone, then do a double take.

Holy.

Fucking.

Shit.

I knew he was built under his clothes, but I didn't think he was *this* built. His muscles aren't bulky, not like Connor's, but they are *incredibly* well defined. I can see his biceps and triceps, his pectorals, and every finely-honed ridge of his six pack that borders on an eight pack. There's a V at the bottom of his navel that disappears into the towel, and I have a sudden urge to lick the water droplets traveling down his abs.

No. Nope. *Abort mission.*

I pointedly glue my eyes back to my phone, frowning when Dorian chuckles as he retreats into the closet. He saw me staring at him, and finds my admiration entertaining.

He emerges wearing only a thin pair of black briefs that do *nothing* to hide the bulge of his cock. I can't stop myself from glancing at it, even though I know I shouldn't, and a quick look is all it takes to tell me that the big-dick energy he's been emanating is very much proportionate. He's *huge*, and a lot of my arousal dims at the realization that he'd be very, *very* painful to take. I don't care that his focal point with women is controlling their pleasure; I have no intention of getting killed by a monster-cock, and he would probably split me in half. I barely escaped going to urgent care today for my shoulder dislocation, I sure as *shit* am not going to go to the hospital after getting torn up by that goddamn giant.

I take out one of my headphones, pointedly looking him in the eyes. "Can I sleep on the floor?"

"No."

"Okay. Can you put on a shirt?"

"No."

"Why?"

"Because I want to feel you if you cuddle up to me in your sleep, or even brush against me," he explains frankly.

"Oh." I frown. "Why?"

"Because I want to find out if your skin is as soft as it looks."

"Why?"

He releases a long breath. "Because it would feel good. Stop asking why and get in bed."

"Which side do you sleep on?" I ask him.

"The middle, usually," he admits.

I nod. "Alright. I'll take the very edge. The bed's big enough that we don't need to touch. Can I build a pillow fort?"

"No." When I open my lips to ask why, he preempts my question with a response. "Because I don't want to. Because I look forward to seeing if you'll wrap around me in the night. Because I want to feel you, and a few fucking pillows aren't going to get in the way of that. Let's sleep, Mira, it's late and we have an early morning."

Chapter Seven

Unsurprisingly, I *don't* cuddle up to Dorian through the night. I'm not a particularly touchy-feely person when it comes to humans. I like to keep to myself, both when I'm asleep and when I'm awake. I awaken teetering on the very edge of the bed when my phone alarm goes off. I pop my headphones out of my ears, return them to their case, and yawn as I sit up. Beside me, Dorian scowls, his eyes half-lidded.

"It's too early," he says grumpily. "What time is it?"

"7:30," I tell him. "Enough time for me to get stuff from my dorm room, talk to my roommates, and make it to my first class on time."

He lets out a long sigh. "Fine." He rolls out of bed, stretching his arms above his head, and squints at me through the early morning sunlight. "You didn't touch me at all last night."

I nod. "Yeah, I'm not big on physical contact with people." I shrug. "I can sense them from afar, but up close it gets much worse. Looking into someone's eyes can be like staring into their soul, but skin to skin contact amplifies everything tenfold. I've already seen all I need to in your eyes, I don't want to overwhelm myself more."

"And what is it that you've seen?" Dorian asks, seeming more alert now.

I gaze at him. "That your morals are as dark grey as it gets, and your soul is even darker. That you've been hurt in the past, so you hurt people in the present. That you," I shake my head, "are a stone-cold killer who will not lose even a wink of sleep over taking someone's life. I've seen that you're very dangerous, and that you don't discriminate much when you kill."

I stand, offering a wan smile. "On the plus side, I have negative zero desire to sleep with you, and I'm pretty sure you're not one to force girls—could still be wrong on that account, but I don't think I am—which means I'm probably safe from you. So you're not as bad as some of the people I've come across." I yawn. "Can we go to Greywood now?"

Dorian's brows are furrowed as he stares at me, his eyes shining with a mixture of confusion and vague discomfort. As if he doesn't like how well I read him.

Trust me, buddy, I don't like reading people, either.

He clears his throat. "Yeah. Breakfast, then we can go."

A knock sounds on the door. Dorian straightens to his full height, instantly going on alert. He glances at me, motioning at the bed. "Sit there and stay."

My brows knit. "I'm not a dog."

"But you are currently in a house with three people you already know are dangerous. You heard more than you should, and you saw more than you should," Dorian says, gesturing to the bed again.

I don't want him to think I'm going to be an obedient girl he can order around; that would not be a good way to kick off my captivity. Last night, I was scared. I'm still scared, but I'm also pretty sure that Dorian doesn't have any interest in hurting me, and that he won't force me to do anything sexual. In fact, he seems unreasonably invested in protecting me.

I fold my arms over my chest. "I haven't seen anything."

Another knock sounds, this time accompanied by a muffled voice. Dorian walks up to me with a sigh. My breath hitches as he grips my arms and walks me backward until my legs hit the edge of the bed. I fall into a sitting position, bouncing on the mattress. He leans over me, and I become *acutely* aware of just how much bigger he is than me, how much stronger, how easily he could break me in half if he wanted to.

But the realization isn't accompanied by fear. It creates another feeling, something far more dangerous that sparks in my belly and begins to travel lower until it reaches my core. I swallow hard, planting my palms on the mattress and leaning back.

"You see more than you should. You might not have witnessed something that could be construed as a crime, but you have *seen* us. Usually, people who know as much about me and my legion as you do are considered dangerous. You've pinned all of us to an insane degree, which could make Connor and Seamus see you as a problem. You've already heard Connor's opinion on loose ends. When I tell you to sit or stay, it's not because I'm being a prick, it is because I'm thinking of how to keep you safe when you present as a threat to guys who are used to killing threats."

That douses the warmth traveling through me, replacing it with chilling cold. "I'm not a threat," I assure him. "I have no evidence of anything. Even if I wanted to tell someone—which I don't, I value my life—what would I say? That I have a *feeling?*" I shake my head. "I learned to keep shit to myself when I was a kid."

"Good, then we won't have any problems. Nevertheless, when I tell you to sit and stay, you should do it for your own sake. Clear?"

I nod silently. Dorian releases me, stalking over to the door. He opens it, revealing Seamus, who's wide awake and well-dressed in a white button-up and black slacks. Seamus looks at Dorian, glances at me, and smirks. "I see you two have gotten cozy."

"Not as much as I'd like," Dorian says, making my cheeks scorch with a blush. "What's up?"

"Thought our guest might like some clothes that haven't been mauled by a feral animal."

"The alpha's possessive," I inform Seamus. He gazes at me, a smile gracing his lips.

He looks back at Dorian. "Looks like your wolf might not be the only one. Anyhow, I was out to run some errands, so I stopped by to grab some clothes for you. Do you like skirts?"

I shake my head. "Impractical. I like to move and sit how I want."

"Good thing I got options, then." He hands a *very* large shopping bag to Dorian, who glances down at it with furrowed brows.

"Are you trying to buy my affection?" I ask mildly, raising my eyebrows.

Seamus snorts. "No, love. You're not a girl whose affection can be bought, are you? I'm just being civilized, since we'll be roommates for a bit. You play nice, we play nice, yeah?"

Sounds good to me. "Yup. I'm not high maintenance—give me music and leave me alone, and I won't make any problems. Unless you try to keep me away from my friends." I frown. "Is my car still parked at the mountain? I'll need it to go see them."

"I'll take you to campus in a bit, you can see your roommates then," Dorian tells me. "Seamus brought your car back this morning, didn't he?"

Seamus smiles. "I did say errands. I also stopped by a local vet's office and picked up some antibiotics for our sickly kitten. Already gave her the first dose."

"How did you know about the sick kitten?" I wonder.

"Dorian texted me about it last night. Figured I'd kill three birds with one stone this morning and earn myself some brownie points with you."

"Oh. Thank you. Back to the topic, I wasn't referring to my human friends, I mean my wolf pack and fox skulk. Both expect me to make my rounds regularly."

"We'll talk about it later," Dorian says. "Thanks, Seamus. We'll be down to breakfast in a bit." Seamus walks away, whistling a merry tune, and Dorian closes the door.

"You guys have a kitchen, right?" I question. "I usually home-bake treats and bring them to my furry friends. I also occasionally bring treats for my human friends, too." Cara and Valerie *love* it when I cook and bake for them; skills I learned from the only positive role model I've ever had in my life.

"You said you're not high maintenance," Dorian remarks drily.

"*I'm* not. The animals I happen to be attached to are. And my roommates do very well when bribed with baked treats." I tilt my head as I consider him. "I could probably win you guys over with my cookies, too. Or a home-cooked meal, which I'll bet you don't get often."

Dorian appears mildly surprised. "You cook?"

"Yeah. I like cooking and baking; it's soothing. It helps me with my anxiety, and it makes people happy, which gives me a fucking break from all the negativity everyone *constantly* emanates."

Dorian blinks slowly. "Okay, I'll see about the kitchen, food, and your pets. For now, get dressed. We'll grab breakfast on our way to campus."

Dorian agrees to stay in the car while I go into my dorm building. I have about half an hour before my first class, so I'll need to be quick. When I unlock the front door to my apartment-like dorm room, I spot Cara sitting on the small living room couch, scrolling through her phone.

She looks up at my entrance, and her cinnamon-colored eyes blaze as she glares at me. "You *bitch,*" she says. "Where the fuck were you? Do you know how worried I've been?"

Cara is the extrovert of our friend group. She is *very* loud, extremely animated, and a little dramatic to boot. Born to a Brazilian model and an Italian businessman, Cara is absolutely stunning. She's all long limbs and grace, standing several inches taller than me. She has black hair that's currently swept into a bun, and the sort of breathtaking body and cleavage that leaves a line of drooling men wherever she goes.

"I sent a text," I say.

"Oh, okay. It's all good because you *sent a text.*" She scoffs. "Mira, your text said, and I quote, *shit went down, I'm alright, I'll see you tomorrow.* Then you didn't respond to my five texts!"

"You sent those five texts in the ten minutes you've been awake," I point out calmly. I received them on my way here.

"Chill out, Car," Valerie says, strolling out of her room with her backpack slung over her shoulder. She looks me over with ice-blue eyes, eyebrows raising. "New clothes?"

I glance down at the crème blouse and dark jeans I wear. Seamus has good style. "Yeah."

"What happened?" Valerie queries, heading over to our small kitchenette and pouring herself a cup of coffee from the ancient coffee machine.

"Why the *fuck* weren't you here when we woke up?" Cara demands.

I sigh. "Look, it's been a long night. The basics? After I left my pack, someone was following me. A guy, I think. I'm pretty sure he had a knife, and I got *super* scared. I ran out onto the road, was lucky enough to run into another guy, one who goes to Greywood. He scared whoever the fuck was following me off—apparently, he's had dealings with the forest stalker. Long story short, I'm pretty sure I got spotted by the sort of person nobody wants to get spotted by, so Dorian Acheron offered for me to stay with him for a bit so that I didn't bring any shit back to campus and you guys."

Cara blinks several times, lips parting.

"Dorian Acheron, as in the guy who's so deep into criminal dealings it's a wonder he goes to college?" Valerie asks calmly. "Yeah, he sounds like an ideal candidate to protect you." Her words are coated with sarcasm.

"Shit," Cara murmurs. "I'm sorry. Are you okay? Being chased through the woods must've been so fucking scary."

It was, but not in the way she thinks. I don't *like* lying to my two only friends, but I see it as a necessity to protect them, so that's exactly what I'm going to do.

"I'm okay," I assure her. "Mainly, I'm worried about bringing stuff back to you guys. I don't know who was after me, whose path I crossed—Dorian won't tell me—but I think it's someone bad. Worse than Dorian. I won't say that Acheron is a *good* guy, and his crew is scary, but they're the lesser evil." My lips twist. "The vibe I got from the guy chasing me was... *not* good. I'm pretty sure he wanted to kill me and bury me in a shallow grave, or worse. So, yeah, I'm accepting Dorian's protection. Just for a bit until he takes care of his own dealings with whatever the fuck is going on, and I'm safe to come back."

Valerie sips her coffee. "That's sketchy," she announces. "You're being sketchy and withholding shit."

"Of course I am," I agree. "I don't want to get the two of you in deep shit. I'm going to keep some stuff to myself for your safety." That much is completely true.

"Fair enough," Valerie says with a nod, looking me over. She brushes a few strands of her long, reddish-brown hair out of her face, giving me a long up and down. "Looks like Dorian's treating you well. Is he into you?"

"I think so," I say. "He's not my type, though. I'm just accepting his protection for now, which was probably extended *because* he's into me."

"Guys don't like to be shirked like that," Valerie replies, blue eyes darkening into a midnight color. "Don't lead someone like Dorian on."

I let out a puff of laughter. "Believe me, *I'm not*. I made it patently clear that I wasn't going to fuck him."

"Dorian Acheron, hmm?" Cara asks, eyes brightening. She is easily one of the most sexual people I know, all about free love, and is known for leaving a trail of broken hearts in her wake wherever she goes. "I've seen him around campus. He's hot. *Really* hot. Like, I'd let that man tie me up and fuck me however he feels like fucking me hot, you know?"

I swallow, trying to keep my nerves from fluttering. I'm trying not to think about getting down and dirty with Dorian; my arrangement with him is temporary. Just until he and his housemates are convinced that I'm going to keep my lips closed. I don't understand why they're so worried; I literally *didn't* see anything, I mainly just inferred. They must be into some pretty dark shit to be so suspicious.

"You're going to get yourself killed one of these days," Valerie says to Cara, finishing her coffee and washing the cup. "You'll let the wrong guy fuck you and then your face will be on the 5 o'clock news."

Cara smiles serenely. "Not while I have Mira around to vet my guys for me." She turns to me. "You've probably saved me from getting killed once or twice."

On the rare occasion when Cara manages to drag me and Valerie to a local bar, she's usually in the mood to hunt down whoever her next fuck-buddy will be. She has a steady rotation of them; they last about a week before she's bored and ready to move on. When she sets eyes on someone she likes, she turns to me and asks what his vibes are. I give her my honest opinion, which prompts her to either go home with him or keep looking.

"Not killed, but hurt or taken advantage of," I agree. My phone buzzes in my pocket. Seeing that it's a text from Dorian, I sigh. "Dorian's acting a bit protective. He's sort of shadowing me for a bit."

"Sounds like a stalker," Valerie says. "You sure it wasn't him chasing you in the woods?"

I have to choke down a laugh and fight *really* hard to keep myself from grimacing. "Positive. He can't be in two places at once."

"Stalker or no, he's hot as fuck," Cara chips in. "I wouldn't mind getting stalked by him."

I feel my lips thin. "Once I'm out of his hair, I'll send him in your direction. I need to pack a bag and grab my school shit, I'll see you guys later."

"Be safe," Valerie says, gaze lingering on me. "Seriously. If something's wrong, you can tell me. You know that, right?"

"Of course," I agree. I *do* know that. I know I could tell them anything and it'd stay here, I just don't want to burden them. I make quick work of packing a bunch of my clothes into a duffle bag, grab my backpack, and head downstairs. Dorian waits in his BMW; I inhale a deep breath before getting in.

"I don't like the fact that I have to stay with you," I say as I close the door. "Seriously. I'm not going to say anything. I'm good at keeping my lips sealed."

"Your roommates believed you?" Dorian queries, ignoring my complaint.

"Relatively, yeah. They won't ask questions. You have a reputation around campus."

He shifts the car into gear. "That I do."

I sigh as he peels out of the dorm parking lot. "Look, you have my phone bugged. You can keep an eye on me from afar."

He glances at me. "I know you don't like having to stay with me, but it's a necessity. The boss demanded it. He's not the sort of person that it's wise to refuse."

"Who's your boss?" I ask. "Actually, never mind, I don't want to know."

Dorian's lips quirk. "Clever girl. It's only for a week. You'll survive. I'll pick you up outside the science department at five, be ready."

I pull my phone out of my pocket and fiddle with it, mainly for something to do. "Fine."

"When do you usually go see your animals?"

"Tuesdays and weekends, when I'm not scheduled for a shift at the animal shelter."

Dorian nods. "And you bring them baked treats?"

I smile a little at the memories that flit across my mind; my foxes and wolves nudging at my backpack and staring at me with those adorably hopeful eyes. "Yeah."

Dorian glances at me again, eyes warming. "If I take you grocery shopping, will you make me something?"

"You gonna pay for additional supplies?"

He looks a little surprised at that. I think I might've overstepped, but then he says, "Obviously. Why wouldn't I?"

Because I usually have to balance my books myself, and it gets fucking hard. Especially when I can't *not* go see my pack and skulk without a container full of treats for them. And I won't go with store bought treats; they have all sorts of unhealthy shit in them.

"If you tell me Connor's favorite meal, I can also make you guys dinner tonight. So long as you pay."

That does *not* appear to please Dorian. "Why Connor? You don't want to make *me* something?"

I roll my eyes. "Connor, because he's the one who would prefer me dead. I'm pretty sure he's utilitarian; if I prove useful, he might start seeing me as less of a loose end and more of something else. Not a person, I don't think, but something *other* than a loose end, which sounds good to me."

"He's not going to kill you," Dorian assures me. "I won't let him"

"It might be good if his inability to kill me hinged on something other than his friends holding him back," I say bluntly. "If you tell me his favorite dinner, I'll make your favorite dessert for you." I shake my head with a sigh. "Men. You're all too much trouble and effort."

Dorian's lips quirk. "Any time you want to see exactly what I can bring to your life, Mira, let me know. I'm *very* much a giver." He sighs, smile dropping. "Connor likes all-American dinner's—steak and potatoes. We have a grill. You know how to grill?"

"Yup. The grocery store I usually hit doesn't have really good steaks, though."

"We'll go to a place I know. Seamus likes anything that's cooked well, so he's easy to please."

"And you? What do you want for dessert?"

"You," he responds bluntly. "But I'll take whatever. Just surprise me."

Chapter Eight

"It's cold out tonight." Chloe Rodgers says, shivering beside me. She rubs her hands up and down her arms as we brave the bitter chill to get to the parking lot behind the science buildings.

The strawberry-blonde, green-eyed enchantress shares my animal science course, even though she's technically on biochemistry track. She's taking one of the hardest courses as a freaking *elective*. The girl is scary smart, scary pretty, and scary nice. The truly terrifying thing is that her niceness isn't a thin shield; she's genuinely a kind person, which is just eerie to me.

"Vermont weather can be harsh," I agree, pulling my blouse tighter around me. It's nice—silk, so soft I could weep. Seamus might be one scary motherfucker, but he's got good taste in women's clothes.

Chloe pulls her phone out of her pocket as we reach the parking lot and sends a text—probably to Mason, her boyfriend. I've met him enough times to deduce he is *not* a good person, but he is so devoted to Chloe it's almost suffocating. When he looks at her, everything about his energy just... lifts.

"Mason coming to pick you up?" I ask her, stuffing my hands into the pockets of my jeans.

She nods. "Yeah, he's running a bit late. I've told him I should get a car, my stepdad has offered to buy me one more than once, but Mase likes driving me."

"He really loves you," I say with a faint smile. "It's kind of sickening."

Chloe lets out a light, ringing laugh. "He scared me at first. A lot. But I love him, too. He's good to me."

I don't think there are many people who can say that about Mason Sieger, heir to a multibillion-dollar empire, but I don't doubt his devotion to Chloe.

"You need a ride somewhere?" she asks me. "Back to dorms? I know they're across campus."

I bite my lip. "A friend's picking me up, so I'm good."

"M'kay," Chloe says, just as Mason's car pulls up in front of us.

She gives my hand a squeeze, smiles, and gets in the car. Mason only spares me the briefest glance before curling a hand around Chloe's neck and drawing her in for a deep, lingering kiss. I avert my gaze, even as something in my chest pulses with want. After a minute, the car pulls away, leaving me alone in the cold, with my teeth chattering.

I'm not left to wait for long before Dorian also pulls up in his BMW. If only I could feel as safe around him as Chloe does around Mason, I could breathe a *lot* easier. Instead, I'm going to endeavor to win over the members of his house by making a really, *really* good dinner that'll hopefully make them want to kill me a little less.

The drive to the grocery store is mostly taken in silence—I can tell Dorian's mind is elsewhere. The quiet doesn't bother me. I go over the notes I took for my classes today until we approach a *super* nice store—the one on the rich side of town. I grab his arm as he pulls into a parking spot.

"Um... can we go to the Speed Mart downtown?" I ask him.

His brows furrow. "This place is better. It has a good meats selection, too, so we won't have to go to a butcher."

I chew my lip. "Yeah, I don't doubt it, but working at an animal shelter doesn't pay much. I have a pretty strict budget for grocery shopping, and I need to get more supplies for my pack and clan. I..." *God,* this is embarrassing. "I can't afford this place."

His expression smooths out. "Oh, don't worry about it. Whatever you need, I'll cover it."

I shake my head firmly. "No. You're paying for dinner stuff, definitely, but not the rest—I don't want to be in your debt."

"You won't be," he replies. "As much as you're trying to make nice with my crew, it'd also behoove me to make nice with you, don't you think?"

"No. Whether or not you're nice to me won't change the fact that I'll keep my mouth shut. I still will." My plan is to avoid getting killed or seen as a loose end for the next week, then return to my life as it was.

Independence is something I've always prized; I worked *really* fucking hard to earn it, and I'm not eager to lose it or have it undermined. I also don't really *want* Dorian to be nice to me. I don't want to start forgetting who he is or how we met—I don't want to be charmed by him. I know he's into me, I know he wants to have sex with me, and I don't want to give into that.

I won't deny that I've experienced moments of attraction to him—he is *really* hot—but I like to think I'm better than sleeping with someone I caught getting rid of a body in the woods.

Dorian sighs. "It's been a long day, let's not argue. You won't owe me anything. This doesn't have to mean anything. It's just groceries."

He gets out of the car without giving me a chance to respond. Reluctantly, I follow, frowning even as I tell myself that it *is* just groceries. I don't even want to know how much Seamus spent on the bag of clothes he presented me with—these jeans alone probably cost at least seventy bucks, and the silky blouse... *yeah.* I'm pretty sure a few hundred dollars would be pocket change to these guys. Shit, a few *thousand* dollars probably wouldn't make a dent in their accounts.

I bite my lip and follow Dorian inside the store, spending the next half hour pointedly averting my eyes from all the price tags. *It's not my money.* Besides, Dorian *did* dislocate my shoulder last night, so I could view this as *his* way of making reparations to *me*. I don't think he feels bad about hurting me, but I can pretend he does, and pretend that this is his way of paying me back.

I find myself sneaking glances at him on the drive back to his gothic McMansion. There's definitely something down about him today, as if he's received shitty news or heard something he didn't want to hear. Part of me is tempted to ask him about it; another part is actually tempted to *soothe* him. I resist both temptations, opting to instead go through the recipes folder in the notes app of my phone. I've tested out a lot of recipes over the years, and I always write down the ones that work best, along with a few personal edits I figure out as I go along.

Growing up, I never had the privilege to cook—there was barely even canned food at home. I only started learning when I began visiting a friend who was a cooking enthusiast. As soon as I left for Greywood and started earning my own money, I spent all of my free time honing my cooking skills. I was pretty crappy at first, even with the practice I'd gotten over the years. Valerie and Cara nearly kicked me out of our dorm because of my disastrous experiments, but after a few months I improved. Now, they *love* it when I cook; they'll even contribute to groceries when they know I'm making a family meal for all of us.

"It's early," Dorian observes. "We usually don't eat until 10. We're night owls in this house."

I release a breath of relief. "Oh, good. Then I'll have time to make everything I was thinking of *and* marinate the steaks."

Dorian throws me a squinty look as he parks his car in front of the House of Horrors. "That's four hours from now," he says slowly. "Are you planning on cooking enough to feed an army?"

I smile faintly, shaking my head. "No, I'm planning to cook enough to have leftovers for a few days. Do you know how rare it is for me to have enough groceries to make *several* dishes? I love cooking. It relaxes me. Tonight's as much for me as it is for you, big guy." I nod towards the back seat. "I'm designating you as my bag boy; help me carry groceries."

Dorian's brows furrow. "You don't have to serve us, you know," he says. "I'd actually prefer if you didn't."

I pat his hand. "Once again, this'll be fun for *me*. Cooking calms me, and weirdly enough, I've had a lot of anxiety since meeting you. You and your psycho roommates just happen to be lucky beneficiaries of my coping skills. And hopefully Connor will start seeing me as something other than a liability—that's also part of the game plan. If not," I shrug, "at least I'll get to spend a few hours engaging in one of my favorite hobbies. Now, seriously. Help me get the groceries."

There are over half a dozen bags brimming with products—vegetables, meats, flour, sugar, dark chocolate. I might've gone a bit overboard once I started viewing Dorian swiping his card as him repaying a debt. "Let's go."

I carry two light bags filled with produce, while Dorian carts everything else. He unlocks the mansion door, taking me straight into a kitchen with appliances that nearly make my mouth water.

Huge marble island. Stainless-steel fridge. Chef's grade six-burner stove and *four* ovens. Oh, I am going to have *fun* tonight. Usually, I have to make do with an oven possessed by a demon and a barely functional two-burner stove.

Dorian spends a few minutes showing me all the cooking supplies, a seemingly endless stockpile. Mixing bowls, whisks, measuring cups, even pasta makers and a mandoline. Excitement sizzles in my veins; I've never had a kitchen or so many excellent tools to work with.

"You need help?" Dorian asks, watching as I lay out the grocery items and start collecting cutting boards, mixers, knives, and pots and pans of all different sizes.

"Nope," I respond. "You'll just get in my way. You're good to go, everything will be ready at ten." I wash my hands and grab several sauces from a cupboard to start on a marinade for the steak. "You guys have a grill?" I ask.

He nods. "Out back. Let me know a half hour before you need it, and I'll fire it up." He seats himself at a small wooden table in the corner of the kitchen, pulling his phone out of his pocket. "I'll stick around."

I frown at him, opening my mouth to tell him I prefer to work in peace, but think better of it. "Whatever floats your boat."

The next hours are spent in a flurry of slicing, dicing, mixing, frying, baking, and preparations. I'm undertaking an impressive menu tonight, and creative ideas are buzzing through my mind. If I wasn't so dedicated to becoming a vet, I'd pursue being a chef—as is, cooking will just remain my beloved hobby.

There will be three kinds of meat today—chicken, filet mignon, ribeye—and a dizzying number of side dishes. Home-made salsa and guacamole. Dauphinoise potatoes. Mediterranean roasted potatoes. A simple chopped salad with my favorite dressing. Several flatbread pizzas with different toppings. Spicy-sweet fried plantains.

As I'm prepping oven temperatures, I glance over at Dorian. He retrieved his laptop a few minutes ago; now he sits in front of it, squinting at whatever he's reading.

"Hey, Dorian?"

He turns to look at me. "Yeah, baby?"

"Don't call me that. Generally speaking, how much do you and your roommates eat?"

"An inhuman amount," he responds drily, sweeping his eyes over the loaded kitchen island. "Your food will be put to good use."

I nod, battering the plantain slices to prepare them to fry. "Good. I'd feel pretty shitty if any of this was gonna go to waste."

"It won't," he says. "Everything smells delicious, by the way. Whatever we don't eat today, we'll finish off tomorrow." A wry smile touches his lips. "Be careful, Mira. You spoil the occupants of this house, and we might get used to it."

I let out a laugh. "I'm spoiling myself—this kitchen is *fantastic*. Once again, you three—"

"Just happen to be lucky beneficiaries, yeah," he interjects with a playful eye roll. "So I've been told." He returns his attention to his laptop, and I return my attention to my cooking.

At 9:15, everything besides the grilling and a handful of potato dishes baking in the oven is done. I send Dorian out to turn on the grills, and of course, that's when Seamus decides to wander into the kitchen.

"Sorry to interrupt, love," he says mildly, walking up to the counter and surveying the many serving bowls and plates covering it, most of them already filled with yummy delights. "It smells absolutely *wonderful* in here, so I couldn't resist. Are you treating us for being good boys and not killing you?"

My lips thin at the reminder of the thin ice I still tread on. "I'm treating both myself *and* you." I snap a dishtowel at him. "Now, shoo. Right now, this is my kitchen."

Seamus's eyebrows raise as he regards me. "That so? I think it's *our* kitchen."

"When you taste my food, you'll be begging me to permanently take over this kitchen," I inform him. "Enough with the veiled threats; I'm *still* not going to talk."

"I'll hold you to that," Seamus says. I feel his gaze on me as I turn to wipe down the counter around the stove. "Your ass looks *fantastic* in those jeans, by the way—*ow!* The *fuck,* Acheron?"

"I already said I'm not going to share. I will not say it again. *Get. Out,*" Dorian growls. I spin around to see that he's returned from firing up the grills and is staring at Seamus with a murderous expression.

"Okay! *Fuck,* okay." Seamus turns and breezes out of the kitchen, but not before tipping me a wink that makes Dorian growl.

I set a few timers on my phone so I don't forget about the dishes in the oven. Turning to Dorian, I request, "Help me carry these to the grill." I pull the bowls of marinating steak from the fridge.

Dorian's eyebrows raise. "Yes, chef." He picks up two bowls while I grab the third, leading me through the kitchen and to a doorway at the end of a hall, which lets out onto a back patio I haven't seen yet. Stone pillars support a wooden roof over the patio, with withering ivy vines languidly crawling over the beams.

The patio is nice, but the backyard is in a state of disrepair. Brown grass sprouts in awkward patches across the uneven, dark soil. There are no flowers in sight, though random tufts of what might be wheat grow at the base of a tall stone wall, which stands guard over the house like a watchful sentinel.

The grill is a masterpiece of design, momentarily making me forget the backyard's disrepair. Stainless steel and four-burner, it boasts sleek metal trays affixed to its sides where I set the bowls, and a gleaming hood that lifts to reveal pristine grates, ideal for crafting perfect cross-hatch marks.

"I'm good out here," I tell Dorian. "I won't run away. You can go back inside."

"I'm staying," Dorian replies, watching as I set two pairs of tongs by a large fork and carving knife. I let out a low moan at the *sizzle* as I plop the steaks on the grate, practically salivating. "I don't think I've ever seen you so... content."

I blink at him. "So far, you've seen me when I was zoned out at a library, with a dislocated shoulder last night, and today while I've been uncomfortable because I want to go home. My circumstances aren't really permitting contentment right now, but cooking? Yeah, that chills me out and makes me happy."

"Need help?" Dorian asks. "Or will I just be *getting in your way?*" He lifts his fingers to mime quotation marks around the words, telling me how ridiculous he thinks I'm being.

I feel my lips quirk. "I might have you watch the steaks in a few minutes when my first timer goes off. I'll need to take the filet mignon and potatoes out of the oven."

Dorian's eyes darken. "I don't want you going into the house alone."

"Because it's not safe?" I query, arching an eyebrow. "You're the one who told me the three of you are under orders to *not* kill me. I don't think Seamus wants me dead—he wants to get in my pants instead—and you indicated that Connor listens to your boss."

"It's not a matter of safety," Dorian growls. "It's a matter of, I don't want Seamus to get any one-on-one time with you—which he'll use to charm his way into your pan*ties*—or for Connor to get the chance to scare the shit out of you."

I contemplate that for a moment, prodding at the steaks with my tongs. "Well, I'm very practiced with resisting guys who want to get in my panties, and I'm used to fear."

"I sensed as much last night," Dorian agrees. "That doesn't mean I want you to feel it."

That'd be sweet if Dorian hadn't already scared me half to death. Deciding to pivot topics, I ask, "What had you in a shitty mood earlier?"

Dorian waves a dismissive hand, but I don't miss the way his shoulders momentarily stiffen. "Nothing. Legion stuff. *Business* stuff."

I give him a long look, pondering whether I should push for more. After a few seconds, I decide against it. Whatever's going on with him is none of my business, and it's not like I care about him. At least I *shouldn't* care, even though I find myself wanting to know more.

My phone alarm for the dauphinoise potatoes and filet mignon goes off. I hand Dorian the tongs, quickly rushing into the house to take the potato casserole and steak out of the oven, smiling at the delicious scents. Since Dorian doesn't chase after me, I figure he isn't *that* worried about his roommates.

Dinner preparations are finished up in silence. Dorian shows me the dining room, which features a gorgeous dark wood table. He helps me set it and bring the dishes over to it. As I take the desserts I whipped up out of the oven and set them under a warming light, I hear footsteps converging in the dining room, signaling the arrival of the two crazy guys sharing this house with Dorian. I inhale a long, steeling breath before joining the men gathering at the table.

I shouldn't care, but I want them to enjoy dinner. I want Connor to stop seeing me as a liability and start seeing me as an actual *human*, though that might be a bit much to ask for. I want Seamus to stop with the veiled threats. Making a nice dinner won't solve all my problems, but it could be the distraction we all need.

In the dining room, Seamus surveys all the dishes with an expression of deep interest and intense longing, while Connor's eyebrows rise as he looks everything over.

I spend a few minutes pointing at the dishes and rattling off what they are before taking a seat and anxiously waiting for everyone to dig in and give me feedback. I *love* cooking, and I also love it when other people like what I produce, what I sometimes spend *hours* on.

At his first bite of the dauphinoise potatoes, Seamus moans, "Holy *fuck.*"

Connor, who went right for the steak, gives me an approving nod. "What'd you use to marinade it?"

"Chef's secret." I turn to Dorian, who eats in silence beside me, throwing me narrow-eyed looks. Almost as if he doesn't like that I'm impressing his roommates or doing anything that could be seen as a service to them.

A *pop* and *crack*, reminiscent of gunshots, sounds off in the distance. Dorian stiffens; Connor drops his fork and knife, expression turning murderous; Seamus sighs. "Looks like we've got company."

Chapter Nine

"No fucking way," Dorian says, his words a furious mutter. "*This* close to campus? They'd have to be insane."

"This gang's not exactly renowned for their sanity," Connor comments drily. "This is pretty daring of them, though. Maybe it's not—"

A crack in the window of the room precedes a bullet whizzing past me, missing my hair by an inch and burying into the stone wall behind me. I gasp, sweat breaking out over my skin as my heart begins to race. Dorian yanks me out of my seat and pushes me to the floor, behind one of the legs of the table. Seamus and Connor also crouch behind the table, exchanging glances and rushed words.

"They've breached the perimeter," Dorian says to Seamus and Connor. My mind reels, going at a hundred miles per minute. "Let's arm up and go give them a greeting."

"What the *fuck* is going on?" I whisper.

Seamus glances at me. "Just some business, love. Unusual, but part of the life. Be a good girl and stay under the table—don't move, don't breathe too loud. They shouldn't be able to get in, but—"

"But I left the back patio unlocked after bringing in the steaks," Dorian says grimly, his words punctuated by several more cracks at the windows and accompanying bullets flying through.

Horrible memories prickle at my mind. This is not the first shootout I've been stuck in the middle of, thanks to the occupation of my stepfather. Consequently, the wave of anxiety that sweeps over me is almost debilitating. *Almost.* I push down the nerves in favor of grounding myself in the present, keeping my mind here. If I dissociate now, that could mean death for me.

Seamus army-crawls across the floor to a wooden cupboard lying against the wall and swiftly opens it. He draws out three black briefcases, sliding two of them along the floor to Connor and Dorian. Each man promptly enters a code on the combination lock of their briefcase, lifting the lids to reveal three guns of different sizes. A door slams somewhere in the house; my breath catches as I realize the attackers are now inside.

"Give me a gun," I tell Dorian.

He glances at me while loading his weapons, shoving a .45 in the back of his pants and holding a pistol in his right hand.

"Don't be ridiculous, Mira," he murmurs. "Just breathe. This'll all be over soon."

Connor chances a look up and over the table, squinting. "I count three in the yard. If they're adhering to standard formation for their ranks, that means there are about six to nine of them here."

"That leaves two or three for each," Seamus responds, cocking his gun. "Let's have some fun, shall we?"

"*Dorian,*" I emphasize. "Give me a fucking gun, I'm serious."

"Mira, you're in shock—"

"*I'm not in shock*—" Several sets of footsteps sound throughout the house, ratcheting my anxiety up to level 1000. I try to control my panting breaths, forcing away memories of home invaders and people who'd break into my childhood house in the middle of the night, wanting to kill my stepdad as revenge for his many heinous crimes.

The people who accidentally killed my mother instead...

Past and present blur as my finely-honed survival instincts overtake me. There was a time when I'd freeze in these sorts of situations; lots of practice at a shooting range and figuring out how to take control of my fate rather than sit in a corner and pray for my life helped me overcome that.

"In the hall," Seamus calls out, training his gun on the doorway. Two shadowed figures dressed in all black run through the hall, one of them holding a semi-automatic rifle, the other a handgun. Seamus lifts his firearm and takes aim. When he tries to shoot, the gun jams, which marks the end of my obedience and restraint.

I grab the third gun out of Dorian's briefcase as Seamus curses and Dorian takes cover behind a table leg. A hail of bullets rain over us. They hit the table, the walls behind us, even the windows, but by some miracle, none make contact with us.

Crouching low to the ground, I load the gun, click off the safety, cock it, and take aim. Two shots go off at once; one from Dorian, the other from me. Dorian's bullet hits the chest of the guy with the semiautomatic rifle, mine hits the forehead of the one with a handgun.

"What—*the*—*fuck*?" Seamus hisses at me.

"You can question me and be suspicious later," I snap at him. "I told you that I've been in life-or-death situations before."

More shots fire at the window of the room, shattering the glass entirely. It rains to the floor in a hail of shards, and I know whoever's on the other side must be close. They're probably planning to get in through the window, so there'll be people coming at us from all sides. Connor runs into the hallway, preparing to take down whoever he meets there. Seamus is glancing at the other hall at the opposite end of the room—he takes off a moment later. I peek over the table, ducking just before another shot whizzes by my head.

I inhale two deep breaths as I wait for the enemies to fire off the next round of bullets, trying to calm my racing heart. I need to be clearheaded if I'm going to make it out of here alive.

"There are three people out there," I murmur to Dorian. "I can get one of them."

He looks like he has questions, but instead he says, "They're too far out *and* they're obscured by darkness. There's no clean shot."

I don't need to see them to sense where they are—I can *always* feel the presence of people, especially those who radiate the sort of oppressive dark energy coming from the invaders. Frustrated, I growl and chance another glance over the table, straining to focus on the faintly visible dark silhouettes outside. The most menacing of the three, a man who practically reeks of death and blood, offers the clearest shot; I aim and take it. A strangled cry cuts through the air, followed by the heavy thud of his body hitting the ground.

"Mira, what the—"

"They're getting closer," I tell him. "I have *not* lived this long only to die now because you decided to keep me as a captive in your House of Horrors. Fucking *shoot*, Dorian!"

I fire off another bullet just as Dorian takes three consecutive shots, finally getting over his shock and focusing on the action.

One of our bullets take down a second man, but the last one standing fires a shot that hits Dorian's arm. My chest pangs with alarm as he jerks and reels back with a low groan. *Shit.* Blood pours from his arm and the bullets *just keep coming*. Dorian falls to the floor with a thud, breathing heavily, face draining of all color. A single glance at his wound tells me that the bullet didn't hit his brachial, which means tending to him can wait. Looks like the hunk of metal skimmed the outside of his shoulder before burying into the wall.

I can *feel* the remaining gunman's anger at the loss of his comrades, and that makes him reckless. Reckless men waste ammunition, and they eventually have to pause to reload or grab their second gun. I wait for the empty *clicking* sound to signal that he's out of ammo; as soon as it comes, I abandon cover and squeeze the trigger of my weapon, hitting the last gunman square between the eyebrows.

Gunfire sounds from both ends of the house, making me flinch and swallow harshly. If Seamus and Connor are on whoever's gotten in, I have to trust that they'll take care of the issue; they're the trained professionals. I'm a rookie who learned how to shoot so she wouldn't feel so fucking helpless all the time—though I was technically trained by a professional, as well.

I close my eyes and try to feel if there are any more presences lurking nearby. The only ones I sense come from the house itself—Seamus and Connor are hopefully taking care of them. My lips thin as I look at Dorian, who's clutching his arm with a grimace. I follow his gaze down to the blood that's seeping out of his skin.

"Let me see," I tell him. He gives me a jaded look, like he might refuse, but then he nods. I empty the chamber of my gun, flick on the safety, and pull out the magazine, quickly pushing the extra bullet back into the magazine before shoving the weapon in the waistband of my jeans. The last thing I need is to accidentally shoot myself after narrowly avoiding getting shot by whoever the fuck came for Dorian.

"Sit up," I tell him. "Prop your back against the table leg."

"Is it clear outside?" he asks me.

I nod. "It is."

His eyes narrow even as he sits up with a groan, following my instructions. "How do you know?"

"I can feel them. They reek of menace and a deep-seated desire to kill you. There's only one left alive in the house," I say quickly, lifting the sleeve of his shirt to get a better look at his wound. "It didn't graze any arteries. I'm gonna feel around it to see if it tore muscle," I tell him. "It'll hurt."

He nods, lips twisting with anticipation. I run my fingers along the edges of the gaping wound, then the sides and back of his arm, closing my eyes so I can focus purely on the feeling of it. "No muscle tears," I tell him, opening my eyes. "It didn't go too deep. It's just a flesh wound—"

"It's time for you to explain how the *fuck* you know how to shoot a gun," Connor says from the doorway, his voice little more than a growl. I wince as I hear and *feel* the anger radiating from him. *He wants to kill me.* I'm sure of it. The purpose of tonight was to *not* be viewed as a loose end or threat, and now, I've turned into a greater threat than I was before.

"Do you want me to stitch up Dorian first?"

Heavy footsteps carry Connor over to me. I brace myself, hissing as he fists a hand in my hair and cranes my neck to stare up at him. What I see makes me wince. He's covered in blood—not his own, I don't think, but it's soaking through his shirt and pants, and there are splatters of it across his face and neck. "Right now, I want to kill you, Mira," he growls lowly. "Fucking. Talk."

"Ease up, lad," Seamus says mildly from the doorway, also having returned.

"You saw her. She can shoot. She's been trained. The background check on her hasn't come back yet. Last night, she was a loose end; tonight, she's a threat."

I whimper when Connor pulls me up by my hair, yanks the gun from my waistband, and drops me in a dining chair. He braces his hands on the back of it, leaning over me. "I find it very fucking suspicious that you made a distracting dinner just before nine guys decided to try to break in. Did the Serpents send you?"

Unable to control my fear any longer, I let out a shaky, "No."

I glance at Seamus, who leans against the wall with thinned lips. He won't help me. Then, at Dorian, who's also watching this exchange without intervening. I give him a desperate *please help* look. His eyes shadow for a moment, as if he's contemplating it. He glances between me and Connor; hope sears through my veins. Maybe he'll tell his psycho roommate to back the hell off. Maybe he'll defend my innocence. *Maybe he's not all bad...*

Dorian gives his head a slight shake. A shard of pain pierces my chest. Last night, he seemed intent on keeping me alive—he's come onto me more times than I can count in the twenty-four hours I've known him. Now, he's leaving me to the resident psychopath? I saved his fucking *life!*

Connor grabs my chin roughly and redirects my line of sight to him. "Don't look at them. They won't help you. Look at me. *Did the Serpents send you?"*

"No," I repeat again, more firmly. "If Serpents refers to the guys who just attacked, then you'll notice I killed several of them. Why would I kill someone who sent me?"

"She did," Dorian confirms, his words little more than a groan. He's in pain—previously, I was going to help him, but now I'm *seething* mad at him. I know I shouldn't be, but he's not helping me or protecting me from Connor, which means he gives a total of zero fucks about me, so I need to give *negative* fucks for him. He can go to hell; all of these crazy fuckers can go to hell.

"That doesn't mean someone else didn't send you," Connor growls lowly, still not looking away from me. "Who? The Southies? Someone who has shit against the Bratva?"

"No one sent me!" I snap.

"Then where the *fuck* did you learn how to shoot a gun?" Connor demands.

As a general rule, I do not talk about my past. It's a graveyard filled with bones, ghosts, and demons. Any time I've tried to talk about it, I ended up unleashing those ghosts and demons on myself. It rattles me so much I always spend the next days in a state of hyper-anxiety. I certainly do not want to tell *these* assholes anything, but I can see just how much Connor wants to kill me. I can *feel* it, too; it causes a perpetual tremble in my limbs.

"Do not withhold anything," Connor snaps. "Either explain to me *in detail* how you came by such an interesting skillset, or stay silent, and you'll never talk again. Clear?"

My throat clicks as I swallow, forcing myself to nod. I don't have an option but to *literally* unearth old wounds to expose myself right now, otherwise I risk getting killed. I've faced death enough times that the prospect isn't as daunting as it should be, but I do *not* want to die by Connor's hands. I'm reasonably certain that his method of killing would put me through the sort of agony that I'm not eager to endure. He's the type to send a message; if he thinks I'm a mole, he'll probably chop me into pieces while keeping me alive. I have a higher pain tolerance than most, but I'm not *immune* to pain.

"Lift my shirt. Left side. Check my ribs," I tell him.

"Is this a trick?" he demands.

I shake my head. "Nope. It's show-and-tell, since you're eager to see me dead. Check." I'd do it myself, but I think any movement from me would drastically increase my odds of getting killed.

Connor doesn't lift my shirt; he tears it straight down the middle, and humiliation at my exposed bra *and* what he's about to see burns in my chest. My torso is a canvas of scars, most so faded that they're barely visible. Cigarette burns, old cuts from flying beer bottles... the left side of my ribs are the worst. That's where there are two bullet wounds. Two injuries that very nearly killed me, one of which was put there by the man who was supposed to protect me.

Connor roughly twists me to the side, and his hands freeze on my waist as his eyebrows draw down.

Seamus sucks in a sharp breath; Dorian goes still as a statue; I clench my jaw, hating every moment of this.

"Explain," Connor growls.

"My mom married a gang member when I was nine," I say. "Clyde. He was not a good person. He did a lot of bad shit that had people constantly trying to kill him. My mom was collateral to one of the shootings; I was almost collateral to another. The lower bullet scar is from a man who broke into our home when I was twelve."

"And the upper one?" Connor questions, no remorse or contrition in his tone.

"From when my stepdad was *very* drunk a year later. He was pissed I didn't die with my mom."

"Jesus Christ," Seamus murmurs.

"Can I please fucking *move now*, or are you planning on finishing the job he started?" I ask Connor, desperate to cover myself. I *hate* the scars on my body—they're constant reminders of what I try to forget.

"That doesn't explain how you learned to shoot," Connor says.

"I started going to a gun range when I was fourteen. The owner was in love with my mom years ago; he was kind to me. I was pretty sure my stepdad would kill me some day, I could feel that he wanted to, so I learned how to protect myself."

Connor releases me. "You're going to stay here. I am going to check what you said. There should be hospital reports to corroborate—"

I bark out a laugh. "There are no hospital reports." I barely refrain from adding *idiot*. "I dug out the bullets on my own and nearly killed myself in the process. There's one for when I had a broken bone in my leg, bad enough that the bone tore through skin and I needed surgery. There are few for my mom, from when Clyde hit her so hard she couldn't heal on her own. That's it."

Connor's quiet for a moment, examining my bullet scars again. "There are sloppy incision scars around the wound," he confirms. "Could've been made by you. Okay. Stay here. I'll be back. If what you say tracks, you'll live to see another day. If you're trying to fucking *play me*, and you got those wounds while training up with a gang or some shit, you're dead."

"Noted," I snap. "I'll wait patiently while you pull your head out of your ass."

Connor shoots me a scathing glare before he stomps out of the room.

"You good, mate?" Seamus asks Dorian.

"Fucking dandy," he replies. "I need this wound stitched up."

I say nothing. I'm sure as fuck not going to bloody my hands helping him when he was content to leave me to Connor's rage. I wrap the tatters of my shirt around myself, cross my arms to keep it in place, and slump back against the chair, thinking. I tune out Dorian and Seamus as they talk to each other, and allow myself to do something I very rarely engage in unless I'm listening to music; I dissociate. Music is vital for helping me zone out safely—dissociation without it is dangerous business, because there's no way to know when I'll come back to myself.

The experience of dissociating is blissful. My emotions fade. My physical being fades. My surroundings fade—it's like I take a backseat in my body. My senses are still active, but easy to ignore. The feelings and energies of the people around me are easy to disregard. I can think in peace without the inhibiting factors of the real world getting in my way.

I need to get out of here. That's my first thought; the need to escape. I tried to play nice, and it did not get me into a desirable position. I *could* wait out the week until I'm let go, but there's no telling how many times I'll have to confront death again. Or how suspicious Connor will be of me, or if he'll decide that it'd simply be easier to get rid of me.

I thought I could rely on Dorian for at least *some* protection since he seemed to like me, but that was clearly a miscalculation. I'm alone in keeping myself safe *yet again.* It's not the first time, but I'd hoped to avoid ever being in such a position again.

Does the universe just hate me?

I try to think through my options. I could try to sneak out tonight or tomorrow, but where would I go? These guys all go to Greywood, and they're obviously armed and connected. I can't just *leave* Greywood; I'm here on a scholarship. I could *try* to transfer schools and transfer the scholarship, but it would be nearly impossible to do that mid-semester. I'd need to wait for next semester at the very least, preferably the end of the school year.

I don't know how long I spend trapped in my own mind, but faint footsteps draw me out of my self-induced stupor. My survival instincts force me to be present once more, bringing me partially out of my dissociative state. Connor enters the room just as I blink repeatedly, my vision coming back into focus.

He stares at me; I stare at him. After a moment, he looks at Seamus and Dorian. "What she said tracks. Reports line up."

I don't get an apology from him or even an apologetic glance, but I don't expect either. He doesn't seem the type to feel sorry for hurting someone, physically or otherwise.

"You need to get fixed up," Connor says to Dorian. "I'll call the doctor for a visit. We need to report this to the boss."

Dorian looks at me. "I'd prefer to avoid a visit from the doc, and the obscene *donation* he'll demand. You know how to do stitches?"

I let out a humorless puff of laughter. *Of course I do.* I offered to do them earlier. "Nope." *Just like I can't shoot a gun.*

Seamus's eyebrows raise and faint amusement flashes across his expression. Connor rolls his eyes. Dorian's brows furrow. "It has been a very long day followed by a very long night," Dorian says lowly. "Trust me when I say, you do not want to piss any of us off right now. You've seen too much and heard too much."

"I try to mess with your wound, there's no guarantee I won't accidentally slice through your brachial artery," I say mildly. "You'll want a professional to take care of it." I *wouldn't* slice through his artery, but I am not doing anyone in this room any favors.

"I'll call the boss," Seamus says.

"And I'll call the fucking doctor," Connor growls. He glances at Dorian. "Can you walk?"

Dorian nods. "I think so. I'll wait in the living room." He turns his gaze to me. "You're coming with me. I'm going to keep you *very* close for the time being."

Feeling my lips thin, I nod. I'm in no mood to get interrogated or threatened more. I don't want to be in the same *state* as any of these crazy assholes right now, but it doesn't look like I have much of a choice.

Chapter Ten
Dorian

As always, the doctor we have on-call takes pleasure in swindling us. *Fifty thousand* dollars for a simple clean-and-stitch job that I'm certain Mira could've done for me. She doesn't flinch or move as the doctor slices around in my arm, taking his sweet time retrieving the pieces of my shirt stuck in the wound. Just sits with her arms folded over her tattered shirt and stares ahead, her eyes glazed.

Once the doctor's done and I've wired him the obscene sum of money he requested in return for his services, I send him on his way with a cursory threat to keep his mouth shut. My phone buzzes with a text from Connor, saying that he's informed Sergei of the situation, and Sergei wants me to call him.

"Mira," I say. She doesn't move, doesn't actually appear to have heard me. I feel my brows crease as I repeat her name a second time, then a third, to no response. It's not just that she doesn't respond; it's that she doesn't even seem to *hear* me. *The fuck?* I shift closer to her and wave a hand in front of her face. She flinches, blinks several times, and turns to look at me.

Last night, she told me she zones out when she's listening to music. It seems she might zone out when she's stressed, as well.

"I'm leaving the room to make a call. Stay here."

Brows furrowed, eyes filled with anger, she gives me a single nod.

I try to gentle my voice as I say, "I can see that you're upset, but—"

"*Don't,*" she hisses. "Go make your call. I'll stay here like a good little prisoner until you get back."

I feel my head jerk back at the heat in her words. I'm tempted to stay right here and have an actual conversation, but Sergei Novikov is not a man to be kept waiting. I stand and leave the room, going to the hallway. Seamus and Connor are probably finishing up with body disposal right about now, but there are still blood splatters along the hardwood that'll need to get cleaned up.

I pull out my phone and dial Sergei's number. He picks up after only two rings.

"How's the arm?" he asks without preamble.

"Fine," I reply. "Flea bite. It barely even hurts."

"Good," he grunts. "The Serpents made a stupid mistake coming for you in your own home, but they also proved they're a threat. Getting rid of them is now your top priority, understand? Make a plan and follow through, exterminate the rats before they spread their diseases any farther."

"Understood," I reply.

Sergei pauses for a long moment, then says, "The girl. Mira."

Something tightens in my chest as I glance back toward the living room. "What about her?"

"Connor had quite the report to pass on. As did Seamus when I spoke to him. I'd like to hear your take on things."

I give him a play-by-play of what happened. She made dinner, shots got fired. She grabbed a gun and started shooting back, quite success-fully. I got hit, she seemed game to help me, then Connor threatened her and scared the shit out of her. She told us about her stepdad, Connor checked the parts of her story that could be corroborated. She's been quietly seething ever since.

"Last night, she was a potential loose end; now she's smack dab in the center of your dealings," Sergei says. "Connor tried to find leverage on her to keep her quiet, unsuccessfully."

"He wants to kill her," I add.

"That would be a mistake. It seems she proved her value tonight, did she not?"

"She did."

"It sounds like she saved your ass. I do not have an appetite for killing people who have been nothing but compliant and helpful, especially women." Relief blasts through me, underscoring Sergei's pause. I say nothing, waiting for him to continue.

"You have two options," Sergei says. "She's in this now, there's no two ways about that. There's no getting out after what she's seen or done. Your choice is *how* she'll be in it. You either recruit her to your legion—initiate her and ensure her loyalty—or you keep her as your woman."

Initiations are brutal, and so is this life. I don't want to subject Mira to that. In fact, I'm quite committed to *protecting* her—I don't want to hurt her. Over the last day, I've found myself growing increasingly partial to keeping her around longer than a week. *Much* longer than a week. If the option is between recruiting her, something I'm loath to do, and keeping her as my own, something I very much want to do, I'm going to go with the latter.

"I'd prefer to keep her as my woman," I say. "There are problems on that front, though."

"List them," Sergei demands.

"Connor scared her *badly*. When he did, she turned to me; I stayed quiet. So did Seamus. Her skillset was suspicious enough that we all had questions. She's been off in her own mind ever since. Has barely spoken a word to anyone."

"Alright," Sergei mutters. "Sounds like she might feel betrayed. How was she behaving beforehand? Last night and today?"

It feels surreal to be discussing my problems over a potential relationship with Sergei, but if he's offering help, I'm in no position to refuse.

"Reluctant but compliant," I say.

"Attitude?"

"Mostly positive, occasionally withdrawn."

"Were you intimate last night?"

"Not really," I reply.

"What do you mean, *not really*?" Sergei queries.

"We slept in the same bed but didn't touch. Nothing sexual."

He releases a long breath. "Okay. Here's what you're going to do. Do *not* threaten her with recruitment, but turn up the heat. Woo her in whatever manner she's receptive to. When I was building a relationship with my Kira, it took a long time to get past her walls. I was not forceful at any point, I was calculated. I did things for her that were meaningful *to her*. Women respond to being spoiled and taken care of, but each of them seek a different kind of caretaking, and many of them expect it to be a two-way street. Be open so that she'll feel safe to open up to you. Don't lie to her whenever you can avoid it. Spoil the hell out of her."

"I don't think she wants to be around anyone right now," I say, peeking into the living room. Mira's in the same position on the couch, feet tucked under her, arms crossed over her chest. Closed off and withdrawn.

"Tough shit. Don't be forceful, but don't let her steamroll you. Keep her close. Blame it on me if you need to. From this moment onward, your operation has shifted to making her yours, and there are few things more difficult than gaining a woman's trust and affection when she's led a difficult life that makes her cautious of people. *Especially* when she feels she's been betrayed or abandoned in a time of need."

"How do you know?" I question. Sergei's wealth of knowledge about women and relationships is strange, but considering he's happily married and word has it he's trying for an heir, I don't doubt his advice. It helps that he is, hands-down, the smartest person I've ever met with an IQ that puts most geniuses to shame.

"Experience, and an affinity for reading people. As for your woman, Connor filled me in on what he found. Admirable that she's in Greywood on a scholarship after such a life. Most people would fracture under the weight of the trauma, men and women alike."

That much I believe; I've seen it happen. The sight of the scars littering Mira's ribs, chest, and stomach are almost too much to bear, and they help me piece together a tentative picture of her life. One that inspires a great deal of admiration and respect for her.

"Keep me updated on your plans with the Serpents, and tell me if there are any problems with the girl," he says, ending the call without a goodbye.

I shoot off a text to my group chat with Connor and Seamus, asking if they need help with cleanup. They respond within a minute, telling me they have it handled, which leaves me to deal with the girl. *My* girl, who's quietly stewing on the couch. I rotate my shoulder, wincing a bit at the pain before strolling back into the room.

"It's been a long night. Let's head to bed."

She slowly turns to pin me with a steady, blank gaze. I don't like the emptiness in her eyes. "I'd very much like my own room."

I consider her request. I don't want her to have her own room, I want her in my bed. *Where she belongs.* The thought startles me, but also feels *right* somehow. She *should* be in my bed. I want to keep her close, both so I can have eyes on her *and* so I have the opportunity to study her. Learn her. Get to know her. Crawl into the crevices of her being and determine exactly what it'll take to successfully claim her. What sort of care does she want—*need?* What can I do for her that'll make her less angry? How can I explain that I didn't intend to betray her or leave her to the wolves?

"Not going to happen," I reply. "Come on, Mira. I'm tired and need to sleep off my injury. You need rest, too. We can argue in the morning."

"*I want my own room,*" she repeats more forcefully. "I am *not* sleeping in your bed again."

The determination in her voice makes me smile a little. "You are. We can discuss more in the morning. Don't make me carry you; I'm not feeling my best right now, so it'll only piss me off. Let's go."

She stares at me for several beats, releasing a low growl that reminds me of a hissing kitten. Even so, she stands from the couch. She's silent as she follows me up to my bedroom, where she promptly picks up the bag of clothes she brought from her dorm and shuts herself in the bathroom. A few seconds later, the shower turns on.

I take the alone time to contemplate exactly how I'm going to deal with her. She disobeyed me pretty blatantly tonight, multiple times. My instinct is to pin her down for a thorough punishment, but that wouldn't be useful at this... *fragile* stage in our relationship. Then again, it would be good to set expectations early on; to show her that while I enjoy her sass, if she pushes me too hard, I'll push back. *Harder.*

With a sigh. I decide I can hold off on any punishment for now. I think she'd appreciate the evening to breathe and adjust—it's been a trying night for both of us.

I lock the door of my room to make sure she can't escape in the night, pocketing the key. I'm sure Mira's at least thought about it, considering how pissed she is. When she comes out of the bathroom, dressed in small shorts and a camisole, I go in without a word. I carefully wash myself, thanking god that the doctor had the foresight to provide me with waterproof bandages. By the time I emerge, Mira's at the very edge of the bed, either asleep or pretending to be. I leave her be for the night, too exhausted to fight.

I wake up in the middle of the night, drawn from unconsciousness by some gut instinct. The bedroom's dark, illuminated only by dim moonbeams streaming through the window. My eyes crack open and instinctively search for Mira. Though I haven't known her for long, I'm already becoming attuned to her and starting to crave her, which is why I know I'll find an empty bed before I even look.

I force myself into a sitting position, rubbing the sleep from my eyes, and throw the sheets off me. My shoulder gives a pang of protest, but the pain's nowhere near as bad as it was earlier, so the painkillers the doc gave me are doing their job.

"I didn't run away," Mira murmurs softly. I follow the direction of the words and find her sitting on the old windowsill, legs drawn up to her chest, the side of her face resting on her kneecaps as she gazes out of the window.

"What are you doing over there?" I question gruffly, my voice thick with exhaustion.

"Couldn't fall asleep. Gave up trying after a while. I would've gotten some reading done, but my phone has once again disappeared, and I didn't want to turn on the lights and risk waking you."

"That's thoughtful," I comment. *Unexpectedly* thoughtful.

"It wasn't out of any consideration for you. If you woke up, we'd probably end up talking, and I'm not in a talking mood." She pauses for a long moment, fingers gripping her legs. "Go to bed, Dorian. The door's locked, and so is the window. I'm not going anywhere." Her tone tells me she is quite displeased with her captivity.

"What's wrong?" I ask her, propping my pillow against the headboard and leaning back, observing her. Bathed by the moonlight, she looks ethereally gorgeous. Her skin seems to glow beneath the beams, and her posture, though withdrawn and shut off, still has an innate grace to it. She is absolutely *stunning,* and the sight of her makes a clawing possessiveness unfurl within me.

"Nothing," she says. "Just couldn't sleep. Go back to bed. Your voice is irritating me."

I can't help the chuckle that slips from my chest. "I'm glad to see that the events earlier haven't dimmed your habit of saying whatever's on your mind."

Her head lifts from her knees, and she slowly turns to look at me. Her hair haloes her face, framing her beautiful features. Her lips seem fuller, eyes bigger, nose cuter. She's somehow grown even *more* gorgeous since I last looked at her. It only takes me a moment to realize that it's not because any of her physical attributes have changed, it's because I now see her as mine. I found her, now I get to keep her.

"I'm not even saying a third of what's on my mind," she says softly, turning her gaze back to the window. I bite my bottom lip as I stare at her. I'm pretty sure there are many insults and protests floating around in her pretty head, begging to be let out, but she's keeping them to herself. Many people hold their tongue out of politeness; I think Mira's keeping quiet because she can't be bothered to talk to me.

"I'll go back to sleep as soon as you join me."

A soft, sardonic breath of laughter escapes her. She doesn't respond, just shakes her head.

"Come on," I coax. "The bed's soft and warm, and I'm supposed to be sleeping off my bullet wound."

"So sleep," she says impassively.

My lips curl in amusement. "I won't sleep while you're over there. Get your ass over here."

"I'm sure you'll manage," she says, sounding completely disinterested.

A long sigh escapes me. "If you won't come over here, will you tell me why you can't sleep?"

"Insomnia, probably. It comes and goes. You really should sleep. I don't want to get blamed, threatened, or executed if your injury somehow worsens."

"Nobody's going to blame, threaten, or execute you," I tell her, feeling my brows draw together. Does she *still* think there are any plans to kill her? I guess we haven't exactly had the discussion of her being mine now—mine to covet and protect—but I thought I'd assured her that no harm would come to her even after Connor's outburst. I might have forgotten to; the painkillers *are* fogging up my head a bit.

"Hmm," she says, unconvinced.

"Mira, look at me," I say.

"I'd rather not."

"Look at me, or I'm coming over there and bringing you over here." My shoulder is starting to throb like a bitch, but a little pain won't keep me from carrying her over to where she belongs, *our bed*.

Once again, she turns to look at me, eyes filled with irritation. I find I like her irritation more than the vacancy, but I'd much prefer to see something else in them. Lightness, or even affection.

"Nobody's going to hurt you," I tell her clearly. "Nobody is going to threaten you. If Connor or Seamus try to blame you for something, they'll be facing me."

Her lips twist for a moment, as if she might protest or tell me she thinks I'm full of shit, but then she simply nods. "Okay."

"You don't believe me."

"You're astute."

Okay, enough. "Get back here," I say, unable to keep the growl from my voice. "If you can't sleep, fine, but sitting on the windowsill won't help you. At least lie on a comfortable bed."

"Do I have to?"

"Yes."

Slowly, she unfurls from her position, bare feet hitting the floor. Arms crossed over her chest, she pads over to me, seating herself on the very edge of my bed before curling into a fetal pose, still facing the window.

I reach out a hand to brush her hair from her neck; she hisses, "*Don't.*"

Something rears inside me at that, at her denying my touch. I want access to touch her whenever I want, I'll *have* access to touch her whenever I want, but not yet. First, we need to get things straightened out between us. I'll deal with that in the morning.

"Stay in this bed," I grumble.

I readjust my pillow and settle back down onto the soft mattress. Despite the tension humming in the air, it doesn't take long for me to fall into a deep sleep.

Chapter Eleven
Dorian

W hen I awaken again, sunlight streams from the curtains, and Mira is once again idling on the windowsill. Yawning, I say, "That's five, I think."

"What's five?" she questions, her tone drowsy and tired.

"Five times you've disobeyed me. Five punishments. First was when you took the gun from the briefcase, the rest were littered throughout the night."

"You going to beat me for my disobedience?" her tone is a blend of resignation and sardonic bemusement.

"Not my style. I've already told you what *is* my style." Her breath catches as she throws me a startled glance, then shakes her head. A flush paints her cheeks, though, so I think my little empath might be intrigued by the idea.

"And what, exactly, have I done to earn these five *punishments?*" She releases a laugh, shaking her head. "If you think that orgasms are synonymous with punishments, I'm surprised you don't have more women chasing you down."

"There are plenty who have tried to chase me," I say dismissively. She's the only one that I would gladly let catch me, though instead *I'm* the one trying to catch *her*. I suppose it could be worse; I'm finding that she is delightful prey to hunt. "And trust me, pretty girl, pleasure can be much more agonizing than pain. As for your punishments..."

I hold up a hand, ticking off a finger for each item. "Stealing my gun. Lying to me about your past. Refusing to help me with my bullet—I had to pay fifty grand to that goddamn doctor. Refusing to come up to my room. Getting out of bed when I told you not to."

Her lips twist. "You know those are total bullshit, right? Seamus's gun jammed, so of course my reflexes kicked in. I did not *lie* about my past, I simply didn't see the need to take a stroll down memory lane with strangers who get off on threatening to kill me. You should be glad I refused to help with your bullet, otherwise I might've... *accidentally* sliced through an artery. I didn't *refuse* to come up to your room, I was resistant to it because you left me to Connor's tantrum. I got out of bed because you tried to wrap yourself around me like a fucking octopus an hour before dawn, and I was *not* having that."

I blink slowly. "I think you just got yourself a number six on that list—refusing to let me touch you. Come to think of it, you did the same during your midnight laze on the window, so wouldn't that be seven?"

"You're being ridiculous. All of those things were perfectly reasonable and well within my rights to do. I am a human being with my own thoughts and sentiments, I am not going to automatically bend to your will whenever you feel like exercising it. I got through life long before you came into my world, I will get back to it once this miserable week is through, *if* I make it out alive."

"About that," I say casually, "timeline's been extended."

Mira stiffens, and the flush in her cheeks is replaced by a paleness that I dislike. Is being here really *that* horrible?

I try to consider things from her point of view. I chased her down in a forest when I thought she'd seen something—which she hadn't—and Connor outright talked about killing her while I pinned her down. One of her shoulders was dislocated at the time; regardless of her high pain tolerance, that shit *hurts*. Then, she was carted here.

The following night, she tried to do something nice for the residents of this house, and that was interrupted by a shootout, which would be traumatizing for most people. Instead of sitting back, she pulled on her big girl panties and *helped*, and her repayment for that was once again being threatened by Connor. I think back to the way her gaze turned toward me, wide-eyed and panicked, and the way I shook my head because the circumstances *were* phenomenally suspicious. Her eyes shuttered after that, and she drew inwards. She's a lot more measured now; the words that come from her lips carefully selected, replacing the strange but adorable word vomit she's previously spewed.

The nicest thing I've done for her is promise not to let Connor kill her, then sit back while he threatened to do just that.

Woo her, Sergei said. *Spoil her.* I have no idea where I should start, but I want to try. I think Mira *could* be susceptible to material gifts, though they'd have to be meaningful and carefully selected. Besides, I think doing things for her, some kind of acts of service, would land with greater impact.

"What do you mean, the timeline's been extended?" she questions in a horrified whisper.

I release a long breath. "You're going to be our guest for a bit longer. We have to report all dealings to our boss; last night's clusterfuck report included your surprising skillset. My superior wants me to keep you around longer. I respect and fear my boss enough to obey."

A swallow works its way down her delicate throat. "For how long?"

"I'm not sure," I hedge. How long would it take for her to accept my claim? A few weeks? A few months? "Potentially for the rest of the semester."

"No." Mira stands from the windowsill, shaking her head. "No, it's only October. That is *unacceptable—*"

"It's not optional," I tell her. "Believe me, this truly is for your safety. But we can set ground rules, things that might make you more comfortable. I don't want you to be miserable, Mira, I'd like it a lot more if you were happy."

"Then let me *go home!*" she snaps.

"You're welcome to go to dorms whenever you want, but you'll be staying here in the interim."

"But... I have a *life!*"

"I'll get you to all your classes."

"I have my pack and skulk—"

Jesus Christ, the animals again. "We can go see them."

"I have a *job* on weekends!"

"You don't have to quit, you're good to keep working there. No conflicts."

"You live with two *psychopaths! I* don't want to live with them—they're fucking *terrifying!*"

"Connor won't touch you. Believe it or not, you earned his respect last night—you might find he treats you a bit differently now."

She folds her arms over her chest. "Yeah, Dorian, I felt *immensely* respected when he tore my shirt in half while talking about *killing me.*"

Fair enough. "As for Seamus, he's harmless unless you give him a reason to be harmful, which you haven't. He likes you, maybe a bit too much. He'll play nice."

She releases a low growl, once again reminding me of a kitten. "I don't have any of my clothes here, or books, or—"

"Pack them after school. I'll help you take them here."

Mira's silent for a few moments, shaking her head from side to side. Finally, she says, "I want my own room if I have to *live here*."

"No."

"Why the *fuck* not?"

"Because I don't feel like carrying you from a different room to this one every night. I could, but I'd rather have you here in the first place."

A shrill laugh escapes her. "If you think I will *ever* willingly let you touch me after this—"

"You will," I cut her off. "You might hate yourself for it. You might hate *me* for it, but you will."

Her lips purse. She shakes her head, turning back to the window. "*Fuck. Off.*"

I check the time on my phone, deciding to let that topic lie for now. "It's still early. We have time for breakfast here, or we can go out to get something."

"I'm not hungry. I need to go to my dorm room and pack all my shit up." A shrill laugh escapes her. "And find a way to explain to my roommates why I'm suddenly moving out."

I'm tempted to fuck the attitude out of her. I'm tempted to say many things in reprimand, or to tell her exactly what her new reality is going to be. Instead, I approach her slowly, cupping her face in my hand and turning her to look at me. "It won't be as bad as you're imagining." *Being mine has many benefits.*

"I'm going to shower," she announces. "Can I at least *drive* to campus, or will I need to rely on you to chauffeur me around?"

"Your car is a piece of shit that's not safe in the cold weather," I say bluntly. "I'm amazed it managed to get you up and down mountains several times; it's a joke."

"You are *such* a prick," she hisses. "Not all of us have 50 grand to drop on a bullet removal, or 100 grand for a car."

"120," I correct mildly. "I can get you a new one." She'd look good behind the wheel of a sleek Mercedes.

She snorts. "I'm not going to be a kept woman, and I don't want to talk to you right now."

"Mira," I say slowly, trying to redirect. "I'm sorry I let Connor threaten you last night. I'm sorry I didn't intervene. I was bleeding and in pain and the scene was pretty suspicious. It won't ever happen again. I *will* protect you."

She pauses. For a moment, her eyes soften. Something approaching hope sparks in them, and it causes hope to rise within me in return. Then, her eyes shutter again, and Mira ducks out of my hold.

"Nobody can protect me," she says. "Nobody can promise to protect anyone. There are scores of unseen variables that people don't actually *consider* before making false promises. I'll go on protecting myself. Just try not to make that too difficult for me."

She turns and strides into the bathroom without saying anything else. I grit my teeth, gazing at the ceiling. I want to follow her and try to have an actual conversation, but that won't help right now. I'm injured; she's functioning on no sleep. We can circle back to this later, when both of us are in a better state of mind. First, I need to figure out how the fuck I'm going to move forward with her.

I'm pouring myself a cup of coffee downstairs when Seamus strolls into the room, shirtless, his chest glistening from his morning jog. He gives me a nod, setting about fixing himself a cup. He leans against the counter across from me while I stir my coffee, staring into the liquid blankly.

"How's the shoulder?" he asks.

"Better," I mumble. "Doesn't hurt as much. The doctor might be overcharging by about 48k, but he's damn good."

"Glad to hear it." Seamus pauses to sip his coffee. "So," he says after a beat. "Mira."

"I will rip your balls off if you try to make a move on her," I say, looking up.

Seamus rolls his eyes. "Don't worry about that one, mate. I get it; she's yours. Even if I didn't get it before, I certainly get it now—you've got dibs and you won't share." He sips his coffee. "Thing is, you need to actually *make* her your girl, and you have no experience doing that."

"I've fucked plenty of women," I say flatly.

"And how many have you dated?" Seamus questions. "Right, none. I've fucked more women than I can count and have dated several of them. Short flings, but still. I understand the art of wooing. You don't, because you've never had to. So." He takes another sip. "You want my help?"

"*No.*"

"Excellent, you're getting it anyways. Mira's not typical, which means the usual shit of buying her nice, random things won't work. She's tuned into energies."

"You make it sound like magic," I mutter.

Seamus shakes his head. "Nothing magical about it, mate. There are people in this world who can feel things that the rest of us can't. You and me, we can sense it if someone's deathly scared or dangerously angry. It's like a..." he pauses to look for the word. "Like a vibration in the air, almost a frequency. It's palpable, right?"

I consider that for a moment before nodding. "Yeah, I guess."

"Right. There are people who don't just feel those intense vibrations, they feel all of it. Joy. Sadness. Happiness. Misery. Anxiety—everything."

I feel my brows furrow. "How do you know all this?"

"Had an aunt who was quirky. She could always, *always* tell what someone was feeling. She knew your secrets before you did. Scared the fuck out of my family, but I was always fascinated with her, and she was kind enough to explain things to me."

I feel my lips twist. "Okay."

He nods. "Okay. So, you and I feel the energies of extreme negative emotions in the air. People who are much rarer, like your girl, feel *all of it*. It's overwhelming. It never ends. My aunt described it as a pool of tar she was forever cursed to wade through." His eyes slide away. "She killed herself a few years ago."

Jesus. "I'm sorry to hear that."

"You'll recover. She's not the first or the last. Your girl seems stable, and she has her coping skills, but keep in mind that she is naturally more vulnerable to stress than you are. Not just her stress, but everyone's. She's vulnerable to a whole spectrum of emotions, but the bad ones—no matter how subtle—will always land the hardest. So, to a person like that, what do you think would be a meaningful gift?"

I blink slowly. "A sabbatical in a monastery?"

"Fucking Christ, no. *Nature,* idiot. Things surrounding nature. Aunt loved to be out in the mountains; your girl clearly also likes the mountains. That's not because they're pretty, it's because of the energy found *there*. Even hardened fucks like us know the soothing vibes that come from nature, yeah?"

I try to follow along as best as I can. "Yeah."

"So, *natural* things. Clothes and cars and jewelry are all good and fine, but not deeply meaningful. Girl like that? Research the crystals known to be calming. Better yet, ask her which one she likes or uses—I'll bet you ten grand she has her own collection. Get her a necklace with those. Support her when she wants to go see her wolf or fox pack or whatever. Take her on hikes. And fuck her as often as you can; I gather there are few better ways to release one's *energies*."

I mentally make a note to research what he's talking about, and gently bring it up with Mira. "I don't think she wants me to touch her."

"Show her why she should."

Light footsteps sound from the staircase. Mira's. Connor's footfalls are far heavier and closer to stomps. She appears in the doorway to the kitchen a moment later.

"Morning, love," Seamus greets.

"Brit," she replies with a nod, then turns to look at me. "I need to go to my dorm room."

I incline my head. "I'll take you. You want coffee?"

She shakes her head. "I'll grab some in my room. What should my expected schedule be now that I'm an indefinite captive? Will you be accompanying me everywhere?"

"Not captive, guest," Seamus says. "A most lovely guest. Didn't have time to properly praise you, but the dinner you made last night was wonderful before things went tits up."

Mira eyes him. "Get fucked, Brit."

Seamus chuckles. "Good to see you too, love." He nods at me. "Remember what we talked about."

Chapter Twelve
Mira

"What the fuck do you mean, *you're moving out?*" Cara screeches. "We had to fight administration to get a mini apartment for the three of us! We were going to room together for the rest of our time at Greywood! How can you just be... *moving out?*"

"Complicated circumstances," I grit, tossing another pile of clothes into my duffle bag. I can't tell Cara and Valerie that I got mixed up with organized crime, but I don't think they'll buy other bullshit excuses, so I have to stay deliberately vague. I look over to Cara. She's standing in the entrance to my room, arms crossed over her chest, looking *furious.* "Cara, if I could tell you, I would." I glance at Valerie, where she idles on my windowsill, looking at the campus below. "You too, Val. I want to. I *really* want to. But, for my safety and yours, I can't. Pushing me is only making me feel shittier than I already do, so please, let it go."

Valerie turns to gaze at me, giving a single nod. "I get it. Bad shit changes circumstances far too often. I'm not happy about it, I'll miss the hell out of you, but I get it. Will you still come around?"

"As often as I can manage," I say firmly. "I plan to spend more time away from that fucking house than I do in it."

Cara perks up at that. "Does that mean we can go out more? I won't have to drag the two of you by the ears?"

I smile vaguely. "Yeah, it does."

Cara's mood changes from furious and confused to excited in an instant. "Yay! Ohmygod, can we start tonight? There's this hip place in the city that I've been meaning to check out. Some of the boys from the swim team are known to frequent it."

What better way to get the hell away from Dorian than go to a bar? "Do they have food there?"

"Burgers and regular bar food, I think," Cara replies. "I'm more interested in the selection of male specimens that will be available."

I feel a smile pull at my lips. "Excellent."

After I load up all my crap in Dorian's car, I tell him I'm going out with my roommates tonight. He's quiet for a long moment, but eventually he nods in acquiescence. Having to ask him for permission chafes at my independence, but I understand my situation with him is extremely precarious.

"So, I'm not going to be a captive in your House of Horrors?"

He slides me a look tinged with faint irritation. "No, Mira. I'm not your jailer. Just your..." he pauses to search for the right word. "Housemate. So long as you don't break rules, feel free to go about your usual life. I *would* like to spend some time with you, though."

And I would like anything but *that.* "What are the rules?"

He shrugs. "Don't tell anyone things they shouldn't know. Nothing about Tuesday night in the forest, nothing about last night. As long as you don't open your mouth, we won't have any problems." He bites his bottom lip. "And you'll stick close to me when you're not otherwise occupied, especially at home."

Which means I won't be at his house any more than absolutely necessary. "Fine."

He glances at me again. "And two nights a week, we're going to do something together."

I feel my head jerk back. "*What?*"

"A date, I think the kids call it. You and me. We can go out, stay in, go to the mountains to see your pets for all I care."

"They're not my pets, I'm *their* pet," I say absently, still focused on his outrageous demand for *dates.*

An amused smile curls Dorian's lips. "Oh?"

"They're wild groups of animals. The wolf pack's alpha sees me as an extended member of his pack, one he looks after and makes sure others don't play too hard with. Ergo, his pet. The fox skulk sees me as an ally, I think. That's besides the point. Why would we go on dates?"

"To get to know each other," Dorian says simply. "I'm not that bad, you know."

"I don't," I say. "And I frankly don't want to know. I don't care to know. We," I motion between us, "are not dating. I'm your kind-of-captive, you're my kind-of-captor."

"Captor and captive," Dorian muses. "I think I'd like that game. Especially if there were ropes involved. You'd make a very pretty captive, tied down and at my mercy."

"*No!*" I snap. "You need to stop doing... *that.*"

"Doing what?" Dorian asks innocently.

"Sex talk. I'm not going to fuck you."

"You're right," Dorian agrees, surprising me. "*I'm* going to fuck *you.*"

"Jesus Christ," I mutter. "What's your deal? Why do you want in my panties so badly?"

He pauses for several beats to think that over. "I don't know," he says after a long moment. "You're... unique. And shiny. And pretty. And very, *very* smart. The way you see the world—*feel* the world—is fascinating to me." Abruptly, he shifts topics. "Does it ever get to be too much? *Feeling* everything and everyone around you?"

I gaze down at my lap, lips pursing. "Only every minute of every day."

From the corner of my eyes, I see Dorian nod. "How do you deal with it?"

"I focus on the pure, untainted things in this world," I respond honestly. "Animals. Nature. Products of nature. Anything with a singular, predictable energy. Even herbal candles help—they're a steady, consistent pulse of not only the same *aroma*, but also the same *feeling*. When I'm in public, I'll partially dissociate by listening to music."

"Have you ever done candle making?" Dorian asks me. "There's a spot in the city I saw once where people can make their own herbal candles. Looked cool."

I feel my brows draw together as I look at him. "You looked into candle making? When? Between terrifying innocents and shooting down home invaders with guns?"

A grim smile spreads on Dorian's lips. "I found a few minutes after shooting up a barrel of puppies this morning." He lets out a long breath. "I'm not that terrible, Mira. You can find that out for yourself."

"What you are or aren't is none of my business."

"Fine. So, you like candles, animals, and nature. What else?"

I think for a moment. "Crystals. Genuine crystals, rough and mined from the earth, not the smooth, tumbled ones. I want them raw and real and consistent." I sigh. "I just like consistency, I guess."

Dorian nods. "The world is a very *in*consistent place. Uncertain, unpredictable to everyone. I can't imagine what that would be like to someone who perceives that chaos on an energetic level. Hellish, I'd guess."

That's surprisingly insightful of him. "It certainly isn't pleasant."

Dorian's lips twist. "I am sorry, you know. I can see you're not happy with being my guest for a while. I don't want you unhappy or uncomfortable. If there's anything I can do to help that, just tell me and I will."

I let out a long breath, turning my gaze to the window. "No, thank you. Focus on figuring out whatever it is you need to so I can go back to my life; I'll focus on myself."

"What about him?" Cara questions, tipping her head towards a blond-haired guy reminiscent of a Viking from ancient times. He's just sent her over a drink.

"No, and toss out whatever he sent you."

Cara's eyes widen as she gazes at me. "*Really?* You think he slipped something into it?" she shoves the strawberry daiquiri away from her; it slides forward a few inches on the polished faux-wood table we sit at, some of the liquid sloshing over the surface.

"I don't know if he did, but he has the vibe like he might do some shit like that," I reply honestly.

Valerie sighs, taking a swig of her beer. "I love you, Mira, but you make it really difficult to have faith in men. Or in our country. Or in people themselves."

I smile grimly, clinking my beer against hers. "Welcome to the club, babe."

Cara's already moved onto her next prospect. Her black hair looks particularly glossy in the low light of the bar, and her cinnamon eyes glimmer as she looks over her options for the evening. I've rarely known the girl to fuck someone more than once, and she seldom dedicates more than a week to a single fling—only if the guy is *very* satisfying in bed.

"So, what's up with Dorian?" Valerie asks me, leaning close. We're both on our first beer of the night—hers is almost empty while I've only taken two sips from mine. Against Dorian's protests, I managed to take my own car here tonight, so I need to be clear minded to drive back to his House of Horrors. Apparently, there's a cleaning crew taking care of all the damage from the shooting there right now. He said that by the time I get "home" the shooting should be a distant memory.

Ha. As if I could ever forget the shooting, *or* call that cursed place my home.

"I've told you everything I can," I say.

"Yeah, and I've gathered that you probably saw something you shouldn't have seen and are being kept close because of it." Val takes another swig. "You're not a total captive, since you're out with us tonight, but I don't think you *wanted* to leave dorms."

I'm not surprised that Valerie's deduced as much; she's brilliant and intuitive to a fault. Still, I slide her a sidelong glance, silently asking her to not press the topic. I know my phone's bugged, but I don't know just how bugged it is. I imagine Dorian can read all of my texts and messages, an uncomfortable prospect, but the most unsavory thing on my phone is the nudes Cara occasionally sends me to get my opinion on how *fucktacular* she looks. I don't know what else Dorian can access through my phone, or if he can somehow listen in on me.

"Remember when Cara's nudes got leaked by that one jilted guy?" I question, trying to switch topics.

Valerie thinks for a moment. "Oh, the one she was with for two weeks?"

"Nine days, but yeah. It was fucking awesome that she thought about starting an Only Fans account. She's legendary."

"*She* can hear you," Cara sing-songs, turning back to glance at us with a salacious smile. "Frankly, anyone who gets to see my body is lucky. They're *welcome.*"

Valerie and I share an amused chuckle.

"What about the redhead?" Cara questions, motioning to the bar. "He looks like he fucks *dirty.*"

I follow her line of sight to look at him, tilting my head to the side as I try to sift through the many energies and emotions crowding the room and focus in on his. It's a low, steady hum, comfortable and neutral. Not erratic, anxious, or desperate—none of the usual red markers that prompt me to tell Cara to keep looking.

"He seems fine," I say. "Bring him over here and I can tell you for sure."

Just like that, Cara stands from her seat. She fluffs up her hair, pushes up her breasts so they practically spill out of the scoop-neckline of her little black dress, and sashays over to the bar on her secondhand Jimmy Choos.

"So, Dorian," Valerie repeats. "I'm not asking to know what happened to make you stay in his house; it's none of my business. What I want to know is what's happening between you and that six-foot-plus modern Adonis."

I release a choked laugh. "Pardon me?"

Valerie shrugs. "I might not get around as much as Cara, but I have eyes. And desires. If I'm being perfectly honest, all three of the boys in that house are hot as *hell,* but there's something coldly calculated about Dorian that's *especially* attractive."

I blink slowly. "You've been acquainted with him?"

"We shared an elective last year," she says. "He never noticed me, but every female in that class noticed him. The men, too. Every time he walked in, I swear the temperature skyrocketed."

I take a small sip of my beer. "He's into me, I think, but I don't return the sentiment. I mean, there's no denying he's hot, but I don't like his vibes."

Valerie's eyes darken as she leans forward. "Has he hurt you?"

"No," I say, shaking my head. "No, he hasn't physically hurt me." *Just left me to fend for myself,* again. I'm sensitive to that kind of thing.

"You know how long you'll be stuck with him?" she asks.

"End of semester, I think," I say. "If it goes beyond that, I'll need to get drastic. I don't think he or his roommates will hurt me," especially if they're under orders from their elusive *boss* not to, "but I don't like that house. I don't like its inhabitants. If I thought I could get away with it, I'd refuse to stay there." I sigh. "The things I've seen will not make the three psychos amenable to letting me go. The fact that Dorian wants in my panties won't help my case."

"What if you just fuck him?" Valerie asks. "Ignore the vibes, and use the sex to control him? Men are easily manipulated when they're pussy whipped."

I chuckle, shaking my head with amusement. "I think *he'd* be the one to try to control *me* if that happened." My brows draw together. "I'm kind of fucked, dude. I don't really know what to do other than wait out the storm, but if the storm doesn't end..." I shake my head. "I can't stay at Greywood. I'd have to try to find a way to transfer schools and scholarships."

Valerie pulls in a sharp breath, frowning. Before she can respond, Cara brings not *one,* but *two* guys over. The redhead she's been eyeing and his brown-haired friend.

"Ronny, this is my friend, Mira," Cara says, introducing the brunette and tipping me a wink. "She's single and ready as fuck to mingle."

I start to give Cara a glare but then pause. Why *don't* I hang out with this guy for a bit? So long as he's not terrible company, that is. He could serve as a palette cleanser before I have to go back to Dorian and his House of Horrors.

"Hey," I great Ronny with a smile and nod, kicking the empty chair beside me. "Have a seat."

I turn my attention over to the redhead, once again doing what Cara likes to call an "elevated vibe-check". It only takes me a few seconds to determine he's as safe as a young male can possibly be. When Cara meets my eyes again, I give her a subtle nod, letting her know she's in the clear.

Ronny begins to make small talk with me and Valerie, who takes out her phone and starts scrolling on it. Evidently, he goes to Greywood and is majoring in economics. His favorite color is blue, he likes to hike, and as he speaks, I notice that I don't mind his vibe. Like his friend's, it's calm, steady, and unthreatening. Almost a little boring. I bet Ronny would like turn-off-the-lights vanilla sex.

After a few minutes of conversation, Ronny leans forward to tuck a stray, stubborn lock of my hair behind my ear. I glance down, feeling my cheeks heat at the gesture. I don't exactly *want* him, but I *do* want to get my thoughts away from Dorian, and Ronny's a convenient person to help me forget the menace currently haunting my life. Even if it's only for a little while.

"So, you're in animal sciences," Ronny says, releasing my hair and taking a sip of his beer. "Does that mean you want to become a vet?"

I nod. "That's the idea. I like animals, I'd love to have a career dedicated to helping them."

"Isn't half of veterinary medicine having to kill them?" he questions.

His words hit me like a bucket of cold water. *Total turn off.* "Euthanasia is a very small part of the practice, actually. Less than 5%. It'd be heartbreaking, certainly, but I think it's also part of the cycle of life. You don't want any living being to be stuck in pain or misery." I'm pretty irritated at his blatantly spoken misconception.

"Yeah, I guess," Ronny says. "There are constant cases of malpractice with euthanasia, though, aren't there? When the vet doesn't put in enough effort before deciding to just kill the dog or cat?"

Right here is proof that energy doesn't speak to everything. It's a good indicator of character and danger, but it's not terribly useful in determining the minutia of personalities. Ronny might have a pleasant energy, but his opinions and words are deeply annoying.

"There are mistakes made in every profession, including medicine and veterinary care, yes." I take a small sip of my beer. "There are also issues with economists, and some could say that the misinformation they spread is the reason we've been careening towards an economic crash of apocalyptic proportion for the better part of twenty years."

Ronny chuckles. "Economists getting things wrong doesn't mean anyone dies. Vets and doctors getting things wrong result in deaths all the time."

Now, I'm *really* getting irritated. "Economists might not cause deaths, but their shitty systems of calculation and prediction are contributing to massive inflation and subsequent decline in population growth. Most middle-class families can no longer afford to have children. The smart ones will wait until their finances are straightened out to have kids, and for far too many, that time doesn't come anymore."

Valerie looks up from her phone long enough to chip in, "In fact, one could say that economists and politicians are the reason that the

American Dream has dwindled down to a fantasy; this country has all but cut out the promise of success and an affordable life for the middle class."

Ronny swigs his beer again. "Yeah, whatever. It's all a matter of opinions."

"Not really," Valerie disagrees. "It's a matter of numbers. Something that you'll need to get damn good at if you yourself would ever like to have enough money to raise a family. Unless you're one of the idiots who will go for it without thinking ahead and planning for the future. In that case..." she trails off with a shrug. "Well. That wouldn't reflect on your career very well, would it?"

I nod. "An opinion is something unsupported by fact. It's a theory, one that can be wrong. See, you have an *opinion* that 50% of veterinary medicine consists of euthanasia."

"Actually, that's not an opinion or theory," Valerie pipes up. "It's just plain wrong."

God, I love this girl.

"I wasn't talking to you," Ronny says to Valerie irritably. She snorts and returns her attention to her phone, dismissing him entirely.

I glance across the table to Cara, only to see that she's now on the redhead's lap, shoving her tongue halfway down his throat while he clutches her ass and grinds her against him. The girl has absolutely no modesty when it comes to public settings—when she's in hunter mode, she doesn't care about anything besides getting a satisfying fuck.

I gasp when Ronny's hand lands *high* on my thigh, looking at him with wide eyes. He gives me a sloppy grin. "Why don't we cut with the bullshit talk and head back to my dorm?"

I might've considered it if he hadn't opened his mouth to spew total crap and be rude to my friend, but he did, and now I have less than zero interest in fucking him.

"No, thanks," I say dismissively. "I only fuck smart people."

"Then that would make *me* an excellent candidate," a male voice says.

Only it's not Ronny who says it.

Dorian strides up to the table, standing behind the idiot I spent the better part of a half hour conversing with. There's an impassive expression settled on Dorian's features—he looks calm. His posture isn't particularly confrontational and he's not glaring. Everything about him is perfectly composed, but I can *feel* the anger radiating from him.

Valerie starts to chuckle with a muttered *shit*. She probably finds this massively entertaining, while I find it completely horrifying.

Dorian casually steps around Ronny and comes to stand by my chair, gazing down at me. My breathing hitches as I stare at him in turn, growing more and more concerned at the barely-leashed rage I can sense emanating from him. What's even more terrifying is that, if I weren't cursed to *feel* people as well as I see them, I'd have no clue that he was upset. Nothing about his demeanor advertises anger—he looks mildly *bored*.

"Mira," he says quietly. "It's time to go home."

"Hey, who the fuck are you, man?" Ronny demands.

Dorian swiftly spins to face him. "Her roommate. Her suitor. Someone who's smart enough to fuck her." He lifts a shoulder. "I'm many things to her. You aren't." Slowly, he tilts his head to the side. "In fact, you're *nothing*."

Ronny stands from his seat. "What'd you just say to me?"

I can sense the tension radiating from Ronny now. He's had a few drinks while we've been talking. He was already agitated with the way

I handled his bullshit comments about vets, but now he's *extremely* agitated at being talked down to. Dorian is definitely spoiling for a fight, and Ronny just might give it to him. I don't feel like witnessing a blood bath, so I stand from my seat and step forward, clearing my throat.

"You should go, Dorian," I say softly. "I'll settle my tab and drive to the house. I'll see you there."

"Bill's taken care of," Dorian says mildly. "For you *and* your friends." Slowly, he turns to look at me again. "Let's go home." He holds out a hand.

I swallow, giving my head a shake. "I'll drive myself and meet you there."

Dorian leans close, until his mouth is right by my ear. "If you don't come back with me right fucking now, Mira, I'm going to beat that manchild to a bloody pulp. You had your little rebellion, now it's over, and you *are* coming back with me. Understand?"

Shit.

Chapter Thirteen

Dorian doesn't let me get in my car. Instead, with a hand firmly wrapped around my arm, he takes me to his. Valerie looks like she wants to protest when we leave the bar, but I stop her with a subtle shake of my head. Dorian's in a dangerous mood right now, and I won't risk his rage turning on either of my roommates—*former* roommates.

I don't speak in the car, too nervous to say anything to him. Dorian doesn't try to initiate a conversation, either—not until we park in front of his house. Then, he turns to me and says, "You're in trouble, Mira. When we get inside, you are going to go directly to my room, where you will wait for your punishment. If you know what's good for you, you are going to strip naked and wait for me on my bed while I assure my crew that you did *not* run away or try to ask for help."

I swallow harshly. If Connor or Seamus think that I tried to run or that I talked, I'm once again in serious danger. "I don't want to be punished."

Dorian's eyes harden. "Of course you don't, but you do need to learn."

"I told you I was going out," I say, feeling my brows furrow.

"You said you were going out to dinner with your roommates. You did not say you were going to a shitty dive bar to pick up guys. You did *not* say that you would let another man put his hands on you."

"Ronny didn't—"

"Do *not* say his name," Dorian snaps. "I'm barely holding on, Mira. I have patience, but I am not a saint. You've tempted my wrath a whole fucking lot tonight. Don't make it worse for yourself. Go to my room, get naked, wait on the bed."

"I'm *not* going to get naked," I say, growing irritated. "I'm not taking my clothes off. Just because you dislike something I did doesn't mean you can punish me like an errant schoolgirl. I am *not* a child, I am an *adult*, and you're being unfair."

"The adult world is unfair," he seethes. "Life is unfair. You're tempting my fairness right now." He inhales a deep breath, nostrils flaring before he opens his door and climbs out.

I stay put. There is no way I am going to follow him into the House of Horrors like a condemned prisoner going to their execution. I'm going to stay right fucking here. Dorian glances at me, shakes his head, and rounds the car to my door. On instinct, I lock it, even though I know the gesture is futile. He releases a puff of laughter, then shakes his head and reaches into his pocket, withdrawing the key FOB to the car. He clicks a button; the car unlocks. Before I can lock it again, he wrenches open the door and leans over me. Ignoring my protests, he snaps off my seatbelt, grabs my arm, and physically drags me out of the car.

"Are you fucking insane?" I demand. "*Stop!* I did *nothing* that deserves a..."

"Punishment? You did. As for insanity," he cuts off with a chuckle, "you are pushing me phenomenally close to the point of no return. Now, compose yourself."

I clench my jaw as he steers me into the house. We pass by the living room; Dorian stops when he sees Seamus and Connor seated there, sharing a drink.

Seamus glances over me impassively. "Looks like you found her. Problems?"

"Nope, our guest just needs a clarifications of the rules of this house."

"You need any supplies?" Connor queries, making me tense. "I have a few toys that could come in handy. Crop, cane, wartenberg pinwheel—"

"No, thank you. I'll handle it. She wasn't running or doing anything dangerous, just rebelling in her own way."

"I was getting *drinks* with my *friends,*" I hiss, coming embarrassingly close to stomping my foot as though I'm a child.

"Not my problem," Connor says, turning back to Seamus. "Your Dorian's charge. What he says goes."

"Are you *fucking* kidding me? Am I not a human being?"

"Not in my eyes," Connor says tersely, looking back to me again. "To me, you're a loose end and a liability. Listening to Dorian is the only thing that will make you less of a problem, so I suggest you do so."

"Connor," Dorian says. "We discussed this."

"I won't hurt your precious girlfriend," Connor says. "As long as she's not a problem."

Seamus casts Connor a nasty look. "Do you ever let shit go? Cut it with the threats. You won't hurt her, period. You yourself said that she's Dorian's problem."

If Seamus had left it at *period*, I might feel a bit warmer to him. As is, they're all discussing me as though I'm Dorian's *property*. It's dehumanizing, incensing, and makes me all the more desperate to get out of this house.

"Enough," Dorian says. "Connor, keep your bullshit to yourself." With that, he tugs me away from the living room. I go willingly at first, but as soon as we reach the staircase, I start struggling.

"Dorian," I say, panic taking root in me. What I've heard about his punishments suggests that they're extremely intimate, and I don't want to experience that. I don't want to give myself to him that way. I nearly trip as he pulls me up the staircase; Dorian steadies me with an arm around my waist, glancing at me before sweeping me into his arms, cradling me to his chest. I start to struggle immediately. "Dorian, please—"

"Hush," he says. "You'll beg me in a bit. Not yet."

"Dorian—"

"Keep talking, sweetheart, and I'll only add to your punishment. So far you're up to twelve."

What?

"No, Dorian—"

"Thirteen."

"You can't just—"

"Fourteen."

I finally seal my lips. I feel his low chuckle rumble through his chest and vibrate into me as he carries me down the hallway leading to his room, opens his door, and slams it shut behind us.

He sets me down on the bed, folding his arms as he stares at me. "Strip."

There's no deterring him. He's going to punish me regardless of if I cooperate, and there's nothing I can do to stop him. Fear shoots through my veins, accompanied by a crushing sense of resignation. Since I can't sway him, I need to find a way to get through tonight.

Despite my unease, I can't deny the sliver of interest that prickles at me. I'm mostly horrified, but there's a small part of me that's curious. I know I shouldn't be, but I can't help myself. Despite my better sense, I can't deny that he's attractive, and everything he's told me about his kinks is extremely titillating.

"Dorian, I—I don't know how this works…" I try to remember the countless stories Cara's told me about her kinky exploits and even her experience at BDSM parties. "Don't I get a safety word?"

Dorian's lips quirk. "Safeword? Sure. I'll even give you an out. Convince me that you're sorry for misleading me with your intentions of going out tonight. And for all your offenses last night. *Beg* for forgiveness, be very earnest about it, and I won't do what I've been *aching* to do to you."

I rear back. "You want me to *apologize* when I've done *nothing* wrong?"

"You have a one-minute window," Dorian says. "Begin."

For a moment, I consider it. While some part of me is intrigued, I'm not entirely comfortable with Dorian touching me, but I'm far more *un*comfortable implying I did something wrong when I didn't.

"No," I say after a long moment of silence. "Absolutely not. You want me to apologize when you're the one who's crashed into my life like a wrecking ball? *You* should be apologizing to *me,* not the other way around. I am *not* sorry for going out with my roommates. I am *not* sorry for refusing to help you with your shoulder last night. Actually—" I cut off with a sardonic laugh. "I am. Then, I could've nicked your artery, and your death would've looked like an accident."

"And that's fifteen," Dorian says with a subtle nod. "Usually, five is quite the punishment. Adding on an additional ten?" He gives a mock wince of sympathy. "Well. You're in for a long night, and I'm in for a *very* enjoyable night. Let's hope you don't have many plans tomorrow; there's little guarantee you'll be able to walk."

He places a knee on the bed, causing the mattress to dip under his weight. I scurry backwards, a mixture of genuine fear and something that might be... *arousal?* Mixing with it. I can feel Dorian's anger, but I can also feel his aching desire. What intrigues me is that his desire is unlike any I've felt from a man before. The other guys I've been with were all selfish, wanting to fuck me to get their own release without caring if I got off. Dorian's desire is entirely focused on me. He doesn't want me for the sake of himself, he wants me for *me*, and that... is a heady sensation.

Dorian tilts his head to the side as he watches me grab a pillow and hold it in front of me as if it's a weapon, trying to wade through the muddled mess of my thoughts and emotions.

"You have an option," Dorian says. "You'll almost always get options with me, Mira, which is a courtesy the others in this house wouldn't give you. Take off your clothes, or I will tie your hands and perhaps even your feet to the bedposts, and rip them off you. You will remain like that, spread eagle and open to me, until I've extracted my punishment." My breath hitches; his lips quirk. "You have thirty seconds."

I should take off my clothes. I may hate myself for it, but I *am* curious to see where this goes. I have no doubt that he will tie me down if I don't give him what he wants, and if I let him do that, I'll have absolutely no control. I don't think I'll have much control tonight, regardless of what I do, but I could have at least *some* if I decide to give in. Then again... I don't want culpability. I don't want the guilt that accompanies giving into him.

"Fuck you, Dorian. You can't always get what you want as soon as you want it."

Dorian chuckles. "You're very right there, Mira. But tonight, I'm going to give you the punishment you deserve, which is *exactly* what I want. I want to watch you fall apart, watch your eyes glaze over with pleasure, watch you turn incoherent with it." He grabs the pillow from my hands and tosses it away, swiftly straddling me and cuffing my wrists in his hands, pinning my arms above my head. "I want to hear you beg, *plead* that you've had enough, only for me to continue on."

"Dorian—"

"I want to taste you everywhere there is to taste you. I'm *going* to taste you everywhere there is to taste you. I'm going to play with you until I've extracted as many orgasms as I can from you with just my touch. And *then*..." he cuts off with a chuckle. "Then I might use toys to finish off the punishment."

Toys?

"First, though, I'm going to start out with these *gorgeous* fucking breasts," he says. He pauses for a long moment, gazing at me, then gives his head a shake. "I changed my mind. I'm not going to tie you down. I want to feel you struggle against me. I want to feel you turn limp from coming."

My thighs clench, and a pulse in my core robs me of the ability to speak.

He grips the collar of my shirt in his hands. The sound of material ripping echoes through the air as he splits my shirt clean down the center and pushes the scraps away, leaving them to hang around my shoulders. He rids me of the tatters with a few sharp tugs. His eyes fall to my bra and flare with hunger as he tracks the rapid rise and fall of my chest. He reaches into his pocket and withdraws a small, folded knife. I shrink back, terrified, but he either doesn't notice or doesn't care. With a flick, he opens the knife, making me wince. He examines the blade for several moments, appearing thoughtful.

"I almost stabbed that fuck who had the gall to touch you tonight," he says conversationally. "I almost did something as dumb as incite violence in a room chock-full of people because of you. That would've been quite the mess to clean up, and it would've been entirely your fault."

I want to scream that him deciding to stab someone could never be my fault, but fear keeps my lips frozen. Dorian must have some mind-reading ability, though, because he looks at me with a small smile. "Yes, Mira, *your* fault. I'm calculated and meticulous; I don't fuck up. You, however, have *already* driven me to the brink of madness. I think it's only fair I return the favor."

I'm frozen with a heady mixture of fear and anticipation as he stares down at me like the predator who's just trapped his prey. He runs his fingers under the wired lining of my bra, lifting it from my skin, then cuts it with a single, precise flick of his blade. A long breath shudders out of him as he gazes down at my breasts, tongue darting out to wet his lips. His hands settle on my waist, giving it a squeeze, before running up and cupping my breasts. He molds the globes in his palms, not seeming put off by the fact that they're on the smaller side, barely enough to fill his palms.

"Gorgeous," he murmurs. "Better than I imagined." He runs his thumbs over my nipples, back and forward, watching as they bead under his touch. A faint smile touches his lips as pinpricks of pleasure run through my breasts, and my back inadvertently arches to push them into his palms.

"Such a good girl," he praises. "Offering yourself up to me like a sacrifice. I think you and I are going to get along splendidly, Mira."

He leans down, tongue laving along my nipple, and sparks of pleasure travel straight from his tongue to my core.

Panic suffuses me, but not because I'm afraid *of* Dorian; it's because I've never felt this way during foreplay. My heart hammers away in my chest as he sucks my nipple into his mouth, making a low, rumbly groan of pleasure. *He* likes doing this; I can feel it, and what shocks me is that his pleasure isn't selfish. There's a synergy between us that I've never experienced before, and it *terrifies* me.

"Wait!" I cry out, finding enough mobility to push his head away. "Wait—" Dorian pulls back, studying my expression, brows drawn. I'm panting, flushed, and trying to unfuck my thoughts and ground myself in reality, because a simple touch from him is enough to scramble my mind.

"Shh," Dorian soothes. "Mira, we've barely gotten started."

Chapter Fourteen

"Wait," I repeat, blinking repeatedly. "I'm... I'm afraid."

My words appear to interest Dorian. Something about my honesty or vulnerability calls to him. He settles himself over me, palms braced on either side of my shoulder, and stares down at me with raised eyebrows. I dig my fingernails into his muscular arms, trying to hold him at bay.

"Why?" he questions. "What's making you afraid?"

"You," I whisper.

His brows furrow. "I'm not going to hurt you. Quite the opposite."

"I know," I say. "That's what scares me. This isn't... normal. You're not supposed to be focused on me, you're supposed to be focused on yourself and your own pleasure. But you're not. You want me for *me*, not for yourself."

"Very true," Dorian agrees. "You're not used to that, are you?" He strokes his thumb over my cheek.

I shake my head. "No. I don't do well with new experiences. If you wanted to *hurt* me for what you perceive to be defiance or whatever-the-fuck, that would be one thing. That makes sense to me. This?" I shake my head. "Not at all. I don't like it."

Dorian tilts his head to the side as he regards me. "Would you *prefer* it if I hurt you? Gave you a spanking instead of what I intend to do?"

"It'd make more sense. I'm used to pain."

Dorian blinks slowly, releasing a puff of laughter and shaking his head. "Jesus, Mira. Are you really *that* inexperienced with pleasure?"

Yup. "No. I can get myself off just fine."

"Let me rephrase," Dorian amends. "Are you really that inexperienced with pleasure... *with a man?*"

I don't respond. He gives me a smile, appearing contemplative as he looks me over. "Tell you what," he says slowly. "I can see you're overwhelmed. I don't want to overwhelm you to the point where you do that thing you do—go blank. So, I'm going to commute your punishment. Instead of fifteen, you'll give me three."

I bite my bottom lip. "Three... orgasms?"

He nods slowly. "I'd rather see how many I can physically pull out of you, but I'll settle for three. Come for me three times... and a kiss." His lips twist. "Only if you want it. I'm not going to force that."

I swallow hard, gazing at him with wide eyes. This whole scene is too much, too intense, but I like that he's listening to me. I like that he's willing to pull back and hold himself back. And, despite my reservations, I truly *am* interested in seeing where things go. I *do* want him. The fact that I know I shouldn't only makes me want him more.

"Are you going to give me a kiss, Mira?" Dorian asks, gazing at me with intense focus. His hand trails across my jaw and down my neck, resting in the center of it. He doesn't apply any pressure, just strokes his thumb over my pulse.

"You really want a kiss from me?" I question, genuinely curious. It seems like access to my lips has a lot of worth to him.

Dorian nods slowly. "Very much so."

I inhale a deep breath. "Then take it."

His mouth curves into a smile. I only catch a glimpse of it before he leans his head down and brushes his lips across mine. He doesn't go straight for a full-on kiss like I expect him to; he starts with brushing his lips over one corner of my mouth and then the other. He kisses my nose, my chin, my forehead, both of my cheeks. He pauses to nibble on my earlobe, and my body softens underneath his.

He continues teasing me for so long that I start to grow nervous, squirming beneath him. My grip on his shoulders turns from harsh to soft. My hands slide over the muscles of his back, up his neck, and then my fingers thread through his hair of their own accord. I use my grip to press his mouth to mine, drawing a low rumble of pleasure from him. My lips part, and his descend on them. The world falls away; the bed, his room, our fucked-up circumstances all fade into the ether.

All that's left is me and him.

His lips. His softness. His gentleness and his desire for me. I feel it; it seeps through his pores and invades me, turning me on beyond anything I thought was possible. His tongue strokes against mine. Softly at first, but then with increasing hunger. Each sensual lick and rub creates a responding tug in my core, and I feel myself grow molten for him. My grip on his hair tightens; he gently squeezes my throat, drawing a soft moan from me and a chuckle from him.

His energy turns to something persuasive and titillating. If energies could have scents, his would be pine and jasmine; an enticing, intoxicating mix that calls to me like a siren's song. My leg creeps up to his waist, hooking over it, heel digging into his ass. He grinds forward, and I gasp as I feel his erection slide over me. Even through the fabric of both of our pants, I can feel him; he's hot, thick, hard, and so, *so* big it's intimidating.

Dorian gently nips my lower lip before pulling back. I gasp in several shuddering breaths, panting. I try to pull him in for another kiss, but he doesn't allow it. He smiles at me and shakes his head.

"We can kiss more later," he murmurs. "Right now, you owe me a debt. Three orgasms. I'm going to take my payment."

I whimper in response, aching for him. My apprehension has all but left the building, and in its place is a scorching need.

Dorian slides down my body, unwinding my leg from around his waist. He settles himself in the cradle between my thighs, then gets to work unbuttoning and unzipping my jeans.

"Lift your hips," he whispers.

I comply without hesitation. He slides my jeans off slowly, inch by inch, his pupils dilating as he takes in every bit of my exposed skin. He bites his bottom lip, shaking his head slowly.

"You're so beautiful," He murmurs as he gets my pants off and tosses them over his shoulder. His palms slide up my legs, caressing my skin. "Creamy skin, smooth as silk. Gorgeous." He stops when he hits a patch of scar tissue on my left leg, tilting his head to examine it. His lips curve down at the corners as he sees the two surgical scars, accompanied by a disgusting, gnarled scar that's a result of my bone tearing through my skin. His thumb rubs over it, and his eyes darken with anger. His energy turns from laser-focused and brimming with desire to something rageful.

"Is this where he hurt you?" Dorian asks. "Your piece of shit stepfather?"

I turn my head away. "Yes."

"And yet you'd prefer pain over pleasure?" Dorian questions sharply. A low, almost angry chuckle escapes him. "Haven't you felt enough of that in your life?"

"I'm used to it," I say lowly. "I can withstand a lot of it."

"I know," Dorian says. "I've seen it. You didn't react to your shoulder like you should have. You should've been crying, at the very least you should've yelled when it came out of place and got put back in.

But you didn't. You blinked and you swayed, but you didn't even shed a tear." He pauses, kissing my scar, and for some reason, *that* makes my eyes sting with tears. "I will *never* hurt you. I will never let another person hurt you. One of these days, sometime very soon, I'm going to find the scumbag who did this to you and kill him."

I don't have a response to that, because I can feel just how honest Dorian's being. He *will* find my stepdad and kill him—I can sense his determination. He *craves* doing it. I didn't think I'd ever want someone killed on my account, but the idea of this man going after the one who hurt me doesn't bother me as much as it should.

Another kiss along my scar makes a single tear drip from my eye. Dorian kisses a spot above the scar, moving his lips higher and higher until he's kissing the crease between my thighs.

"Jesus," he murmurs. "I can *smell* you, Mira. You're wet for me already, aren't you?"

Embarrassment seals my lips and keeps me silent; Dorian's response is a dark smile. "It seems you enjoyed our kiss as much as I did, didn't you?" He shakes his head. "Do you know how much that fucking turns me on?" He hooks his thumb under the waistband of my panties, making quick work of pulling them off my legs. I startle and jerk when two of his fingers slide through my slit, top to bottom, and then back up again. He releases a low groan. "You *are* wet." His words hold a note of wonder. "What got you wet, pretty girl? Kissing my lips? Hearing me talk? Knowing what I'm about to do to you?" When I don't respond, he prompts, "Mira, look at me." I whimper, shaking my head. He rubs his thumb up and down my clit, startling me. "I have no problem adding to your punishment, baby."

Pursing my lips, I force myself to turn and look at him. The sight I find is immensely, ridiculously erotic. Dorian, settled between my thighs, looking at me with glittering eyes. My body open around him, his fingers glistening as the continue to play with my wet, sensitive flesh.

"Are you ready?" he asks me.

I shake my head. He smiles, focusing his attention on my pussy. He wedges his shoulders firmly between my thighs, spreading me open, leaving me completely vulnerable to his gaze. He spends a long, *long* time just staring at my pussy, until I think I might spontaneously combust.

Slowly, one of his fingers nudges my entrance. It slides into me easily, aided by the wetness spilling out of me. I release a low moan as my entire body tenses at the intrusion, and the noise only grows louder as he adds a second finger.

"Yes," he breathes. "Give me your noises. All of them." His thumb swipes around my channel to gather some of my wetness before gliding over my clit in a single, smooth circle. Shockingly, abruptly, and completely out of the blue, I come. My channel tightens around his fingers, fluttering, and Dorian sucks in a sharp breath as he feels it. His gaze rises to meet mine, and an irritatingly smug smirk tugs on his lips as he rubs several strong circles over my clit, again and again, turning my orgasm from tenuous to powerful, until my back bows. Warm waves wash through my body, tightening my nipples and forcing my belly to clench. A loud, drawn-out sound of pleasure escapes me. My orgasm is slow to subside, and as soon as it's over, Dorian releases a groan. "Do you have any idea..." he shakes his head. "How fucking *perfect* you are for me?"

He doesn't give me a chance to respond. He pulls his fingers out of me and lowers his head, replacing them with his tongue. I can't help myself; I cry out. One slow, languid lick turns into a thrust as he practically *drinks* from me, making noises of enjoyment that wind me up. I feel myself approaching a second crest almost immediately, and this one is more intense. I know it's coming, I can feel it approaching, a high peak of a mountain that threatens to toss me into the oblivion of the valley beneath.

I reach down with my hands, intimidated, wanting to push his head away; Dorian grabs my wrists and pins them to my lower stomach, continuing to lap at me while rubbing my clit with his thumb. Up and down, small circles, from side to side... it doesn't take long for my second orgasm to wash over me, and as expected, this one is *much* more intense. It goes on longer, draining me of strength and the ability to do anything but cry out with pleasure. I try to twist my body to the side, but he holds me in place with his grip on my hands.

"Dorian," I whimper. "Please, too much."

"One more," he says, pulling away. His thumb leaves my clit, and *three* fingers glide right into me, causing tears to spark in my eyes. They hook upwards, finding a spot on my upper walls that makes my legs tense and toes curl as my belly clenches. "One more, then it's over," Dorian says.

I shake my head. "I can't."

"You can," he disagrees. "Your body responds to me so beautifully. I know you can. I could pull another dozen out of you if I was so inclined, but we made a deal. You gave me an *excellent* kiss. So give me one more, Mira."

"I can't, I'll die," I press.

A laugh brushes over my clit like the most tantalizing feather. "You know that in French, an orgasm is called *la petite mort?* A little death. You'll have one more of those, but you won't *actually* die."

His tongue laves over my clit in two pulses before his lips wrap around it. His fingers tickle that spot on the top of my channel, and my vision blackens as I come again with a *scream*, accompanied by full-body convulsions. My head tosses from side to side, my body writhes, and through it, Dorian continues suckling on my clit and insistently rubbing his fingers over that magical spot in my channel, not letting up until I'm truly crying and babbling, begging for a reprieve. One last strong suction from his mouth nearly makes me pass out before he's finally satisfied. His fingers pull out of me, his head pulls back, and he releases my wrists. My entire body trembles in the aftermath of my orgasm, and I finally understand what all the fuss is about with sex. That was just *foreplay;* I can't imagine what Dorian will be capable of if we actually fuck.

He crawls up my body and his lips cover mine again. I taste myself on his tongue, the tang of my release. I moan again, clutching his shoulders, wrapping my legs around his waist. I cling to him like he's a lifeline while he kisses me, demanding everything I have to give.

"Mira," he murmurs against my lips. "You're *so* fucking beautiful. So fucking perfect. So fucking *mine.*"

His words penetrate deep, reaching within me and warming some dark recess of my soul. Maybe it's a result of all the pleasure hormones currently working their way through my brain, but I *like* the sound of being his. I want it; crave it, even. I've never really belonged to anyone other than myself; I've always had to take care of and look after myself.

I learned how to handle my weapons because I knew living in my household was deadly. I took on odd jobs throughout high school—mowing lawns, gardening, teaching at summer camps—to save up money and get away from my house. Since my mom died, I've taken on life all by myself, and the world has not been particularly kind to me. What would it be like to have someone else who also looks out for me?

But it wouldn't just be someone else, it would be Dorian. I get the strong sense that Dorian would take over my life completely if given half the chance, and I can't have that. Not only because he proved he's incapable of protecting me barely a day after I met him, but also because I don't *really* know if he's reliable, and I don't want to be robbed of my independence. I've worked too hard for it.

I turn my head to the side, breaking our kiss as my post-orgasm haze starts to fade. My entire body aches and I feel sensitive and thoroughly wrung-out. Three consecutive orgasms took a substantial toll on me; I already understand why Dorian refers to this as a *punishment.* I was in agony for the third, having *fifteen* in a row would be a devastation on my senses.

Dorian presses one last kiss on my cheek before rolling off the bed. Strangely, I feel cold without him on top of me and near me, vulnerable and awkward. I shouldn't want to curl up against him, but I do.

Before I can think it through, I ask, "Where are you going?"

"To get a washcloth and clean you up," Dorian calls out. "Then to take the coldest fucking shower in history."

As promised, he returns not moments later, holding a warm washcloth. When he runs it between my thighs, I whimper and wince, which makes him *smile* with satisfaction.

"Stay here," he tells me. "I'll be back in a few minutes."

I nod, curling up on my side, eyes fluttering with exhaustion. I barely hear the shower turn on before sleep lulls me into comfortable darkness.

Chapter Fifteen

"*What t'fuck are you doing here?*" *An ominous, terrifyingly familiar voice demands of me.*

My stepfather's *voice, one that haunts me day and night. "I..." I fumble through words, trying to speak through the terror overtaking me. I know he's going to hurt me. I can see he's in a foul mood; the small kitchen table he's seated in front of is littered with half a dozen empty beer bottles, and one of his burner phones has been smashed to bits, presumably in a fit of his temper. When I'm not around to serve as a punching bag, Clyde tends to destroy objects.*

In the morning, he'll rant at me about how everything is my fault; he'll find ways to blame me for all that's wrong in his life.

"You?" Clyde prompts, blinking his bloodshot, mud-brown eyes. He pushes his chair away from the table, and I wince at the sound of it screeching across the floor. "You what? You wish you were never born?" He releases a dark, grating laugh. "Not yet."

"My friends are waiting outside," I say, attempting to be brave. "I have to get to the science fair. I just left a few things at home."

I'm lying, of course; my friends aren't waiting for me outside this shitty, rundown house. They're already at the state science fair, waiting for me to join the exhibition we spent the last months painstakingly putting together. We won the fairs in our county and district; now we're hoping to win state.

Clyde makes a point of peering out of the grimy window above the sink, looking at the street beyond the house. "I don't see anyone," he says, turning back to me. "You're a lying bitch, just like your mother."

I want to tell him not to talk poorly of my mother, not to speak badly of the dead, but the words are stuck in my throat. Clyde is going to hurt me; I know it. I can feel his desire to. It's like an acrid scent hanging in the air. He fumes with it.

"She wasn't even a good fuck, but at least she could cook—you can't even do that," he continues rambling, some of his words so slurred I can barely understand them.

"Clyde," I say slowly. "There will be questions if I don't show up to the state fair. Please, let me go."

His upper lip curls into a sneer. "Trying to run?" he says, taking another step forward. "You can't run from the mob. Learned that the hard way."

He advances another step, and I contemplate sprinting to the second floor of the house and barricading myself in my room to call the police. But I've tried that before; the local PD is on Clyde's boss's payroll. Clyde will take an extra job, and his boss will make everything go away. Until I can get out of this goddamn town, I'm effectively a prisoner.

"Please," I say again. "I'm sorry I make you so angry. I'm trying t-to…" I trail off as he stops a foot away from me. In a flash, his hand snatches out and grabs a fistful of my hair, then he throws a punch to my stomach that knocks the breath and strength out of me. I double over, falling to my knees, only for him to yank me back to my feet with the hand still gripping my hair. I barely see the move when he kicks out his booted foot, slamming it into my calf sideways, and a blinding pain overtakes me—searing agony, worse than anything I've ever felt before. Several cracks sound, followed by the squelching of flesh, and the pain is so terrible, I heave and crumple to the floor.

I know for a fact I won't be making it to the science fair tonight; I don't know if I'll ever walk again.

Phantom pain searing its way down my leg drags me out of my horrific nightmare. Sweat slicking my skin, I shoot upright and reach down to my leg, frantically ensuring that the skin is smooth, not torn by my own bone.

Someone else also sits up in my bed, startling me so much I release a yelp. Confusion overwhelms me as the past and present try to meld, and I struggle to comprehend where I am, who's with me, and what the fuck is happening. A hand clasps around my arm, scaring the shit out of me. I claw at it frantically, trying to orient myself.

Dorian. His energy assaults me, seeping into my senses, and somehow, it helps ground me. I'm in *his* bed, in *his* house, and he's speaking to me, urgently saying something, but I'm still too out of it to understand anything. "Give me—a second," I manage to say through strained breaths, attempting to get my racing heart under control.

I'm not under Clyde's roof anymore, though I am being forced to stay in a house with three men who have relations to the bratva, are probably members of it. I scrub a hand down my face, trying to focus on small things. The cool sheets beneath me and around me, Dorian beside me, moonlight streaming through the window. Little things that cement me in *this* reality rather than the traumatic memories trying to pull me back to another place and time.

My hearing is the last sense to return, and the first thing I perceive is Dorian speaking to me in an oddly calm, soothing voice.

"You're okay," he murmurs, as if gentling a wild beast. "You're safe, Mira. Nobody here will hurt you." He's turned on the lamp on his nightstand, and it casts a dim glow on the room, enabling me to see despite the late hour.

I release a rattling laugh. "You know that's a lie."

He reaches out to put a hand on my arm, softly sliding it up and down my bare skin. I realize that the only article of clothing I'm wearing is a shirt—an old one that dwarfs me, probably belonging to Dorian.

"It isn't," he assures me. "Nobody here will hurt you, Mira. If they try, they won't like what I do to them. You're safe."

"Stop saying that to me," I say harshly. "I am *not* safe. *Nobody* on this fucking planet is safe."

In the wake of my panic attack comes a rush of anger that I'm relatively used to. My emotions are always volatile after bad nightmares. Sometimes I sob for hours with no real reason; other times I have to physically stop myself from throwing things at the wall. Right now, the only thing—*person*—I want to hurt is Dorian, which is unfair.

"I... I need to shower," I say. "I'm sweaty and disgusting—"

I cut off when Dorian leans forward, grabs my waist, and lifts me. Without asking or even giving me a heads up, he sits me on his lap and holds me tightly to his chest, nestling me against him. My knees straddle his hips, my hands press against his hard, hot chest. My internal reaction to this development is so mixed it fucks my brain sideways. Part of me is terrified at whatever's happening here, of actually being *held* after a nightmare. That's never happened before. Part of me revels in the contact, in the physical comfort that he offers. And another part of me absolutely *seethes*. I want to melt into Dorian's embrace, scream in anger and fear, and go at him like a cornered dog all at once.

I don't know how to control this confusing mix of emotions as they bubble up inside of me, *needing* some sort of release. Usually, my response to nightmares is to shower and listen to music, isolate until the hyper-emotional episode that always follows my flashbacks has passed.

"Dorian," I prompt. "I need you to let go of me. I need to be alone."

He pulls back to study my expression; whatever he sees makes him shake his head. "No," he says quietly. "You don't. Being alone is the last thing you need right now."

My anger rises, squashing the fear and longing. "How the *hell* would you know what I need?"

"Admittedly, I'm not as good as you, but I am still *very* good at reading people," Dorian says. "If you're alone after whatever dream you just had, you'll suppress your emotions. They might go away for a while, but they'll eventually come back to haunt you. I know because I've been there, too. You should *not* isolate. I'm not going to *let* you isolate."

"I want to hurt you," I say through gritted teeth. "I want to break shit and cause pain."

He nods. "Fair enough. What else do you want?"

Fair enough? The way he accepts my words as if they're a given, as if they make perfect sense, somehow only makes me madder. "Are you *dumb?* I want to scratch your fucking eyes out."

"I'm not dumb," he replies. "My IQ clocks in at around 145. I am, however, experienced in more ways than one. What else do you want?"

My mouth opens and closes. How can I verbalize that I want to claw him bloody, but I also want to be held by him? That I want to scream my lungs out, and also curl up into a silent ball? The emotions are conflicting; mainly, I want to do what I *always* do, which is go somewhere alone.

Dorian's thumb strokes over my waist. "I'm not going to judge you. What else do you want? *After* you scratch my eyes out." His lips tilt up in the corners with the beginnings of an infuriating smirk.

"I want..." I shake my head.

"Go on," Dorian encourages.

"To be held."

He nods. "Okay. Here's what's going to happen. You can claw at me, scratch at me, whatever. Neck, chest, anywhere but my face. Through it, I'm going to keep a hold of you. Then, I am going to *keep* holding you."

"No," I say instantly, even though his suggestion sounds extremely appealing.

"Yes," he agrees. "I'm not letting go of you until you've let all your emotions out, Mira. You will remain right here, in my arms, until I know you've diffused. Not *suppressed*, which it sounds like is your go-to. Suppressing creates problems for later; diffusing takes care of the problem entirely."

"What are you, a fucking therapist?" I snap. "Dorian, you know absolute *shit* about me. You know *nothing*. Don't presume to talk about my life like you understand it, or about my emotions like you know how to handle them, because *you don't*."

"Do you?" Dorian asks, gazing at me unblinkingly.

No. "Yes. I've never had a public outburst, I've never embarrassed myself, I've never come close to stabbing someone in a fucking *bar*."

Dorian isn't offended at my jab. "I did come close to stabbing someone because of you," he freely admits. "Then, I composed myself by punishing you. I'm giving you free leave to do the same. Scratch me, bite me, whatever. I have not been easy on you, and that won't change. If you need to claw at me to lift some of the pressure building inside of you, *do it*."

I swallow as I gaze at him. I *do* want to hurt him. I'm remarkably pissed at him, at what he's put me through, at the way he treats me like his property, and most of all, at the way he *sees* me. He looks beneath the surface and peers right into my soul. It's alarming, disconcerting, and remarkably infuriating. I don't want to be *seen*, I want to be left alone, and with him, I don't have that option. Maybe it *would* make me feel better to just... let it all out. Let everything loose.

"Take off your shirt," I say raggedly, my hands curling into fists.

I only catch the barest glimpse of Dorian's victorious smile before he releases me, pulls his shirt over his head, and slowly lays back on the pillow. I stare at the smooth, unblemished skin of his chest, imagining what it would be like to see *my* scratch marks and bite marks on it. I envision him wincing tomorrow when he moves at a certain angle, remembering *me.* The thoughts send a pulse of arousal straight to my core.

"Do your worst, Mira," he invites softly.

I don't go at him like a caged animal. Instead, I place my fingernails on his chest, just under his collarbones, and very slowly, very deliberately rake them downwards. I don't apply enough pressure to break skin, but enough to leave red marks that stand brightly against his pale flesh. Dorian sucks in a sharp breath, and I feel his cock twitch beneath me. Upper lip curling, I shift forward, away from his growing erection. I don't want to be turned on by him right now; I want to *hurt* him right now.

"Really?" I question lowly. "You're getting hard *now?*"

"You're on top of me, digging your fingernails into my chest," Dorian says coolly. "What did you expect would happen?"

"God, you are *so* irritating."

"That's not going to stop or change," he warns me. "I am going to get turned on by you. Eventually, I am going to fuck you, and you're going to like it. Until then, I'll continue indulging myself by playing with your body like it's my favorite instrument. Like it's an object that exists solely to please me."

I know he's taunting me, trying to get me to lose control. Logically, I know it. Unfortunately, the logical part of my brain isn't at the wheel right now. My emotions are steering me right now, so his taunt works. I claw him again, gouging deep with a low growl, then slap his chest. My vision turns red as sheer rage overtakes me; I don't even realize what I'm doing. I slap, claw, even lean down to *bite* him like I'm a vampire, wanting to do anything that'll bring him pain. I want him to be as uncomfortable in his own skin as he makes me. And, somewhere deep down, I think I might want to mark him as much as he wants to mark me.

Eventually, hot tears start rolling down my cheeks, and my attacks turn from vehement and crazed to sloppy and pathetic. I cry for many things; not just the indefinite loss of freedom I'm experiencing because I had the misfortune of crossing Dorian's path, but also grief for just how hard I had to fight to earn that freedom in the first place. Every day was a battle for survival with my stepfather, and the fact that I came out alive is a miracle. I barely slept, I barely ate. I never ended up making it to my science fair because he broke my leg so badly, I spent the next week in the hospital. I got out from under Clyde's control, never to return, only to find myself under Dorian's control just a few years later.

I *deserve* to be free. I *deserve* to be able to live my life. I've earned that right through bloodshed and hardship, and yet, it's nowhere within reach. Each time I think I've finally achieved freedom, something happens that ends up proving the opposite. Freedom is a finely-spun web of illusion. If I'm not beholden to my stepfather, then I'm beholden to the whims of the United States' broken education system. Beholden to the control of men like *Dorian*. There's a catch *everywhere, nothing* is free, and I am *sick* of it. If I could feasibly run away into the forest and live out my days in nature, with a pack of wild animals, I suspect I'd be far happier than I am now.

"Shh," Dorian soothes, cutting through the whirlwind of thoughts cluttering my mind. "Shh, Mira. You're alright. You're okay. I've got you."

Dimly, I realize that he's sat up once again, and he's holding me. My eyes are squeezed shut and I'm hitting his shoulders with my fists, but the gestures are weak. Mostly, I'm just sobbing, mourning.

What *really* sucks is that this feels better than my usual routine of isolating until I can make the anger and rage go away. Dorian was right, this is a genuine release, and I hate him all the more for it. What happened before was merely creating problems for later, pushing my emotions down until they became humongous and built to a boiling point. Now, I feel lighter. It's not a happy lightness, though. It's merely an absence of weight. Really, it's just... numbness, emptiness that carries vague whispers of cold with it.

Dorian chases away the cold with his own warmth and presence, invading the emptiness with himself. His scent, his energy, the feeling of him holding me tight.

"I hate you," I whisper. "I hate you *so* much."

"You don't," he disagrees gently, stroking my back as if I'm a child he's trying to soothe. "You should, but you don't. I like that a lot, you know that?"

"I don't care what you like," I sniffle.

"I know," he says, sounding vaguely amused. "You don't *have* to dislike me, though. That's a choice you make. I wish you didn't." He pauses for a long, long moment. Exhausted, I let my head slump forward, my cheek resting in the crook of his neck, my gaze trained on the moon beams spilling through the window.

"You could like me, Mira. You could *allow* yourself to like me. I'm *not* like your stepfather. I do *not* hurt little girls and leave them to fend for themselves. Choose me, be mine, and I'll give you the entire world. I'll lay it at your feet. I'll deliver your stepfather's head to you on a silver platter."

"I want you to leave me alone," I murmur. "I want to get through this particular trial that life has seen fit to throw at me in one piece. I want to... be free."

"You're not my prisoner."

A soft, sardonic puff of laughter escapes me. "Can I go back to dorms, then?"

"No. But you can *choose* to be here. You can enjoy being here."

"I don't know what you want from me," I admit quietly.

"I just want you," he says. The declaration is simple, quietly spoken, and absolute. It almost sounds like a foregone conclusion; he wants me, so he'll have me.

"I'll never be yours," I say. "I'll never belong to anyone but myself."

Dorian places a tender, gentle, misleadingly affectionate kiss on my head. "We'll see about that."

Chapter Sixteen

Somehow, I fall asleep after the insanity of the night. When I awaken, it's to puffy eyes and a somber demeanor, though I feel lighter than I did last night. I'm still angry at Dorian—I don't see that going away any time soon—but I no longer feel quite so weighed down by my anger.

Dorian's already awake, sitting up on his side of the bed and squinting at something on his laptop. When he hears the sheets rustling as I stretch, he glances over at me and smiles. I pointedly avoid looking at him, instead opting to stare at the mattress. "Morning." In the corner of my eye, I see him notch his chin at the nightstand next to me. "I brought you coffee. It's probably cold now, I can go refill it if you want."

I sit up straight, cracking my neck from side to side and reaching for my phone, which is charging by a blue mug of coffee. Dorian must've plugged it in while I slept last night, since I don't remember doing so.

"It's nine," he says calmly. "You had an... emotional night, so I thought I'd let you sleep. Besides, you have all your classes online on Fridays. You usually use the day to get ahead on homework so you can have free-ish weekends, right?"

"You're not endearing yourself to me, you stalker," I mutter, scrolling through my messages. My lips quirk at the ridiculous text chain Cara sent me last night.

> **Cara**: Have fun getting your tits fucked off your body.

> **Cara**: You vetted my guy wrong. He wouldn't even give me oral.

> **Cara**: Let me know if you're not dead in the morning.

> **Cara**: I'd be V sad if you die.

> **Cara**: Unless cause of death is too many orgasms. That must be one helluva way to go.

There's also a single text from Valerie.

> **Valerie**: Let me know that you're not dead when you get the chance. BTW: Got into a fun debate with Ronny-boy after you left. I now carry his balls in my purse. I'll tell you about it next time we see each other.

Valerie's version of fun often entails emasculating men, and I have no doubt Ronny walked out of the bar feeling like he was two inches tall.

"I need to get to work," I tell Dorian, taking a sip of the lukewarm coffee. I don't feel any more comfortable around Dorian than I did last night, and I'm eager to distance myself from him and try to find a way to leave him permanently. I don't want to have to take extreme measures, but if he leaves me with no other options, I'll have to uproot my life.

I lived under the rule of a gang member once; I'm not going to let that be upgraded to living under the rule of a bratva member. A few weeks of this shit can be tolerated, maybe even a month or two, but an indefinite timeline? No.

"You can work here," Dorian says. "Or in one of the living rooms."

I shake my head. "No, I need to get away from this house. I'll go to the campus library."

"Will you?" Dorian questions mildly. He doesn't challenge my statement outright, but his words are enough to get the message across. If I want to get to campus, I have to go through him. If I want to do *anything,* I'll have to go through him.

I release a deep breath. My best bet right now is playing his game, lying low until I can figure out plausible next steps.

"Can I *please* go to campus to get my work done for the day?" I ask, trying to keep the tetchiness from my tone.

Dorian nods. "Of course. I'll take you." He pauses. "And stay with you. I also have a bit of homework, so a change of scene might be helpful."

Naturally, I won't be allowed to go alone. I shouldn't have expected anything else.

"Dorian."

"Mm?"

"How long am I going to be kept in this house exactly? How long are you going to be *chaperoning* me?"

"Not chaperoning," he says, giving a mock shudder. "You're not a child or a debutante. I'll be *accompanying* you until I'm sure you won't pull the same shit you did last night, blatantly flirting with other men even though you know I want you."

"Just because you *want* me doesn't make you *entitled* to me," I point out, trying to keep my tone calm. "I don't need you to accompany me places." His response is a mere shrug. Thinning my lips, I press forward. "How long am I going to be staying in this house? Concretely?"

"A while," he responds mildly.

"How long is a while?" I press. "A few weeks? A few *months?* How long, Dorian? How long am I going to be a captive—"

"Guest," he interjects.

"—Here? How long am I going to forfeit my freedom? Will it have to be until the end of the semester? Will it be *longer?*"

He sighs, growing irritated. "I don't know, Mira. Until not only *I*, but my *boss* is convinced that you're not a threat. You obviously have a past that's given you a certain skillset. He wants to keep you close for the time being. He becomes dangerous when he doesn't get what he wants."

I inhale a deep breath. "It's not... it's not *forever*, right?"

Dorian doesn't respond. The fuckwad does not say a single word, which makes my blood chill. He's either not speaking because he doesn't know the answer, or because the answer is *yes*.

"Dorian," I say. "You're... you're going to let me go, right? Eventually?"

He shuts the screen of his laptop. "I'm hoping you won't *want* to go after a while, Mira."

"That's not an answer," I say, my tone becoming shrill. "You're going to let me go eventually. You *have* to let me go eventually. I can't stay here for the rest of college—"

"I'm done talking about this," he announces, standing from the bed. "Get ready, shower, do whatever you want to do. I have some shit to get done."

He walks out of the room, slamming the door behind him, leaving me a puddle of uncertainty on the bed.

We get to the library an hour later. The drive is taken entirely in silence. Dorian is quiet, seeming somewhat ruffled, and I have no desire to make any conversation with him. Instead, I start to think through my options.

I can't stay at Greywood if it means being under Dorian's rule permanently. I won't put myself through that. I had excellent grades in high school and have done very well in Greywood so far; there's a slim chance that I might somehow be able to transfer to another school and retain a scholarship. I make a decision that the sooner I get the transfer, the better; I need to start looking *now*.

While I'm in front of Dorian, in his line of vision, part of his life, I understand I'll remain a complication and potential threat that needs to be kept close. If I were gone, though... if I left, went to another school out of state, and kept my mouth closed about everything I've seen and done, maybe there's a way he'd let me go. I might not be worth the effort of a retrieval.

That, of course, leaves behind the problem of his boss, who's been mentioned to me several times in passing. I don't know who the boss is, but I know enough to understand that he's a very dangerous man. I *also* know that the boss is the reason Connor didn't kill me the night I first met him and is probably the reason I survived the night of the shootout. Hopefully, that means he's disinclined to kill an innocent girl.

If I leave in the right way, write a letter or contract that can convince whoever the boss is that I'll keep what I know to myself, maybe I'll be given reprieve. Maybe I'll be able to get away, have a clean break.

I *hate* the very idea of leaving. I hate being driven out of the place that I've made my home, where I have friends and *had* safety for the first time in my life. Now, my safety is being threatened by Dorian's presence in my life. I can't risk staying here, with him, indefinitely. The more I think about it, the more a school transfer—*if* I can pull it off—makes sense. I *have* to be able to pull it off.

We're nearing the end of October right now. I can try to talk to my guidance counselor and ask her to put out feelers for a transfer. If I could, I'd draft her an email this very moment, but my phone is bugged and I don't have a personal laptop. I usually do my schoolwork on a laptop I share with Valerie.

The library has computers available for student use, though. I could sign into my school email on one of them and send a message to my guidance counselor. Or I could try to meet with her in person.

My head starts to prickle with an oncoming headache as Dorian parks in the parking lot of the library. Despite his surly silence, he still opens my car door for me and keeps a hand at the small of my back as we enter the building. After I check out a school laptop from the librarian, we set up in one of the private rooms at the back of the library, one that has walls lined with bookshelves holding dusty textbooks and a large wooden table. As I pull my things out of my backpack and open the laptop, I worry my lip. If I tell Dorian I'm meeting up with my guidance counselor, I'll have a chance to negate his suspicions, but if he finds out in some other way, I'll be in trouble.

"I'm going to try to see my guidance counselor," I tell Dorian.

He slowly looks up from his laptop, arching an eyebrow at me. "Why?"

I try to muster a brave face. "I need to talk about doubling up my spring semester schedule. The sooner I graduate, the faster I can get to vet school, and the better chance I'll have for a scholarship. If I can double up on spring classes and take extra summer semester courses, I'll graduate fall of next year. Then I'll dedicate the rest of the year to my work at the animal shelter while also applying to vet schools."

Dorian blinks a few times, and his eyes warm. "Overachiever much, Mira?"

I shrug. "I have to be. The more I do, the faster I get ahead, and the farther away I get from my past."

He tilts his head to the side. "I'm sorry you had a nightmare last night. Do you want to talk about it?"

I shake my head. "No."

He nods, seeming pensive. "You know you can, though, right? You can talk to me about whatever you want."

I'm sure I *could*, but I have no guarantee that any information I give Dorian will actually stay with him. I don't *think* he's one to gossip, I don't get that vibe from him, but even so, I also don't want to give him more ammunition against me.

"Thanks," I say noncommittally.

Dorian nods. "Yeah. Why is it you want to get so far ahead?" His eyebrows furrow as he contemplates me. "Is it because you want to get away from me?"

It takes all of my control not to stiffen. I need to choose my wording carefully to avoid his suspicion.

"No," I say blandly. "It's because I want to get ahead in life, like I said. Besides, you didn't give me a solid timeline for how long I'd be staying with you. You mentioned end of semester, but didn't reiterate it when I asked again. In any case, what does it matter? I don't assume that I'll be spending next year as your *guest,* will I?"

He doesn't respond for long moments, which makes me swallow harshly. "What if you did?" he asks. "What if I told you that I want to keep you? Not as my prisoner or guest, but as my woman?"

I force a laugh. "Then I'd tell you you're completely insane."

He doesn't get offended; instead, he nods. "Fair enough." He pauses. "You could be, though. Mine. If you wanted to be."

Despite myself, my thoughts wander in a direction they shouldn't. I see a clear image of Dorian and I together, some time in the future. Me coming home from a long day at vet school, him smiling softly and welcoming me back with a kiss.

But then... it wouldn't just be us. I have to keep Connor and Seamus in mind. I wouldn't be returning to Dorian, I'd be returning to his crew—legion, as he calls it. Seamus can be okay, sometimes, but Connor is a non-starter. I don't want anything to do with him; I loathe being in the same house as him. If it were *just* Dorian, if he weren't part of some gang or mafia gig, things might be different, but they aren't. I've already gotten plenty of experience with one gang member; I don't need more.

"We're not compatible," I tell him. "The life you lead is triggering to me. I might seem like I can hold my own, and I can, but that doesn't mean that I *want* to. I don't want to live in fear."

"Contrary to what you might've gathered the other night, my life is no more or less dangerous than the average person's," Dorian remarks. "That was an odd-out situation. One I'm working to ensure won't repeat itself. I might have dealings in the dark, but that's not the whole of my identity. I won't always be working solely in illegal circles. I intend to go into legitimate lines of business."

"That's wonderful for you," I say. "It doesn't change things. Even if I *wanted* to like you, I couldn't. You stress me out."

"What if I worked to change that?" He asks. "I know you don't like living in a house with the others. How about we get a place away from them?"

I blink slowly. He's saying a lot of extravagant things, even talking about us moving in together *separately*, theorizing about a future exempt from criminal work.

"Dorian," I say slowly, "why are you talking about all of this? What's with all the what ifs? What's with the *we* shit? Do you really like me that much?"

He glances to the side before once again meeting my gaze. His is uncommonly open and unguarded, allowing me to see the stark desire and longing that it holds. More, there's something lonely there. Some untold yearning for connection to replace a sense of emptiness. I feel in his energy the same thing I see in his gaze; a soul-deep desire. A want, a *need* for something between us.

"I feel a connection to you," he admits, his expression sober and tone sincere. "More than I've ever felt with another girl. I want to explore it. I *really* want to explore it, Mira."

The stark honesty and openness of his admission is touching. So touching it almost makes me want to lean in and kiss him. Almost, but not quite.

"Can't you see that we're wrong for each other, though?" I ask quietly. "I feel something for you, too. There's a pull between us, but it's superficial. It can't possibly stand the test of time and life." I shake my head. "You only know snippets of what I went through with my stepfather, Dorian, things I had to tell you under duress. My life with him was bad. Bad enough that at fourteen years old, I knew I had to learn to defend myself, or I would never make it away from home. I did, but only just. I beat *so many* odds by getting out of there. I worked my ass off to get a scholarship, to get my freedom, and I gathered so much blackmail on my stepfather that he *had* to let me go. I spent years mowing lawns and doing other unpleasant odd-jobs to save *just* enough money to be able to support myself at Greywood. Money that

I had to hide from my stepfather, or he would've taken it from me. I—" I cut off with a sigh, looking back to my laptop. There's no point in ranting or rambling; it won't get me what I want. It won't get me to where I want, *need* to be.

Dorian reaches across the desk, placing his hand over mine. His palm is calloused and rough, but his skin is warm. The touch is unexpectedly soothing. I'm tempted to lean in, to cover his hand with my free one, to climb onto his lap and let him help me forget all of my difficulties.

Instead, swallowing, I pull my hand away. I fold my arms over my chest, thinning my lips and looking at my keyboard.

"I'm not your stepfather," he says quietly. "I don't get off on hurting innocents or children. I don't have a boss that would demand or condone such behavior. In fact, my boss is known for routinely killing people who deliberately target those who can't protect themselves."

"You might not be my stepfather, but you're in the same line of work as him," I say, a bit sadly. I start drafting an email regarding a meeting to my guidance counselor. "That means there can never be an *us*. We can never be together." I shoot off the email, then switch over to my virtual classes for the day. Most of my work today can be done online—I have an option to attend the classes through zoom, but I can also listen to pre-recorded lectures and do the accompanying assignments.

Dorian withdraws at my words. He resumes typing away at his laptop, and the angry clicks on his keyboard fill the ominous, tense silence. I can't help but feel like I hurt him—no, I *know* that I hurt him. He was open, vulnerable, and I shut him down. Guilt steals across my chest, making each breath I take heavy with regret, but I remind myself that I'm doing what I have to.

I'm doing what almost nobody in my life has done since the death of my mother; choosing myself.

Chapter Seventeen

Dorian

I work side by side with Mira for several hours. Her words ring in my head in repeat, creating a deep ache in my soul. That bastard trained her to distrust the world and all the people in it; he made sweet, empathetic Mira into the wary, closed off person she is now.

I know Connor's doing a deep dive into her life and background, and I'm planning on taking a close look at whatever he ends up compiling. I would ask her, but I doubt she'd spill her deepest secrets to me.

I intend to hunt down Mira's stepfather and take care of him the same way Sergei Novikov takes care of child abusers; tear him apart limb by limb until there's barely anything left of him. Make an *example* of him. Tell the world that anyone who hurts Mira is going to get an extended, extremely painful death.

"Oh," Mira says, sounding pleasantly surprised as she blinks at her borrowed laptop.

I peel my gaze away from my screen, glancing over at her. "What is it?"

"My guidance counselor has room in her schedule for a chat today. In an hour." She turns to look at me head on, something I can't quite name flashing through her gaze. "I'm going to talk to her. Please don't stop me."

Jesus, does she really think *that* lowly of me? Like I'd prevent her from trying to achieve her educational goals. I admire her for her determination, grit, and hard work—I would never try to impede her. I want to *empower* her.

"I won't stop you," I assure her. "I'll wait here for you. I assume you'll be going to the admissions offices for the meeting?" The admissions building is just a five-minute walk from the library. Even if Mira wanted to run away, she wouldn't get far; I have a GPS tracker on her phone.

"Yes," she nods. "It shouldn't be too long. Half an hour, maybe." She shifts nervously in her seat, and her throat works as she swallows.

She's probably worried her meeting will go awry and she won't hear what she wants to from her counselor. I offer her what I hope is a supportive smile, trying to emulate what I intend to be: an encouraging boyfriend. *Her* boyfriend. I'm irritated with her continued rejection, but I won't fault her for being wary of me. The demons in her past have left their mark. In her shoes, I would be wary of me, as well.

"I'm sure it'll go well," I tell her. "Do you have a lot more work left to do after it?"

She glances at her laptop, clicks around on it, and shakes her head. "No, I've already gotten through the bulk of it. Friday's one of my lighter days. After my schoolwork, I usually do meal-prep for the weekend and for my pack and clan."

A smile pulls on my lips. "Right. Well, you're welcome to do that, but I want to take you out first."

She blinks slowly, hesitant. "Take me out... where? Not to kill me, right?"

I give her an exasperated sigh. "No, Mira, not to kill you. I want to protect you, not harm you. We've been over this." I suspect it'll take time and a great deal of effort to get her past her preconceived notions of how people in organized crime conduct themselves.

There are certainly bad actors in our world. *Terrible* ones. People who take advantage of the weak to get ahead, who have free reign to give into their worst desires and darkest perversions. But those are actually the *minority*. The majority of those in the mob, mafia, or bratva started out with legitimate businesses, then found that cutting corners and going underground with certain dealings got them ahead faster. They're not law-abiding citizens and they're certainly not *good* people, but they aren't child-beaters, either.

Then, there are the Sergei Novikov's of the underground. People who do bad things, *terrible* things, but follow a code of honor. Sergei's known as a legend in organized crime circles; mafias around the world are terrified of him. He's ruthless, meticulous, calculated, and unnervingly effective. He's known to be a master of torture and is *absolutely* a sadist, but anyone who's seen or heard him with his wife have gotten glimpses of his gentleness, of his reverence for his woman, of the way he worships the ground she walks on.

There are rumors that he keeps a rival bratva Pakhan captive in the dungeon below his primary residence. Apparently, the idiot tried to take Kira from Sergei, and Sergei now uses that man as a guinea pig to invent new torture methods on.

Perhaps he's onto something with that. Each time I think of Mira's stepfather, I have an undeniable urge to disembowel him and garrote him with his own viscera, but I also have the urge to play with him. Take my time with him; spend days, weeks, months, perhaps even years on him. After all, he hurt *my* woman for years, and turnabout's fair play.

Huh. *My* woman. The title feels undeniably right. I'll find a way to make it into a reality. I *have* to. I won't allow anything to come between me and Mira. *My* Mira.

I watch her from the corner of my eye for the next forty-five minutes, gazing at her intermittently as she types away on her laptop. When she leaves to retrieve a textbook from the science section of the library, I briefly scan the open tabs on her computer and take a glimpse at her email, in case she's planning anything nefarious. The email to her counselor is exactly what she said it'd be; she asked for a meeting regarding her academic schedule and her counselor offered her a time slot.

I move away from Mira's computer just as she returns and begins packing up her things.

"Good luck, baby," I say. She pauses at the endearment, as do I. Both of us are startled. I didn't intend to call her that—it just slipped out—but it feels right. It feels *good*. It's endearing and possessive at the same time, laying a claim to her.

Instead of responding, she hurries to finish stuffing all her things into her backpack, giving me a nod before rushing out of the room. I take a few minutes to make a reservation at a nice restaurant, book a slot at a nearby candle-making boutique, then call the local zoo to inquire about an idea that's been swirling around in my mind. As soon as I'm done setting up plans with the zoo administrator, I get a call from Connor.

I'm not happy with him right now. Usually, we get along well enough, but things have been tense between us since Mira came into the picture. He's made his disdain for her clear, and he's scared her and made my pursuit of her unnecessarily difficult. I don't think she'd be half as uncomfortable as she is if it weren't for his unpleasantness.

"Yeah?" I say, picking up the call.

"You're right that your girl is trustworthy, as in she won't talk," he says. "She is, however, going to try to create some problems. I tapped into the bug you have in her bag. Her conversation with the guidance counselor is *most* interesting. You should take a listen."

He hangs up on me. My chest tightens and my heart speeds as Connor's words burrow deep, creating a hum of anxiety that tingles through my body. I navigate over to a secure browser on my laptop, pop in my headphones, and connect them to the bug I have in Mira's backpack.

Static greets me at first. Crackles and pops that quickly morph into two distinct voices. One belongs to Mira, the other to an unfamiliar woman who must be Mira's guidance counselor.

"Are you *sure* you're interested in that? You have an excellent record at Greywood. As your counselor, I'd advise you to avoid transferring altogether, but if you *must* transfer, then at least wait until next year. A mid-year transfer will be difficult to execute, and there's no guarantee you'll retain any scholarships at your new university. *If* you're accepted in the first place."

What—the—fuck? A goddamn *transfer*? Mira wants to *transfer* away from Greywood?

"I'd like to explore my options," Mira responds, her voice steady. "If you could guide me in the right direction, recommend programs that offer scholarships or grants—ones that I have a decent shot of getting into—I'd appreciate it."

A long pause ensues, during which my blood pressure shoots through the roof. The shuffling of papers sounds through my headphones, underscoring my rising anger.

"There are a couple options that might be worth looking into," the guidance counselor says. "No guarantees, but possibilities. Mira..." she trails off. "Is everything alright? Is there a reason you want to get away from campus? You're one of the animal sciences department's brightest pupils; you're one of Greywood's most promising students. We don't want to lose you. If you're having troubles on campus that you're trying to run from—"

Mira coughs. "No, there are no... troubles. No. I just, um, want a change of scenery. The... the Vermont weather doesn't agree with me."

While I'm furious that Mira's taking such pains to try to run from me, I'm also consumed by relief that she says nothing about me, Connor, or Seamus. This conversation isn't a guarantee that she'll never talk about us, but it's a good indicator that she intends to keep her mouth shut. After this, maybe Connor will stop seeing her as nothing more than a liability.

"The weather?" The guidance counselor repeats dubiously.

"Please let me know which programs you'd recommend," Mira says, attempting to shift gears. "I'd like to start sending out applications and getting recommendation letters as soon as possible. If a transfer isn't feasible, I understand, but I'd like the option."

"Very well," the guidance counselor says. "If that's truly what you want."

"It is," Mira confirms firmly.

I listen as Mira says her goodbyes, popping out my headphones and *seething*. I only let myself stew for a few moments, though; then I get down to doing what I do best: *think. Plan.* Strategize a way to get past this hurdle.

I'm furious with her for having the gall to try to run, and yet, I can't truly blame her. She's still afraid for her life. She must see this as the safest option for her—the best way out. While my base instinct is to carry her back to the house and show her exactly how bad a punishment from me can get, I push that aside for now.

I'm serious about Mira. I shouldn't be, it's too soon, yet I feel a surety when it comes to her; a certainty that she's the one for me, and I'm the one for her. If I want to keep her in the long run, I have to be strategic. Fear is not a good way to build a relationship; connection is. Punishments can frighten her into obeying and make her beholden to me for a time. But if she comes to care for me and truly connects with me, forms an attachment to me, I can keep her forever.

I need her to be content. I need her to be *happy*. I need her to not only be afraid of the punishments I am *so* looking forward to delivering, but to also feel drawn to the happiness and opportunities I can offer her. She likes animals? I'll get her a house full of them. She wants to be a vet? I'll get her into the best, most prestigious program. She wants safety and security? I'll deliver that in spades. She wants to be free of the fear of her stepfather? I'll kill him with my bare fucking hands.

First, we're going to have a good day together. I'm going to pretend that I never heard her unfortunate conversation until tonight, when we come home. When I have her in my bed. Then, I can get to the correction; now, it's time for something more lighthearted.

Fortunately, a part of living my life means becoming an excellent actor. She will have no clue that I know anything until it's too late. I'm still going to treat her, give her a wonderful afternoon, get to know her and take interest in her, and *then* I'll pounce on her like the prey she's just morphed into.

I take a few minutes to compose myself, compose my emotions and muster my facial expression to one of neutrality. Some of those minutes are spent fantasizing exactly what I'll do to Mira once we get back to the house tonight, but the rest are spent focusing on the plans between now and then. For tonight, I already have all the props and toys I could possibly desire. For now, I want to see Mira smile. There'll be more than enough time to extract every drop of agonized pleasure she's capable of giving to me tonight.

When she returns to the library, I'm scribbling away in my note-book, working on an accounting assignment. She seems a bit nervous and out of sorts as she takes the seat beside me, but relaxes when I offer her a calm, casual smile.

"How did your meeting go?" I ask her, taking care to keep my voice even.

She has a chance right now. A chance to admit why she had her meeting, what she talked to her guidance counselor about. If she does, her punishment will be significantly less severe, and both this day and this evening will be spent bonding.

Mira briefly bites her bottom lip, seeming unsure. I think part of her *wants* to tell me. Then, a mix of fear and desperation flashes through her eyes before her face goes blank.

"It went well," she says. My heart falls to my stomach. "I'll see what comes of it soon enough. How's your schoolwork?"

"Coming along," I reply, my voice faintly strained. "Let's wrap up here. I have a surprise for you."

Several surprises, and not all of them will be nearly as fun for you as the first one.

Chapter Eighteen

Dorian

Our local county zoo is about a thirty-minute drive from campus, at the base of one of the largest canyons in the area. This time of year, as staff prepare for the upcoming winter, it's closed on weekdays. Fortunately, the hefty donation I wired earlier makes the staff and owners reconsider my request for a private tour and private showing.

"I've never actually been here," Mira says. "God, the leaves are so pretty. Do you have any Halloween plans?"

My lips tilt up at the corners as I regard her. She's at least partially returned to what seems to be her usual self; switching tracks of conversation at nearly the speed of light.

"We usually host a party," I say. "A costume party, obviously. Things can get pretty rowdy, though, and we have a lot going on this year, so I'm not sure if we will. Do *you* have any plans?"

She shrugs. "Last year, I went to a party with Cara—mainly to chaperone her and make sure whichever flavor of the night she picked was safe and sane. Valerie and I ended up in the corner of the room, talking about climate change."

"So you didn't go anywhere with a flavor of the night?" I query.

She shakes her head. "I'm not into one-night stands. I'm not really into sex; you already know this."

Masculine pride warms my chest. "But you do like it with me."

Her breath audibly hitches. She casts me a sidelong glance as I park the car. "I wouldn't know. We haven't had sex, and we're not going to."

How wrong she is. I smile faintly but don't push. This little fieldtrip is for her enjoyment—no point in diluting it. I'll get my enjoyment when she's sobbing, begging me for mercy later tonight.

She doesn't wait for me to open her car door, which makes me frown. We'll have to work on that.

"Hold on, the sign says the zoo is only open Saturday and Sunday for the fall and winter season," Mira says, frowning as we approach the entrance.

I curl an arm around her waist, enjoying the little shiver that courses through her. "I got us a special tour. Don't worry, we won't get in trouble."

As expected, we're greeted at the entrance by one of the staff members, an attentive young man who ushers us through the wrought-iron gates of the zoo. The intricate designs catch the glint of late fall sunlight.

We follow him into a labyrinth of stone paths, edged with frost-dusted bushes and carpeted with golden leaves that crunch underfoot. We pass vacant animal enclosures where skeletal branches of barren trees rise like sculptures against the sky. The air is crisp and chill, so most of the animals are probably sheltered indoors, though the distant call of a bird echoes faintly from somewhere in the grounds.

"I like how spacious everything is," Mira says approvingly. "I've heard good things about this zoo. They only take in rescues, animals that would struggle to survive out in the wild. If they're successful in their rehabilitation, they return their charges back to their natural habitats."

"That's right," the staff member says, grinning at Mira. His eyes linger on her a beat too long, and I draw her closer, giving him a warning glare that makes the man clear his throat and look away. "We, uh, pride ourselves on both the living conditions we create for all of our rescues, and our dedication to rehabilitating them."

"That's wonderful," Mira says, smiling happily. "What percentage of animals are rehabilitated and then released?"

"About fifteen percent," the man—*boy*—responds. "It's a better turnaround rate than we expect; the ones we take in are usually in pretty rough shape. We have an excellent veterinary department, with three vets and nearly a dozen assistants that work miracles. You'll actually get to meet Dr. Woods later today—"

"Careful not to ruin the surprise," I warn him.

"Of course. We're almost there, anyways." The boy smiles at Mira again. "I'm Richard, by the way. I graduated Greywood last year. I'm interning here now, gaining some experience before applying to vet schools. I think I saw you around the animal sciences department a few times."

Mira blinks. "Oh. Honestly, I don't remember, but that's really cool. I'm Mira, junior at Greywood. So you're one of the assistants?"

The warmth in her tone and sparkle in her eyes as she watches Richard bothers me. She should only look at *me* with those glittering eyes that shine with approval and interest. She should only talk to me in that smoky, beautiful voice that feels like a fist wrapped around my cock. I can see the effect she's having on this manchild—he keeps glancing at her like he can't help himself. I don't blame him, but if he does anything beyond looking, he and I will have a not-so-pleasant conversation.

"Part-time assistant to the vets," Richard says. "Full time staff member." He leads us up to a large stone building attached to the back of an outdoor enclosure that mimics dry, open-plane terrain. "Here we are," he says, opening a glass door for us—for *Mira*, really. I release her so she can go in, then step into Richard's personal space, fixing him with a glare.

"She's mine," I say lowly, staring him right in the eye, letting him *feel* the warning as well as see it.

He swallows. "Got it. After you, uh—"

"Dorian," I say. "Dorian Acheron."

Recognition flashes in his gaze. Considering he went to Greywood, it's no wonder that he's heard of me, and the caution that quickly follows his recognition pleases me. I walk through the door, smiling at Mira, who's reading a large plaque on the wall.

"So this is for the lions?" she asks.

Richard rushes in, closing the door behind him. "Yes, we have a nice indoor enclosure to keep them warm when the weather becomes too chilly. If you'll follow me, you're actually in for a real treat today, courtesy of your... boyfriend?"

"No," Mira says, at the same time that I confirm, "Yes."

"Um, okay," Richard says. "Right this way, guys." He leads us through three doorways, and into a sterile room with bright lights, wooden cubbies, and a metal sink with industrial-grade hand soap. "You'll need to take off anything that dangles or can easily be ripped off. Sweaters, jackets, any jewelry. Then, please wash your hands, scrubbing hard for at least two minutes."

Mira turns to me with an excited smile. "I know that protocol. We're going to see some baby animals, aren't we?"

I bite my bottom lip, loving the way her eyes light up with pleasure and anticipation. "Get scrubbing and you'll find out."

Five minutes later, the attendant moves to stand in front of a wooden door on the far wall of the room. "Okay. Inside, please do not interact with the animals unless they come to you. I will be there, as will two other very experienced handlers, so if you feel like the furry guys are getting too aggressive, let us know and we'll safely escort you out."

"They're lion cubs, aren't they?" Mira questions, bouncing on her toes. "Do we get to feed them? How old are they?"

I stroke a hand up and down her back, enjoying her little shiver. "No more questions. Richy?" I say, looking to the boy.

"It's Richard—never mind," he cuts off, unlocking the door. "Step right in when I open this, please. One at a time."

Mira doesn't need to be told twice. Richard cracks the door open just far enough to allow a person through, and she slips into the room. I follow quickly, not wanting to miss even a second of her reaction.

Her hands are pressed to her chest, her eyes are lit up with adoration, and her gaze is trained on the nest of blankets at the far side of the room, where three little lion cubs are playing with each other. Two handlers stand in the corner of the room, both women, and they smile at Mira and me, waving in greeting.

"Oh my god," she whispers, clutching my arm. "They can't be more than a few weeks old! How did you set this up?"

"I donated a significant sum of money and told the staff that my girlfriend is Greywood's top animal science student, on her way to becoming a vet," I respond.

Mira's too delighted to dispute me calling her my girlfriend. She takes a step across the sand-dusted floor, looking like she wants to run up to the cubs and embrace them but knowing better.

Richard slips in after us, closing the door with a decisive click.

"Welcome," one of the women says, stepping forward. "We heard you're interested in playing with the cubs a bit today; we could use an extra set of hands feeding them."

It appears to take Mira monumental effort not to squeal as the woman gestures to a small wooden table set with three milk-filled bottles.

The woman crosses the room, approaching Mira and me.

"I'm Sam, the head handler." She and Mira exchange pleasant greetings, and Sam takes care to thank me for my donation.

After a minute of chit chat and asking Mira about her experience with animals, Sam briefs her on the correct way to approach the cubs and offer them milk. I lean against the wall, watching as Mira picks up one of the milk bottles and kneels on the floor not far from the cubs, patiently waiting for them to come to her.

The largest male cub turns to face her, sniffing the air. He slowly takes a step towards her, then another, padding his way over to her with a regal posture and inquisitive air. The little creature seems to like either her scent or the scent of the bottle she holds, because he wastes no time standing on her lap and butting his head against her shoulder, releasing a yip that's presumably a request to be fed. Mira absolutely melts, eyes glittering and face warming even more. Carefully, she offers the cub the bottle. The little lion latches on quickly and easily, resting his front paws against Mira's knees and nursing from the bottle she holds.

"Would you also like to join?" Sam asks me, her smile flirtatious and posture invitational.

"Sure," I say casually, not smiling back. I accept the bottle she hands me and walk up to Mira, pausing when the cub she's feeding releases the bottle and shoots me a glare. He growls at me while pawing at Mira's leg, almost like he's warning me away. Not from his bottle, I don't think, but from *her*. Christ, my girl really *is* an animal whisperer—on *steroids*.

Mira gives a laugh of pure delight; Sam's eyebrows raise with faint surprise.

"Looks like Hunk likes you," Sam says, nodding at the cub, who licks Mira's shoulder before once again latching onto the bottle. "He's a fiery one."

"Animals tend to feel comfortable around me," Mira says brightly. "Which is good, because I adore them."

I end up sitting cross-legged a solid seven feet away from Mira, and Sam takes a spot on the floor beside me. The two other cubs make their way over to us. I'm a lot less graceful than Mira and Sam, practically shoving the bottle's nipple into my cub's mouth. The creature doesn't seem to mind, even though the second female handler arches an eyebrow at me and reminds me to be gentle.

"What made you take interest in our zoo?" Sam asks, batting her eyelashes at me.

"My girlfriend," I respond. "Mira." I have no problem making it patently clear that Mira belongs to me. Soon enough, her rebellion will fade, and we can have more days like this. First, though, she needs to accept her place at my side.

Patience, I remind myself. I'm showing her the good before demonstrating the punishments she can earn. Fun first; punishment later.

Chapter Nineteen

Dorian

Mira's in a good mood for the rest of the day. Once we finish up with the cubs, we take a drive through the canyons, and then I bring her to the candle store where we spend an hour making candles. I let Mira choose the scents for my candle as well as hers, because she's so adorably excited about the project. Finally, we head to one of my favorite Italian restaurants so I can feed her. She's talkative and wonderfully random with her topics; I soak up every moment of her attention. Occasionally, there's a flicker of guilt in her eyes when I slip our future into the conversation, but she doesn't confess.

We get back to the house and go straight to my bedroom after a nice long walk around the city. I close my door and lock it, setting the bag with our candles on the floor. Anticipation thrums in my veins, speeding my heart and sending blood rushing to my cock. I have a slew of ideas of what I'm going to do to Mira tonight, and I literally cannot *wait* to get started. She appears a little uncomfortable being alone with me, but not afraid.

Not yet.

I slowly begin removing the cufflinks from my button-up, un-screwing them and leaving them on my nightstand. Mira swallows, idling in the middle of my room, alternating between looking at her phone and glancing at me. She knows something's coming; I'm sure she can feel the tension in my energy, or whatever it is her sixth sense perceives. She just doesn't know *what's* coming, or what *I* already know.

I toe off my shoes and roll up my sleeves, turning to gaze at her. "Is there something you want to tell me?"

Her grip on her phone tightens, so much so her knuckles turn white. She gives me a jaded, startled glance, and I watch her delicate throat work with a swallow. My gaze falls to her bare neck. I want to get her a collar—not the traditional leather one used during scenes or with some dom/sub couples, but something that's sparkly and pretty, something that only we'll know the meaning of. A symbol of both my ownership and my worship. She's not going to be my pet, sub, or slave, though she will submit to me in the bedroom. Mira will be my *queen*.

Before the night's out, I am *going* to own her. We'll agree on the fact that she belongs to me, even if we disagree about everything else.

"No," Mira says with surprising steadiness, though her breaths quicken. I allow myself a few moments of watching the swift rise and fall of her chest, remembering the way her gorgeous breasts looked when her breathing was laborious last night. The way her nipples tightened, the way she submitted to me so beautifully.

"Let me rephrase," I say, taking a step forward. "Is there something you *should* tell me?"

She pauses for a long time, gazing at me. Contemplating her answer. I see it the moment she realizes just what I know. She doesn't say anything; instead, she picks up her backpack, sits down on the floor, and begins rifling through it. Her hands sift through her belongings, neatly stacking two textbooks beside her, two notebooks next to the textbooks, and a leather pencil pouch on the notebooks. Then, she turns her backpack upside down, dumping out the contents and searching through the stray pencils and pens that fall out.

I know what she's looking for; the bug I carefully placed in her backpack the first chance I got. One I didn't have use for before today. I let her search, enjoying the thought of her anticipation and worry building as I retreat into the closet. I head over to the chest of drawers lying along the back wall and squat down to the lowest drawer. I open it, taking a moment to survey my options.

Most of the toys I keep here have gone unused. I've known for some time that my desire to dominate women came in a much different form than the kinky people around me; my acquaintances and friends dabble in power-play, but those dynamics often return to delivering pain. Connor's sadism is legendary, his need to cause pain to find pleasure is absolute. Seamus is more malleable, his brand of domination changes from girl to girl, but it also often includes pain. Hurting my partners doesn't interest me; controlling their pleasure is far more titillating.

And yet, I've never had the desire to do to someone what I want to do to Mira. I'm not just interested in setting a number of times I want her to come and achieving it; I found last night that I'm fascinated by watching her orgasm. It's the most arousing, exciting thing I can imagine, and I want to watch it over and over again. I want to be the cause of her coming so many times she's spent and exhausted; I want to hear her screams turn into hoarse, barely-there cries. I want her to be so tired in the morning, she can barely walk. That's how I want, *need* to dominate and control her.

Some of the toys in front of me are non-starters; things I tried once and decided I had no interest in. Things that were more painful than pleasurable. I don't *mind* exerting control through pain, it can be entertaining on occasion, but it's not what I really *crave*. My hands ghost over several whips, a few of which were Christmas presents from

Connor and Seamus, along with the intense nipple clamps. I gaze at a dusty selection of toys, and find myself ignoring the ones I've used before. I don't want to recreate past scenes with Mira, I want to make new ones. I settle on a slim, manageable dildo, two different types of vibrators, a crop, and a blindfold. I eye the selection of sensory play oils but ultimately decide against them. I can have fun with them another time, but they might be a bit much for Mira her first real go around with toys.

I leave my selected props on top of the drawer, only taking the blindfold with me back into the bedroom. Mira sits in the same spot where I left her, holding up a small, porous metal device that's not even as big as a fingernail.

She glances up at me, lips thinning. I'm sure she's displeased with the invasion of her privacy, but truthfully, the best way to keep her safe is to bug her. If she'd said the wrong thing to someone, I would know before my roommates, hide the evidence, and mitigate the damage before it could blow up into a scandal.

She drops the bug on the floor, lifts up her thickest textbook, and brings it smashing down on the device. I feel my lips curve with amusement at her nonverbal *fuck you*.

"You were a very bad girl," I tell her, meaning every word. "Asking your guidance counselor to transfer you?"

She *was* a bad girl. I can't fully blame her, but I desperately wish she would've talked to *me* rather than looking for a mid-year transfer to another school. Not only would that be a lacking method of solving her problems, it could also throw her education and career off track, potentially setting her back. She doesn't deserve to be set back; she deserves to fly into the atmosphere.

We're going to establish some very direct, very open communication tonight. Work on the fundamental building block that every relationship needs to have.

"What other choice did I have?" she asks quietly, looking down at the textbook.

"Talking to me," I reply. "Expressing your fears. Working *with* me rather than against me. You won't win against me, Mira. Not in the world we live in. You could win a great deal by teaming up with me, by choosing to be on *our* side."

"So today was a trick?" she asks, sounding saddened. Forlorn in a way that grates at me. "The zoo, the candles, the nice dinner... all of it was to lure me into a false sense of safety?"

I shake my head. "Absolutely not. I set up the day-date before I tapped into the audio of your meeting with your guidance counselor. I went through with the date because I wanted to show you the bright side of being with me. The fun we can have together, the enjoyment we can find with each other. I decided to allow my anger to cool down while reveling in my day with you, so I could be level-headed for your punishment."

"I don't want to be punished," she says. Louder, she continues on, "I don't *deserve* to be punished. I haven't done anything wrong."

I gaze at her, pursing my lips. "You went behind my back, trying to do something that would effectively get you away from me. That is *wrong*. Now, I understand that we haven't established the boundaries of our relationship, or opened up a steady, reliable channel of communication, which we're going to do tonight. We're going to have a nice, long talk, and then I'll ensure you *thoroughly* apologize for your indiscretions. Am I understood?"

Mira swallows again, but nods, folding. I notice guilt on her features, but she doesn't express it verbally. She doesn't need to—I can see the discomfort and contrition stamped over her entire body. Her eyebrows are pinched, her shoulders are slumped. I recall that she was withdrawn and occasionally guilty looking during dinner; it's possible that she hasn't felt very good about her ploy to get away from me, either.

I walk over to the bed and take a seat on the edge of it. "Come here."

Mira slowly rises and crosses the space between us, footsteps tentatively padding along the floor. She stops two feet away from me, wringing her hands in front of her.

I pat my thigh. "Sit."

Biting her bottom lip, she slowly takes a seat sideways on my lap. I set the blindfold down beside me, wrap one arm around her back, and plant my free hand on her thigh, supporting her and holding her in place. Mira's weight is light, her build is small, and holding her like this feels so utterly right, I'm filled with a righteous anger that she had the audacity to try to leave. To try to run away from *this*. I know she feels our connection the same way I do; her breathing hitches when I stroke my thumb over her knee, and she relaxes against me with a soft sigh. I muster the anger running through me. I don't want to rage at her; that won't get us anywhere. I want to understand why she did what she did from her perspective, tell her mine, then get past this.

"Explain why you felt the need to go to your guidance counselor," I say, keeping my tone carefully even.

"I'm sorry," she says. The words sound like they're ripped out of her. "I can feel that it hurt you, and I don't want to hurt you."

"I appreciate the apology," I say sincerely, "but that isn't what I asked for. I asked for an explanation." I give her thigh a warning squeeze.

Mira releases a long sigh. "Fear."

"Fear?" I repeat. When she merely nods, I prompt, "Of?"

"You."

That does *not* sit well with me. "I've assured you repeatedly that I am not going to hurt you, and I'm not going to allow anyone else to kill you."

"I know," she says simply.

My frustration mounts. I contract the arm around her back, holding her tighter to me, forcing the side of her body against my chest. I almost wish ridding the physical distance between us could also close the gap of the emotional distance. "Then what are you afraid of?"

"Your life."

I swallow, feeling my eyebrows furrow. "What about my life, exactly?"

She lets out another sigh. "We've already been over this, but I guess we'll have to do it again. Your life is not safe. You have some sort of gang war going on that brought enemies to your house. They shot at you. They shot at *me.* When I tried to shoot back, Connor's immediate assumption was that I'm a threat, and he wanted to kill me. For some reason, I'd just *assumed* that you'd intervene—when you didn't, that crushed me, and I got angrier than I've been in a long time. I withdrew, dissociated, did the things that I avoid doing because they're *dangerous.* Do you know *why* I dissociate and zone out?" she pauses, glancing at me. I shake my head. "Because when the noise of the real world becomes too overwhelming, I need a safe space away from it. Do you know *when* I started to do that?" I shake my head again, and she looks down at her hands. "When home invaders shot my mother and stepfather full of bullets. He survived; she didn't. I dissociated to the extent that I didn't come back to myself for weeks." Her lips pinch. "I was eleven."

My heart pangs at the image of her at such a tender age, eyes vacant, demeanor withdrawn, her mind in a far away, unreachable place. "I'm so sorry."

"I'm not telling you this because I want your pity," she says harshly. "I don't. It doesn't interest me. I'm saying this to explain. I almost died several times in my youth; one of them was because of a home invader. My mom *did* die because of a home invader, and I subsequently developed a mental disorder that I have to grapple with every day of my life. My life was nearly taken several times because of my stepfather's involvement in criminal activities. You are involved in criminal activities." She sucks in a deep breath, shifting her body away from me. I loosen my grip, allowing her the small bit of freedom. A deep ache pangs in my chest at the life she's lived, at the things she's survived. It's accompanied by a deep admiration of her. "Do you understand why I need to get away from you? From this house?"

"I understand why you think you do," I reply. "You're correlating my connections with those of your stepfather. Let me tell you now, they are *nothing* alike. From my understanding, your stepfather is involved with local gangs that peddle drugs, run strip clubs, and have a dirty chief of police on their payroll. I do not engage in those activities. My boss is a brutal, dangerous man, but he's also an honorable one. The shootout you were present for was unfortunate, an example of you being in the wrong place at the wrong time. Things are not usually like that. I've actually never been attacked in this house before. My legion is currently enshrined in exterminating a dangerous local gang, and we were targeted for it. The gang that targeted us will be wiped out before they have another chance to pull a similar stunt.

"As for Connor... he sees the world in black and white. Either you're an ally or an enemy. A threat or a nobody. A problem or a solution. He saw you as a potential foe and problem; he doesn't anymore.

Now, he sees you as *mine*. He understands that if he has problems with you, he is to come to *me* with them, and he will respect that." Unable to resist, I lean forward and press a kiss on Mira's neck. She doesn't pull back or flinch, which pleases me. "I understand you're uncomfortable here. I was serious earlier when I said we can get a different place. I know of an apartment building in the city that a few students live in—it's safe and will get you away from the house."

"You keep saying *us*, as if we're a foregone conclusion," Mira murmurs. "I don't think we are, Dorian. I don't *feel* like we are."

Chapter Twenty

Dorian

I inhale a deep breath, trying to temper my immediate urge to quite simply fuck her until she changes her mind.

"We're not," she goes on, causing anger to replace the pain in my chest. "I know you're into me, and despite my better judgement, I'm into you." Her voice quiets. "Really into you, actually. Today was wonderful, but I can't reconcile the side of you that pulls out a gun, gets *shot*, then recovers so quickly it's almost miraculous, with the side of you that set up a lovely date that was *perfect* for me." She shakes her head. "Or the side of you that just sat there when Connor was a hairbreadth away from killing me."

I tighten my arm around her again, pulling her closer. Pressing her head against my shoulder and stroking her arm. "Listen to me," I tell her firmly, allowing a hint of the dominance I'm going to unleash on her seep through my tone. "I understand you have trauma from your stepfather, but you need to understand that I—am—*not*—*him*. The reason my legion went after the gang that attacked us is *because* they were trying to charge bullshit protection money from local small businesses and Greywood students who couldn't afford it. When people refused to pay, the Serpents would send someone to beat them half to death. We dismantled their operation, cutting off their profit and killing most of their people; they went underground to regroup, making it more difficult than normal to pick them off. But we *will* pick them off. I won't pretend to be a good man, but I have morals and standards that I stick to religiously. You like me, I like you. You want me, I want you so much sometimes just looking at you makes my chest feel tight. Let us have each other, Mira. Give in, and let's see where this goes. I don't just want you for a few weeks; I want you, period."

A soft, astonished puff of laughter tickles my neck. "You barely know me."

"I know more than enough," I counter. "I know you're a sensitive soul and an empath, though you hate that term. I know you have the ability to ensnare humans and animals alike, though you prefer the company of animals. I know you're resilient and *so* strong it puts me to shame." I brush a kiss over her head. "I know you're stubborn, driven, and so damn smart it's downright irritating at times." I kiss her cheek. "I know I feel things I've never felt before when I'm with you."

"Classic line," she quips.

"It's not a line," I retort. "It's the fucking truth, Mira. I want to take care of you. I want to support you. I want to be your partner. I want to see you smile and know that I'm the cause of your happiness." I move my lips across her jaw and down to her neck, lightly sucking the skin there. "When we're in bed together, I want to possess you. Make you mine in every sense of the word. I want to dominate you, but not in the cliché way. You already know that I get off on controlling a girl's pleasure, but it's different with you. I discovered an obsession with making you come last night." I feel it the moment she begins to grow flustered, squirming on my lap, her breaths quickening. "I want to feel you fall apart around my cock, my fingers, my tongue. When you're bad, I want to spend hours indulging in the more sadistic side of pleasure. Seeing how many times you *can* come. Knowing that your abs will be sore in the morning, and you'll feel like you ran a marathon.

Knowing that, after a while, orgasms aren't just overwhelming; they're painful, yet so, *so* pleasurable at the same time."

"Dorian," she gasps, her hand grasping mine.

"We'll get to that," I assure her, skimming my lips up the column of her neck and pressing a kiss to her jaw. "Soon. First, I need you to agree to become mine. At least give it a genuine shot. Explore what we could be alongside me." My hand trails up her thigh, coming to rest on her navel, fingers splayed out across her belly. My pinky sits just above the seam of her jeans, and I can't fucking *wait* to peel them off and get to work. "Agree to it," I breathe.

She swallows. "Then what?"

"Then you get a true punishment for trying to run from me, and soon, I'll get us an apartment. We'll live together."

"T—that's moving very fast," she says breathlessly.

"I'm still supposed to be keeping an eye on you," I remind her. "If it's us in an apartment, you'll be away from this house. I won't worry that Connor will scare you or Seamus will come onto you. It makes sense. Agree to it, Mira."

She bites her lip, shaking her head. "I... don't know."

"Agree to it," I coax, nipping her earlobe. If she doesn't give in soon, I'm liable to do something drastic.

"I want the cats to come with us," she says petulantly.

I chuckle. "Done. Any other requests?"

She blinks a few times. "Many, I'm sure. I'll let you know when I remember them."

I suck my bottom lip into my mouth, loving that I can have this effect on her. She really is the perfect submissive for me.

"Okay," I say, reigning myself in. "Now, I'm going to punish you. Do you understand *why* you're being punished?"

She gives me a wary glance. "Because I did the sensible thing."

"No," I disagree. "Because you didn't communicate. Communication is vital to any relationship, even more so in ours. If you have a problem in the future, if you want to run, you will tell me. We will talk it over. I will adjust whatever I can to make you feel safer."

She contemplates this for a long moment before giving a nod. "Okay."

"Okay," I repeat.

"Since I agreed, can we forgo the punishment?" she asks, blinking at me adorably.

I hide a smile, shaking my head. "No. The function of a punishment is correction. You'll have thoughts of fleeing in the future, I'm sure. You're a flighty girl—it's part of your survival mindset. When you have those thoughts, you will remember tonight, and you'll reconsider."

"Dorian," she says softly, "I'm afraid."

I lean forward, planting a chaste kiss on her lips. "I know."

"Will you... explain to me what'll happen? Then talk me through it while it's happening?"

The fact that she's not resisting right now speaks volumes. She might be afraid, but she's also curious. She wants to know where this will go, even if it makes her nervous.

"Are you familiar with the concept of a pleasure sadist?" I ask her.

Frowning, she shakes her head.

"In the kink community, I'd be considered a pleasure dominant by most."

Her frown deepens. "You're in the kink community?"

I shake my head. "Not really. Connor certainly is and Seamus dabbles in it—I've tagged along with them to a few local parties, but it wasn't really my scene. Parties or play meet-ups are usually done in a group setting, and I'm not into doing things in public. I prefer to keep things behind closed doors."

She bites her lip. "I've never done anything that wasn't considered vanilla."

I smile. "What we did last night was far from vanilla. I was in the dominant role; you were in the submissive one. I had the power in the scene, your only real option was to lie back and take what I gave. You seemed into it."

She nibbles on her bottom lip again, and my dick twitches, stiffening against the generous curve of her ass. She feels it, squirming a little. Her hips rock back into it, and I hiss out a breath, gritting my teeth. I want to fuck her very badly, but I won't do that until she asks for it. In the meantime, I am more than happy to just play with her body.

"It was... strange, but good," she says, a bit breathlessly.

Her hips rock back once again. I grip them, stilling her movements. I have better control over myself than most, but my restraint has limits.

"Careful," I say lowly. "I don't want to fuck you tonight."

She deflates at that, seeming almost offended. I squeeze her hips. "Not because I don't *want* to fuck you—I do. Desperately. But because our first time shouldn't be during a punishment."

"So scrap the punishment," she breathes. "I shouldn't, but I want you. Badly."

A low groan rumbles from my chest. I sink my teeth into the soft skin of her shoulder, growing harder at her soft, breathy gasp. "No," I tell her, kissing the spot I bit. Hopefully it'll turn into a mark. "You're getting punished tonight, Mira. No way out of it. Back to what we were talking about before we got off track... pleasure sadist is a fairly new, not often used term. Conventional sadists are known for getting off by delivering pain and humiliation."

She stiffens. "That doesn't sound like something I'd like."

"Good, because that's not much to my tastes, either," I assure her. "What's more to my tastes is the sadistic aspect of pleasure. After a certain number of orgasms, the female body sort of... lets go into an oblivious state. Coming becomes agonizing, sometimes painful, and simultaneously *too* pleasurable. I haven't played a whole lot with pushing those boundaries, the girls I've been with usually said their safeword long before I really started setting new limits for what they can handle."

Mira's breath hitches again, and she gazes at me, eyes wide and filled with intrigue. "What was it... um, what was it like for the other girls?" Her brows pinch when she says *other girls*, and it probably makes me a bastard to hope she's jealous at the thought of me with another.

"A new experience for them," I say simply. "Some liked it and got into the scenes. Others, not so much. All tapped out just when *I* was truly hitting a flow, because it was too much for them. I don't blame them for that, but I do wish I could've taken things farther."

"You actually get off on making a woman come?" she questions, disbelieving. "Men are usually in it for their own orgasm. If a girl comes, it might be good for their pride, but not much more."

I smile faintly. "You tell me, Mira. You can feel people in a way that astounds me. What did you get from me last night?"

She thinks for a moment. "Arousal. Excitement. I think you wanted to push more, but you didn't want to scare me."

I nod. "That's correct. Tonight, I want to push hard. I'm going to get at least a dozen orgasms out of you, but you will have a safe word you can use if you *really* need to stop. If you say it, everything immediately halts, and we talk. After that, the scene either ends, or you can choose to keep it going. You can choose to surrender and let me lead. I'm pretty good at reading people, as I've proved, and there are several limits for women."

"Oh? What are those?" she inquires.

"The first one is based on their experience and immediate comfort," I tell her. "That's the softest limit. With some women it's passed after orgasm one, but for most it's between two and three. Then there's the second limit, where they *really* think they're done. That's usually between three and five, when they genuinely don't think they can come anymore." I allow my lips to lift into a smirk. "With a skilled enough touch, they absolutely can. Then comes the third limit, at around a dozen, and pressing past it is transcendent, I think. That's where coherency fades, thoughts fade, the ability to speak fades. Getting past that one is *the* most exciting thing to me possible, but I never have."

Mira swallows. "You can really coax a dozen orgasms from a girl?"

"Yes. I'm pretty sure I could get into triple digits, but that's outright sadism. The balance of pain and pleasure shifts and the focus becomes pain. I haven't been with a girl who's into that, and frankly, *I'm* only into whatever gets the right reaction from my partner. The balance has to be right; a girl's response has to be right."

"What's the highest number of times you've ever made a girl come?" Mira sounds positively titillated.

"Thirty something," I reply. "It took over two hours, and it was *extremely* hot. Not as hot as watching you come last night, though."

"You really find me that desirable?"

"You're the most desirable woman I've ever come across, and not just physically. Emotionally, intellectually, all of it. It's all a massive turn on for me. Of course, I'm into the idea of scrambling your brain with pleasure."

A soft noise, almost like a whimper, escapes her, and I damn near lose control of myself.

"Does that answer your questions?" I ask, my tone gravelly. I need to get to the part where I start playing as soon as possible. I literally can*not* wait.

She nods. "I think so. What will it be like tonight? Will it be like last night?"

"It'll go farther," I tell her, lowering one hand to her thigh and stroking it. "I'm going to strip you and put you in cuffs attached to my bedposts to keep you open. I'm going to use my fingers and mouth like I did last night, but I'm also going to use some toys."

She raises her eyebrows. "Toys like vibrators?"

I incline my head. "Among other things."

"Don't guys usually get unmanned by those things?" she asks curiously. "I don't have any personal experience with them—I could never afford one—but Cara swears that they can get a girl off quicker than any man."

I shrug. "I'm not emasculated by toys. I'm perfectly confident in my own ability to incite an orgasm; toys are there to aid me in my quest. They're a tool, not competition." I kiss her neck. As much as I'm enjoying this conversation and Mira's evident curiosity and willingness, I'm eager to get started. "We're going to use a simple, common safeword system. If you feel your boundaries being pushed, say yellow. I'll ease up and check in. If you need an immediate stop, say red. It won't end the scene, but it'll bring it to an abrupt halt, and if you tell me you need to end it, I will." I raise one of my hands to her chin, turning her head toward me so I can have access to her lips. I kiss her once, twice, then take a deep, long drink from her lips, a low noise rumbling from my chest when she submits to my kiss. "Are we understood?" I ask, pulling back.

Mira blinks a few times, adorably dazed. "Yes."

"Repeat your safe-words and their meaning," I prompt. I might not be hardcore into the BDSM life, but I am mindful of the parameters and limits.

"Yellow means slow down and talk, red means halt everything and check in," Mira breathes.

"Good girl," I praise. Her eyelids flutter, and I don't bother suppressing the smirk that spreads on my lips. "Lay down on the bed, head on the pillows. Get comfortable, baby. You have a long night ahead of you."

I plant one final kiss on her lips before releasing her. She wastes no time crawling up the bed on all fours, her ass swaying from side to side. It's tantalizing as hell; everything about her is unbelievably fucking hot, but her ass is truly a thing to be worshipped.

Once she's in position, head on the pillows, I rise and round the bed until I'm standing beside her. "Do you want to take off your clothes, or do you want me to do it?" It's a simple question and a simple choice, but her answer will be indicative of her mindset, and of her comfort with this.

"You do it," she says quietly.

I kneel beside her and take her shoulders in my grip, sitting her up. I finger the hem of her top, raising it up and over her head, revealing a plain blue bra. I run my fingers along the underside of it, gently scratching her with my nails, loving the little shudder that races up her spine. I flick the clasp open, and she helps me pull the straps down her shoulders.

"Lay back," I tell her softly. I reach over to the bedpost nearest to me, running my hands over smooth wood until I feel the edge of a chain. I clasp the leather cuff it's attached to and pull it from beneath the mattress. The material is sturdy, and the chain clinks as I pull it onto the bed, letting Mira see it.

Her eyes widen but she doesn't protest or try to stop me.

"You ready?" I ask her.

"I don't know."

"You're ready," I assure her. "The goal is at least twelve. That's your punishment. If you need to stop for the night, you know what to say, and we'll finish in the morning. Give me your hand."

She holds out her wrist. It trembles when I wrap my hand around it. I'm not sure if it's from cold, fear, or arousal, but I like it. I like her vulnerability, her hesitation. I like knowing that all of those thoughts cluttering her mind will soon disappear under the thrall of consuming pleasure.

I wrap the cuff around her wrist, tightening it. Enough so that she can't slip out of it, but not so much that it cuts off circulation. I repeat the process with her other wrist, and then my hands move to her jeans. I unbutton them, unzip them, and hook my thumbs under the waistband of her panties and her pants, simultaneously pulling both down her legs.

I stop to gaze at her, a long breath shuttering out of me. She is absolutely *luminous*. Ethereally gorgeous, so beautiful it's almost painful to look at her. Her soft, platinum hair fans out over my pillows, and her slight breasts tremble with each one of her breaths. Her flat stomach and dipped waist give way to the curve of generous hips and the soft mound of her pussy, which is dusted with light-blonde hair so fine it's barely visible. I run my hands up and down the soft skin of her thighs, fantasy after fantasy overtaking me.

Pushing those back, for now, I secure her legs in place with the cuffs at the bottom posts of the bed and squeeze her thigh. "I'm going to go get some things. Then we'll get started."

Chapter Twenty-One
Mira

As Dorian retreats into the closet, fear takes over. While he was next to me, touching me, speaking to me in a calm, soothing voice, everything felt manageable, and something about us actually seemed right. Now that he's walked away, even for a moment, I'm struck by the wrongness of this situation.

I am chained to his bed—*tightly*. I couldn't escape if I wanted to. I know he gave me safe words to slow or stop the situation, but what assurance do I have that using them will amount to anything? *None.* He hasn't broken his word to me yet, but he's never put me in such a vulnerable position before. I am quite literally bound in place and completely helpless.

When Dorian returns and I see the items clutched in his hand, my fear skyrockets. He's holding a vibrator—a wand-like object as long as his forearm with a thick, bulbous head—a slim black dildo, and most concerningly, a fucking *crop*. Like the one used to train or direct horses.

While he was talking about his desires, the things that get him going, I was reluctantly excited and a little aroused. At no point did he say he'd whip me like an animal.

"Wait!" I exclaim when he drops the toys and *crop* at the foot of the bed. "You didn't say anything about a *crop*!"

He picks up the object in question, turning the braided handle in his hand, running his thumb over the thin flapper at the end. "It's not for pain," he assures me in a steady, calm voice that's infused with sheer dominance and confidence. "It *can* be used for pain, but that's not why I have it."

I yank at my wrists and legs, shame licking through me when wetness gathers between my thighs. I've never been bound like this, and I never expected to actually be turned on from being bound like this. "Dorian—"

"Shh," he hushes, planting one knee at the foot of the bed. "Give me a little fucking trust, Mira. I said pain wasn't my trade; I meant it. If it was, it would be in my interest to tell you about it up front and try to seduce you into enjoying it, but it isn't."

My breaths quicken as he makes his way up the bed, until he's kneeling between my knees. He grasps one of my shins in a warm, firm grip, squeezing my flesh. "Close your eyes," he says.

I shake my head.

"Close your eyes, Mira," he repeats. "Looking at it is frightening you. Instead, I want you to *feel*."

Inhaling a deep breath, I squeeze my eyes shut, and brace for a painful blow.

It never comes.

Instead, what I feel is smooth, slightly cold leather running up my leg, teasing the crease where my thigh meets my pussy, and ghosting over the top of my mound before slowly dragging up my navel. A noise of surprise escapes me; the brush of the crop is feather-light, and while the danger it represents of a potentially painful blow is there, it instead feels... good. The contact of cool, firm leather brushing over my soft, prone skin is intriguing. A low moan makes its way past my lips when the crop circles my left nipple, brushing over it until I feel the peak stiffen. Then comes the gentlest of taps, with barely any force behind it. It's not a slap or even a smack; more like a caress with minimum downward pressure. It feels oddly arousing.

"There we go," Dorian murmurs, giving me another tap. My eyes open and my gaze meets his; he's watching me with intense focus, eyes swimming with desire. My stare travels over his face and then traces a path farther down, taking in his body. He's still fully clothed in a black button-down and beige slacks; he looks ready to go into a business meeting, and the stark difference between him being fully clothed and me being naked and vulnerable is an intense turn-on.

"See what I mean?" he asks, giving me another, slightly stronger tap. This one has more of an impact, but still no pain. Just stimulation.

I nod. "Yes."

"You need to learn to trust me," he admonishes with another tap. "When I say I'm going to do something, that's what I'll do. If I change my mind, you'll be the first to know. I won't fuck either of us over by lying to you, okay?"

"Okay," I agree.

"Good girl." The words send a rush of warmth coursing through my body. I *love* it when he calls me a good girl; I love it even more when he calls me beautiful and praises my body, but nothing compares to when he admires my mind and the parts of me I find weird.

He spends several moments tapping away at my nipple, and after a while, the skin grows sensitive. It becomes an intense erogenous zone that feels like it has a direct connection to my pussy. The pressure of his hits remain steady—sometimes going softer, but never hard enough to hurt. Soon, the impact morphs. It doesn't become painful, but it gets intense. He pauses, brushing his thumb over my nipple, and it feels surprisingly sensitive. I arch into his touch, moaning, and he smiles, circling the bud with his finger. He turns his attention to my other breast, giving it the same treatment.

There's patience in each of his movements, focus and precision but also serenity. I don't think I've ever seen him so in his element, so relaxed. He might be good at giving off the impression of being constantly at ease, but his energy rarely matches his demeanor. Right now, even his energy is peaceful. Titillated, aroused, but also calm and satisfied. It's bizarre and fascinating.

After several moments, he sets aside the crop again, and lifts both of his hands to my breasts, massaging them. His fingers periodically circle over my nipples, the touches ranging from gentle to intense, all of them ridiculously erotic.

When he leans down and runs his tongue over one of them, I can't contain my moan of abandon. I'm almost painfully sensitive, and the heat of his tongue is nearly too much to bear, but it feels insanely good. The arousal pooling in my core magnifies tenfold, until I'm embarrassed that I'll leave a wet spot on his sheets.

"There's my good girl," he coos, pulling back. He settles himself in the cradle of my thighs, and his warm palm cups my pussy. A harsh breath hisses out of him when he finds out just how wet I am, and my cheeks heat.

"Jesus, Mira," he says lowly. "I think you might've liked that as much as I did."

Two fingers run through my slit repeatedly, almost like a massage. His fingers move up to my clit, rubbing the bud up and down, side to side, and in circles. Noises of pleasure escape me—whimpers, gasps, moans. It doesn't take long before I feel myself building to an orgasm, and my back arches as my hips buck. Dorian smiles faintly, amusement evident in his expression and his energy, but he doesn't change his pace or intensity. Just continues in that same, steady, *maddening* rhythm.

"Dorian," I gasp. "I—I think I'm going to..." My voice cuts off as my body stiffens. Dorian pulls his hand away, and I release a whine as my impending orgasm dies as fast as it came.

"Not yet," he says patiently.

I shake my head. "Wait—I was so close!"

"I know," he says, amused. "I'm not ready for you to come yet. Trust me when I say, you'll wish I were still edging you once I really get started. For now..." he picks up the crop, running the flat end through my slit, and I nearly choke on my gasp. The cool leather against my heated skin is too intense to bear, and when he delivers his first tap, I nearly come. It's agonizing, invigorating and so, *so* frustrating.

"Settle in, Mira," he says. "We're just getting warmed up. You'll come when I'm ready for you to come, and once I'm ready, you'll come as many times as *I* want you to come. You don't get a say here. You don't have any control here. Sit back, relax, and let me work."

I turn my head away, whimpering into my arm. He starts to gently tap my clit and pussy at a quick, staccato pace. Every few taps, he gives a slightly harder smack that jolts and shocks me, making me cry out. Perversely and completely out of the blue, I start to feel myself building to an orgasm again, just from him tapping my pussy. It's taboo, wrong, and unreasonably hot.

My cries take on a higher pitch as I start to climb—just as I reach my crest and my stomach muscles tense, Dorian stops. He sets aside the crop and refocuses his attention on my breasts, returning to playing with my nipples. He pinches them and rubs his thumbs over them with firm pressure, all while I toss my head from side to side, panting harshly and begging, willing to do *anything* for him to make me come already.

I never thought foreplay or any sexual play could be like this; I'd always assumed that guys were wired to do the bare minimum before getting to the main event so they could get their orgasm. This here feels freaking *amazing,* yet the denial is so frustrating I'm tempted to scream insults at Dorian.

After a while, he starts massaging my pussy again. I'm much closer to the edge now, my orgasm is *just* within reach—he barely has to rub me for thirty seconds before I'm there. The bastard pulls away *again*.

"You are *such* an asshole," I whine. "Why won't you let me come?"

"Because I'm enjoying this far too much," Dorian replies, laughter in his voice. "You're so fucking needy right now, Mira. It's adorable and obscenely arousing. I honestly think I might come in my pants like a fourteen-year-old." He smirks. "You'd let me do anything I wanted to you right now, wouldn't you?"

"Do you need me to beg?" I try. "*Please*, Dorian."

He shakes his head, massaging my thighs. "No, baby, I don't need you to beg, though I don't mind the sound of it. But you should know that begging will get you nowhere. I'll still do what I want on my timetable. You'll get what's coming to you when *I'm* ready. Hearing you say *please* in that breathy, needy voice is a lovely bonus, but it won't change my mind."

"You *are* a sadist," I realize.

A sadist who's decided to torture me for his own amusement...

Chapter Twenty-Two

D orian shrugs. "According to some, yes. This is barely scratching the surface of my sadism, though. If you think a bit of edging is sadistic, I'm interested to find out what you'll call me when I ignore your pleas for me to stop or ease up." He lands an open palm slap on my pussy; my back arches and a loud cry escapes me. "Enough talking for now, beautiful. I think I'm almost ready for you to come." He gives me another slap, and I choke on a yelp. "How close are you?" he asks, sounding genuinely curious.

"I'm *right there*," I moan. "I can't take it."

He rubs his thumb up and down my labia. "You don't have a choice, baby. You'll take whatever I feel like giving you. Won't you?"

I nod emphatically.

He smiles. "Good girl. You can come now. I've been dying to taste you again; holding myself back while you're laid out beneath me, bound and helpless like the most beautiful sacrifice, has been *torture*." He leans down between my legs, spreads my pussy open with his thumbs, and gives me a long, slow lick along my slit. Tension threads through every bit of me, stiffening my muscles as I reach the crest once again. This time, Dorian doesn't pull back to try to delay it or edge me. Two of his fingers slide easily into my channel, curving upwards and hitting a spot that make tingles explode across my skin while he lavishes my clit with attention. The orgasm that's eluded me slams into me with the impact of a freight train. My back arches and I yank at my wrists, unable to control my body's reaction as I come *loudly*. So loudly I'm afraid my cries will be heard through the entire house, but I'm too lost in abandon to *really* care. My stomach contracts, my thighs tremble, and Dorian makes a growling noise that damn near drives me out of my mind.

His fingers set a slow, patient pace of sliding in and out of me, hooking over that magical spot inside me. He continues eating me through my orgasm, prolonging it and making little noises of enjoyment that drive me wild. "Too much," I whimper after an eternity. "Dorian, please, it's too much."

He pulls his mouth away and stills his fingers, meeting my eyes. His have a wicked gleam that makes me genuinely anxious, because I understand that he completely meant it when he said he was just getting started. I already feel spent, and yet he's barely begun.

"That was one," he murmurs. "I want you to count for me, Mira." He places a kiss on my stomach. "Each time you come, count. If you really want to please me, thank me for making you come."

"One," I whimper. "Thank you."

"For?" he questions, lips tilting at the corners.

"Making me come," I rush out.

His hint of a smile turns into a full blown one. "You're very welcome." His mouth returns to lavishing me with attention before I've truly come down from my first orgasm, sending me careening straight into a second one. Somehow, I manage to remember to count and thank him, even though my mind becomes fogged and dazed. Another orgasm follows, and then another, and by the time I've thanked him for my *sixth* orgasm, the attention to my pussy really becomes too much. I'm hypersensitive, too aroused to handle it, which doesn't bother him the slightest bit. I start to struggle to come from his mouth—after a few minutes, he pulls away and pulls his fingers out of me. He takes a moment to kiss me, letting me taste myself on his lips, then picks up the crop again.

My eyes widen. "No—"

"That word has zero relevance to me right now," he says, trailing it down my navel. "You know what you have to say to make things slow or stop. Unless I hear *those* words, I won't stop. I won't change what I'm doing. I don't give much of a shit what you say right now, baby, because I am enjoying myself *far* too much to ease up."

A tear sneaks out of my eye, and I consider using one of my safe words. Consider making him stop altogether, but something holds me back. I can see and feel how much he's enjoying this scene. I don't want to interrupt that unless I'm *really* done and genuinely can't do any more. I'm not at that point yet; I'm still somewhat coherent, just painfully sensitive.

When I don't say anything, he spreads my pussy with one hand and taps the crop right against my clit. My back arches and I suck in an agonized breath, eyes watering at the pulse-pounding sensation. He taps me once, twice. On the third time, the impact makes me come. It's a different sort of orgasm; shorter, quicker, yet no less intense than the others. Surprise flares in Dorian's eyes as he looks at me. His gaze darkens, and he growls, "*Fuck*, that was hot."

I whine in response.

He smacks my clit more intensely, and reminds, "I didn't hear you count *or* thank me. That's displeasing."

"Seven," I manage to say. "Thank you. I'm sorry."

He nods. "Good girl. I think I'm ready to test the toys out on you now. You're primed and prepared for them, aren't you?"

Although he phrases the words as a question, I know he's not actually *asking* for my opinion. In this moment, unless I safe word, my opinions are completely irrelevant to him. He's doing what feels good to *him*, and what feels good to *him* is watching my reactions, witnessing my pleasure, knowing that *he's* the one reducing me to a puddle of need and sensitivity.

He retrieves two of the other toys he brought; a vibrator that suddenly looks deeply intimidating, and a slim, long dildo. "God, I want to fuck you right now," he says wistfully.

"Please do," I respond eagerly. I want to feel him inside me; I want to get him off the way he's getting me off.

He shakes his head. "Not tonight. Soon, I hope, but not now. This is a punishment, Mira, remember? I think I've been very nice to you and pretty lenient, easing you into this scene." The desire in his eyes darkens, and I sense the exact moment that the true sadist in him rears its head. It's not out for blood or pain; it's out for complete surrender and obeisance to its wishes.

The hot pink dildo slowly prods at my entrance and gently slides inside of me. Its passage is eased by how obscenely wet I am, and as it slides over my g-spot, my eyes roll into the back of my head. Dorian twists it around a little bit, lips quirking when I squirm and yank at my bindings.

"Take a deep breath for me," he murmurs. "Things are only about to get more difficult for you, and a hell of a lot more entertaining for me."

He presses a button on the handle of the vibrator, and I jerk as a low buzz fills the bedroom. Dorian presses it to the inside of my thigh, letting me feel the rumbling intensity of the vibrations, chuckling at my whimper. My channel clenches around the dildo, and I squeeze my eyes shut, at once terrified and titillated. His mouth was insanely good; the crop felt like heaven and torture against my overstimulated pussy; I can't imagine what a vibrator will feel like when he's already spent what feels like an eternity playing with me.

"Are you ready?" he asks.

I shake my head. He smiles, eyes dancing with glee. "I think you are."

He presses the smooth, rounded head of the device against my clit, and I nearly black out. It is so fucking intense, so overwhelming that I can't help the scream that tears out of my throat. It takes less than a second for me to start coming again. Dorian rumbles out what a good girl I am, then reminds me to count.

Eight...

Nine...

Ten...

By the eleventh, I feel like I'm fighting for my life. I can barely breathe through the pleasure, and the numbers scramble in my mind; I can't remember how many times I've come, I can barely remember my own name.

"Count," Dorian reminds me, swirling the vibrator along my swollen clit.

Tears stream down my cheeks. "I... I don't know."

He shrugs. "You skip a number, I'll take that as an invitation to start over. *Eleven*, Mira. Count and thank me."

"Thank you," I whimper. "E—eleven."

"Very good." His voice is filled with pleasure. I think he might give me reprieve, but instead, he *turns the setting up*. Reality becomes warped as renewed, powerful vibrations assault my entire body. My vision dims and blurs, potent heat slicks my skin with sweat. I yank at my restraints so convulsively I feel the strain in my burning muscles.

My stomach contracts with such intensity it cramps and aches, and I squeeze around the dildo so hard I think I might snap it in half.

I can barely think, but I know what I need to say. The number I have to utter to please and satisfy Dorian. My lips form around the word, but my brain doesn't have the capacity to actually make any noise aside from a loud, consuming cry. Dimly, I hear Dorian reminding me to count again. I clench my teeth to cut off my endless cry, and with all my focus I manage to breathe, "Twelve."

It's barely audible, but he hears it. He turns off the vibrator, tossing it to the side, and slowly, gently pulls the dildo out of me. Every inch of me feels hypersensitized and overstimulated; not just my pussy, but my entire body. I can't seem to stop whimpering *or* crying tears of pleasure-pain, and even though I haven't uttered either of my safe words, Dorian begins to release my bindings, all the while quietly praising me for being such a good girl, taking what he wanted to give so well, following his instructions perfectly and coming so beautifully. He wraps my body in his arms, not seeming to care about my sweat-coated skin, or the way I can't stop trembling in the aftermath of *twelve fucking orgasms*. He spoons me, holding me close, and while I feel his erection pressing against my ass, he doesn't do anything about it. Doesn't make any moves to take care of it. He just holds me tight, fluttering kisses along my neck and shoulder.

"Easy," he murmurs as I sob softly. I don't know *why* I'm crying or why I'm emotional—I'm free, he's no longer playing with my body as if it's a toy, yet I can't seem to get control of myself. My hormones are completely out of whack, and I'm uncharacteristically needy and clingy.

I turn around so we're chest to chest, cuddling up to him and crying into his shirt. He murmurs soothing words of praise, telling me how well I did, how proud of me he is while stroking my hair with one hand and spine with the other.

"I... I don't know what's wrong with me," I whimper as the tears start to slow.

"Sub-drop," he says calmly. "After the scene, when reality sets in, things start to feel weird and sometimes unpleasant. Overwhelming. Emotions get a bit twisted up, and most submissives are left with an intense feeling of vulnerability. Tears are pretty common. This is perfectly normal."

He sounds so confident, so in control, so *experienced* that I trust him. I trust him to hold me, take care of me, and give me what I need. I lay the side of my cheek on his chest, not caring that I'm getting his shirt wet, and let him console me and murmur to me.

"I can see why you called that a punishment," I say once my tears have slowed. "I feel thoroughly punished and sore."

He kisses the top of my head. "Good. In the future, you will *not* sneakily try to get away from me. If you have a problem, you *will* come to me. Or that bit of edging and dozen orgasms you just got will seem like child's play. Got it?"

I nod with a whimper, cuddling closer to him. "I'm sorry."

"I know," he soothes. "I'm not angry anymore."

He's... not? I know he liked what he just did to me, but was his form of punishing me really enough to negate any anger he might've been feeling?

"You're not still mad?" I ask, dubious.

"No," he replies simply. "We settled it physically. We talked, I delivered a pretty clear message. I'm over it. As long as you don't do it again, we won't have a problem, Mira."

I frown, trying to concentrate on him, on his energy. I don't get any negative vibes, don't feel any residual anger—merely contentment and satisfaction. I sense that he likes holding me like this, and he likes the way we got past our conflict. It helped him channel his anger and upset through a physical punishment, and I think he feels it sort of… put me in my place. Not in a demeaning way, but in a way that forces me to understand where we are.

"What now?" I ask after several long moments.

"Now, I clean you up," he replies. "A quick shower, and then a nice long soak in a warm bath."

"I don't think I can walk," I admit.

I feel his smile more than see it. "I know. That's why I'm here." He slowly removes his arms and scoots to the edge of the bed. Cold overwhelms me, and the intense vulnerability comes crashing back; tears well in my eyes. I don't like this sub-drop thing very much. It's making me clingy, and I'm not a clingy person.

Dorian stands from the bed and leans over to gently scoop me up in his muscular arms. He carries me in a princess-hold as he walks to the bathroom, flicking on the lights with his elbow. After setting me on the counter, right between the sinks, he turns on the shower. He waits a few seconds and tests the temperature of the water, then begins to strip. I watch as inch after inch of smooth, tan skin is revealed. His body is something sonnets should be written about; each of his muscles are perfectly-honed. His biceps bulge and his six-pack almost hints at an *eight* pack. A dusting of dark hair trails down his naval, leading to a gorgeous cock that peeks out of his boxers. When he catches me looking at him, he smirks.

I avert my gaze; he chuckles. "Stare all you want, baby. It's all yours."

I like the sound of that. I remind myself that I shouldn't get attached. Just because we had a scarily intimate scene and I enjoyed a day-date with him doesn't mean that what we have is long term. At some point soon, I'm going to need to sit him down and have a serious conversation about what this thing between us is, and what it can amount to. As much as I'm finding I like him and we *could* fit together, I don't see him as part of my life moving forward. I'm going to vet school, and he's going to stay embroiled in gang wars and criminal activities. Those two things can't possibly click.

I don't want to talk about it now, though. Right now, I just want to be close to him. As if sensing my train of thought, Dorian plants a kiss on my lips before moving to the marble bathtub and turning on the faucets. He selects a vial of blue liquid that stands on the edge of the tub, drizzles in a bit of it, then scoops me up and takes me into the shower.

Patiently and with something bordering reverence, he holds me up with one hand while using the other to wash my hair. He lathers it with a shampoo that smells of cedar and sandalwood, massaging it into my scalp, and rinses it out. The same process is repeated with conditioner, before he takes his time washing my body with a body wash that smells like an enticing mix of fresh mint and sage. I like the way he washes me with the utmost care and attention. When he gets to my pussy, I whimper, and he kisses my shoulder. "I know it's sore," he murmurs. "I'll put some cream on it before we head to bed for the night, it should soothe the worst of the aches." He's even gentler with my pussy than he is with the rest of my body, though no less thorough. He kneels as he rubs my legs, even my feet, planting kisses on my skin as he goes along.

He washes himself as a quick, succinct afterthought and carries me to the tub, which is about two-thirds full and brimming with bubbles from the serum he poured into it. He turns off the faucet and helps me in, climbing in behind me.

I don't think a man has ever given me this much attention. I know that no one's ever cared for me enough to wash me like I'm a delicate doll made of glass. I feel worshipped and valued, sensations that could easily become addictive if I'm not careful.

When Dorian climbs in behind me, settling me between his legs, I feel the press of his erection against my back. He's *still* hard—so hard it must be painful.

"Let me take care of you," I murmur, turning around and wrapping my fist around his length, trying to keep my eyes from widening when my fingers can't touch. His thickness is... a *lot*.

"No," he shakes his head. "Not tonight. I'll get myself off later, or in the morning. Tonight's about you, not me."

I blink slowly.

I know this isn't *entirely* selfless on his part; he got a fuck-ton of pleasure from what just happened, but he didn't get what most men chase—release. He's hard as a steel pipe and I *know* he wants me, but he's making no move to get his own orgasm. He won't even let me jerk him off. In a way, that scene was about *both* of us; him showing me what he likes and what turns him on, me getting thoroughly punished for what he sees as an indiscretion.

My eyes start to droop after a few minutes in the bath, and I go lax against Dorian's chest. It doesn't take long for me to fall asleep, right here in the bathtub, lulled into darkness by my own exhaustion and the feel of his heart beating against my back.

Chapter Twenty-Three

In the morning, I wake up before Dorian. He's behind me, an arm slung around my waist and a strong leg curved over mine, wrapped around me like some sort of barnacle. Although I don't think *he's* awake, a certain part of his anatomy is—I feel his erection pressing insistently against my back, demanding attention. A quick shift of my thighs reveals what I already suspected; I am *sore*. Not as sore as I expected to be, I should be able to go about my daily activities, though I'm quite certain I'll wince each time I sit.

I bite my lip when Dorian's dick thickens even more, nudging against my skin, almost demanding to be satiated. I don't know what kind of headspace he's in today—he said that punishing me last night alleviated his anger, but he might've been exaggerating. Maybe a wake-up call in the form of a blowjob will put him in a better mood and give me a higher chance of him allowing me to go about my usual Saturday tasks. Baking for my wolf pack and maybe even making a midnight trip to visit them.

I also *want* to go down on him. I want to find out what he tastes like, what he feels like, the noises he'll make when *he* comes. I don't understand the intimate mechanics of the whole pleasure-dom thing, but surely he enjoys getting off just as much as he enjoys getting *me* off.

Slowly, carefully so as not to wake him, I shift my position, pressing my ass back against his erection. I'm only wearing a long shirt, something he must've dressed me in after I passed out in the bathtub, and he's only wearing what feel like very thin boxers.

His hard-on hardens even *more*, and my eyes widen as I swallow. I saw Dorian's size last night when we showered, but that was a brief glimpse. I knew he was big, but this feels... intimidatingly big. Substantially bigger than any of the guys I've slept with before, and probably more than my sore pussy can handle at present, or possibly *ever*.

I want to try getting him in my mouth. See how far down my throat I can manage to take him.

I grind back against him again, and his arm around my waist tightens as he releases a low, sleepy groan. Smiling, I gently grab his arm and try to remove it from me; that has the adverse effect of making his hold on me contract.

"I hope you're not just planning to tease me," he murmurs, his voice low and thick with sleep. It's an intimate bedroom-voice that raises the hairs on my arms and makes me give a faint shudder of pleasure.

"Turn around," I tell him. "Lie on your back."

"Giving commands now?" Dorian sounds vaguely amused. "I prefer to be the one telling *you* what to do when we're in bed together."

"I'll do my best to blow your mind," I say honestly, grinding into him again and drawing a hiss from his lips. "Turn around, Dorian."

"Mmm. I guess I'm willing to see where this goes." He presses a kiss to my shoulder and another to the back of my neck before releasing me. I hear the rustling of sheets as he follows my directions, and when I rise up to my knees, I'm treated to the sight of him shirtless, with the morning sun illuminating his body. He's wearing a pair of boxer briefs that sport a considerable tent in the center, making anticipation and a touch of worry rise up in me.

I reach forward, lightly dragging my fingernails down his abs before tugging at the waist of his boxers. "A little help?" I ask.

With a small, amused smile, he strips out of them. I straddle his legs, leaning down until I'm face-level with his cock. It's a thing of beauty; long and thick, with a bulging vein running along the bottom of it, and several smaller veins decorating the edges of his smooth shaft. My mouth waters as I stare at him, and my breath hitches.

"You keep staring like that, I'm going to start charging you for an Only Fans subscription," Dorian says, laughter in his voice.

I blink a few times. "Yeah. Uh, sorry, it's just..." I wave at his dick. "Big. Like, *really* big. Like, holy shit, I don't know if I'll be able to get the tip in my mouth big."

"You're under no obligation to deep throat me," Dorian says mildly, threading his hands behind his head and settling in. "Do what feels good for you. Explore. I guarantee it'll be amazing for me."

I like that. I've only given head a few times, and the blowjobs were gross and nauseating. The guys grunted and held my hair as they thrust into my mouth, holding me with grubby hands... I was *not* into it. I just did whatever it took to be done quickly.

In this moment, I actually *want* to go down on Dorian, and he seems happy to let me do whatever I wish.

I grip the base of him in my hand, sucking in a sharp breath when the tips of my fingers don't touch. I try to recall the videos I've watched, giving girls advice on how to blow a guy's mind, and the unsolicited input I receive from Cara regularly.

I gently cup his balls with my free hand, softly massaging them. Dorian's six pack clenches. Smiling, I lean forward and run my tongue over the vein on the underside of his cock in a long, languid lick. His breath shudders out of him when I gently lave my tongue over the head of his cock, lapping up the bead of salty pre-come that's gathered.

"*Fuck*," Dorian groans.

I wrap my lips around his head, meeting his eyes as I start to suckle gently, firming my suction to see what works best for him. His eyes briefly roll into the back of his head, and he releases a moan that makes heat gather between my thighs.

I work his head while massaging his balls for several minutes, until drool starts to gather in my mouth. I use it as lubrication for the rest of his length, gathering my saliva with the hand on his base and starting to jerk him. Even though my jaw feels stretched too wide and I don't think I'll be able to get him down very far, I'm determined to try. I start bobbing my head in time with my jerking motions, trying to take him a little deeper with each pass, encouraged by his noises of pleasure. Quickly, I get too enthusiastic, and he hits the back of my throat. I gag and pull off, giving myself a second to breathe before going at him again.

"There's a good girl," Dorian rumbles, watching me as I labor over his cock, testing out different speeds, levels of suction, and massaging motions on his balls. "*My* good girl. Fuck, Mira, I'm close. Are you ready to swallow me?"

"Mm," I moan around his length, and that's all it takes to send him over the edge. His hips jerk up, pushing more of his cock into my mouth. My eyes water, but I fight the gag reflex. I take him as far back as I can, squeezing his balls, jerking his shaft faster as he starts to come in my mouth. Warm, salty bursts of his seed shoot directly down my throat, and I swallow all of it, even though I'm a little overwhelmed at the volume.

"Good fucking girl," he croons. "That's one hell of a way to wake up."

I give his length one last loving stroke before releasing him. He stares at me with warmth and affection brightening his gaze, paired with a dark possessiveness. I try to attribute it all to the post-orgasm glow, though it's hard to write it off as the hormone hit of an orgasm. Suddenly nervous, I scramble to the edge of the bed.

"I'm, uh, going to take a shower," I say awkwardly, frowning down at the band T-shirt I'm wearing—his, presumably.

He nods. "Alright, baby. I'll make coffee. There's a tube of lotion on the bathroom counter; it should help with your soreness. I put some on you last night, but it might be time to reapply." With that, he rolls out of bed and leaves the room, and I'm left feeling strangely bereft.

Chapter Twenty-Four

I shower quickly and apply the cream Dorian left for me, one that succeeds in instantly soothing my soreness. Once I'm done, I venture back into the bedroom to search for clothes, wrapped tightly in a towel. The shirts and pants I brought from my dorm are already neatly folded in the closet. I select a pair of forgiving yoga pants and a cropped navy-blue sweater. Dorian comes into the bedroom carrying a tray that has two plates piled high with food and two accompanying cups of coffee.

"Breakfast in bed," he says with a smile.

I raise my eyebrows as I look at the heaped servings of bacon and stacks of pancakes on each plate. "Did you make all of this yourself?"

He chuckles, setting the tray down on a nightstand. "Admittedly, I'm not as good as you, but I can still cook." He straightens his dark bedspread, takes a seat on top of it, and gently sets the tray down over the covers. "Come on," he says lightly. "You had quite the workout last night. We need to replenish your body with nutrients."

"This looks like a very healthy selection for replenishment," I quip drily. "Carbs, cholesterol, sugar, and fat. What could be better?"

Dorian gives me a long, deliberate once-over. "We can both afford the calories. Sit."

As soon as I join him on the bed, he wraps an arm around my waist and pulls me right up against him, offering me a gentle smile.

"I never got a good morning kiss from you," he comments.

I raise my eyebrows. "I think you got something better than that."

"While I very much enjoyed your wakeup call, it can't compare to a kiss." He leans his head down until his lips hover right above mine. "Open for me."

My lips instinctually part under the weight of his softly-spoken command, and he presses his against them in a lazy, slow, yet passionate claim. He pulls away after a few moments, kissing the top of my head before nodding at the plate. "Eat."

Swallowing, a little dazed, I obey him. While I'm munching on a piece of perfectly crispy bacon, I glance at him. "Can I ask you a question?"

"Whatever you want," he replies easily, pouring syrup on a pancake.

"What do you get out of your style of dominance?" I ask curiously. "I don't know much about kink, only what I've read and heard from one of my roommates. I understand that people who are dominant in bed are usually focused on the reactions of their submissives, but that often takes the form of hurting them, then following it up with a few orgasms. You forgo the former and put all the focus on the latter. Why?"

Dorian exhales a deep breath, brows furrowing. "It's a combination of things for me, I think," Dorian says. "First of all, I don't get off on causing pain, even if the person I'm with enjoys it. Second of all, I guess there's an element of pride. Few men actually know how to satisfy their female partners—your bodies and pleasure mechanisms are a lot more complicated than ours. It takes focus and practice to please you. I'm competitive, so I guess my kink really started with me wanting to be the best in bed I could possibly be. Then, I realized that

I was both fascinated and *really* turned on by controlling my partner's pleasure. When they get to come, how many times they get to come. I liked making all the decisions. A submissive's responses to too much or not enough pleasure were extremely erotic, so I started playing around more. I've never been with someone who fascinates me as much as you, though. You take arousing to a whole new level—you're fucking ethereal when you come and when you beg."

I feel my cheeks burn as I glance away. Dorian takes my chin in his hand and gently guides me to watch him once again. "Don't be embarrassed," he says firmly. "It's okay to enjoy it. I *want* you to enjoy it."

"It just seems selfish on my part," I murmur. "You didn't come last night. Only I did. How is that fair?"

"It's fair because watching you come, being the reason for it, was hotter to me than you getting me off," he says simply. "I enjoyed what you did this morning, but I would've liked it even more if *I* had woken *you* up to a solid half hour of teasing you with an orgasm before giving you several. I'm not like most other men; what really arouses me is different. Sucking and fucking is fine, but it doesn't titillate me as much as what I did last night, knowing what I *can* do to you. Don't feel selfish; ultimately, I'm still doing what *I* want to do, and you enjoying it is part of the package. Okay?"

"Okay," I whisper, still struggling to comprehend how making me come can be more satisfying to Dorian than coming himself.

He raises a fork to my lips. "Open."

I part them, allowing him to feed me a slice of fluffy, sweet, delicious pancake drenched in the perfect amount of syrup. After I've chewed and swallowed, I say, "I'm not a child. You don't need to feed me."

"But you *are* mine, and I like taking care of you," Dorian replies. "If you don't want me to hand-feed you, just say so."

My cheeks heat again. "I... think I like it."

He smiles. "Good."

The rest of breakfast is spent in comfortable silence. Dorian eats quick bites in between feeding me, holding my chin, stroking my cheeks, watching me with the utmost attention. Once we're done, he stacks the plates and hands me my coffee. I sip it for several minutes before forcing myself to address the elephant in the room.

"About me being yours..."

Dorian glances at me. "Yes?"

"I'm not. Not really, or at least not permanently. You know that, right?"

He shrugs. "It's true for now, and honestly, I hope it'll keep being true for a long time."

I open my mouth to argue the point, then seal my lips, scrambling for a coherent way to word my thoughts. "I get that you like me, and I like you too, but we're really not sustainable. What I said yesterday—"

Dorian cuts me off by pressing a finger against my lips. "Listen to me, Mira, and please listen well. I don't like *having* to say this, frankly it's fucking offensive, but I understand you need to hear it. I am *nothing* like your piece of shit stepfather. The men I work with are *nothing* like your piece of shit stepfather. The organization I'm a part of is *nothing* like the organization he's in."

I tilt my head back, and his fingers slide from my lips. Apprehension and fear tightens my gut as I gaze at him. "How do you know?" I question softly. "You know nothing about him. You don't know all that much about *me,* despite whatever background check you might've run."

"People are looking into your stepfather on my behalf; I'm digging into him."

"Why?"

"Because I can't kill an enemy I don't know."

My coffee cup freezes halfway to my lips. My eyes widen as I meet Dorian's gaze, which swims with dark intentions. I fear I must've misheard him, but his response leaves little room for doubt. He intends to kill my *stepfather*?

"Why?" I whisper.

Dorian's jaw ticks. "Because he hurt a girl he should've protected. A girl who, against all odds, grew into a magnificent woman that I have decided to claim. A woman who is fighting my claim because of the things she saw under his care." His features twist. "Not care, more like *reign*. He hurt you, which means he will die." Dorian blinks slowly. "I think I'd be willing—more, *eager* to kill anyone who wanted to hurt you."

I swallow thickly, my breath catching, and take a sip of coffee to distract myself from the warm feelings burrowing their way into my chest. Dorian wants to kill *for* me. The notion should be gruesome and a complete turn-off. It should scare me away, *especially* considering my upbringing. But it doesn't.

In the animal kingdom, the patriarchs or matriarchs of the strongest clans, packs, and prides will kill to keep their own safe, and among the species who mate for life, they'll kill any animal that comes sniffing around their mate.

In the real world, killing for love might be frowned upon, but sometimes it's justified. My stepfather is a man who should have died long ago; he should've died instead of my mother when his house was broken into years ago. He's a stain upon this world, and I've wished him dead more times than I could count, though I've never had the power to execute him myself.

Dorian does. Despite my aversion to most things involving organized crime, I feel no repulsion at the thought of Dorian killing a scumbag like Clyde. I almost lost a leg because of that man.

"Would you like that?" Dorian questions, rubbing a hand up and down my arm.

I nod slowly. "I think so."

He smiles. "Good. I'd do it anyway, but it'll be nice not to have to hide it from you."

I frown. "If we're going to be... whatever we are, you can't hide anything from me. I need to know that when I ask questions, you'll give me honest answers."

Dorian's lips thin. "That requires a great deal of trust and certain concessions from you, Mira. I can only be open with you if you give yourself to me fully, if I know for sure that you'd never repeat anything you heard. Open yourself to me, and I'll give you the same courtesy. Otherwise, I have to protect myself through silence, because lives depend on my ability to keep my mouth shut."

I swallow. "Like Connor and Seamus's?"

Dorian nods. "They're my legion. I'll protect them to the end."

I feel a faint smile pull on my lips. "Your legion? I thought legions require more than three men."

"In ancient times, sure, the concept of legions were large military units with several subdivisions. Legions prized courage, respect, loyalty, competence, obedience, and hard work. All of those things apply to the self-made legion whose members live in this house. We might just be a trio, but we work hard to exhibit those traits, and we work very well together."

"I don't know that I like your fellow legionaries very much," I murmur, frowning. "Seamus is fine, but Connor's a fucking fiend. I'm pretty sure he still wants to kill me."

"Connor is difficult," Dorian allows, nodding. "He sees things in black and white, and you're a grey spot to him. A complication. He prefers to kill complications before they can harm him. He's calmer now that I've claimed you and made clear that you're *my* complication, one I'll take care of. That removes his responsibility and liability. He'll ease up in time."

"Maybe, but I don't like this house, minus the cats." My lips twitch. "The cats are cute. I want to keep them. How is the little one with the respiratory infection doing?" I frown, realizing that I've forgotten to check on the litter during the chaos of the last days.

"She's fine; the antibiotics Seamus got her are working, and she seems to be doing better," Dorian says with a smile. "If you want the cats, I'll share custody with you." His expression sobers. "I'll do some research to see about finding us a different place today and talk to my boys about it. They should understand, even though there might be some complaints."

I should feel uncomfortable at the idea of moving in with Dorian, but at this point, I'm starting to understand that him keeping me close is about *both* of our safety. Even if I don't see long term potential between us, I'd like to explore what there can be in the short term. Get inside his brain and pick it apart like the puzzle it is. There's definitely *something* between us, and while his lifestyle means I won't stick around for long, I can try to enjoy the perks of being with him for *now*.

"I'll agree to an apartment for this school year," I say. "Beyond that, we'll see."

Dorian watches me for a few moments, then nods. "End of the year," he concurs. "After that, we'll decide on next steps."

I smile. "Wonderful. Just to give you a taste of what's coming, how would you feel about me inviting Cara and Valerie over for a girl's night later?" The idea is impromptu, but I miss living with my former roommates, and I don't want to become estranged from them.

Dorian thinks for a few beats. "We don't have anything incriminating out in the open, and we'll seal up what we have in random drawers or cupboards. As long as your girls don't snoop or act suspicious, I'm fine with it. I'll talk to Connor and Seamus. Connor's planning on being out of the house tonight anyways." He winces. "Seamus might try to fuck your friends."

I snort. "Cara would be all for it."

Dorian kisses my lips. "Let's finish up, and I'll see what I can do about having your friends over."

Chapter Twenty-Five

S omehow, Dorian manages to get his roommates to agree to me having a girl's night. Connor has to leave for some overnight assignment—one I suspect has nothing to do with school—while Seamus seems weirdly excited and spends the afternoon asking me about my roommates. I'm learning to roll with his weirdness, so I don't give him shit.

Dorian and I spend the day doing oddly domestic activities together. In the morning and for some of the afternoon, we do homework. Later on, he agrees to take me grocery shopping so I can bake some goodies for tonight and make a few batches of treats for my wolf pack. I hope to visit my wolves tomorrow.

When Valerie and Cara arrive at eight p.m., I rush to the door to let them in. I'm eager to see them again. I miss living with my girls, and while Cara can be annoying, I also miss her endless rambling about topics that range from the weather, to why religion is bullshit, to the latest fashion trends, to the world of BDSM.

"Hey, bitch," Cara says when I open the door, hefting up a bag of Chinese food. "Hope you're hungry, I brought reinforcements." She's decked out in all pink—a hot-pink blazer over a light-pink shirt and matching skinny jeans.

I smile. "I hope you guys are in the mood for cookies, brownies, *and* cupcakes. I spent the last two hours baking; I just need to frost the cupcakes."

Valerie, wearing all black, lifts up a brown paper bag that clinks with glass bottles. "I brought the booze, and a bullet-pointed proposal on why we should watch a horror movie tonight."

Cara huffs. "I thought we agreed to a rom-com."

"Horror movies are fucking hilarious," Val deadpans, giving Cara a look of vague disgust. "Sometimes they're romantic, too."

I grab a fistful of both of their shirts and pull them into the house, giving them loud kisses on the cheek in greeting.

"Dorian will be around, his psycho roommate is out for the night, and the British roommate has been told to stay out of sight."

"Mira, love, you should know by now that I'm not very good at listening to orders," Seamus says from *directly behind me*. His voice startles me so much I nearly jump out of my skin.

Cara practically salivates. "That *accent*. That *face*." She clears her throat. "What's your name, handsome?"

"Seamus Archibald the Third, darling," Seamus responds. "And you are?"

"Just Cara," Cara says, eyeing Seamus like he's her next meal. "You single?"

"Miserably so," Seamus says, giving Cara a mischievous grin, though I get the sense his flirting is a sign of friendliness rather than interest. When his gaze falls on Valerie, who's looking at something on her phone, his eyes sharpen and his energy changes from watchful to alert, as if he's a Doberman whose ears have just pricked up. "And who might *you* be, love?" Valerie's eyes flick over to Seamus.

She gives him a critical up and down, snorts, and returns her attention to her phone. "Uninterested."

Just like that, Seamus's focus *locks* onto Valerie, and I heave a silent sigh. I can already tell I should've bargained with Seamus to stay out of the house tonight.

"Well, that's unfortunate," Seamus murmurs. "See, I have a condition that makes me prone to only fall for women who are notoriously uninterested."

"I'm pre-med," Valerie comments drily. "I say you'll live." She powers off her phone and puts it away, turning to look at me. "So, food and a horror movie?"

"*No horror*," Cara says with a shudder.

I shrug. "I'm kind of on board with Valerie on this one. It *is* spooky season, and horror movies *are* usually funny. Thrillers are even more hilarious, though."

Seamus gives me a strange look. "You're full of surprises, aren't you?"

Dorian strolls into the entryway, slinging an arm around my shoulder and dropping a kiss on my lips before offering Cara and Valerie an enigmatic smile. "Ladies," he drawls. "Apologies for intruding on girl's night—"

"You can intrude on me or in me *any* time," Cara says with a smile.

Dorian doesn't even look at her. "Sorry, I'm spoken for. Oh, and keep Mira out of your whole bar pickup routine unless I'm *also* invited. Now, dinner?"

Half an hour later, the five of us have settled in the living room, but we still haven't managed to pick out a movie. Dorian and I are seated together on the blue couch, while Cara's curled up on an armchair to the right of us. Valerie and Seamus are seated on a two-cushion sofa to our left. I'm actively shielding my box of sesame chicken from Dorian, who still manages to steal a piece every time I try to argue the merits of watching a horror movie.

"Oh, *enough*," Valerie says with a loud sigh. "Let's get some alcohol in Cara and she'll agree to whatever." She looks at Seamus. "You have a cocktail mixer? This place looks fancy enough for one."

Seamus smiles. "I sure do, love. It's in the kitchen—care to see it?"

Valerie's gaze flicks over to me and she raises her eyebrows, silently asking me if it's safe. I don't think Seamus would hurt her, but he might come onto her *really* strongly, so I say, "I can show you. The cookies and cupcakes have probably cooled enough to frost anyways."

Valerie's gaze sharpens. "Vanilla cupcakes?"

I smile. "Yup."

"With that vanilla buttercream frosting?" she says, her voice faintly breathless.

I nod. "Indeed."

She stands. "Yeah, I'll mix drinks while you frost cupcakes. And one or two might disappear in the interim."

Seamus makes a humming noise. "Vanilla, hmm? That's disappointing."

Valerie releases a low, taunting chuckle, swooping down to pick up the paper bag she brought. "Seamus, there is *nothing* about me that's vanilla."

"Oh?" Seamus says, sounding like he wants to know every sordid detail of Valerie's sex life. I quickly pull her into the kitchen by her hand, cutting him off before he can start interrogating her.

"He's hot, if not a bit arrogant," Valerie says once we get to the kitchen. "I might fuck him. You cool with that?"

I blink. "I thought you weren't interested."

"I'm not interested in his *personality*," Valerie says. "His body, on the other hand, looks excellent. Bonus points if he's kinky." She pauses, unloading several liquor bottles. "Is he kinky?"

I feel my cheeks heat. "Um… there's a good chance, but I'm not sure. You'd have to ask him."

She shrugs. "I don't have to. He's a total dom—I can feel it. I would not mind spending a night having my brains fucked out by him." She gives a low laugh. "The rest of the time? He strikes me as insufferable."

"You're not wrong about the insufferable part. How are things in the apartment?" I ask, redirecting the topic as I pull the buttercream frosting out of the fridge and set the baking pan of cupcakes on the kitchen island. I rifle through the drawers until I find the professional frosting pipe that I convinced Dorian to buy for me earlier, a request he was all too happy to indulge. He seems happy to indulge *every* request I make, no matter how frivolous. *Except the ones that involve us going our separate ways.*

"I haven't killed Cara yet, so I'd say they're going well," Valerie says blithely. "Moscow Mule?"

"Make it light," I tell her. "You have a heavy pour."

She shrugs. "I also have a high alcohol tolerance and don't really get hung over." Her eyes flick up to the doorway and she releases a groan as Dorian and Seamus file in, followed closely by Cara.

I eye the four of them as I spoon frosting into the piping bag. "If you're all here, you might as well help out. Cara, get yourself a drink and make your peace with a horror movie. Seamus, please plate the chocolate chip cookies, and try not to eat all of them. Dorian, how steady is your hand?"

"Extremely steady," Dorian responds.

I nod. "Wonderful. Come help me frost."

"You're doing quite well in your role as lady of the house," Seamus comments, tipping me a wink. While Dorian and I get started frosting, Seamus quickly plates all the cookies. He moves to stand right beside

Valerie as she mixes up drinks, leaving barely a few inches of space separating them. "You going to make me a drink, love?"

"What do you want?" Valerie asks, sliding a Moscow Mule across the counter to me.

"That depends," Seamus says with a mischievous smile. "Are you on the menu?"

Not pausing in shaking her cocktail, Valerie says, "You can't afford me."

Seamus's smile widens. "I beg to differ, darling. I'm a *very* generous person in the right circumstances."

"You clingy?" Valerie asks.

Seamus releases an astonished laugh. "No. You a brat?"

Valerie looks at him jerkily, tilting her head to the side, as if he's just spoken some sort of code word that only she understands.

Dorian whispers in my ear, "A brat refers to a submissive that has attitude."

Oh. My hand falters as I vacillate between frosting cupcakes and watching the exchange between Valerie and Seamus. Valerie has her fair share of flings, but she's not as out there as Cara is, and she doesn't ever stick around for more than just sex. She's also pretty private about her sex life, never blistering my ears with details like Cara does.

"Brat*ty*, but not necessarily a brat," Valerie says mildly, eyeing Seamus. "What do you want to drink?"

Seamus grins. "Surprise me." Valerie tilts her head from side to side, considering him.

"Do you have cinnamon sticks?"

Seamus nods. "Of course."

"Matches? Round glasses? Good whiskey? Old Fashioned supplies?"

"Yes to all of the above," Seamus says, sounding intrigued. "I'll fetch them, and perhaps we can talk more about your... *proclivities* over a drink."

Valerie shrugs noncommittally. "We'll see how it goes. You seem like an annoying person, so perhaps talking *shouldn't* be on the menu."

Seamus leaves the room with a chuckle, and Cara says she's going to go find a horror movie she can stomach, leaving Valerie, Dorian and me alone in the kitchen.

"Be careful with that one," I advise Valerie. "He's dangerous."

Valerie looks at Dorian. "Is he gonna kill me?"

Dorian smiles, shaking his head. "No."

"Is he a cannibal or child-beater?"

Dorian's smile disappears, replaced by faint disgust, while I don't bother suppressing my laugh.

"*No*," Dorian emphasizes. "Where the hell are those questions coming from?"

"A girl's gotta have standards before engaging in some fun." Valerie shrugs. "Is he a good debater?"

"I certainly fancy myself one," Seamus responds, strolling back into the room and setting an expensive-looking bottle of whiskey in front of Valerie. Val watches as he gathers cinnamon sticks and the other supplies she requested, arching an eyebrow at him.

"You trying to impress me, eye-candy?"

"I don't need good alcohol to impress you," Seamus replies, setting all the ingredients of an Old Fashioned in front of her. "There are *plenty* of other ways I can do that."

"Cupcakes are done!" I say, a little shrilly. "If you two want to fuck, go for it, but please do your flirting out of earshot. It's getting uncomfortable." Dorian grabs a plate and helps me organize the cupcakes. I slide one across the counter to Valerie, then flee the kitchen as fast as I can manage.

"Seamus *won't* hurt her, right?" I ask Dorian in the hall.

He shakes his head. "No. He's into some heavy kinks, but he's also very conscientious of limits and safe words. If they get together, they'll talk and negotiate a scene that works for them. The only way he'll actually hurt her is if she wants more than sex from him."

I throw my head back and laugh. "Valerie never does more than just sex. She has an aversion to relationships."

Dorian smiles faintly. "Sounds like someone else I know."

"I don't have an aversion to relationships," I correct. "I have an aversion to gangsters."

"Lucky for you, baby, I'm not a gangster."

"Then what are you?" I ask curiously.

Dorian blinks slowly. "Many things. Ask me what I *want* to be."

I swallow at the tension that electrifies the air between us. "What do you want to be?"

"Yours."

He reaches out to ghost his thumb over my bottom lip. I look away, feeling my cheeks heat at his frankly spoken admission. I'm not ready to explore the feelings that his declaration stir, so I duck past him and head to the living room, holding the plate of cupcakes up. "Sugar's here," I announce.

Seamus and Valerie arrive shortly after Cara's grabbed a cupcake and reluctantly agreed to watch *The Conjuring.* We all settle down as Dorian puts on the movie, each of us with a cupcake and drink in hand.

My phone starts buzzing with a phone call about halfway through the opening credits. The caller ID is *Unknown,* so I assume it's a scammer and send it to voicemail, returning my attention to the movie.

Everyone's retaken their positions from before. Cara's clutching the edges of a fur blanket I gave her, staring at the screen with wide, frightened eyes. Valerie's leaned forward in her seat, munching on a cupcake while gazing at the TV screen with a steadily-deepening interest. Seamus is watching *Valerie* instead of the movie; when he catches me looking at him, he tips me an unabashed wink.

My phone starts buzzing again about thirty minutes into the movie—again, I send the call to voicemail and settle further into the comfortable cushions of the couch. Dorian sneaks an arm around my waist and tugs me into his side.

"Excuse me," I murmur, casting him a glance. "I wasn't aware that girls-night meant I'd be cuddling with my b—" I cut off with a swallow, cheeks heating at the realization that I nearly called him my boyfriend, which he's *not*. He might've been really sweet to me yesterday and today—aside from the punishment last night, when he was being downright cruel—but I haven't outright *agreed* to being his. I just haven't argued. He's stated and reiterated multiple times that he wants me to be his and considers me to be his, but that doesn't make it true. There are still fundamental problems between us.

"Your what?" Dorian murmurs, eyes glittering with interest.

I clear my throat quietly. "My captor."

His lips quirk. "I'm not your captor, Mira. Since you're my guest, I suppose that makes me your host."

I nod. "My host, then. I wasn't aware that having a girl's night with my roommates—"

"Former roommates," he corrects.

"—would involve me cuddling with my *host*."

"Well," Dorian says with a shrug, "that can't be helped. See, I'm actually scared of horror movies, so I need you to protect me from the ghosts and demons. I'm considering you my good-luck charm, which means I'll be keeping you close." When I raise my eyebrows, he pushes his bottom lip out in an adorable pout. "You don't want to let me get eaten by demons, do you?"

I can't help the smile pulling on my lips. "I don't think the demons in this movie will eat you."

"Semantics."

"Are you two going to flirt for the whole movie or actually watch it?" Seamus questions loudly. "You're being distracting."

"If you were watching the movie instead of Mira's former roommate, you wouldn't be so distracted," Dorian says back, not looking away from me.

Cheeks burning, I pointedly avert my gaze from him and turn my attention to the screen.

Again, my phone starts buzzing. This time, I welcome the distraction, unfolding myself from Dorian's grip. "I gotta take this call," I murmur, hurrying out of the room. I make my way into the kitchen, gazing at the *Unknown* ID pasted on my phone screen, knowing it's probably a scammer sitting in a call center in India.

I wind through the house and head out of the back exit, flicking on the patio lights. It's chilly outside, but I don't want to risk running into Dorian if I head back in to grab a sweater. I'm flustered and unsure of where I stand with him, even more uncertain of which direction we're heading in. I feel like we're evolving in a way I'm not ready for.

Taking a seat at the wooden table, I pick up the call, pressing it to my ear. I expect to hear a scammer telling me that my credit card information has been stolen and the only way to fix it is to give him my social security number and all of my personal details.

"Hello?" I say, already preparing how I can blow off some steam by fucking with the operator.

"Mira."

My blood runs cold. My heart stops. Goosebumps spread over my arm and neck like a rash, and nausea rises in my esophagus. Everything in the world seems to come to a halt as I hear the cruel, *cruel* voice speaking to me. The evening birds stop chirping, the distant sound of cars driving by disappear, and even the low hum buzzing from the patio lights seems to fall silent. *Everything* goes still.

"Clyde."

Chapter Twenty-Six

My voice sounds faint, almost as if it's coming from a different person. My thoughts fog up as my brain reverts to the survival mindset I learned while living with the man on the other end of the line. The scar on my leg starts to itch, as if reminding me of what Clyde's capable of.

How did he get this number? I changed all my personal information when I managed to escape him and go to college. I have a new phone number, new last name, new *life*. With the threats I dropped on Clyde before leaving, I thought he'd let me go.

He has to let me go, I remind myself. He can't do anything to me without me fucking him over and getting him killed. One conversation with his boss is all it'll take to bring his carefully-constructed life crumbling around him. One whisper in the right ear and he's done for.

I move to hang up on him; Clyde stops me with a single phrase. "It's been a long time, Mira. Years. You really thought you could leave me in the past?"

Anger overtakes my fear. "I *have* left you in the past, Clyde. We're of no consequence to each other, and that's how I'd prefer to keep it."

He clicks his tongue. "I thought that was the case, too," he says calmly, "until I found out that you've been getting in bed with some *very* bad people. I always knew you'd grow up to be a whore, just like your slut of a mother. I just didn't think you had it in you to spread your legs for a criminal." A low, rattling chuckle escapes him as bile churns at the back of my throat. "Like mother like daughter, I guess."

"You have no idea what you're talking about," I hiss furiously.

"Oh? So, you're *not* the side piece of one of Sergei Novikov's foot soldiers? A boy who goes to that fancy university with you?" He hums. "I must've gotten bad intel, then."

My fear reignites, a consuming dread that freezes me in place, dissipating my anger. So Sergei Novikov is the boss Dorian keeps referring to; no *wonder* Dorian's religious in sticking to Sergei's orders. I've heard of Sergei Novikov—anyone who doesn't live under a rock has heard of him. He's an infamous Bratva boss who owns all of Russia and most of Eurasia; rumor has it he has several international operations, too. One that I'm apparently caught in the middle of.

Clyde should have no way of knowing about my connection to Dorian or of Dorian's connection to Sergei; both men are completely out of his reach. He's with a local gang in a town in Pennsylvania—an organization that's made up of a collection of wife-beating imbeciles. From what I've heard about Sergei, he runs an *international* criminal empire.

"I don't know what you're talking about." Even though I try to make the words strong, they come out coated in fear.

Clyde chuckles. "*Right*. Here's what you're going to do for me, Mira. Carver wants in with Sergei Novikov. He wants to go into business together. You are going to get him a meeting with Sergei—"

"*No*, I am *not*," I hiss. I refuse to be pulled back into Clyde's world; I refuse to enable him by getting his boss a meeting with Sergei. Clyde is nothing but a bad memory for me. I will *not* allow him to invade my present. "You can't make me. If I ever talk to Carver, I won't be arranging a meeting with whoever the fuck Sergei Novikov is. I'll be telling your boss exactly what you did six years ago and who died because of it."

My senior year in high school, I managed to find out about a crime Clyde committed that not even his boss would be horrible enough to overlook. Clyde liked to keep pictures of his victims for his own sick amusement, and I happened to stumble upon a stack of them while cleaning the house.

One of those pictures was of his boss's late wife. I found indisputable evidence that Clyde killed the woman years ago—but not before he brutally tortured her.

That particular woman was a heinous person. I am not sad she's dead. I remember her suggesting that Clyde should force my mother to work at one of the gang's strip clubs; she even said to do the same with me. She obviously had a hand in some terrible operations, so she deserves to be dead. If Carver ever finds out what my stepfather did, Clyde would die a torturous, painful death.

"You won't," Clyde says, full of an eerie confidence. "Because, if you do, I'll be sure to implicate *you* in that bitch's death. Maybe your mom put me up to it because she didn't like how Maria talked about her. Your mom's not around anymore, so Carver will look for someone else to take revenge on alongside me. *You.*"

My eyes flutter as my breaths turn shaky, stuttering in and out of me. In a fair world, Clyde's threat would hold no weight, but I know that I don't live in that world. I live in an absolutely brutal one. There's a chance, no matter how slim, that Carver would believe Clyde's bullshit, and subsequently come for me. Then, everything I've worked for will have beeen for nothing.

"Here's what's going to happen, cunt. You'll talk to your soldier and tell him your dearest stepfather has a boss who's interested in doing business with his boss. You'll get your little boyfriend—if he's even that much—in contact with me. We'll run things up the hierarchy. Got it?"

I do the only thing I can think of doing; I hang up on him. Then, I sink into my chair, and for once, I allow myself to dissociate without the aid of music. The pain and panic from Clyde's threats is just too much, so I slip away from those feelings. I let the world become muted, and I gradually feel my problems and worries fade into the ether, replaced by a blessed numbness.

The numbness isn't cold or cruel; it's placid. Steady. Almost content. It's a bubble outside of space and time that I try to avoid, because it can become *too* comfortable, and I can forget the importance of being present. Right now I just don't have it in me to care about the consequences of uncontrolled dissociation.

The phone rings again, and then again; I watch it vibrate on the cool tabletop, feel the echoes of the vibration from where my thigh rests against one of the table's legs. No fear accompanies watching Clyde's number flash across my screen, not anymore. My detachment frees me from the fear. The pain. The memories. It envelops me in a cocoon of nothingness that I could comfortably inhabit until the day I die.

I feel my body start to grow stiff from the cold outside, but I'm in no hurry to react or warm myself up. It's as if I'm experiencing the world from under a layer of water, as if nothing can actually touch me.

It could be moments or hours that pass before I hear the patio door open with a loud creak. I don't care enough to find out who opened it, so I continue staring at my phone screen, which still vibrates with an incoming call every few minutes. I wonder how many times Clyde has tried to call by now, or how many more he will. If he keeps it up, my phone will die, and I have no intention of recharging it.

"Mira," Dorian says, sounding a touch alarmed. His footsteps echo across stone as he makes his way over to me. My eyes shift to his as he walks into my line of sight and leans over the table, peering at my phone. His eyebrows draw together as he sees it light up with yet another incoming call.

"Who's calling?" he asks, glancing at me. "Jesus, Mira, you're turning blue." My phone temporarily forgotten, he rubs a hand up and down my arm, and nearly recoils at whatever it is he feels. "Christ," he mutters. "It's thirty fucking degrees outside and you've been out here for the better part of an hour—why didn't you grab a sweater?"

I gaze at him for a moment, deciding if I want to put in the effort of responding to him. Then, my phone lights up yet again, and Dorian glances at it with an irritated scowl. "Who the *fuck* is calling you repeatedly?"

He reaches for my phone, and that's what finally spurs me into speaking. Even in my disconnected state, I can grasp the implications of how bad things could get if Clyde got talking to Dorian; I just can't find it in me to care as much as I should.

"Clyde," I murmur.

Dorian rears back, recoiling from the phone, and gazes at me with shock. "Your *stepfather?*"

I nod, just once.

"What the *fuck* does he want with you?" Dorian demands, sounding shocked. "Did you talk to him? Are you okay?"

I spend a few moments trying to formulate a response, then realize there's too much emotional effort involved. Instead of answering his questions, I say, "Ignore him. My phone will die eventually."

Dorian grasps my chin in his hand and angles my head, forcing me to face him. I gaze at him, not bothering to pull out of his grip.

He rubs a thumb over my cheek, brows furrowing, eyes filling with what might be comprehension. "You're dissociated right now, aren't you? Zoned out, whatever you call it?"

"Yes," I nod. He's already caught on; there's no sense in refuting his assessment.

"*Fuck.*" Dorian takes a few deep breaths, then gently wraps his hand around mine and pulls me up from the chair. Once I'm standing, I notice the way my limbs tremble, either from the cold or the adrenaline coursing through me. Just because I no longer *feel* the effects of my anxiety doesn't mean it's *disappeared;* I've simply removed myself from it.

"Alright, baby," he says, picking up my phone and pocketing it. "We're going inside."

"Val and Cara will get spooked if they see me like this," I say factually.

"They're distracted by the movie. We're going to our room; I'll let them know something's come up, then we can handle your piece of shit stepfather." He pauses, rubbing a hand up and down my arm. "Is that okay?"

I... don't know. I don't really *care.* "Sure."

My vague answer seems to concern Dorian more than relieve him. He pulls me inside and leads me directly up the stairs and to his room, where he sits me on his bed. He wraps me in a blanket, brushes a kiss over my forehead, and tells me to stay.

He leaves, and a few minutes later he walks back in, holding a plate with a cupcake on it. He sets it on his bedside table, taking a seat next to me and wrapping his arm around me. "What do you need?" he asks.

"Nothing," I respond easily. I'm perfectly okay as is, though the pesky shiver coursing through me isn't going away.

He releases a small sigh. "Not good enough, Mira. What do you need in order to snap out of it?"

I feel my brows furrow with vague confusion. "Why would I want to do that?"

Dorian squeezes his arm around me. "Because zoning out isn't the answer. Because you can trust me to have your back. Because going through life without feeling, with that empty look in your eyes, isn't good for anyone. Least of all you." He kisses my cheek. "Because this version of you scares me, and I want my Mira back."

His words do something to me. They reach deep inside, accessing the person buried under layers of dissociation, stirring something odd. Making me *want* to snap out of it, which is a brand-new experience for me.

My brows furrow as the fog surrounding me lessens by the faintest margin. It doesn't disappear entirely; it just recedes a tiny bit, only enough for me to perceive the warmth of Dorian's arms around me, for me to start feeling curiosity accompanying the questions floating around in my mind. Faint worries that accompany the thought of Val and Cara downstairs, alone with Seamus.

"Stop," I murmur, glancing at Dorian. He's trying to ground me, but I don't *want* to be grounded right now. If I come back to myself, I'll have to talk to him about my conversation with my stepfather. I'll have to face the reality that I'm getting sucked back into the life that nearly killed me once, one I fought hard to escape.

"No," Dorian says immovably, his tone hardening. "When shit gets difficult, you do not get to disappear into yourself. You face it. And you don't *ever* face it alone; you come to me and let me stand by your side, or at your back, or in front of you as a shield. Whatever it is, whatever that fucking monster wants, we'll figure it out together. You will *not* zone out; you will come to *me*." His voice softens as he plants a kiss on the nape of my neck. "Come back to me, Mira. Trust that I'll protect you."

"*Stop*," I repeat, because his words are working. I yearn to trust him, to believe in him, in *us*. I long to believe that he'll protect me, to be able to trust *someone* after a lifetime of only being able to trust myself.

My mother, though a good woman at her core, was weak. She tried to shield me as best as she could, but when push came to shove, Clyde would hurt us both. She could do nothing to stop him because she didn't have the strength or will.

Then she was gone, and Clyde only had me to hurt.

"No," Dorian says again. "Give me some trust, Mira. Just a little. Give me a chance to come through for you and I will."

His words snap me back to reality. Everything slams into me at once—every feeling that faded with my dissociation. The abrupt return of all my emotions, all my fear, everything that's built over the last hour yet was pushed into the background as I dissociated rather than processed, is too much. It feels like a freight train ramming into me. It's crippling. It's devastating. It physically and emotionally shatters me, making me hunch forward.

Breaths saw in and out of my chest, harsh and quick and grating. The tremor in my limbs feels overwhelming. My entire body *burns* with anxiety, and the nausea that sweeps over me is so overwhelming, I heave. Knowing what follows when I come back from a dissociation at a bad time, I drop the blanket, rushing to the bathroom on shaky legs.

I barely get to the toilet before my dinner makes a reappearance. My nose burns, my eyes water, and my stomach contracts with painful cramps as I vomit until there's nothing left inside me. Until I feel empty.

Dorian's there beside me an instant after I flee. He stays with me, holding my hair out of my face, rubbing my back, murmuring words of reassurance that I can't hear between all the choking, gasping, and puking.

Once I'm done throwing up, I slump to the side, my face contorting at the powerful cramps twisting my stomach into knots. It feels nearly impossible to get a full breath in between everything. I'm hollowed out yet filled with a swirling, angry swarm of emotions that threaten to tear me apart from the inside out.

The only stabilizing force is Dorian. Heedless of how clammy and gross I am, he flushes the toilet and takes a seat on the floor beside me, pulling me into his arms. He snags a washcloth from its resting place on the counter and uses it to clean me up as best as he can. In the complete absence of my own strength, his starts to seep into me, like sunlight penetrating the leaves of a flower in the warmth that follows a frost. The process is instinctive, almost biological, and incredibly powerful.

At any other time, I might fight it. Now, I have neither the strength nor the will.

"Clyde called," I say, my voice a haunting whisper.

Dorian holds me a little tighter. "I know."

"He wants me to use you to get him in contact with Sergei Novikov, who I guess is your boss." I squeeze my eyes shut. "He wants his local, piece of shit gang boss to go into business with Sergei."

Dorian tenses. "I see."

"You…" a shrill laugh escapes me. "You probably would've found out anyways, considering you have my phone tapped, or whatever the fuck." I release another laugh, this one sounding like it comes from a cackling witch. "The monster from my past wants to get connected with the menace in my present. It's gotta be fate."

"Don't go there." Dorian's words are spoken in a mild tone, but there's something razor-sharp beneath them. "I might be a menace, but I am not harmful to you. I never will be."

"You *kidnapped* me," I rasp.

"I made you a reluctant guest for the sake of your own safety," he retorts calmly.

"You won't even tell me *when* I'll stop being your guest—I might never get out of here!"

"You're not a prisoner. You can leave whenever you want."

Yeah, right. "If that's the case, give me keys to my car. Let me leave right now."

"In your current state you'd wrap us around a tree," Dorian says, brushing the backs of his fingers up and down my arm.

"*Us?* There's no—"

"Enough," he cuts me off. "I get that you're rattled. I get that you're afraid. I'm trying not to hold what you're saying against you, but please, don't press your luck. This is *not* a you versus me situation. This is about *us*, and what *we* can do together. Don't alienate yourself from me. Not just because it's the stupidest fucking thing you could do right now, but because it *hurts me*."

The vulnerability in his last two words makes me deflate like a faulty balloon. I go quiet, guilt creeping in. Dorian's not at fault here. He *is* my best hope of getting through this relatively unharmed. He's rough around the edges—*very* rough—but I can't deny he's been good to me. He could've taken advantage of my being here, in his house; he could've taken liberties with me many times in very bad ways. In ways *Clyde* wouldn't have hesitated to. Instead, all I've received are punishments that came in the form of orgasm control.

"I'm sorry," I murmur.

"I know," he says soothingly. "I'm not mad. Just, please, stop making me your enemy. I don't want to be, and you don't want me to be."

I nod; he kisses my head.

"Good. Here's what's going to happen; you're going to hop into the shower and get clean. I'm going to send your roommates home with apologies and tell them you're not feeling well, then I'm going to talk over some things with Seamus. He's good when it comes to dealing with bad actors. Take your time in the shower, I should be back by the time you're out." He squeezes me again. "We'll get you a new, secure phone tomorrow and figure out a comprehensive game plan."

Chapter Twenty-Seven

Dorian

The movie's rolling credits when I make a reappearance downstairs. Seamus is still staring at Valerie with a look that suggests he's found his next conquest. Cara has made her way through no less than four cupcakes. Valerie's stare is glued to her phone.

"Ladies," I say amiably, turning off the TV and flicking on the lights.

Valerie casts a glance at me. "Where's Mira?"

"Upstairs," I reply. "She has an upset stomach, isn't feeling well."

Cara rises from her seat immediately. "I'll go check on her."

"That would be ill-advised," I say mildly. "She's showering off her date with the toilet bowl at the moment and then going straight to sleep. She'll give you a call tomorrow, I'm sure." From a new phone and new number with better encryption and protection, though I don't bother saying that.

Valerie and Cara share a glance, and some silent communication passes between them. They both stare at each other for several long moments before Valerie nods and Cara shrugs. Whatever discussion they had through eye contact appears to have been settled.

"Well, we better get going, then," Valerie says, also standing. "Thanks for playing host, even though this was supposed to be a *girls-only* night," she mutters pointedly.

Seamus also rises, stepping beside Valerie. He brushes a hand down her spine; a light shudder shakes her shoulders.

"Let me get your number before you leave, love," he says, giving Valerie a suggestive smile.

I'm glad that he's found someone new to fix his attention on; if he had continued making passes at Mira or even looking at her for too long, I'd have ended up beating the shit out of him. A single punch between friends like us can be forgiven, but an extensive fight that I'd have ensured left him with a broken nose? Yeah, that would have disturbed the dynamics in the house.

That's precisely why I think it's best for Mira and I to get our own place as soon as possible. I'm becoming too possessive of her; my obsession has already crossed the point of no return and become a danger to the other inhabitants of the house. The last time Connor threatened Mira, I was ready to kill him. When Seamus flirts with her, even if it's harmless, I don't think he understands just how much he's courting death.

In any case, I find deep satisfaction when Valerie stares at Seamus, considering him for several moments before shaking her head. "Nah, I'm good. If I'm interested, I'll find you."

She takes Cara's hand in her own and both of them flit right out of the house, leaving a stunned Seamus in their wake. After snapping out of his temporary stupor born of rejection—something he does *not* experience often—he takes a step forward, probably intending to catch Valerie before she drives off.

"I wouldn't," I tell him. "Don't chase, it's beneath you."

He slides me an irritated glance. "I never chase. I'm the one who *gets* chased."

I raise my eyebrows, waving at him. He's mid-step, but his focus briefly wavers from following after his newest object of interest. Realizing my implication, he immediately straightens and relaxes his posture.

"I don't usually chase," he amends. "But that one is interesting."

Maybe he's found himself a new point of fixation, one that'll divert his attention from *my* Mira. Speaking of my Mira, there are several things I need to take care of so I can get back to her without guilt weighing so heavily on my shoulders. I'm supposed to protect her, yet I failed in that tonight.

"Go after Valerie in a few days if you really want. For now, there are greater worries."

Seamus hears the serious undertone in my words and immediately switches gears, turning to face me fully.

"Problem?" he queries. His entire demeanor changes, morphing from the lighthearted tease to the well-learned strategist who's very good at putting together solutions and has used his skillset to earn the favor of a remarkably dangerous man.

"Mira's stepdad, Clyde, called her. He requested she set up a meeting between Sergei and his own boss."

Seamus blinks slowly. "That *is* a problem. Do you need solutions, or do you already have one in mind?"

"I'm going to run this situation through Sergei," I say. "He's already aware of Mira; I'm sure Connor also sent him the report he put together on her." The full background check came through today, and I read it while Mira was baking in preparation for girl's night. Seeing the evidence of what Mira's been through, what *Clyde* put her through, made my blood boil. "Sergei's the one who told me to choose how I wanted to keep Mira and follow through—he'll want to stay updated on progress, and he'll *certainly* want to know if his name is being dropped by a thug with relations to Mira."

"Have a plan first," Seamus advises. "Sergei won't like it if you come to him without a plan, or at least the start of one."

"My plan is quite simple, and it hasn't changed," I tell Seamus simply. "I am going to kill Mira's stepdad, and I will happily kill anyone associated with him, as well. He deserves to die for what he's put her through, what he's done to her." Killing Clyde has been on my to-do list since the night I saw Mira's scars; now, it's just moved higher on my list.

Seamus shrugs. "Fine, just don't sound dumb in front of the boss. He hired us because we're smart, capable, and agile; he won't want a bumbling, revenge-driven mess on the phone with him."

"Don't worry about me," I say, a bit sharply. "Worry about your-self."

"I can worry for both of us," Seamus says, eyeing me. "Be careful you don't isolate yourself, Dorian. Connor and I have had your back for years. That girl in your room has been here for less than a week. Don't let her take over your life."

"I'm not angling to let her take over my life, I'm aiming to integrate her into it," I tell him. "When you meet the one for you, you'll feel the same way. I'm not trying to shut you or Connor out, but the fact of the matter is that my priorities have shifted to include her, not to exclude you."

Seamus's lips thin, but he nods. I'm not sure how he feels about what I've said; his face gives little away.

"Do what you need to do, then," he says. "Let me know if you need me, mate." He walks away.

I watch him leave, something stirring inside of me. Worry over our friendship, perhaps. Seamus has become a brother to me in the last years; he's had my back and saved my life so many times, I've lost count. Likewise, I've had his back and protected him.

I have no desire to alienate him. I am not actively trying to allow Mira to come between me and my legion. I want her to join it, even if not in full capacity. *If only my roommates would make that a simpler endeavor for me...*

Chapter Twenty-Eight

Dorian

Shaking my head with a sigh, I head to the kitchen so I can make my call in private. While it's true that Sergei will want me to have some semblance of a game plan on how to address the issue I'm about to bring to him, I think he might be a touch more forgiving than Seamus might assume, simply because my current problem revolves around Mira. Sergei's obsession with his wife is legendary; he kidnapped her when he was incarcerated in the States several years ago and brought her to Russia with him, then spent the next months making her fall in love with him.

If anyone can understand how frazzled I'd be over Mira's abusive stepfather trying to get her back under his control, it's Sergei. He'd lay waste to entire countries to keep his wife safe or make her happy.

I give Sergei a call while putting away the cupcakes in the kitchen. He doesn't pick up, which makes my heart drop to my stomach, but he calls back a minute later. Sergei made it clear from day one that my legion is his personal pet project; he'll delegate many things when it comes to business, but for whatever reason, he wants to maintain a close relationship with me, Connor, and Seamus.

"Dorian." The voice that greets me is markedly unexpected, because it's a *female* voice. I imagine only one person in the world has the ability to pick up Sergei's phone in lieu of him, and that would be his wife, Kira.

"Mrs. Novikov," I greet, trying to mask my surprise. "I'm sorry to disturb you—"

"No disturbance at all." Her voice is pleasant, almost like a melody, but something about it is off-putting. There's an eerie flatness to her words that reminds me very much of Sergei. "And, please, dispense with the Mrs. Novikov nonsense. I only took Sergei's surname because he won a bet."

It's on the tip of my tongue to ask precisely what bet could have possibly culminated in the woman who tamed Sergei doing anything she didn't want to do, but I manage to refrain. I don't know Kira, so I don't have the liberties to ask any errant questions.

"My apologies," I say, fighting to keep my tone even. "If Sergei's otherwise occupied, I'll call back at a better time—"

"He's in the shower," Kira says mildly. "The water's just shut off, so he'll be out soon. Tell me, what is it the two of you have been discussing during your late-night chats? Or the early morning ones...or any of the ones in between. I often find him stepping aside to take a call from you or one of your... *legion* members. I always mean to ask him directly, but distractions persistently arise."

I bite my bottom lip, unsure of what to do or say. If Sergei hasn't told Kira anything about my legion, I assume that's because he doesn't want her to know. While that doesn't *sound* like Sergei—from my understanding, he tells his wife everything—I won't risk getting cut off by saying something to her that I shouldn't.

"I hope you won't have me killed for saying this, but I can't disclose anything without Sergei's permission."

A long, thick silence stretches between us. I'm almost tempted to reach for the knife block to cut through it. I'm half-afraid that my words have somehow earned me a direct ticket to the afterlife, but then, Kira speaks.

"*Very* good. Sergei will be pleased with your loyalty." Kira laughs, sounding vaguely amused. My building anxiety rushes out of me in a stream, and I suppress an audible breath of relief. "You really don't think I know everything that goes on with my husband's dealings? I help orchestrate half of them." She sighs. "You've been having trouble with a woman recently, yes? Miranda?"

I nearly flinch at hearing Mira's full name. I've only ever known her by Mira, and the name suits her. "Yes," I say slowly. "She prefers to go by Mira." I'm not sure why I add the last bit, but I can't help myself.

"Ah," Kira says. "A bit similar to my own name, but that shouldn't be too much of a problem. Tell me, what are your troubles in paradise?"

This time, I'm the one to initiate the silence, because I'm not sure how to respond or if I want to have a discussion about this. I called Sergei to inform him of the potential issues that might arise because Clyde is starting to get smart, not to discuss my love life with a woman who's rumored to be a psychopath.

"I won't force you to tell me," Kira says after several moments. "But I was once an incredibly well-respected psychologist in the States. I am capable of giving good advice."

"Weren't you a *criminal* psychologist?"

"The line between loving someone and killing them is surprisingly thin, believe it or not. Both are often rooted in *passion*. Besides, I have a superior understanding of the human mind and emotions. However, if you don't care for what I have to say, I won't waste my time on you."

"No," I say, a tad too quickly. I clear my throat. "Um, perhaps I'd benefit from hearing such a well-respected woman's perspective."

"Good save," Kira says. "Give me the premise of the situation in two sentences."

I take a moment to think my words over carefully. "I have a growing attachment to Mira, and I believe she's growing fond of me as well. However, she sees me as a criminal, and her experience with criminal men in her life has been life-*threatening*."

"I see," Kira says. "Well, the solution is simple."

I bite back a laugh. "Would you care to impart your knowledge onto me?"

"Since you asked so kindly, yes," she agrees. "Be consistent. In your moods, in your actions, in your *reactions*. If Mira's been traumatized at the hands of a criminal man, I believe it's safe to say she's used to instability. Offer her stability, stick with it for the long haul, and you should be fine. Do with that advice what you will. Now, I believe I'll return Sergei's phone to him so the two of you can chat."

I stiffen. "Return—I thought you said he was in the shower?"

"I lied," she responds simply. "He *will* be needing to go to the shower soon since he should just be finishing up with his favorite toy in the basement."

I don't have the guts to ask exactly what she means by that. I have an inkling that by *toy* she might actually mean *captive*.

I hear the faint echo of footsteps, and a few moments later, the phone changes hands.

"Dorian?" Sergei says, sounding a tad perplexed. "Ah, Kira got a hold of you, did she? My condolences." Kira says something in the background; Sergei chuckles and gives a muffled response. "It's late for the both of us. What is it?"

"Mira's stepfather," I say, still reeling from the advice I got from Kira. She's right, consistency *is* laughably simple, and it's precisely what I'd wager Mira requires to settle. "Clyde Brenner. He's asking her to arrange a meeting between your boss and his."

"And his boss would be...?" Sergei questions calmly.

According to the report Connor compiled, "Wagner. Carver Wagner."

"I've never even heard of him," Sergei says, sounding mildly bemused. "What does he run?"

"He has a county in Pennsylvania locked down with his connection to the sheriff. Carver runs drugs, taxes people who work or live on what he considers to be his territory, and has a few strip clubs. He's small-time, completely inconsequential."

"Hmm," Sergei hums thoughtfully. "And how did this Mr. Wagner come to know about you *or* me?"

My blood thrums at the implication behind his words. He's hinting that Mira might've had something to do with Clyde poking around, that she might've passed on information, which is fucking ludicrous.

I've seen the scars on her body. I've held her after she woke up from a nightmare. I saw her earlier *tonight*, when she was so dissociated from the world it genuinely frightened me. The placid, empty look in her eyes is something that's going to haunt me for some time to come. I commit myself to ensuring that, if I ever catch her in that state, I'll pull her out of it. We'll deal with her problems together—they'll be *our* problems.

"I say this with the utmost respect for who you are and all you're doing for me," I start carefully, "but don't *ever* fucking question Mira's loyalties. They may not completely be mine, *yet*, but they sure as *shit* don't lie with the man who nearly killed her on several occasions."

A low chuckle escapes Sergei. "Point taken. You're growing into a man, Dorian."

I feel my eyebrows inch up. "I wasn't aware I was a boy beforehand."

"I was a boy well into my thirties, until I met Kira. I might've had money, power, and influence before her, but *she* made me into a man. I look forward to watching the same transformation take hold in you. Onto the little problem; I assume it's in your plans to exterminate Clyde?"

"It's now pretty high up on my to-do list," I affirm. "If Carver makes himself into a nuisance, I'll take care of him, as well."

"Good," Sergei says. "Get your legion on it. I want all of you to take care of this as a team. If you want them to accept the shifts in your life, they need to continue being part of your dealings. Connor and Seamus have to *want* to protect your girl just like you do, though perhaps not with the same vigor."

"Connor isn't protective over anyone," I say. "I'm working on Seamus."

"Yes, Connor's always been a bit of a lone wolf. He's fit in with the two of you, though, so there's hope for him yet. Put together a plan on what you'll be doing for your woman and keep me apprised. How is your other mission going?"

"The Serpents in the city have gone underground or moved away. There are a few locations we'll be checking out in the next weeks. I hope to be done with their bullshit by the end of the year, though the timeline might be extended."

"Fine." Sergei pauses. "Go take care of your woman. And, if Kira gave you advice, follow it to the letter. That's an order."

"Got it. I'll keep you updated." Sergei hangs up without saying goodbye; I make my way directly back to my room.

The bathroom door is still closed and faint tendrils of steam curl out from beneath it, but there's no sound of running water. Only a minute passes before Mira makes her appearance, and my heart nearly stops when I see that she's wearing *my* sweater. It's old, a team sweater back from my high school football days, and it falls nearly to her knees. She looks fucking *ethereal* in it.

She stares at me; I stare at her. Several long moments of silence stretch out. If I had my way, this is the moment I'd sweep her into my arms and fuck her into next year, but she's had a long and very trying night. Now isn't the time for sex.

"I, uh, hope it's okay that I took your sweater," she murmurs, sounding adorably bashful. "I liked the way it smelled."

I guess I'll be dousing all of my clothes with the cologne I wear, then. If she wears nothing but my clothes for the rest of our lives, I'd die a happy man.

"More than okay," I say, stepping forward and tentatively taking her hand in mine. She's flighty, and I don't want to spook her. "I like it very much. I might instate a new rule that the only clothes you're allowed to wear to bed are *my* clothes."

A reluctant smile spreads on her lips, and she allows me to pull her into my arms. I hold her close, resting my chin on her head, breathing in the fact that she's here and she's mine, whether or not she's ready to admit that part yet. Slowly, her arms wrap around my waist, and my heart *soars*.

"I'm sorry I snapped at you earlier," she mutters into my chest. "I didn't mean to."

"I know," I say evenly. *Consistency is key.* "I'm not mad at you; I get that it's been a whirlwind of a night. But, please, stop putting us on opposite sides. That's not where we're supposed to be. We're a team."

"I don't know if we're a team, but I don't think we're enemies anymore," she says. Her fingers idly pluck at the fabric of my shirt.

"We were never enemies," I say, allowing a note of teasing in my voice. "If we were, I wouldn't be nearly as nice to you."

"Nice to me," she repeats drolly. "Are you referring to that time you literally chased me down in the woods at night? Or when you proceeded to hold me captive here? Or—"

"Hush," I say, not masking my exasperation. "It's all working out, isn't it?" Without waiting for her to respond, I tug her over to the bed and settle her under the comforter. It's the work of a few seconds to strip down, throw on a pair of sweats, and climb in behind her. I pull her right into my chest; again, she comes willingly, and this time, something frighteningly possessive unfurls deep within me. A ravening, ravaging beast that screams to claim his mate and lock her down for eternity.

"Are you okay now?" I murmur into her hair, stroking my hands over her belly.

I wonder what it'd be like if and when it swells with our child.

Not if, I decide. *When.* I've only ever thought about kids in passing, and the thoughts were fleeting. The turns my life took as soon as I hit college essentially removed even the idea of children from the equation; I couldn't imagine bringing them into my world. While I share a close comradery and bond with Connor and Seamus, the activities we partake in aren't the safest. Having a kid always seemed cruel.

But now... now I want to find a way. It'd amaze me if Mira *didn't* want children; she has a naturally maternal presence. I want to have those children with her; I want to watch our baby grow inside her. I want to raise the kid *with* her.

I hold Mira until I'm sure she's asleep, then I gently slip my fingers beneath the hem of her sweater and circle my fingertips over the soft skin of her navel. *One day*, I promise myself. *One day I'll put a baby there.*

Chapter Twenty-Nine
Mira

I wake up in the morning to a soft, pleasant sensation of something fluttering against the back of my neck. It almost feels like the wings of butterflies beating against my skin, accompanied by the heat of a hot body against my back. The pleasant sensation is quickly upended by a sharp sting as Dorian sinks his teeth into my nape, causing me to arch against him with a gasp. I fist the sheets in front of me when he snakes an arm around my waist and slips his hand beneath my borrowed hoodie, wrapping it around my breast and squeezing it tight.

He releases my neck from his teeth and trails his lips over to my ear. "Good morning," he rumbles.

A small moan is my response as he squeezes my nipple, causing warmth to spark in my core.

"Dorian…" My words trail off, lost to a groan as he twists my nipple and snakes his other arm around me, fingers gliding between my folds.

"You're not wet," he observes, sounding extremely displeased at the fact.

"I just woke up," I gasp. "Keep doing that and it'll change pretty damn soon."

"Good," Dorian says lowly, sinking his teeth into the juncture where my shoulder meets my neck. "I'd like to fuck you before we get out of bed this morning, Mira. If you're not on board with that, say so now. Otherwise, settle in for the ride."

I bite my lip as my breathing speeds. His fingers below find my clit, idly circling and plucking at it, igniting a low, molten warmth that quickly causes a trickle of arousal to seep out of me. He dips his fingers lower, sliding just a centimeter inside of me to scoop up the wetness. He smears my juices over my clit, allowing him to play with me more easily.

"I need to hear a yes or a no," Dorian whispers, punctuating the words with a kiss on the shell of my ear, then a light nibble on the lobe.

"Y—yes," I stutter. After the events of last night, I am very much in the mood to forget all about the harsh realities of the real world. I want to lose myself to the sensation of Dorian's touch, let him take the lead and make me forget my own name. We've only gotten sexual when he's decided I need to be punished; I don't know if he'll be quite so dominant now, but I'm sure he'll still make me come so hard I see stars.

"Good girl," he praises. "Sit up," he breathes.

I follow his instructions without argument. He spreads my legs and settles between them, fingering the hem of my sweatshirt and tugging at it. I lift my arms up overhead, allowing him to pull it off. He tosses it over his shoulder, and it lands in the corner of the room with a light *thump.*

Dorian's eyes travel a slow path over my body, his gaze so heated it feels like a physical sensation. Icy-hot fingers caused by his stare travel a path over my lips, down my neck, and linger for a while on my breasts. Then, they go lower, until they're brushing over my pussy, further down to my thighs and legs.

"You are so fucking beautiful," he says quietly, giving his head a shake. Almost as if he can't believe that I'm real, I'm here, and at least for now, I'm his. "*So* gorgeous, Mira, it kills me." His eyes darken with desire as he meets my gaze. "I don't like administering pain, but this is going to hurt a bit."

Well... "You do have a monster cock."

His lips quirk, and amusement briefly brightens his eyes. "Pardon?"

"A monster cock," I repeat, waving at his crotch. "That thing is set to send me to the hospital." My brows furrow. "In case I *do* actually end up making a trip to the ER after this, I hope you know I'm not paying for my punctured lung. I'm sending you the bill."

Dorian chuckles. "Jesus, Mira. You're funny in the mornings. But I think we've talked enough. I'm not going to *actually* injure you, you goof, but it might hurt at first." He hooks his hands under my knees, rears back, and gives an abrupt yank on my legs. I nearly choke on my inhale as I slide down on the bed. My head hits the pillow with enough force to make me dizzy.

"First, I want to dine," he says, spreading my folds with his thumbs and leaning down. "I've missed your taste. Have you missed having me between your legs?"

"Not when you make me come so much I can barely stand," I murmur, half-teasing. He really does have a tendency to take things overboard, but then again, this isn't a punishment. I *hope*. I was pretty terrible to him last night, but he didn't seem truly upset about it.

"You'll come as many times as I want you to come," he murmurs, leaning down. "When we're having sex, I'm in charge, and I think that's how you prefer it. You don't have to do any of the work; just lie back and take it like a good girl. Do you like that?"

His breath ghosting over my pussy makes me squirm with anticipation. When his gaze flicks up to meet mine, I nod with a whimper.

"Good girl." His tongue gives me a long, slow lick over my folds and swirls around my clit. My back arches, and I dig my nails into the sheets with a long moan as he goes to fucking *town* on my pussy.

He alternates between thrusting his tongue inside me, fucking me with it, and laving it over my clit. I squirm and moan and whimper as he drives me up and up into an orgasm that promises to shatter my world, but just when I'm on the precipice, he pulls away.

"Dorian," I whine, panting. *"Please."*

"You want to come, pretty girl?" he asks, his voice a teasing coo. "You will. I promise you will, but only when *I'm* ready for you to. Do you understand?"

"Please," I repeat.

He smiles faintly. "I love the sound of your pleading, Mira. Keep begging me, but know that it won't make much of a difference."

The total loss of control pricks at my pride a little bit, but it's overwhelmingly sexy. Dorian isn't shy or demure about sex; he's *really* damn good at it, and he takes charge as if he was born to lead. It's impossible not to want to submit to his desires, so that's precisely what I do. I let him take over, I forget about doing any of the work, and I whine and whimper and damn near cry as he edges me nearly into oblivion. *Five times* I beg him to let me come; five times he leaves me high and dry, until my entire body aches with the desire to come.

"Good girl, taking everything I have to give," he praises gently. "How badly do you want to come?"

I toss my head from side to side, legs trembling. *"So* badly."

He presses a kiss to the top of my mound. I crane my neck to watch him. The sight that greets me is so erotic I nearly come from it alone. Dorian's hands gripping my thighs so tightly the skin creases under his hold. His eyes, fixed on me with complete attention. His lips shining with the evidence of my desire.

He licks my taste off his lips, and I nearly lose it right there and then.

"Then come," he says simply. He wraps his lips around my clit and suckles gently. My back bows painfully, and an agonized cry escapes me as I come with a jerk and full-body shake. My channel clenches convulsively; two fingers slide inside me, and Dorian groans against my flesh as he feels me fall apart around him.

"Fuck, fuck, *fuck*," I chant. "Oh, god, Dorian—" I cut off as the pleasure becomes too much, as sensitivity causes goosebumps to break out over my skin. "*Dorian*. I—I can't—"

"Come for me again," he demands, pulling back. "I want to hear you call my name."

It doesn't take me long to oblige him on both fronts, especially when he curves the fingers buried inside me upward, tickling a spot on the top of my channel that makes my toes curl and breasts ache for attention. My second orgasm is faster than the first, but no less potent. He keeps stimulating me until I ride it out completely and am left a trembling, sweating puddle on the bedsheets.

"Look at all this arousal," he murmurs, pulling his fingers out of me and scooping up the wetness glistening over my pussy. He brings them to his lips, and my eyes nearly roll into the back of my head as I watch him suck them into his mouth, as if he can't get enough of my taste. He climbs his way up my body and slants his lips over mine, letting me taste myself. I moan into the erotic kiss, wrapping my arms around his neck and legs around his waist, keeping him close.

"You're going to need to be a very good girl for me and take deep breaths," he murmurs, pulling away. "If it hurts too much, tell me. This is not meant to be painful. Okay?"

I nod, chasing his lips for another kiss. He's warm, masculine, and so utterly in charge, it frees me of any burden or responsibility. I want everything he has to give; I want to take his cock, take all his desires, let him turn me into his personal toy.

"Fuck me, Dorian," I whisper against his lips. "*Please.*"

He smiles into our kiss. "Anything my girl wants. Anything you could possibly desire, Mira, I'll give to you. If you want to watch the world burn, I'll strike the match that sets it on fire. If you want to see the people who hurt you die, I'll bring you their heads on a silver platter. If you want to be loved, cherished, and adored, I'll spend hours reminding you just how much you mean to me."

"What do I mean to you?" My voice is quiet now, filled with shyness and uncertainty. I don't think I've had anyone care for me the way Dorian does in a long time, if ever.

Dorian blinks slowly. "*Everything.*"

He shucks his boxers with a few quick tugs while my breath catches and my eyes flutter at his admission. He hooks one of my legs high on his waist, gripping it under the knee, and uses his other hand to bring his hot, *hard* cock over my pussy. Instead of thrusting right into me, he glides it up and down my slit, getting it wet with my arousal and teasing my clit until I think I might come again.

"Deep breaths for me," he murmurs, plucking at my nipple before bracing a hand by my head. "It's going to be tough for a bit."

I moan my agreement, nodding enthusiastically.

He positions his dick at my entrance; I arch with a gasp as he slowly starts to slide inside me, wiping my mind of all thoughts that aren't centered on him. There's an immediate prickle and burn as his thickness stretches my inner muscles. I've never had a cock as big as his, and I haven't had sex in well over a year, so the intrusion *hurts*, but it's also accompanied by a deep, aching pleasure that makes me want to brave the pain. He slides in a bit farther, and I can't hold back a low whine. Dorian freezes immediately, cupping my cheek with a hand and stroking his thumb over the hollow beneath my eye.

"Easy," he breathes. "Take it easy, baby. Nice and deep breaths for me, now."

"Keep going," I beg. "Please."

He shakes his head. "Not if it's hurting you."

"It hurts in all the right ways," I moan. "*Please*, Dorian."

He releases a low, shuddering breath. A small shiver travels over him, as if my words are almost too much for him to bear. "*Fuck*, Mira." He slides in farther, slowly sinking deeper and deeper until his balls tap my ass and my eyes roll into the back of my head. I dig my nails into the nape of his neck so hard it's a wonder I don't draw blood. "You feel so *fucking* good." He pumps in and out of me, harsh thrusts that force the breath from my lungs and make my entire body tighten. My nipples scrape over his hard chest, and I throw my head back, moaning with each of his thrusts, lifting my hips to meet him.

His pace is steady, reaching deep with each surge forward. Sweat slicks both of our skin, setting us aglow in the wash of morning light that filters through the windows. I gasp and whine and gouge deep scratches down his back with my nails.

"Faster," I urge him. "Harder, Dorian. *Please*."

A low groan escapes him, and he speeds his pace. His thrusts turn forceful and overwhelming, and though it burns, I love every moment of it. I love bathing in his energy, in the deep satisfaction and overwhelming pleasure that radiates from him, mingling with my own and driving me higher and higher. The feeling of connection between us is as potent as all the physical sensations I'm experiencing, winding me tight.

"Ask me to come," he rasps. "Beg me to come like a good girl."

"Please," I gasp. "Please, can I come?"

He wraps his hand around my neck, not applying any pressure, just resting his thumb on my pulse. His jaw clenches as his eyes burn with desire and satisfaction.

He gives his head a single shake. "Not yet. Hold it." He pulls out, and my orgasm dies right on the cusp. He flips me over onto my hands and knees, pushing my upper body to the bed with a palm between my shoulder blades. He fists a hand in my hair, turning my head sideways so I can breathe even while he's pressing my face into the pillow. His cock slides back into me easily, and he starts fucking me with the same harsh, eager pace again.

My eyes squeeze tightly as I gasp and whimper, clawing at the sheets. Dorian's thumb slides between the cleft of my ass, pressing against the tight ring of muscles that's already slick with my pleasure.

"Have you ever had anyone back here?" he whispers lowly, kissing the small of my back.

I shake my head with a low whine.

"Good girl," he breathes. "I'm going to fuck you here soon. I'm going to claim every single one of your holes for my own." He twists his thumb around, and the taboo sensation raises the hairs on the back of my neck, even as it drives me *wild* with pleasure and need. Slowly, his finger sinks into my rosebud, and the feeling of him breaching that forbidden hole makes a loud, tortured groan escape me.

"Fuck—*please* let me come," I beg.

"Good girl," he praises. "Come, Mira. Come *hard* for me."

Reality shifts and distorts as my eyes squeeze and I jerk, coming with such violence all the muscles in my body stiffen. My convulsions are so intense I'm surprised they don't hurt Dorian. His thrusts speed and turn harsher, jerkier, until he goes still inside of me, also finding his own release. I feel warmth bathe my channel as he spills himself inside me, and my clenching muscles seem to pull his seed deep.

Thank fuck I'm on birth control. My body seems primed and ready for him in *every* way; if I weren't on the pill, I wouldn't be surprised if I fell pregnant, even just from a single night with him.

He rocks into me a few more times, leaning over me to press a kiss to the nape of my neck. "Very good, Mira. *Such* a good girl for me. Fuck, I love the way you feel, the way you sound." He strokes his fingers over the small of my back as he slowly pulls out, and I feel a rush of warmth drip out of me as I bathe in his praise.

He flips me over to my back and kisses me deeply. "I'm going to have this pussy often," he murmurs. "Daily—*several* times daily if time permits. And I won't be sharing it, *ever*. Are we understood?"

I nod.

"Good girl." He kisses my neck, taking the skin between his lips and sucking hard enough that I'm sure he'll leave a mark. I wouldn't be surprised if I'm covered in bruises of his making.

"That was the best sex I've ever had," I breathe. "Jesus *Christ*, are you even human?"

Dorian chuckles, an amused sound brimming with masculine satisfaction. "You're amazing for my ego. Thank you, baby."

He gathers me in his arms and stands, taking me to the shower. I'm still feeling pretty limp and boneless from my three orgasms, so I'm grateful when he keeps me upright in the shower with an arm banded around my waist and washes my body with a deep-seated reverence. He takes his time running his soapy hands over every dip, valley, and contour of my form. He massages my head gently, making me moan with pleasure, and kisses along my neck as he rinses me off.

I could definitely get used to princess treatment like this from him. If we stay together, I expect I might actually get used to it and become a bit spoiled.

"How are you feeling?" he asks, slipping his hands between my legs and rubbing his fingers over my pussy. I hiss and wince a little—I'm sore from his ministrations, but I also feel incredibly, deeply satisfied.

"Sore but good," I breathe, rising on my toes as he cups me hard. His middle finger strokes over my clit, and I squirm. "Dorian—"

"Give me one more," he says, pressing my back firmly to his chest. "Just one more, Mira. I fucking *love* watching you come. I love *making* you come."

I grip his arm with my hands, digging my fingernails in. "Dorian, I don't know if I can—"

"You can," he encourages, rubbing my clit with his middle and index finger. "I know you can. You're capable of a lot more than you think, Mira. You can take it." He kisses my neck. "Come for me again. Be my good girl—"

His words set me off. I jerk as I come, scratching his arm, wriggling my ass against his cock, which starts to harden against me. Even though I'm spent and exhausted, ready to go back to sleep, I can't deny my growing desire. The orgasm is wonderful, but after having Dorian inside me, I think I've caught an addiction. I want him to come inside me, even though I'm pretty sure I'm too tired to come again.

I brace my hands on the tile wall and push my ass against him, making a clear invitation. I hear Dorian's breath catch over the sound of the shower—I guess he wasn't expecting me to offer myself up to him so soon. Maybe he's aware that he has a vagina-destroyer dangling between his legs—whatever the case, he doesn't hesitate to take me up on my offer. He grips my hip with one hand, using the other to guide his thick length inside me. We both groan at the same time, and I rest my forehead against the wall, trying to breathe through the stretch of his intrusion. I think it'll take a while before I'm used to his size. If he plans on fucking me every day like he promised to a few minutes ago, it might not be too long.

Besides, I *like* the bite of pain. I'm not a masochist by any stretch of the imagination, but I like knowing that I'll feel twinges to remind me of this long after he pulls out.

"You good?" he asks.

I release a moan in response; he lets out a harsh chuckle. "Hold on, baby. This is going to be quick and rough."

He makes good on his promise, fucking me with short, harsh strokes that tickle me in all the best ways. One of his hands grips my breast, while the other snakes lower, zeroing in on my clit.

I gasp, *way* too sensitive to be played with again. "Dorian, no—"

"Either use your safeword or fucking take it."

I don't even have to think about it. I don't think I'll ever use my safeword unless I'm well and truly done, and while I'm stretched a bit thin, I'm not there yet. He's set new limits for what I'm capable of taking.

Defeated, I slump forward and let him have his way with me. After a few more strokes, he gathers my hands in his grip and fixes them behind me, holding them tightly at the small of my back. My upper body is left sagging against the shower wall while his other hand lavishes attention over my clit. I whimper, wriggle, shake my head, and beg him to ease up... and he doesn't, which I absolutely *love*. He just takes exactly what he wants, not giving me an option but to stand and accept it. I have no control, and it's liberating.

"Come with me," he orders. "*Now*."

As if he's the master of my body, I comply before my thoughts even catch up with his command. My orgasm is so intense I'd topple over if it weren't for his grip on me, and he follows right behind me, letting out a loud groan as he comes.

"Now I'm dirty again, and I want to go back to sleep."

Dorian releases a short laugh, pressing a kiss to my shoulder as he pulls out of me. "I'll clean you up, and you're welcome to go back to sleep. You're too much of an early bird—it's not even 7am."

"*You're* the one who woke *me* up this morning," I remind him. I am an early bird, but he beat me to the punch today.

"Because you were stirring, as you usually do before you wake up." He spins me around, pressing a soft kiss to my lips. "We can get another few hours, but then we have an apartment tour set up."

Chapter Thirty

Dorian agrees to let me go to the mountain later today on one condition: he accompanies me and I introduce him to my wolf pack. I argue with him on the way to the apartment tour he set up; he ignores all common sense, stating and restating his intention to meet my wolves. I only pause arguing long enough for a realtor to show us around a beautiful, pre-furnished one-bedroom apartment with a walk-in closet, large living room, and state-of-the-art kitchen.

Dorian says we'll take it; he doesn't listen to any of my protests pointing out that moving away might make his situation with his legion more complex. He's determined to have his own place with me, to have me all to himself, and he's both rich and well-connected enough to pull that off.

After signing some paperwork, he takes us to a cute little lunch place, where I resume reminding him that I am heading to see a pack of *wild wolves* tonight. Ones that could tear him apart on a whim. His argument is that if they don't tear me apart, they wouldn't harm him. I don't know how to explain that I can't guarantee his safety on the basis of my own. The pack is kind and gentle to me because the alpha has formed a bond with me and recognizes me as fragile, but the huge wolf has no bond or allegiance to Dorian. He could see Dorian as his next meal.

"Dorian, just let me do this *one thing* alone," I urge on our way home. The sun will be setting soon, so I plan to pick up the treats I baked for the pack yesterday and head straight for the mountain. By the time I get there, it should be dark.

"If we're going to be part of each other's lives, we need to get acquainted with each other's families, don't you think? You've met my legion."

I blink slowly. "And you've met Valerie and Cara."

"Not the same thing," Dorian says with a subtle shake of his head. "You seem to have chosen a wolf pack as your found family. Odd choice, I'll admit, but—"

"*I* didn't choose the wolves, *they* chose *me*," I stress. "I don't think they'll choose you. You're not like me, and I don't want you to get hurt."

"I won't get hurt," Dorian assures me, squeezing my knee.

Groaning, I scramble for a change in topic, trying to find something to distract him.

"You know, you've never told me about your actual family," I say. "I don't know where you're from or anything about your parents—"

"My parents are gone," Dorian replies, his mood turning dark. His expression blanks, going as stagnant and still as a statue, but his energy becomes a strange mixture of angry and withdrawn.

I swallow. "You don't have to tell me anything about yourself, but I'd like to know."

Dorian releases a sigh, glancing at me from the corner of his eye. We pull past the mansion's automated gates, and he parks his car in front of the ginormous home. Hand in hand, we walk through the front door. Seamus and Connor are absent, probably off wreaking havoc somewhere, so Dorian leads me over to the living room couch and pulls me down onto his lap.

"You really want to hear about my life?" he asks. "I'll warn you now, Mira, it's not a pretty story."

"Of course. I want to know you better, especially since you just bought us an apartment." I shift to straddle him, my knees on either side of his hips.

His lips quirk. "Technically, I didn't *buy* it; I signed a six-month lease."

"Semantics." I cup his jaw, bracing my free hand on his shoulder. "Tell me, please."

He deflates at hearing me say *please*. In the bedroom, he likes hearing me beg, though it has no bearing on his actions. Outside of it, saying *please* and asking for things seems to be the right way to approach him.

"My mom died giving birth to me," he says after a long moment. "She came from money; my dad didn't. They married because they were desperately in love, but he always resented her a bit for having a rich, albeit estranged, family. Dad had custody of me as I was growing up, but he was absent. He left me at our house alone a lot. When I was ten, he disappeared for three weeks, and that's when social services caught up with me. I was put in a foster home."

Imagining a young Dorian, confused and alone, makes my heart pang. I let out a soft sigh and lean forward, resting my forehead against his, silently letting him know I'm here for him. He steals a kiss before pulling away, fixing his gaze on the arm of the couch, avoiding my eyes.

"I got into trouble a lot. Nearly ended up in juvie for stealing several times, but always managed to escape at the last second. I fell in with the wrong crowd during high school and learned a lot of things about crime. My foster family at the time only wanted me because of the monthly paycheck I brought, and because they knew that Mom left me a trust fund that'd open up when I was eighteen. They enjoyed smacking me around while waiting for me to grow up so they could steal my money."

"What about your grandparents?" I ask. "You didn't have any relatives to take you in?"

He shakes his head. "Dad's parents died when he was young, and Mom's parents died shortly after I was born. They also left me money, but I never actually met them. Anyway, my only redeeming grace in high school was that I was smart. I nearly failed out of my first year because I missed so many classes, but eventually, I focused on my education. I didn't want to become a deadbeat who blew through his money; I wanted to make more of it, to find what I was good at and become the best. I started showing up to school and doing the assignments. I realized that school was pretty fucking easy for me, and the structure felt good." I slide my hands into Dorian's hair, playing with the silky tresses, and his eyes flutter with appreciation. He grips my hips, pulling me flush against his body, and I feel his cock start to harden against me. I bite my lip, attempting to remain focused.

"And then?" I ask, trying to keep from moaning as he grinds his cock right into my core, rocking forward.

"And then I did very well. When I was eighteen, my trust funds unlocked, and I became wealthy overnight. My foster family tried to steal the money from under me, but I got accepted to Greywood and moved out before they could. Here, I met Connor and Seamus." He fingers the hem of my shirt, tugging it up. I raise my arms over my head, allowing him to yank it off. "Our first year, we got up to some shit. There used to be several gangs in the area, and some of them were trying to fuck with Greywood students—charge protection money from the scholarship kids who worked in the city. We made it clear that they couldn't do that anymore. End of freshman year, Sergei found us and offered us jobs. He suggested we band together, form a legion, and work for him. Protect his interests in the states and prepare to become close affiliates with him after college. He promised to give us assignments that'd make us rich and offer us a leg up in future business dealings." He unclips my bra, drawing the straps off my arms and tossing the material aside. "It was an arrangement that worked for everyone, so that's what we did. Now, we're embroiled in a few conflicts while trying to wipe Greywood and the surrounding areas clean of all crime that doesn't go through us and Sergei."

He kisses the swell of my breast, running his thumb over my nipple. My back arches and my eyes squeeze shut as I try to remain focused.

"I have... questions," I say, gasping as he leans down and sucks my nipple into his mouth. I feel Dorian's smile against my flesh.

"I can answer them later. For now, I'm done talking. I'm more interested in getting into that tight pussy again."

"But Seamus and Connor—"

"Are out of the house for the day."

Before long, I'm fully naked, with Dorian controlling my movements as I slide up and down his cock, occasionally wincing at the twinge of soreness. Sore or not, he feels *really* good. The way he gazes at me with reverence makes me feel like the most powerful woman in the world; the way he rubs his thumb over my clit makes my toes curl with pleasure. I gasp and moan and whimper as I ride him, digging my nails into his skin so hard it's a wonder I don't draw blood.

I fuck myself on his cock until I shatter around him, jerking and crying out loudly as I come. He follows not long after me, groaning from deep in his throat.

In the aftermath, we hold each other, and I come to a very startling realization; I like being held by him so much that I don't want to stop. Not now, maybe not *ever*.

I'm at serious risk of actually falling in love with this monster of a man.

Despite my many, many protests, Dorian comes with me when I head up the mountain to see my pack. We park in my usual place in a small, hidden dirt parking lot, and hike up to where my wolf pack usually hangs out, near their den. I hope they don't maul me as well as Dorian for daring to bring an outsider.

Once we get to the clearing where I usually find the alpha, I take Dorian's hand and lead him to the oak tree where the alpha and I often sit side by side.

"Where are they?" Dorian asks, looking around, attempting to peer through the darkness. "I can barely see anything. Why can't we use a flashlight, again?"

I set my backpack on the forest floor. "No flashlights. We're in their territory; I try to respect their animal nature. On clear nights, the moonlight is plenty enough to see."

"It's not a clear night," Dorian points out. "I can barely see—"

A low growl to the left of us cuts him off. I recognize the growl as belonging to the alpha; it's loud and menacing, a clear warning for us to get off his territory. He hasn't growled at me like that for quite some time, so I assume it's Dorian's scent that's throwing the wolf and making him defensive.

I squeeze Dorian's hand, warning him to remain silent. I told him what to do and expect on our way up here, though I still *thoroughly* disagree with his presence. "It's me," I tell the alpha, searching the darkness to try to get a glimpse of him. Slowly, I unzip my backpack and withdraw the container of cookies. My movements earn me a much louder, much more threatening growl, but I persevere. I uncap the container, grab a cookie, and gently toss it in the direction where the growling stems from. Abruptly, the growling cuts off. A few moments of daunting, hair-raising silence pass, before I hear paws crunching the dead leaves of the forest floor.

The alpha comes into view, eyes narrowed and ears high. His jaw works as he eats my offered cookie. His gaze fixes on me, and his ears perk with recognition, but when he looks at Dorian, they flatten against his head and he growls again.

Praying to whatever higher power exists that I haven't made a colossal mistake by coming here and bringing another human with me, I pull Dorian close, rubbing my hand up and down his arm.

"This is my friend," I say, hoping the alpha realizes that Dorian's no threat because he's here with me. We're near the alpha's den, which means we're near the pups of the pack, which makes bringing a stranger even more dangerous. Wolves are extremely protective of their young.

Slowly, I sink down to my knees. Dorian follows suit, and we both showcase our submission to the alpha. The wolf's growls slow down, then cut off completely. He's still snarling, showing us a flash of yellow teeth as a warning.

I hold out the container with cookies, inviting him to take as many as he wants. Usually, I'm careful with how many treats I give him, but tonight, I'm willing to cater to this wolf's whims if it means he doesn't maul Dorian to death.

The alpha takes a step forward, sniffing the air. When he catches Dorian's scent, he releases another bone-chilling growl. His posture goes from defensive to a crouch that announces he's gearing to attack.

My heart pounds with such vigor I'm afraid it might beat out of my chest, and fear curdles the blood in my veins.

On instinct, I shuffle forward, snagging the alpha's attention. This wolf knows me, he's claimed me as a member of his pack; I helped his mate bring their beautiful pups into the world. I can get him to settle down.

As soon as I'm a few feet away from Dorian, the alpha calms, and that's when the realization hits me. He wasn't growling and gearing to attack because he perceived Dorian as a threat to him, he was doing that because he perceived Dorian as a threat to me, or perhaps as a contender for the alpha's claim over me. The wolf breaches the distance between us, cookies forgotten, and butts his head into my shoulder. I stroke my fingers through his fur, murmuring and cooing to him, assuring him that I accept his claim. When he's settled enough that his fur's no longer standing on end, I give him a stroke over his muzzle.

"Shuffle forward slowly, Dorian," I murmur. "*Very* slowly."

Silently, Dorian follows my instructions. The alpha tenses, his eyes switching over to watch Dorian carefully, but he doesn't growl or adopt an attacking stance again. Over the course of several minutes, I encourage Dorian closer and closer, keeping a careful eye on the alpha's demeanor to gauge whether I'm pushing too far.

When Dorian's directly beside me and the wolf, I take his hand in mine and gently guide it forward. The alpha watches, eyes narrowed, teeth slightly bared. I know I'm risking both of our fingers, but since Dorian insisted on coming, I either have to get the alpha to accept him or hope to god we can run fast enough to escape a pack of angry wolves.

The alpha sticks his nose in the air, inhaling my scent combined with Dorian's. He releases a low chuff, licking his lips. *Not great, not terrible.*

"This is my friend," I tell the wolf. He can't understand me, but he'll catch the cadence of my words and the energy behind them. I hope. "He's very nice, and he wanted to meet you, since you're also an important friend." I rub my thumb over Dorian's knuckles. The alpha inhales deeply again, nostrils flaring. His attention focuses on us, alert and watchful but no longer threatening. His head leans forward until his glimmering teeth are a mere few inches away from Dorian and I's hands. After a moment, he chuffs again and turns around. His head tilts back and he releases a low howl, communicating something to his pack.

I hope to hell he's not telling them to attack.

Only a second passes before the faint noises of rustling sound from all around me, and several wolves emerge into the clearing. They all approach the alpha for direction. Some pause to paw at me or chuff at me in greeting, but Dorian goes largely ignored, thank god. The alpha turns his attention back to the container of cookies.

"You're in the clear," I breathe, relieved. "He gets it, I think. He won't hurt you." If the alpha was going to attack, he would've done it by now.

"Jesus fucking Christ," Dorian murmurs. I glance at him, seeing an expression of sheer shock written on his features. He stares between me and the wolves with a mixture of awe and trepidation. His Adam's apple bobs as he swallows hard, giving his head a faint shake. "I thought I was going to die."

"There's a reason I didn't want you coming with me," I say drily. "What did you expect? A warm and cuddly greeting? These are wild wolves, Dorian. They had us surrounded. If provoked, they could've killed both of us."

"I don't think they'd ever hurt you," Dorian says.

A few yips draw my attention away from him, and a wide smile spreads on my face as the pups of the pack come tumbling towards me. They've grown a bit since I've seen them last; at this age, they grow like damn weeds. They're still adorably clumsy and eager for attention.

They clamber over themselves as they get to my lap, whining and yipping for attention. Their mom takes a seat nearby, watching me interact with them. She's usually comfortable with me holding them, but I think Dorian's presence right beside me is making her uneasy.

I take Dorian's hand and gently guide him to the wolf pup who's curled up over my legs. He's the calmest of the three, and barely even stirs as I guide Dorian to pet him.

"Can't say I've ever petted a wild wolf cub before."

"Pup," I correct.

"Pup," he echoes, vague amusement coating his tone. "Christ, they're cute."

The alpha finishes with his fill of the cookies and trots up to me, butting his head against my backpack and releasing a whine.

"Sorry, my dude. I didn't bring any more. What you see is what you get," I say, smiling faintly.

He chuffs, spins in circles a few times to get comfortable, and lays down beside me, his huge body pressed up against mine.

"What the *fuck*," Dorian breathes.

"Yeah," I agree. "Honestly, I think he sees me as his pet. Cute, isn't it?"

"I don't know if cute is the word I'd use," Dorian murmurs, clearing his throat. "How long do you usually stay?"

"An hour or two," I reply. "Settle in, Dorian, and don't forget that you asked for this."

Chapter Thirty-One

"**I** can't believe he fucking *bit* me," Dorian says later that night. We're back in the house of horrors, and we just finished showering together. The bathroom is all steamed up, and the mirror is fogged over.

"He didn't bite *you*," I correct. "He bit your shirt—there's a difference. It's actually a good thing; it means he wanted us to stay." I smile. "Besides, you have plenty of shirts to spare. If he ripped any more of mine, I'd go into debt buying new ones."

"No, you wouldn't," Dorian corrects. "You're my woman. I'm your man. I'll take care of you. Want to go shopping? Clear out a fucking mall for all I care."

I blink slowly, taken aback by the ease with which he offers me his money. "Um, thank you, but I can make my own money."

"You spend all the money you make on necessities or stuff for your animal friends," Dorian points out drily. "I have too much money; you don't have enough. Solution is simple." His brows furrow. "I meant to get you a credit card but forgot—I'll have it to you by the end of the week."

"Dorian, no," I say firmly. "I don't want to feel like a spoiled, kept woman. I want to make my way in this world."

"You are and will continue to make your way in this world, but you will do it comfortably. I'm not asking, Mira. You work too hard, study too hard, do too much. If I can help you with some of your burdens, it would make me feel like I'm doing my job as your man."

My lips twist as I grab a hairbrush and start working it through my hair. "That seems very old-school. Maybe a bit misogynistic."

"No, it seems like a man committed to his woman," Dorian corrects. "Don't be too proud to accept help. When we get married, my money will be your money—"

"Woah," I cut him off. "*Marriage?* I haven't even agreed to be your girlfriend yet."

Dorian's eyes darken. "You *are* my girlfriend. You'll be my fiancée before long, then my wife."

I regard him with wide eyes. "You might actually be crazy."

"Crazy for you," he agrees. "Finish up—I want to fuck you on our bed before we go to sleep."

"I *just* got clean," I remind him, exasperated. Dorian has had me at least five times today, and he *still* doesn't seem to be satisfied.

Dorian's brows crinkle. "Yeah, you're right. Might as well do it in here, so we can wash off right after..."

A low moan awakens me in the morning, accompanied by a wet, aching heat between my legs. It takes me several seconds to realize it's the heat of a tongue lapping over my pussy, pulling me out of my slumber. A scrape of teeth over my clit makes my back arch and draws a low moan from my throat.

"Good morning," Dorian rumbles, kissing my thigh.

"It is," I agree with another moan as he suckles my clit. "*Fuuuuuuck me*," I gasp when he slides two fingers inside me.

"Gladly," Dorian chuckles, pulling his fingers out of me. He climbs over my body, braces himself, and slowly slides his huge, hard cock into me. I hook my legs over his waist, eyes fluttering as he fills me so completely I can't tell where he starts and I end.

He doesn't waste time or tease me; instead, he fucks me hard and fast, pushing me into an orgasm that's so intense it makes my vision go out. I gasp and pant and moan, digging my nails into his back so hard it's a wonder I don't draw blood.

In the aftermath, he rolls off me and pulls me into his body. I lay my head on his chest and flatten my palm against his abs, trying to catch my breath.

"How high is your sex drive?" I ask when I'm no longer panting. "I'm not sure if I'll be able to keep up with you." Yesterday was wonderful, but my pussy's already sore from the multiple poundings it took. If Dorian keeps up with this pace, it's going to take some getting used to.

"Normally?" Dorian asks. "I'd say medium. A few times a month is plenty to keep me satisfied. With you?" He chuckles. "Infinite. I can't get enough of you."

"As flattering as that is, Dorian, I'm breakable," I murmur. "I can't go all day every day. I'm already sore as hell from yesterday, and now I'll be even *more* sore."

He smirks. "Good. That way. You'll feel me every time you move."

I smack his chest, even though my cheeks warm at the thought. "No, Dorian, *not good*." I glance at the clock on the nightstand; it's barely 7am. "I have school at ten, and I'd really prefer it if I could walk straight. That monster between your legs is a vagina-destroyer."

The jerk chuckles. "You'll get used to me. In order for that to happen, we better keep fucking a few times a day. Eventually, your gorgeous pussy will learn how to take a beating."

I sigh. "We'll revisit this conversation later."

Dorian's phone starts buzzing on the nightstand. He reaches for it, eyebrows furrowing. "I gotta take this, baby. Go shower, we'll eat after."

I glimpse the caller ID over his shoulder: *Sergei Novikov*. It's crazy to think that Dorian has a direct connection to a man who's feared and revered in every corner of the world. His business with Sergei makes me uncomfortable, but I'm far less uncomfortable than I would be if he worked for a small-time gang. Even the media hints that Sergei has a few morals—he's been instrumental in dismantling several trafficking rings over the last decade. He might be wanted in most countries with multiple warrants out for his arrest, but he never *actually* gets arrested when he visits. He's too powerful for any justice system—the one time he was incarcerated years ago, he escaped in a phenomenal bloodbath. It was all over the news for months.

I slip out of bed as Dorian picks up the call, heading to the bathroom on unsteady legs. I shower quickly and brush my teeth. Once I'm done, I walk into the bedroom wrapped only in a towel, running a hairbrush through my hair.

Dorian's just finishing up his conversation.

"Is that an order?" he says. "I don't mean to be disrespectful, but I don't want to do this to Mira." My heart speeds up and my chest prickles with anxiety as he glances at me, his brows drawn and lips thinned.

"That's a lot to ask," he says after a long moment. "You're married, Sergei. Tell me, would you do this to your wife?" After a few more beats of listening to whatever Sergei says, he sighs. "I'll talk to her, but

I'm not ordering her to do anything. If that means we have to part ways, so be it."

The anxiety in my chest comes to an abrupt halt, immediately overshadowed by other, stronger emotions. Dorian's protecting me; whatever he's talking about with his boss, he's willing to go out on a limb for me. He's willing to dissolve his relationship with one of the most powerful men in the *world* for me. Sergei Novikov could easily have him killed for shirking whatever order Dorian's refusing, but he's doing it anyways.

Jesus.

"Yeah, I'll get back to you. Bye." Dorian hangs up the phone, his jaw clenched. He inhales several deep breaths, trying to calm himself before he holds his hand out to me. I step forward and take it, allowing him to pull me onto his lap. He's seated on the edge of the bed, feet on the ground, me balanced on his thighs.

"What was that?" I question, wrapping my arms around his neck. "What is it Sergei wants me to do?"

Dorian swallows. "Apparently, Carver is more of an issue than we previously anticipated. He runs a local chapter of a trafficking ring that has international roots, so Sergei wants to take him down. The easiest way to do that would be to get an in-person meeting, and the easiest way to get an in-person meeting is to have you reach out to your stepfather." He shakes his head again, leaning forward and burying his face in the side of my neck. "Sergei's visiting the states in a few weeks. He suggested that he might drop by your home town, taking me, Seamus, and Connor as backup to help cut the head off of the snake. He figures that Carver should be his next warning to the trafficking world; break Sergei's rules and get killed, *painfully.*"

I swallow harshly. "He wants me to reach out to Clyde."

"Yes," Dorian nods. "Reach out, set up a meeting in three weeks' time. You don't have to be there. You also don't have to do this."

I clear my throat. "I thought Sergei was known for brutally killing anyone involved in human trafficking," I murmur. "Why would Carver want to do business with him?"

"Because he doesn't think Sergei knows about his stake in the skin trade," Dorian replies. "He's looking to partner with Sergei on drug trafficking, not on peddling human flesh. He thinks he has a shield of anonymity protecting him."

"I see," I murmur.

I don't want to talk to Clyde. He's been the monster under my bed for a long, *long* time, but I also can't just stand back and allow him and his boss to steal innocent girls and force them into sex work. I couldn't live with myself if I didn't take action. Protecting those who can't protect themselves is more important than my fear.

Besides, I have Dorian protecting me. He said I won't have to show up, and I believe him. All I have to do is make a call to Clyde, tell him a time in place, and let Dorian's legion and Sergei handle the rest. I don't *want* to, but I *have* to.

"You don't have to do it," Dorian says. "I can reach out to Clyde, but Sergei thinks that Clyde will assume anything from me is a setup. To be fair, I can't imagine myself being civil to the piece of shit who made your life a living hellscape. I can't promise I wouldn't make any death threats." He gently drags my towel up my leg, stroking his hand over the scar tissue that represents the most painful time in my life. His eyes darken as he gazes at the raised flesh and he shakes his head, rubbing his thumb over my skin.

I cup his cheeks, redirecting his gaze to me. "I'll do it," I tell him, shoring myself up.

Dorian releases a long sigh, almost as if he wished that I *wouldn't* agree to call Clyde.

"I can't stand by and do nothing," I say gently. "Not when women and girls are suffering. Not when I *know* how cruel Carver's operation is, how they treat the people around them. It wouldn't be right." I swallow. "So, I'll do it."

Dorian nods slowly. "Thank you, baby. I'm sorry to ask this of you."

"It's okay," I murmur, even though it's not. "I'll live. Just... don't be surprised if I kind of zone out afterwards." It's instinct for me to dissociate when I deal with all the emotions that accompany thinking about, let alone talking to, Clyde.

"You have something on him, don't you?" Dorian asks out of the blue. "Otherwise, that fucker never would've let you go."

I turn my head away, unable to hold his gaze any longer. "Yes," I say quietly. "I have something on him. Something that would get him killed."

"What is it?" Dorian asks.

I swallow hard. I don't want to tell him because I don't want him to think less of me. I know for a fact that Clyde brutally tortured and killed Carver's late wife, and I've kept that information to myself. That's a phenomenally shitty thing for me to have done, but it's also my best form of protection. Otherwise, Clyde would've already come for me, maybe even killed me.

I suck in a deep breath. There's no use hiding this from Dorian, not when I'm about to set up a meeting between him and Clyde. "Please don't judge me," I whisper. "I'm not proud of this."

Dorian gently squeezes my thigh. "I've done a lot of bad shit, Mira. I'm in no position to judge you."

"But you are," I say. "It's bad."

He cups my jaw, turning me to face him. I gaze at his chest, not having the courage to look into his eyes.

"Tell me," he murmurs. "Trust that I won't turn against you, Mira. Please."

I squeeze my eyes shut. He might never look at me the same after I say this, but I don't have much of a choice.

Chapter Thirty-Two

"When I was seventeen, I found a stash of photos Clyde keeps. Fucked up trophies of his most atrocious acts."

"What kind of photos?" Dorian asks.

Bile rises in my throat, and I shake my head slowly. "Pictures of women. Most of them dead, all of them bloody and brutalized. The gang got up to terrible shit, and Clyde got off on beating and raping women. Killing them, too. I think he was the man Carver sent when he wanted to give a rival a message. Clyde would take the rival's wife, torture her, rape her, and sometimes kill her."

Dorian stiffens beneath me, but he doesn't say anything.

"One of those pictures was of Carver's late wife. I think she might've had something on Clyde, something she threatened him with. Whatever the case, she became one of his victims. Every photo has a date, a few words, and Clyde's signature. I took the photo of Maria, Carver's wife, got photocopies of it, and stashed them in several places. If and when my death certificate or a missing person's report is filed in any database, that photo will be sent to Carver."

Dorian sucks in a sharp breath, going even more tense. The energy radiating from him turns angry, *furious*. He's restless and gearing for violence, and I happen to be the person nearest to him. Fear sparks in my chest.

"I know it's terrible to keep what I know to myself," I rush to say. "But I didn't feel like I had another choice. I *had* to get away, and holding Clyde's worst deed against him was the best way to do that. I'm sorry—"

"Shush," Dorian says, pressing his index finger against my lips. "I'm not judging you, baby. I'm not mad at you. I'm fucking furious that you lived with a man like Clyde for years." He inhales, lips pressed into a flat line. "Did he ever...?"

I shake my head. "No. For a while, I was too young, but I knew he would've eventually. That's why I was so desperate to get out, to find leverage on him." I examine Dorian's expression. "You're... not mad at me?"

He shakes his head. "No, Mira, I'm not mad at you. I'm mad that you had to live with a vile man who hurt you. You did what you had to do, baby." He kisses the corner of my mouth.

"It helps to know that Maria was a genuinely awful person herself," I say quietly. "I'm almost positive she had a hand in trafficking, because she threatened to turn my mom into a stripper and *put her to work* more than once. She was truly, truly evil—she and her husband were an excellent match." I purse my lips. "This is awful of me, but I'm glad she's gone. The world is a bit less evil without her. I'm not happy about the things Clyde did to her, the atrocities she experienced that no woman ever should, but..."

"I get it," Dorian assures me, kissing my forehead. "It's okay, baby. It's alright."

"Thank you," I whisper, relief chasing away my anxiety.

He strokes his thumb over my jaw. "Do you want to try calling Clyde now to get it over with, or do it later?"

The sooner it's over, the better. I don't want to give my stepfather a second's more thought than I have to. He doesn't deserve to take up space in my brain.

"I'll do it now," I say. "Should I use my phone?" Dorian presented me with a brand-new phone that has a new number and better encryption yesterday.

He shakes his head. "No, I don't want him knowing your new number. Use the old one."

I slowly get off his lap, taking deep breaths to try to prepare myself. I throw on shorts and a camisole, then fish out my old phone from the bedside stand's drawer. Ironically, it's lying right next to a few sex toys—items that I figure Dorian will be using on me tonight. At least there's something to look forward to in my near future.

I pull out my phone, take a seat on the side of the bed, and unlock it. My finger hovers over Clyde's number in my recent contacts, and I feel my heart start to race. My chest tightens and beads of sweat break out over my body. A fine tremor settles in my limbs, and I feel the urge to dissociate sweep over me. It's almost an instinctual reaction when it comes to Clyde.

Then, Dorian takes a seat beside me and wraps his arm around my waist, and the worst edge of my anxiety melts away. I'm still wound tight, still anxious, but the wish to zone out disappears. I know I can handle this with Dorian next to me.

"Give me a date," I request. "A date for the meeting."

"November 7th," Dorian replies. "9 p.m., at the brewery in town."

Either he or Sergei have done their research. The brewery in my home town has a basement that's often utilized for gang meetings.

I hit Clyde's number. The phone rings only twice before he picks up. The sound of his heavy breathing is enough to make me curl into myself; I draw my knees up to my chest and rest the side of my face against them, trying to remain grounded.

"You've been ignoring my calls," Clyde says darkly. "That's not very nice of you."

Breathe, Mira. Just get through this. "I was doing what you asked," I reply, my voice admirably firm. "It wasn't simple, but I managed to get you a meeting with Novikov. He'll be in your neck of the woods on November 7th; he'll meet you at the brewery at 9 p.m. He'll bring some of his underlings."

A long pause ensues, raising the hairs on the back of my neck. "Good. I'll pass it along."

"We're done now," I tell him. "I did what you asked, that's it. Ask anything else of me ever again, and I'll tell Carver what you did."

"The fuck you will, bitch, because I'll make sure you burn for it if you do," Clyde snaps, raising his voice. Dorian's arm tightens around me, silently showing his support. "Besides, Carver wants to see you again. He's curious how you grew up, what you've made of yourself. You remember that he always liked you, don't you?"

The words are spoken in a sinister tone, and the threat is clear. I only met Carver a handful of times, and each time I did, he gave me looks that raised the hairs on the back of my neck. His energy was teeming with darkness and malice—it's not surprising to know that he's into some darker shit.

"I'm never going back to that shithole again," I tell Clyde, not bothering to keep the derision from my tone. "You and I are done."

"We're done when I say we're done," Clyde responds harshly, losing his patience. "And I say we're not done yet. Drop the uppity cunt act; I know you're still just a scared little girl who needs a man to tell her what to do and correct her when she fucks up. You and the guy you're whoring yourself out to will both attend the meeting."

"The fuck I will," I hiss. "The answer is no, Clyde."

"Then the meeting is off, and your boy will need to explain to his boss exactly what happened to make it fall through. We have a good operation running here; I'm sure Sergei will want in on it. He'll probably be disappointed if it falls through because of his underling."

I look to Dorian with wide eyes. He watches me with a harsh expression, his anger evident in the bulging veins and tendons on his neck. He subtly shakes his head, silently communicating that I should push back against Clyde, but I don't see how. Sergei ordered Dorian to have me set this up; my failure to do so could result in Dorian getting reprimanded, maybe even cut off. He already went out on a limb for me with Sergei, I can't let him down now.

The operation Carver's running has to be shut down; for that, this meeting needs to take place. If that requires me to come along, then I'll do what I have to do. I squeeze Dorian's hand, snuggling close to him. The heat radiating from his body is almost enough to penetrate the cold settling in my bones.

"Fine," I say. Dorian's grip turns to steel and he shakes his head, but I ignore him. "If your blackened heart is really set on having me there, so be it. But the *boy* you keep referring to is actually a *man*, and he happens to be *my man*, so I hope you're not planning on attempting to pull anything with me."

"Are you fucking *threatening* me with the little boy you're selling yourself to?" Clyde all but shouts.

"No. I'm guaranteeing that if you put a finger on me, he will cut it off. Then your wrist, your arm, and finally, your empty head. Sergei doesn't want you; he wants Carver." I pause, letting my threat settle. "Don't contact me again, *ever*. And should any harm befall me at the meeting, know that there are dozens of copies of the photo with your handwriting that'll get sent to your precious boss." I hang up, resisting the urge to throw my old phone at the wall and break it.

Without any preamble, Dorian pulls me onto his lap. "Why the fuck would you agree to that?" he asks, his voice a furious whisper. "I don't want you anywhere near that piece of shit—"

"You'll protect me," I cut him off. "I know you will. He won't touch me, not when I have you."

Dorian swears under his breath. "Of course I'll protect you *physically*, but what will seeing Clyde do to your emotions, Mira? I don't want you to dissociate so far that you disappear. I couldn't handle that." He growls. "Why would you do that? Why put yourself in such a shitty position? You're smarter than that, there has to be another way—"

"There isn't," I interrupt again. "I know Clyde, Dorian. I lived with him for years. Once he has something in his head, there's literally no dissuading him. As for why I did it..." I trail off, biting my lip. "I heard what you said to Sergei. You were willing to defy an order for me. You were willing to dissolve your working relationship with him for me, which I'm sure would've been a dangerous move. If you'll jeopardize your future for me, there's no reason I won't agree to show up to a meeting for you."

Chapter Thirty-Three

I can't verbalize how much Mira's words mean to me, what her sacrifice means to me. As she relaxes against me, hooking her arms around my neck and pressing her forehead against mine, a confidence I haven't yet experienced fills me. One that promises everything will be okay, because I have Mira—*truly* have her. She's no longer just my reluctant guest, she's something more.

She's willing to stick out her neck for me and trusts that I'll protect her. She cares for me, pretty damn deeply if she's willing to go to a place that holds a lifetime of bad memories for her. I press a kiss to her nose, her cheeks, her chin, trying to find a way to showcase my gratitude, my own affection for her. My *love* for her. The words to tell her how I feel are on the tip of my tongue, but I hold them back. Mira's always been flighty, and I don't want to scare her into trying to flee.

I'll wait until I'm certain she loves me, too, and *then* I'll tell her. Then, I'll put a ring on her finger and a baby in her belly. She'll never be able to run after that.

Christ, sometimes my thoughts around this woman are enough to take me aback. I'm not someone who grows obsessive over people—I've never found someone interesting enough to obsess over, until Mira. I'm willing to do just about anything to keep her.

"Thank you, baby," I murmur, kissing her neck. I find her pulse and suck on it, needing to leave my mark on her. "I'll keep you safe, I promise."

"I know you will," she says. Her confidence is enough to undo me. If I didn't know for a fact that she's sore, I'd showcase my gratitude physically. As is, I want to spoil the fuck out of her, starting with taking care of her needs.

"Let's get something to eat," I tell her. "I can make French toast and bacon—"

"I'll cook," she disagrees. "Then I have to get to school. Where are Connor and Seamus?"

"Home," I reply. "I'll talk to them while you command the kitchen." I kiss her neck again. "I have to go out with them tonight. We've located the last members of the gang that attacked us, and we're going to take care of them."

Her nails dig into the back of my neck and she stiffens on my lap, gazing at me with wide eyes. "Dorian," she breathes. "That sounds dangerous."

"No more or less dangerous than the things I've done dozens of times." I kiss her lips, trying to make the gesture reassuring. "I'll be fine, baby. I promise. I need to get rid of anyone in the area who can pose a threat to *us*, and more importantly, *you*. Then we'll take care of Clyde and Carver, and then everyone who opposes us will be dead."

"Cut off the head of a snake and three more will grow back," Mira murmurs. "How can you ever feel safe with what you do? With who you are? How can you ever be sure that you can keep those around you safe?"

I suspect this will be a constant point of contention between me and Mira. She'll always worry over my involvement in organized crime, she'll always hate it, and I don't want to spend my life arguing with her and making her miserable with my refusal to change. I can't leave altogether, and I don't intend to stop being active in the dark parts of my legion until after college. Down the road, however, I've always planned on stepping into an administrative role, moving away from the blatantly illegal operations I carry out.

"I can feel safe by destroying my enemies so thoroughly that none can stand against me," I reply. "This won't be forever, baby. I'm graduating next year, and I plan to go into business. I won't abandon my legion, but I'm going to back off from the illegal shit that leads to shootouts." I kiss her lips again. "Bear with me for now. Trust that I'm doing what I need to, and trust me to keep you safe."

She releases a long sigh, nodding reluctantly. "I'll never like it, but I can tolerate it. Just, please... be safe. Be careful. I—" She looks away, biting her lip. "I don't want to lose you."

"I know you don't, baby, and I don't want to leave you." I pat her ass. "Come on, let's get breakfast. If we stay here much longer, I'll end up fucking you again, and you're already sore."

I find Connor and Seamus in the basement. They're kicked back on the couch, playing Call of Duty. Seamus pauses the game when he notices me, which earns him a glare from Connor. Credence peeks her head out of the cardboard box, gives me a cursory hiss for having the gall to exist, and disappears.

"Boys," I greet, tilting my chin. "How did things go last night?"

"We learned what we needed to know," Connor says shortly. "You're coming with us tonight." His words aren't a question, they're an order. Connor's used to being in charge; being part of a legion where we all hold equal power was challenging for him at first. Now that Mira's disrupted our flow, he's regressing to his old ways.

"I am, but not because you proclaimed it," I say calmly, leaning against the arm of the couch. "I'm coming because I'm in a good enough place with my woman that I'm not afraid to leave her for the night."

Connor's eyes darken as he glares at me, but after a moment, he gives a grunt of assent. "She's settled, then?"

"Yup." I pause, glancing at Seamus. "We're moving into an apartment in the next few weeks. Not much will change; I still plan on spending plenty of time here."

"Abandoning us for pussy," Connor mutters. "I expected more from you."

"Enough," Seamus sighs. "Can't you see the man's in love? Loving Mira doesn't make him love us any less. If you'd stop scaring the living hell out of her, Dorian wouldn't need to move out to keep her safe. Stick a sock in it, Connor, we're fed up with your shit."

"You're taking his side?" Connor demands, tossing aside his remote and sitting forward.

"No, asshole, because there are no sides—at least none that aren't of your own making. You think it's us versus them; it's not. Mira's part of this legion now, even if it's just in essence instead of in name. When I find a girl to settle with, *if* that ever happens, it'll be the same deal. And if you ever find someone who can tolerate you for longer than a night, I expect it'll be a similar setup. Ease the fuck up, man. You're being ridiculous."

"Connor," I say quietly. "I will never be against you and neither will Mira. She's upstairs, in our kitchen, making all of us breakfast even though you've been a complete ass to her. You need to give her a chance for my sake. Please."

Connor's lips thin, but his posture relaxes with dejection. I love the guy; I don't want to alienate him, but he makes it very damn difficult to be his friend.

"Fine," he says after several moments. "I'll give her a shot. If she betrays us or fucks us, though, you'll need to handle her."

That's the best endorsement I can hope for from him.

Seamus stands from the couch, stretching his arms above his head with a loud yawn. "Well, I'm starving, and the scents wafting down here are delightful. I'm heading upstairs to see what's cooking."

Even though Seamus has given up his quest to fuck Mira—he now seems more focused on her friend, Valerie—I still don't want him alone with her. I don't want *any* man other than myself alone with her. I follow him upstairs, making my way into the kitchen. Mira's dressed in a tight shirt and even tighter jeans, back turned to us as she hovers over the stove. Bacon sizzles on one pan, and she's flipping slices of French toast on another. On the kitchen island sits a large glass bowl filled with cut-up fruit.

"If you guys want to start setting the table, it'd be much appreciated," she calls over her shoulder.

Seamus sighs. "Here I was hoping I'd manage to jump-scare her. The girl has eyes in the back of her head." He moves to follow her instructions nevertheless, just as Connor makes an appearance.

"Smells good," he grunts.

"Tastes better," Mira retorts, bending to pull a pan from the oven. Connor's eyes fall to her ass, glimmering with appreciation; I damn near stab him in the neck for looking. Instead, I glare at him until he averts his gaze and walks away, shaking his head with derision.

I walk over to Mira, wrapping my arms around her from behind and resting my chin on her head. She gives my arm a squeeze before loading several more slices of soaked French toast onto the pan, sprinkling them with cinnamon and brown sugar.

"Bacon's about ready if you want to plate it up," she says. "The croissant casserole is also ready. Just another few minutes for the French toast."

"Thanks, baby." I kiss her neck, smiling when a little shudder runs down her arms.

Once everything's done, we settle in the dining room for breakfast. Mira's quiet, and it takes me a few minutes to realize that she keeps glancing at the window, her expression nervous. She must be remembering what happened the night I got shot. Home invasion is a touchy, difficult subject for her, and she had to experience it *here*.

I stand, pick her up, and deposit her on my lap. She melts into me instantly, back relaxing against my chest, resting her cheek against my neck. She presses a kiss to my jaw, and my cock twitches. I inhale a deep breath and try to focus on food. Getting a hard-on when I *just* negotiated a fragile peace with Connor is not the way to go.

Mira, however, isn't on board with my thoughts. When she feels my dick start to stiffen, she sucks in a short breath, then *wriggles on my lap*. My jaw clenches as I reach around her and focus on slicing off a piece of French toast, holding it up to her lips. She stares into my eyes, wraps her lips around the fork, and hollows her cheeks as she sucks the French toast off of the tines. I suppress a low groan. The little minx is *teasing* me.

"As riveting as this foreplay is, I have places to be today," Seamus says. "I'll meet you lot back here at five. Mira, do say hello to that lovely little firecracker next you speak to her. And tell her to text me back."

Mira's eyebrows rise as she quickly chews and swallows, turning to face Seamus. "You're talking to Valerie?"

"Talking's the minority of what we've done," Seamus replies with a suggestive smile. "Tell her to respond, love. I'm eager to see her again."

Mira bites her lip. "Um... I should see her at school today, but Val doesn't usually date."

"I'm well aware. We're not dating."

Mira clears her throat. "She doesn't usually... spend more than one night with a guy."

"Ah, but I'm not just *any* guy," Seamus says with a smile. "Tell her to answer, love. I'll take care of the rest." He tips Mira a wink, stands, and leaves. Connor exits shortly afterwards, taking his and Seamus's plate to the kitchen.

"Trying to get me hard in front of my legion?" I growl in Mira's ear. "That's not very nice."

"I don't have to do much," she says with a breathless laugh. "I don't know if anyone's ever told you this, but you're very excitable."

"Only for you, baby," I say. "But unless you want to get fucked over this kitchen table and be late to school, I highly recommend you ease up. You're sore and I'm insatiable; there's no need to tempt the beast."

Mira gives me a demure look. "What if I like the beast?"

A long breath escapes me. "Then you better be ready for him to feast on you, because he is *ravenous*."

Chapter Thirty-Four
Dorian

I give Sergei a call after a late-afternoon fuck. When I brought Mira back from her classes at Greywood, she started working on her homework in our room. She looked so damn adorable, lazing on the bed and scribbling furiously in a notebook with a pile of textbooks surrounding her, I couldn't resist. I should probably start being a bit more considerate if I want to keep fucking her every day... but I also don't see that happening. I literally cannot get enough of her, and I don't think I ever will. My cock is always semi-hard around her, and getting to full mast doesn't take more than observing Mira being herself. Quirky, sexy, cute as fuck.

Leaving Mira in bed, where she's catching her breath, I head out to the hallway and dial Sergei's number. He picks up on the first ring.

"And?" he asks without preamble.

"She did it. The meeting's a go. Her piece of shit stepfather threatened her into also attending, so she's going to be my priority when we're there. I'll have your back, of course, but not before hers."

I decide to go with straight up honesty from the get-go and tell Sergei exactly where we stand. My loyalty to him hasn't diminished, but my loyalty to Mira is superseding any loyalty I've felt before, *ever*.

"I see," Sergei says after a moment. Tension raises the hairs on the back of my neck as I wait for his condemnation, his dismissal, or even worse, a threat to come after me. He could perceive me as being a liability now that I've fallen for a woman—many mob bosses forbid love altogether in their ranks. "Well, it sounds like you're becoming a man. I'm glad to hear it." The relief that blasts through me at his words is incomprehensible. I don't *require* Sergei's approval, but having it is a very nice benefit.

"Thank you," I say quietly. "I think I know what you meant when you said that Kira turned you into a man." Loving Mira is changing me for the better.

"Don't get sentimental on me now, Dorian. Save it for your woman." Sergei chuckles lowly. "Progress with the Serpents?"

"We're raiding their last stronghold tonight. It sounds like they might have a hand in trafficking rings—we'll get all the info we can on that."

"Good," Sergei says, his tone faintly tinged with approval. "I suppose I'll be seeing you in two weeks. Try not to get killed between now and then." He pauses for a long moment. "Does your woman love you back?"

I gaze at my bedroom door, not surprised that Sergei's already caught on to the depth of my feelings. "She cares for me, otherwise she wouldn't have reached out to Clyde or agreed to his condition. I don't know if she loves me."

"Give it time. You're obviously on the right track. Well done, Dorian." He hangs up without further chit chat. I head back into my bedroom, and my gaze instantly falls to Mira. She's pulled on the shirt that I discarded and is sitting cross-legged on the middle of the bed, chewing the end of a pen as she reads over her notes. Even dressed down, she looks beautiful—especially since she's just been freshly fucked. Her eyes are glazed from the three orgasms she got, and she practically glows in the sunlight filtering through the window.

I climb onto the bed and take a seat beside her, pulling my laptop from the bed stand and opening it, deciding to get a bit of work done before I split at 5 p.m. Mira offers me a lazy smile that I reciprocate, and the two of us fall into comfortable silence, each plugging away at our work for the day.

The compound where intel suggests that the remaining Serpents are hiding out is a warehouse in a shitty, largely abandoned part of the city. I can hear the low thump of bass pulsing from inside the building even before I enter.

Seamus and Connor are with me, all of us armed up to the gills in tactical gear. Bullet proof vests, multiple guns and knives, even night vision goggles hanging from our necks. We're prepared to go in and end these fuckers once and for all. I expect there'll be a brief torture session to extract the information we need from the Serpents still left alive, but other than that, this should be a simple op.

"Right, lads," Seamus says, pulling a gun out of his back pocket. "Let's make this nice and easy. Everyone dies except for the top dogs—we all know who they are. Odds are they'll be drinking in the back, so our first step is to kill everyone in front."

"No quarter asked, no quarter given," Connor mutters, nodding.

"Fuck asking for quarters; kill 'em all," Seamus replies with a grin. Without further preamble, he points his gun at the metal front door and blows off the lock.

After that, everything happens quickly. Connor slams his shoulder into the door, forcing it open with a loud creak, and we come face-to-face with about two dozen Serpents who are evidently indulging in a private stripper party.

The dim warehouse interior is illuminated by grimy overhead lights, their flickering glow casting long shadows across cold steel beams and piles of crates stacked haphazardly against the walls. Women sway and twirl on the laps of men, and in any spaces not occupied by sleek black duffle bags scattered across the stained concrete floor. A few poles are positioned under the harsh lights, where strippers perform their routines to the beat of music playing from portable speakers. The air is thick with cigarette smoke, along with the scents of stale sex and sheer desperation.

The presence of the strippers escalates our mission's complexity; we can't just open fire when we might accidentally hit one of the girls.

Seamus throws a grenade to the left side of the large warehouse, where there's a roundtable of Serpents guffawing over their drinks. A flash is followed by a deafening *boom* as the grenade explodes, sending a plume of smoke billowing upward. Blood sprays out from the explosion, painting streaks across the concrete floors and metal walls. The music abruptly cuts off, and every bastard in the warehouse scrambles for the nearest weapon.

Connor starts shooting before they can, using his semi-automatic rifle to take them out. Enemies start to drop like flies, and the cadence of the music is replaced with screams from the girls as they run to the walls, huddling up together.

I scan everyone who's in the compound, looking for the two men that we need to leave alive. I spot one of them standing at a makeshift metal bar near the back, looking like a deer caught in headlights.

Fucker doesn't even have a weapon. He really didn't expect us to find him.

Intel suggests that he's one of the leaders of the Serpent's ground-operation in this city, peddling drugs on the streets and demanding safety payments from local small businesses. Apparently, they also kidnap homeless girls and send them to a nearby city for another operation they have their hands in.

Time to take out the trash.

Connor, Seamus and I get to work, systematically killing every man, taking gunfire and returning it threefold.

Connor releases a grunt as a bullet grazes his arm, but he doesn't slow down or even pause to check the wound. He's a fucking machine with a single goal; destroy the enemy. His eyes are bright, eager, and filled with bloodlust.

Seamus, on the other hand, seems giddy—not because of bloodlust, but because he always sees these ops as good fun. He smiles and even *laughs* each time he gets a kill, taunting the Serpents every chance he gets.

It takes less than ten minutes to subdue the enemy. The girls are smart enough to stay out of the way, and the Serpents are too focused on us to use them for leverage. When the last visible body has dropped, Seamus sheaths his weapons and makes his way over to the girls, getting to work on calming them down.

Connor and I make for the bar. Halfway across the space, the leader pops out from behind the counter and open fires on us with a semi. If his aim weren't so shitty, I'd be in trouble—as is, I'm almost tempted to chuckle as I duck. Connor doesn't crouch alongside me—he takes aim with his own gun. A single shot from him hits the Serpent right between the eyebrows, and the pudgy man crumbles to the ground, dead.

"Fuck," I mutter, turning to glare at Connor. "We were supposed to take him alive."

Connor lifts a shoulder. "It was a reflex. We'll find his partner and interrogate him."

"Where?" I ask. "The other guy might've fled—he might not even be in the city anymore. This was the Serpent's last stronghold, now their ranks are wiped and most of the leadership is dead. All but one man, Arson, who might've abandoned the ship when he saw it was sinking. We might never see him again."

Connor shrugs again. "Then we never see him again. Good fucking riddance."

I release a long breath. "You aren't thinking, man. You really think Arson's going to let this go? No, he'll be back, and we'll have to live on high alert until we find him." I curse under my breath. "He might be the bridge between this local gang and the trafficking op—if he comes back, he could bring serious manpower. He could start going after *Greywood students*." Fuck, he could come after *Mira*.

"We'll take care of it when the time comes," Connor says, irritation slithering into his tone. "When did you become such a pussy? That girl is fucking you up in all sorts of ways."

"That *woman* is making me into a *man*, asshole," I snap. "One day, you're going to fall head over heels for someone—their happiness will be your happiness. Their pain will be your pain. Their success will make you feel like you're soaring the skies, and their failure will chip away at your heart."

"I don't have a heart," Connor deadpans. "At least, that's what I've been told multiple times, by many girls."

There's no sense in reasoning with him. Connor is too detached to hear anything he doesn't want to hear.

"This is why I'm moving out," I say. "I get that you have your issues. We all do. But not all of us let them rule our lives the way you do. Try actually forming an interpersonal relationship rather than collecting someone as your property; you might find it extremely rewarding."

When we get back to the house, Mira is waiting for me on the living room couch. She has my laptop open on her lap, and is squinting at something on the screen. Usually, anyone else touching my laptop would freak me out, but I gave her the passcode and told her to have at it earlier today. I don't have any sensitive information on it, but even if I did, I wouldn't mind her having access. After what she did for me with Clyde, I trust her completely.

"Hey, baby," I greet, shucking my vest. All the guns are already safely stowed away in the gun vault underneath our gardening shed, so I'm unarmed.

"Oh, thank god," she says, shutting the laptop and gazing at me with wide eyes. She rises from the couch and rushes at me like she's been launched from a rocket, wrapping her arms around my waist and burying her head in my chest.

I chuckle, wrapping my arms tightly around her and holding her close. "Were you worried about me?"

She nods into my chest. "Yes."

"Hallo, love," Seamus greets, striding up beside me. "Do I get the same reception?"

"Get fucked," I snap.

He smiles. "I intend to. I'm off for the night, chaps; try not to miss me too much."

In the back of my mind, I wonder if he's going to meet up with Valerie. He's been pretty hung up on her since we crashed girl's night, hasn't shown interest in anyone else since. He's even gone as far as to *chase* Valerie. He and Connor both thought I was being ridiculous for chasing Mira, but now, I think Seamus might be starting to see where I was coming from.

He heads up to his room, presumably to shower and prepare for whatever booty call he has set up for the night.

Mira steps back from me, running her hands up and down my arms, eyes searching my skin for wounds. "Were you hurt?"

"Nope. I'm just fine. Connor got a bit scraped up, but—"

I cut off when Mira's eyes widen, fixing on Connor. He's striding through the hall, staring at his phone. From his arm comes a steady dribble of blood that creates a puddle on the floor.

"You're leaking," I call out to him, jerking my chin at the mess. He stops and glances at his arm, brows furrowing.

"Damn." He resumes walking.

"Call the doc to take a look at that graze—"

"It's a scratch," he cuts me off dismissively. "It'll heal on its own."

"It's *not* a scratch," Mira says, surprising me. She does her best to avoid Connor and shies away from addressing him at the best of times. Seeing his blood drip everywhere must bring out her nurturing instincts.

Connor freezes again, slowly turning to look at her with a challenging expression. "You got something to say?"

"Yeah, dumbbell," she snarks. "Scratches don't leak like that. If you have a good first aid kit, I can probably stitch you up. Save you the doctor's visit and the subsequent bill." She gives me an apologetic glance, probably thinking back to the time when she refused to help me out.

I'm not mad about it anymore. I'm almost certain that if I was the one who got shot tonight, she'd be offering her services to me. In fact, this might help Connor stop viewing her as an adversary for my attention and loyalty. Maybe she can work her magic on him the same way she's worked it on Seamus and me.

Connor stares at her for a long time. "How do I know you won't fuck with the wound just to hurt me?"

She scoffs faintly. "Easily. You're not that important to me. Besides, it would hurt him," she jerks her head at me, "and that's something I will *never* do. Not intentionally."

My chest warms. I curl an arm around her waist, tucking her into my side. I'm going to reward the shit out of her for this later tonight.

"Fine. I'll get the first aid kit." Connor continues down the hall.

"Bring hydrogen peroxide and rubbing alcohol too," Mira calls out. He doesn't respond, but I'm sure he heard her.

Mira turns to me. "How did it go?"

My lips twist. "Not as well as it could've, but not bad. One of the guys we thought would be there wasn't, and he's a top-dog of the Serpents. We killed his partner prematurely, before we could get the information we need out of him."

Mira searches my eyes, her lips pressing together. "Let me guess. Connor killed him?"

It doesn't take brilliant intuition like hers to deduce that. Aside from being the coldest and most detached out of us, Connor's also a man who functions based on instincts, abandoning logic when shit hits the fan. That's how things end up getting skewed. The loss tonight isn't terrible, but it isn't good, either. Sergei won't be pissed, but he'll probably be disappointed.

"Yeah," I say after a beat. "Connor killed him. We'll figure out another way to get to his partner down the line, but we'll also be stepping up protection around here. Better security, close monitoring. Seamus will be setting up a bunch of techy shit here and at our apartment so we're safe once we move in."

Mira exhales a deep breath, nodding. "That's fair."

Connor strides back into the room, holding a duffle bag in his hands. He dumps it on the coffee table, then goes over to the bar, pouring himself a few fingers of whisky.

"I'm going to wash my hands before we start," Mira murmurs, kissing my jaw. "Be right back."

I turn to Connor when she disappears. "Be nice. This is a gesture of peace on her end."

Connor snorts. "If I were at war with her, she'd already be dead."

"Then stop treating her like an enemy or outsider," I press. "She's doing you a fucking favor. Ease up on it already. If you keep being a cold asshole to everyone around you, you'll eventually have no one left."

Mira walks back into the room before Connor can respond. He glowers at me but sits on the couch and strips off his shirt. I like that Mira doesn't ogle his body the way just about all girls do; she gives him a brief up and down, her gaze clinical and detached, before focusing on his arm. She rifles through the bag, pulling out several first aid kits and packs of gauze and bandages.

"The graze is superficial but still deep," she says. "I'm gonna clean it, sew it, and patch it. The bandage will be waterproof, so you can shower, but it'll need to be changed every three or so days."

"Fine," Connor mutters.

I seat myself in an armchair, watching as Mira gets to work. Her movements are calm and confident, her hands steady, as if she's done this before. A flash of the scars covering her ribs overtakes my mind, reminding me that she probably learned how to stitch people up on herself. The trauma she's endured and the woman she is because of it is extraordinary.

"Why do you think colonel is pronounced like kernel?" she wonders aloud. My lips quirk, while Connor narrows his eyes at her like she's insane. She blinks at him. "I mean, the prestigious title sounds like a corn kernel. It's weird."

Connor grunts. "No clue."

Mira nods sagely. "Yeah. The English language is strange." She starts on the stitches; he doesn't even wince at the needle piercing his flesh. "I've always wanted to learn new languages. Do you know any others?"

Connor stares at her again, appearing to try to make sense of her. "I know some German."

"Oh, can you teach me?"

"No."

"Why?"

"You talk too much."

She nods again. "Yeah, that's fair."

"Stop being a dick," I warn Connor.

He gives an aggrieved shrug. "What? It's fucking true. Who the hell asks questions like that from nowhere?"

"Guilty as charged," Mira says brightly. "At least I'm not a six-foot-plus walking dumbbell and can hold an actual conversation."

Surprisingly, Connor's lips quirk with the hint of a smile. "Fair enough."

Chapter Thirty-Five

Mira

"*Fuck...*" I awaken to the swear word leaving my lips, accompanied by a scorching, consuming heat between my thighs. The warmth comes from Dorian's fingers rubbing my pussy and circling my clit, getting me ready for him. It's the middle of the night; the moon is shining high in the sky, and the house is dead silent. "Dorian—"

"Shh. I just need to use this pussy, then you can go back to sleep."

His words should be humiliating, but instead they cause the heat between my thighs to burn all the brighter. I *love* it when he uses me to get himself off, though he's never a selfish lover. Even when he's borrowing my body for his own ends, he's still attentive to my needs. *Overly* attentive.

"Dorian, I've come so many times today already, I don't know if I can—"

"I don't care. Either safeword or take it." He doesn't stop his movements, as if he's already certain that I'll choose to take it.

He's right. I'm tired and this is pushing me, but not too far. I want to make him feel good too, to get him off, and I know that the reciprocation when we have sex is what gets him most excited. He doesn't get off *unless* I get off. *How did I get so lucky?*

"What time is it?" I mumble, back arching as he slides two fingers into me.

"Three."

"I have classes early tomorrow morning—"

"If you have the bandwidth to think about school right now, I'm clearly not doing my job." He positions himself between my thighs, then wraps a hand around my neck. "Look at me." His thumb rubs circles over my clit, making me gasp. I find his eyes even in the darkness of the room. The green of his irises glow, almost like his passion is enough to light them up. My toes curl as we watch each other, and he blinks slowly. "Come."

I'm helpless to do anything but obey. My body jerks, and I muffle my moan with my hands. I don't want to wake up anyone else, not when there's finally a fragile peace in this house.

"Good girl." Dorian flips me onto my hands and knees without giving me warning. His hand wraps around the back of my neck, pressing my upper body into the mattress. I turn my head sideways, loving the cool sheets against my face. I'm burning up with both my body heat and Dorian's, and I get the feeling that things will only get hotter from here.

I'm proven right when he starts to slide inside me, one thick inch at a time. He releases a low grunt, digging his nails into my hips. "Fucking *hell*, that's hot."

"You should open the window," I breathe. "It's too warm in here."

"Not what I was talking about." He gives my ass a light slap. "*This* is hot as fuck. You're hot as fuck. Jesus Christ, what did I do to deserve you?"

He's echoing my own thoughts, but I can't resist teasing him. "Chased me down in a forest, kidnapped me..."

He releases my neck, gathers both of my arms in his hands, and pins them at the small of my back. "You'll pay for that, baby."

He makes good on his threat, pumping into me with deep, hard strokes that make my eyes roll into the back of my head. I moan and whimper and try to wriggle my hands, but he only tightens his grip. He doesn't play with my clit like he usually does, but he doesn't need to. The feeling of him inside me, the force of his desire and passion, is enough to get me off.

I come with a cry that I muffle into the bedsheets, fingers grasping air and body shivering. Dorian lets out a long curse before also orgasming, buried so deep inside me I can't tell where he starts and I end. He releases my wrists, letting them fall limply to my sides. After laying down flat on the bed, he pulls me into him, arranging our bodies so they fit together like pieces of a puzzle.

"You're making me coffee in the morning," I say with a yawn. "And bringing it to me before I wake up."

"Can I fuck you first?" At my glare, Dorian chuckles. "Just kidding. Kinda." He drops a kiss on my forehead. "I like it when you're bossy. I'll make you as much coffee as you want *and* breakfast in bed, as long as I get to fuck you before school."

I let out a grumble that lacks any real rancor. I'm *very* sore, but I'm also addicted to the feeling of him inside me, so I won't complain.

"Deal."

The week passes without incident. I fall into a routine with Dorian; breakfast together, classes, then back to the House of Horrors. On

Thursday night, we officially get the keys to the apartment he rented, but decide to hold off on moving in for a couple weeks. I'm not quite as opposed to living in his house as I once was; not now that Connor seems to tolerate me.

Seamus disappears every night for a booty call, and I keep the growing suspicion that he's hooking up with Valerie to myself. On Friday, I have another girl's night; Seamus and Dorian once again crash it, while Connor bows out. The tension between Val and Seamus is palpable and electric, but they don't make any moves to act on it. Seamus spends long stretches of time just staring at Val, but she seems content to ignore him altogether.

On Sunday, the first day of November, we have a house meeting. Dorian, Seamus and I all take seats in the living room and talk strategy for the showdown that'll take place in my hometown. Dorian and I have domain over the couch, while Connor and Seamus take their positions on armchairs.

"It'll be tough," Seamus says, resting his chin on his hands. "It's not on our territory, which puts us at an instant disadvantage."

"We can overcome that with enough firepower," Dorian murmurs, wrapping his arm around my waist and pulling me onto his lap. I go willingly, relaxing against his chest. "We have training, discipline, and loyalty that doesn't just hinge on money."

"Sergei's bringing five men," Connor grunts. "That puts us at nine fighters."

"Ten with Mira," Seamus says, gazing at me. "You know how to handle your guns, love. If you're at the meet, we'll want you armed and armored, ready to attack or defend."

"Don't tell her what to do," Dorian snaps. He kisses the shell of my ear. "If you want, you can sit it out. Pretend to be sick. You don't have to do anything you don't want to, baby."

"I want to help," I say firmly. "I want Clyde and Carver dead."

"Never knew you were so bloodthirsty," Seamus says with a grin.

I raise my eyebrows, giving him a droll look. "I'm not a mean person, but I can be vengeful. Clyde and Carver are the reasons my mother is dead. They're the reasons I have scars that will never go away, on my skin and in my soul. If you don't think I want them dead, you're crazy. I'll pull the trigger without losing a moment's sleep."

Seamus whistles. "Well. With that sort of endorsement, you'll certainly be useful."

"Not if you're acting out of anger or vengeance," Connor says seriously, leaning forward and pinning me with a hard gaze. "If your approach is emotional, then it'll be volatile. If you're volatile, you become a liability. If you become a fucking liability, you can make mistakes that get us all killed—"

"Give me a little credit," I cut him off. "I know how to control my emotions. I think I've already proven that."

Connor examines me with drawn brows for several moments before giving a nod. "Fine. You can come."

"Thank you, oh benevolent overlord," I say drily. "I wasn't asking for your permission, jerk."

Seamus and Dorian chuckle; Connor shoots me a glare, but his gaze is devoid of any genuine rancor or anger.

"Sergei did say that he has a problem with sneaking sufficient firepower into the states," Dorian says. "We can only take so many weapons; we only *have* so many weapons, and getting each one into Pennsylvania means shelling out cash for copious bribes."

"There's gotta be a place we can raid near the town," Seamus says thoughtfully. "I'm sure there will be gun stores we can rob..."

"That won't be necessary," I interject. "I still have one friend in my hometown. He owns a shooting range." I swallow, feeling an odd mixture of sadness and affection swirl in my chest as I think of the one man who showed me kindness and care when nobody else did. Asher Calder. His love for my mother extended to me in her absence, and he took care of me as best as he could. I was at his range nearly every day after school, sometimes because I simply didn't want to go home, and he was kind to me. Gave me food, taught me to handle my guns, and gave me basic self-defense lessons.

"The bloke who taught you how to handle your weapons?" Seamus asks.

I nod, recalling the night when I had to tell these guys everything. It was under shitty circumstances, but I'm glad I don't have to rehash it all now—they already know the relevant details of my past. "His name's Asher. Asher Calder. If I ask him for help, he'll give it."

"How are you sure?" Connor challenges. "You haven't seen this person in years, I assume. Have you spoken with him? Kept in contact?"

I swallow. "I haven't, aside from phone calls on my birthday. I know he'll help because my mother was the love of his life, and he's wanted to kill the fuckers who led her to a horrible death for years. He just hasn't had the right opportunity yet. If I talk to him, he'll help." *I think.* No, I *know.* Asher had my back then, and he'll have my back now.

"Right, then the issue becomes evading detection while we get his help," Seamus says. "I assume that Carver will have eyes on us the second we step into town."

"The shooting range is about thirty minutes outside of town, well out of Carver's jurisdiction," I say. "It's a different county. If he even bothers to put people there, I don't think it'll be very many."

"Fine," Connor nods. "We go two days early, which means we leave Wednesday, and find a motel in driving distance to the range."

"I'll take care of getting the guns alongside Mira," Dorian says. "We can go visit her old friend and mentor together."

"I'll tag along," Seamus offers. "You're too hotheaded and protective of your girl; you might say the wrong thing. I'll be there to smooth things over if need be."

He makes a good point. My man can be a bit over the top when it comes to me; I can barely walk around campus with Dorian without risking him threatening any guy who looks at me twice. Asher has no interest in me romantically; I think he sees me as a daughter figure of sorts. He and my mom had a passionate affair a few years before I was born, and though things didn't work out for them then, I know they loved each other very much.

"I'll go with Seamus," I decide. Seamus is an expert in charming people.

"No," Dorian says immovably, tightening his hold on me. "You stay with me."

"Bad call," I say. "Asher's tetchy. He was a marine way back when. Recon Marine. He's sensitive to crowds, and if he feels like he's being ambushed, he won't be receptive. He's always had a soft spot for me, but..."

"Got it," Seamus says. "Vets are tetchy but very useful... if they're functional. Which I presume he is, considering he owns a shooting range. Alright, we leave here on Wednesday night. Meet with your contact on Thursday, and then rendezvous with Sergei Thursday night. The meeting between Sergei and Carver will be on Friday. We'll all be present for that, suited up and armed to the gills." Seamus nods. "Yeah, we'll manage just fine." He turns to me. "How many men does Carver command?"

I try to think back. Business was seldom discussed in front of me, but I became a very proficient eavesdropper during my time with

Clyde. "I heard three dozen mentioned once, but that was years ago. Things could have changed."

"I'll scope out the town after we meet with Asher," Seamus says, standing. "Try to get a sense of what we're up against before we report to Sergei." He clears his throat. "Right, lads. It's late; I'm turning in for the night. Everyone make sure you get time off school."

"I'll let my professors know I'm sick and do classes remotely this week," I say.

"Good call. The law probably won't come for us, but just in case, we ought to have alibis," Seamus says. "Night, all. Sleep tight. Prepare yourself for a great big bang at the end of the week."

He and Connor both depart, leaving just me and Dorian.

I sigh. "I don't know about you, but I need something sweet to combat the salty topics."

Dorian perks right up. "Late night baking session?"

I smile. "Nope—just reheating cupcakes from the other day and frosting them." I pat his hands. "Let me up and I'll feed you."

"The only sweet thing I want to eat right now is you," Dorian says teasingly.

I turn and kiss his jaw. "Wait until you taste the frosting."

Silving, Pennsylvania is a small town with a population of less than ten thousand people. Part of Aesop County, it's a scenic little place with lots of farmland on the outskirts, accompanied by many trailer parks. The town itself is made up of two- or three-story buildings in the center, and smaller houses surrounding them. There's only one main street, two grocery stores, and a handful of shops.

We don't stay in Silving; we stay in a city about an hour over, Creymont. It's a thirty-minute drive to Asher's gun range, and another thirty minutes to Silving.

We get into Creymont's airport late Wednesday night and check into a hotel under assumed names. I haven't slept well since the meeting on Sunday, too wound up with fear and anticipation, so I fall face-first onto the hotel bed I'm sharing with Dorian and pass out.

Thursday morning, we all have breakfast together at the hotel restaurant. Connor tells us that Sergei's in transit and looking forward to having access to weapons; Dorian tries to insist on accompanying Seamus and me to see Asher, but I adamantly refuse. Besides not wanting him to spook Asher, I also want to talk to Seamus about Valerie.

After a long kiss goodbye with Dorian, Seamus and I get into the car we rented for the trip. He insists on driving, of course, so I get to sit in the passenger seat.

"So," he says, pulling onto the freeway at my direction. "You and Dorian are getting serious."

"Seems that way," I agree lightly.

"It *is* that way," Seamus corrects. "He's falling for you. You're falling for him. I don't see the two of you splitting up—he won't let you go." He pauses, letting that sink in. "How are you feeling about that?"

"Taking things a day at a time," I reply. Truthfully, I don't want to leave Dorian. I don't like his lifestyle, but I trust him when he tells me he's going to step back from organized crime once he's graduated. He's committed to being on the above-board business side of things, and I'm okay with that.

"Hmm," Seamus hums. "Just do us all a favor, love, and don't try to leave him. It'll create a shitshow that I don't feel like witnessing or handling."

"We're not here to talk about my relationship," I say bluntly. My business with Dorian is between us—I don't need any interlopers.

"Oh?" Seamus queries. "Very well. It's a long drive, so what is it you want to speak about?"

"Valerie," I say bluntly. "The two of you are hooking up."

"Correct," Seamus says.

"You've been hooking up for a few weeks."

"Also correct."

"Valerie doesn't do relationships, and you don't seem the type, either."

"Are you worried I'll hurt her feelings?" Seamus asks with a faint smirk.

"No. I'm afraid she'll hurt yours. Val has a... complicated past," I say carefully. "She doesn't really connect with people easily. She only connected with me and Cara because we didn't give her much of a choice. I just want to make sure you're managing your expectations and not expecting more than a short-term physical fling with her."

Seamus smiles, but a muscle jumps in his jaw and his shoulders tense, giving away that he's not quite as easy going as he'd like me to believe. "Don't worry about me, love. I have no expectations beyond a few good fucks."

I watch him for a few moments. "As long as it stays that way, everything will be fine."

Chapter Thirty-Six

The gun range Asher owns is in a repurposed factory. Long and triangular, the building rises two stories high, with a hidden basement known only to a select few. Inside, the brightly illuminated lobby features a granite counter standing before gleaming display cases filled with an array of firearms. More guns hang on the walls behind the front counter, their sleek exteriors glimmering under the bright, fluorescent light of the room. The faint scent of gunpowder lingers in the air, a subtle reminder of the building's purpose, while the industrial past of the space is hinted at by exposed beams and weathered brick walls.

Standing at the counter is a young man who looks to be high school age. He's reading a *porn* magazine and loudly chewing gum. He looks up when Seamus and I walk in, quickly folding and putting away his playboy.

"You two have reservations?" he asks, powering on an ancient-looking computer.

"Nope, we're walk-ins. I'm actually here to see Asher, the boss."

The boy frowns. "You know Asher?"

It's a fair question—Asher is a bit of an introvert. He doesn't have many friends, though he *does* have endless connections.

"Yep. Tell him Mira Greene's here, please."

The boy smacks his gum. "Your funeral." He disappears up a staircase in the corner of the room, one leading to Asher's office and personal apartment on the second floor.

"Charming place," Seamus drawls. "Not many people, it would seem."

"It's a weekday morning," I point out. "Not a lot of people choose this time to visit the range. It crowds up on weeknights and weekends, though."

Two sets of footsteps sound from the staircase. The boy working the counter comes down first, closely followed by Asher.

Asher's dressed in army-green pants and a black shirt. His hair has greyed since the last time I saw him, now a salt-and-pepper color. He has a strong, stubborn jaw, piercing grey eyes overcast by bushy eyebrows, and a permanently severe expression. Tattoo sleeves on his muscular arms show off several symbols with personal meaning, though the largest and most eye-catching is a stamp representing his time as a Recon Marine.

Asher stops on the bottom step, eyes narrowing as he gazes at me. There's affection in his steely orbs, along with a great deal of worry.

"Mira," he says, exhaling a long breath. He shakes his head, as if in disbelief, and swiftly crosses the room to fold me into a warm, comforting embrace. He's a big guy, and he's stayed in excellent shape after his time serving. To most other people, I figure he looks intimidating; huge biceps, thighs like tree trunks, an eternally angry resting face. To me, though, he represents the calm in the storm. In another life, my mom might've ended up with him, and none of the bad shit that happened to me would've come to pass.

"Asher," I respond, giving him a squeeze. After a long moment, I step back, looking him over. "It's good to see you."

"The feeling's mutual, though I have to wonder what the fuck you're doing back in this shit hole." He folds his arms over his chest. "You got out. We agreed you'd stay out, sweetheart."

Asher's the one who bought me the plane ticket to Greywood. I didn't have the money, and though I tried to refuse, he insisted. He said it was a gift with the condition that I make something of myself and stay the hell out of town.

"I'm not back permanently," I assure him. "Not even for long."

Seamus clears his throat, prompting Asher to turn a dark, threatening stare on him. I take a few steps back to stand next to Seamus. "Asher, this is my friend, Seamus." I swallow. "Is there somewhere we can speak in private?"

Asher glances at Counter Boy. "Go take your lunch break."

Counter Boy pops his gum again. "It's ten in the morning."

"Then you're off for the day," Asher growls. "Go home and do some fuckin' homework, kid. Or go to school for once. Ditching class may seem cool now, but it'll make your life a lot more difficult than it should be."

Counter Boy doesn't need to be told twice. He picks up a backpack from behind the counter and strolls out, closing the front door behind him.

"How serious is this talk gonna be?" Asher asks me.

I glance at Seamus. "Pretty serious, and extremely private. Everything that's said here needs to stay here."

Asher gazes at Seamus for several moments, trying to get a read on him. Seamus folds his hands into his pockets and adopts a neutral expression, meeting Asher's stare unflinchingly.

"You trust this posh boy?"

I nod. "Oddly enough, I do."

"Fine," Asher says. "Let's go upstairs. You kids want coffee?"

"Please," I say, following him up the staircase. We emerge into a hallway; he leads us to the first door on the left, which is a small sitting room connected to a kitchen. Asher disappears to make the coffee while Seamus and I take seats on a faded grey sofa in front of a coffee table.

"Evidently, you've been acquainted with quite a few dangerous men in your life," Seamus says thoughtfully. He nods at the kitchen. "That one puts me to shame."

"You have no idea," I say grimly. Asher is brilliant, disciplined, and *very* good at killing people. He'd have killed Clyde and Carver years ago if he weren't severely outnumbered. Unlike many vets I've crossed paths with, Asher's emotions do not outweigh his common sense.

Asher stalks back into the room, holding a tray with a French press, several mugs, and a cup of creamer. He sets the tray on the coffee table, drags an armchair across from us, and takes a seat.

"What's this about?" he asks.

"First I need your word that you take everything said here to the grave," I request.

He nods. "You know I'd never betray you. You have my word of honor on your mother's memory. Now talk, and kindly explain pretty-boy's presence. You here to get my blessing or something?"

I spend about half an hour filling Asher in on my situation. He takes everything I say in stride; doesn't flinch when I gloss over my time as Dorian's guest and the danger surrounding him. The only time he shows any outward reaction is when I mention that Dorian works for Sergei Novikov. Then, he has plenty to say.

"Sergei *fucking* Novikov?" he repeats, disbelieving. He looks to Seamus. "The fuck does the Russian Bratva boss want with some American college students?"

"He's expanding business," Seamus responds smoothly. "He'd like a few footholds in America. My legion caught his interest when he was looking into some problems at Greywood for an old acquaintance of his."

"Owning Russia isn't enough? He needs to come here?"

"Of course Russia isn't enough—he also owns Eurasia," Seamus says with a charming grin. In the blink of an eye, his expression turns serious. "He has contacts and teams in every corner of this world. Of course he'd want to assemble a trustworthy force in the United States, as well. Are you truly surprised?"

"No," Asher mutters, shaking his head. "Everything I've heard about the man suggests that he's a power-hungry tyrant. Naturally, he wants to expand the empire he's built. My question is what does that mean for the safety of American citizens?"

"The answer is quite simple: they'll be safer." When Asher gives Seamus an incredulous look, Seamus goes on. "My boss doesn't condone some of the most harmful illegal activities going on in the underbelly of this country. Do you have any idea how many trafficking rings there are in America?"

Asher grunts. "A lot."

"Quite right, and as Sergei moves forces here, he aims to dismantle every single operation—one by one. He will not accept the skin-trade in any of his territories. Carver is a partner to a rather large trafficking ring, so naturally, Sergei will use this opportunity to eliminate him and destroy his operation."

Asher looks at me with a sigh. "You just *had* to get caught up with gangsters, didn't you?"

The faint note of worry and condemnation in his tone makes me practically shrivel beneath his gaze. His scrutiny is well-deserved, but it's not like I had much of a choice. I wasn't *asked* if I wanted to be with Dorian. I've settled and I'm finding that I'm quite happy with him, that I care for him deeply, but this lifestyle and these connections weren't my choice.

"We aren't gangsters," Seamus says, his voice hard. "I'm part of an elite, small legion with stellar men who I'd trust with my life. Mira was pulled into it because she was in the wrong place at the wrong time, but she's now dating the most exceptional man in our legion."

"Your legion consists of three people, yes?" Asher says, challenge in his gaze. "That doesn't sound like a legion to me, it sounds like a gathering of boys playing at being men. With a boss who's giving them far too much fucking power."

"My legion might be small, but it's certainly not made up of boys," Seamus says, quiet fury in his voice. "It's comprised of men who will die for each other, who have bled for each other, and who are committed to protecting innocents. That's how we banded together in the first place. Now, instead of shaming Mira for something she can't control and attacking me for my decisions, why don't you tell us whether or not you're willing to help. If you're not, I think we're done here."

Asher looks at me again. "Tell me the truth, sweetheart. Are you with your man of your own volition, or do you need a rescue? Don't fear pretty boy over there—I can take care of him with both eyes shut."

"I'm here of my own free will," I say immediately.

Things might have *started* without my consent, but now, I don't *want* to leave Dorian. I don't think I'll ever want to leave him. "Carver's late wife threatened to put me and Mom to work in a strip club—which was probably code for trafficking. Carver always looked at me weird, and Clyde nearly killed me or got me killed more times than I can count." I gaze deep into Asher's eyes, letting him see the truth of my words. "Help me get out from under Clyde and Carver's thumbs. I wouldn't be here if you couldn't trust my legion."

"*Your* legion?" Asher repeats, eyebrows raising. "Have you been indoctrinated?"

"I'm in love with one of its members," I say, only to freeze when Seamus gives me a wide-eyed look. I part my lips to backpedal, but can't get any negative words out, because they'd be a lie. Somewhere during the insanity of the last weeks, as Dorian's kept me captive and shoved me into his life, only to bare his soul to me, I truly have fallen for him. I didn't intend to—I was committed not to.

But, if I had the chance to go back and *not* stumble on Dorian in the woods, I don't think I'd take it. I'm glad I met him. He centers me in a way nobody else ever has. He invigorates me, makes me feel alive. He takes care of me, genuinely cares *for* me, and puts all his focus on me. How could I *not* fall for him?

I know it's too soon. I know that I shouldn't feel this way yet or be so certain of my emotions, but I am. I don't care about the timeline or the way we met; all I care about is that I have Dorian now, and I'm not letting him go.

I clear my throat. "Considering that, I'd say I'm part of it just by association."

"And you would be correct," Seamus says, giving me an approving nod.

Asher sighs. "I won't pretend to know your own mind better than you do, but I want to meet this boy of yours. And the other one, too." He frowns. "Why didn't you bring your man with you? Why take pretty boy?"

"We had a few things to talk about, and Dorian is very... protective. He has more emotions than sense when it comes to me. I didn't want the two of you to end up at each other's throats."

Asher folds his arms over his chest. "What is it exactly that you need? How many weapons are we talking? Guns? Rifles? Semis? AR's? Make? Ammo?"

"As many as you can spare," Seamus says. "We can work with any type of weapon."

"I can spare a lot, boy," Asher says. "Call in your... *legion*, and we'll talk."

Dorian and Connor arrive within half an hour, and we greet them in the lobby.

Connor's quiet, as usual, casing the place with sharp eyes while Dorian makes a beeline for me and wraps his arms around my waist, planting a kiss on my lips.

"You should've let me come from the get-go," he says. "Then we wouldn't have rented an extra car."

I scoff. "You just got us an apartment—I'm sure you can afford the expense of a rental. Besides, I needed to prep Asher."

I take a step back, folding my hand into Dorian's, and turn to face Asher. "Asher, this is Dorian. My boyfriend."

Dorian perks up at my side, casting me a glance of surprise. I haven't called him my boyfriend yet, even though he's been insisting that we're official for a while. He'll get a real punch in the gut when I work up the nerve to tell him I love him.

"I can see why you chose him," Asher says drily. "He's not bad to look at." He steps forward, looking Dorian up and down. After a moment, he offers Dorian his hand. "Asher. You got any brains in that good-looking head of yours?"

"One or two brain cells for sure," Dorian responds, taking Asher's hand and giving it a shake. "My woman says you're the man to talk to for firepower."

"Your woman, huh?" Asher repeats, glancing at me. "She's right on that account. First, why don't you and I have a nice little chat?"

"Asher," I say warningly. He's always been protective of me, so I'm sure that his *chat* with Dorian will involve threats of dismemberment should any harm—physical or emotional—befall me.

Asher gives me a deceptively innocent look. "What? I just want to get to know him."

"More like *threaten* him," I say flatly. "Save that shit for later; we have things to do now. *Please.*"

"Fine," Asher sighs. He looks at Dorian, eyes hardening. "I'll make this quick, then. Hurt her and you're dead. Let her get hurt and you're dead. If you want to be her man, then your job is to be her protector, defender, and the person who worships the ground she fuckin' walks on. If I hear that you're not keeping her happy, that you're not prioritizing her needs above your own, you're also dead." He tilts his head to the side. "Clear on all that?"

"Perfectly," Dorian says. "I'll take care of her. I already worship the ground she walks on, and I'll keep doing so. You will never need to worry about her safety or care—not for a moment. I've got her now." Dorian appraises Asher, his brows drawing together. "Who is she to you?"

Asher gazes at me for several beats, his lips thinned. Emotions flash in his eyes, and his energy crackles with something meaningful, as if he wants to say something but is holding himself back. We lock eyes for several moments, and something tugs at my gut. Questions begin to swirl in my mind.

Asher had my back when no one else did. He bought me things when Clyde wouldn't, took care of me when my own stepfather ignored and abused me. Got me clothes when I grew out of mine. New shoes when I wore holes through old ones. Backpacks at the top of every school year so I wouldn't have to carry all my supplies by hand.

In the past, I always assumed that Asher looked out for me because he loved my mother and lost her. I wasn't in a mindset to look into our relationship too deeply; I was too desperate for survival. But now that I really think about it, I believe there's more to the matter. He went above and beyond for me repeatedly—treated me like a relative.

I slowly tilt my head to the side as I stare at him—*really* stare at him. His eyes are grey; an endless, almost translucent grey that reminds me of *my* eyes when I look in the mirror. My thoughts start racing with possibilities.

I knew Mom dated Asher when she was younger, a few years before my birth. *Maybe even up to nine months before I was born.* It couldn't be... but it could be...

The possibility that I might be staring at my biological father smacks me square in the esophagus, nearly robbing me of breath. The idea itself seems ridiculously far-fetched—if Asher's my father, why wouldn't he tell me? Why *didn't* he tell me? Why didn't he raise me? *Why would he abandon me?*

I didn't even know about him until *after* Mom married Clyde. But once Asher showed up, *he showed up.*

Clyde told him in no uncertain terms that he'd kill my mom if Asher kept hanging around us, so he backed off. Mom got really depressed when that happened, and not long after, she was killed. Asher reached out to me when Clyde wasn't around, telling me that if I ever needed anything, I should go to him.

He was in the hospital when I woke up from surgery on my leg. I never found out for sure, but I'm reasonably certain he *paid the bill* for my surgery. Clyde never mentioned any payments, but if my stepfather had dropped thousands of dollars on me, I never would've heard the end of it.

"Asher," I say slowly, "is there something I should know?"

It's the wrong time to have this discussion. I'm a few hours out from meeting with a legendary bratva boss, and the legion is here. We need to get our weapons and our shit together. I don't want to have it out right now, but I can't help myself. I'm seeing things I was too close to see before, and now I have to know.

"Yeah," Asher says quietly. "I think you *do* already know, sweetheart."

I swallow hard. His lack of denial is enough to tell me the truth. "Why didn't you say anything?"

He shrugs, looking away. Connor and Seamus busy themselves perusing the selection of guns, while Dorian stays right by my side, squeezing my hand.

"Because your mother and I split for a good reason."

"That reason being?"

He sighs. "My drug habit. After I left the Marines, shit got difficult. I didn't know who I was or what to do. I was traumatized and did not know how to cope with my PTSD. Your mom got pregnant, and I was hooked on shit nobody should be hooked on, so she left. By the time I pulled my head out of my ass and was ready to show up, she'd already remarried. Clyde would've sooner killed her than let her go, so that was that."

My lips twist. A million emotions swarm through me like a buzzing, angry nest of wasps, so quick and jumbled that I can't make a single one out. Knowing this years ago would've been helpful. Knowing that I *truly* wasn't alone... it would've given me the strength to leave sooner. It's unreasonable, but I can't help but feel like Asher literally left me for the wolves.

He seems to read my mind, because he says, "When I threatened to go to court for custody after your mother's death, Clyde said he'd kill you before giving you away. I believed him, so I stayed on the sidelines. But I was always watching. I had your back." His head lowers. "I couldn't have the spotlight, so I did what I could from the shadows. I got you out of here, which was the best gift I could give you."

"You should've told me," I admonish faintly, feeling my eyes sting with tears. "You really should've told me, Asher."

"I know. But doing so would've put you in danger, which I couldn't bear. I'm sorry."

"Touching as this moment is, we've got shit to do," Connor says drily. "You gonna help or not?"

"Of course I will." Asher stares right at me as he says the words. "I'll always help you when you need it."

I force down the emotions bubbling in my throat. It's not the time or place. We can unpack this when there aren't trafficking rings to be dismantled and people to be killed. "Right, then. Let's get to it."

Chapter Thirty-Seven

Asher takes us down to the basement, where he has an almost unimaginable arsenal of weapons stockpiled in a vault. The vault itself, hidden behind a nondescript bookshelf, is made of cold, unyielding steel. Its interior is a chaotic array of lethal tools. Steel shelves lined with sleek rifles and handguns. Blades of every size and shape glint menacingly from their mounts, while crates of explosives sit ominously against the walls. It looks as though Asher is entangled in his own shadowy dealings—or perhaps preparing to single handedly fight World War III.

"Cozy," Seamus remarks. "Any chance you can explain why you've got so many weapons, mate?"

"Call me mate again and find out what it's like to live without precious limbs," Asher says flatly. "As for the weapons... well. Once a Marine, always a Marine."

"Surprised you don't have a section for crayons," Seamus quips with a sly grin.

Asher glowers at him but doesn't respond.

"What if we had Sergei meet us here?" I suggest. "He could have his pick." I look at Asher. "If you're okay with it."

Asher shrugs. "I'm not against currying favor with Sergei Novikov. Especially when he means to *finally* end the people who got away with hurting you." His jaw tightens. "I should've done that a long time ago."

"You couldn't do it alone," I say. "You were outnumbered three dozen to one."

"I've fought worse odds and lived," Asher tells me, a note of sorrow in his tone. There's turmoil swimming in his eyes, accompanied by a wealth of regret. I release Dorian and wrap my arms around Asher, hugging him again. That should've been another giveaway in my youth; I was never big on hugs or anything touchy-feely, but I always enjoyed the warmth and strength of Asher's embrace. If I'd paid attention, I would've seen the signs everywhere.

"Thank you for having my back and doing what you could," I murmur. "I'm angry that I didn't know sooner, but glad I know now."

I don't know what this means for the future—I have no clue how my relationship with Asher will change or evolve, *if* it will. But my gut tells me that he's going to start showing up a lot more, and I am more than okay with that.

Asher gives me a strong squeeze. "I'll always watch your six, kid. Especially when you choose to shack up with danger."

"At least it's a good kind of danger."

"I'm starting to see that." Asher steps back, and I notice a glimmer of moisture in his eyes. He quickly blinks it away; his face hardens. "Right. Tell Novikov I'm welcoming a rendezvous here. I'll close down shop and cancel all appointments for the next few days so we aren't disturbed. What time's the big boss coming to town?"

"Late," Dorian responds. "Eight or nine, maybe ten."

Asher nods. "Fine."

"I'll be leaving to case Silving soon and get a headcount of how many men we'll be up against," Seamus informs.

"First, I want to see you shoot," Asher says. "I'm not loaning out my guns to little boys who don't know how to handle their weapons. Show me that you can." He jerks his head at the vault walls. "Each of you pick three—handgun, AR, and semi. Sniper rifle, if you want. Let's take 'em up to the range, and you can show me your skills."

Connor frowns at Asher. "Us three? You're not going to make your daughter shoot, as well? I'd have assumed you'd prioritize ensuring *she* knows how to handle her weapons."

Hearing Connor refer to me as Asher's daughter is a gut-punch, but it also feels fundamentally right. I *am* Asher's daughter. I *do* have a father, and he's a good man despite a complex past. *I'm not alone.* I never have been, even when I felt like it.

Asher rumbles out a scornful laugh. "She can outshoot you three in her sleep."

Connor raises his eyebrows doubtfully, flicking me a dubious glance up and down. "She's alright, from the little I've seen."

"Then you haven't seen much. Sweetheart," Asher says with a nod to me, "Why don't you pick out some guns, as well."

He doesn't need to tell me twice. I *want* to show off to the legion and prove myself worthy. I also want to make Connor shit himself with surprise. I select a Glock, M16, and C15.

The shooting range upstairs is pretty typical. There are twelve aisles, each about 200 yards. The targets hang from adjustable automated pulley systems. Connor, Seamus, and Dorian all shoot first, showing off a pretty impressive skillset. Seamus is the best shooter out of them, but they're all *very* good. There are bullseye's all around, though only Seamus manages to fire off all his rounds dead center.

Connor turns to me with a condescending smirk after emptying his AR cartridge. "Your turn, greenie."

Time to show off what Asher taught me when I was a teenager. I'm a bit out of practice, but Asher was always a brilliant and extremely strict teacher. He'd have me take apart and rebuild weapons until I could do it in under a minute, and made me practice shooting until my hands blistered.

My selected guns all rest over a towel on a steel table. I pick up the Glock first, empty the chamber, unload the gun, and take it apart to examine it, just like Asher taught me. My movements are swift, precise, and careful as I put it back together and reload it.

When I look up, Connor's squinting at me with confusion, Seamus is watching me with interest, and Dorian is smiling at me with obvious pride. I feel a warm glow bathe my chest. *These legionaries aren't going to know what hit them.*

"Target distance?" Asher asks.

"You choose." No matter how far it is, I know I'll hit it exactly how I want. Asher taught me very well, and shooting a gun is like riding a bike—it's hard to forget the basics. After a while, everything just becomes instinct.

Asher sets the target to 100 yards. Maybe he's worried that I've gotten rusty, and I'm all too happy to show him that I haven't. His lessons were my lifeline at a time. I remember the look of anguish he'd adopt every time I had to go home to Clyde—he looked like he was in genuine pain. I'd attributed that to his remaining love for my mother, but maybe he loved me, as well.

All the men part as I step up to the window facing the range. I train my eyes on the target.

"Just because you can disassemble and reassemble a gun doesn't mean you can shoot," Connor mutters. "It's not—"

He cuts off as I start firing. The target is in the shape of a man, so I hit all the relevant points. From the fifteen bullets in the magazine, five go into his head, creating a burning hole in the center. Five more are shot at vital organs in his torso. The remaining five go into his crotch. Seamus winces.

When I'm done, I set the gun down and turn to Connor. "You were saying?"

His frown deepens. "The target was close."

Without asking if I'm ready, Asher moves the target back to two hundred yards. I pick up the M16, check it for any faults, and get to work. The same result ensues; I hit every bullet in the designated bullseye.

The C15 is where I really shine—so much so that I decide to challenge myself by hitting the targets in neighboring lanes.

At the end of it, Connor's staring at me with narrowed eyes and his arms crossed over his chest. Seamus looks at once repulsed and intrigued, as though he can't look away even though he wants to. Dorian watches me with a subtle smirk on his lips, his hands folded into his pockets. Once I set down my weapon, he comes right over to me, wrapping his arms around me and planting a soft kiss on my lips. "You never told me you were *that* good," he murmurs.

"You never asked," I retort.

He runs his bottom thumb over my lip. "Well, then, I suppose I'll need to find a way to extract all your secrets from you."

I smile. "For that, my friend, you'll just have to wait patiently."

"Friend?" Dorian growls.

"Lover," I correct. "Better?"

"Alright, fuckbirds, that's enough—you're too sickening to look at," Seamus says. He turns to Asher. "I'm off to Silving to case the place. Any hot spots I should look for?"

Asher promptly lists off several locations—trailer parks, diners, and of course, the infamous town brewery.

"I'll be back in time for the rendezvous."

"Sergei's agreed to the change in location, on the condition that this place is safe from prying eyes, ears, and enemies. His men will thoroughly sweep the premise," Connor says,

"The walls and windows are bulletproof, the doors are thick enough to be vaults, and anyone who tries to break in will find themselves in for some nasty surprises," Asher grunts. "The police know better than to annoy me—I supply them with most of their weapons. I promise you it's safe."

Dorian insists on taking me out to lunch—I agree only when Asher retreats into his office, wanting to get through his work for the day.

We settle at a local spot—Pixiedust Diner. The place has a retro 50's vibe going on, with checkered floors, waitresses wearing short red dresses featuring flared skirts and aprons, and a jukebox in the corner. Dorian and I take a booth along the left wall, which is decorated with a mixture of tasteful graffiti and colorful prints.

"What's good here?" he asks, flipping through the menu.

Asher used to bring me here when I was younger, when I'd take the bus and walk to his shop just to get away from Clyde. I lied to Clyde and told him I was going to some after-school activity, and the bastard never cared enough to double check. I'm not sure if the food here is actually as delicious as I remember, or if I was so starved that it tasted amazing to my adolescent self.

"The milkshakes are legendary—I highly recommend Oreo. And the burgers are creative and delicious. Ohh, they also have seasonal truffle fries—" I cut off with a sigh. "I'm going to get fat. I want the entire menu."

"You won't get fat, and even if you did put on weight, you'd still be the most beautiful girl I've ever met," Dorian murmurs offhandedly. He's gazing at his menu, so his words aren't planned or carefully structured. He genuinely means what he says, and it makes my cheeks heat. "Get the entire menu if you want—then we can take the leftovers to feed Connor and Seamus." He shuts his menu, looking up at me. "Order for me. I trust your judgement."

A young, blonde waitress walks up to our table, deliberately fussing with her dress, pushing out her breasts and trying to catch Dorian's eye. He gives her a single, uninterested glance before returning his attention to me.

The blonde clears her throat. "What can I get y'all today?"

"Two Pixie Special Burgers, two Oreo milkshakes, and the truffle fries to share, please," I say.

The waitress glances at Dorian. "Can I get you anything else?"

"Nope." He pops the p, not bothering to look at her. "I trust my woman."

Her brows furrow with dejection, but she scribbles our orders on a notepad and walks away. "Hopefully I'll prove worthy of that trust," I say, my words half-teasing.

"You already have," Dorian replies seriously. "Sergei's requested to meet you tonight, before the big meeting tomorrow. He wants to get a read on you. Don't be nervous, but do be clever. He won't hurt you, he doesn't go after women or children, but it's important he doesn't see you as a threat to our legion."

I tilt my head to the side. "I still don't understand why Sergei works with you three, sponsors you, whatever. Surely there are more established people he wants to team up with—not just a few vigilante college students."

Dorian shrugs. "He's taking a slightly altruistic but mostly strategic approach. The entire world sees him as a threat, so most people would be reluctant to join his operation. Only the bad apples would want to be part of his empire. My legionaries are young, ambitious, and extremely good at what we do. By getting us to join him now, he's guaranteeing that he'll have a hand in our future plans, and we have a lot of future plans. I've always been clear that I'm aiming to be above-board after school, but Connor and Seamus are looking to start a very substantial, very large operation that spans the entire East Coast. Sergei will have a direct link to them, and they'll owe him their loyalty—as will I. It's a smart move."

"He must really believe in you."

Dorian glances away. "Yeah. He's one of the only people who ever has."

I reach across the table, taking one of his hands in mine. "I believe in you."

His eyes brighten as he locks gazes with me. "Yeah?"

I nod. "Definitely."

He grins. "Good. Keep up with that attitude, and you will be *thoroughly* rewarded." He interlinks our fingers. "Watching you shoot today was hot. I hope you know, I'm going to fuck your brains out at the hotel."

I smile back at him. "Can't wait."

We stay at the diner for over two hours, killing time talking. Dorian loves the food, and orders an extra milkshake to go—I also get a burger and additional milkshake to bring to Asher.

Seamus is already at the range when we get back. "Thirty men," he says without preamble when we walk into the lobby. He's seated on the counter, legs dangling over a glass display case. With his laptop open on his lap, he looks at home and at ease, as if he does work from a gun range all the time.

"That'll be about three for each of us," Dorian says with a nod. "I call dibs on Clyde. He's my kill."

I don't protest. I want Clyde dead, but I don't necessarily want to be the one to kill him. I already have enough blood on my hands; I'd prefer to avoid racking up a higher body count.

"Sergei's early," Connor says, walking into the room. "He just messaged that he's touched down. He'll be here in an hour."

I find Asher upstairs and deliver his burger and shake. He smiles at me gratefully, taking his food from the paper bag and setting it up on the coffee table. I idle awkwardly in the doorway to the sitting room, a thousand questions settled on the tip of my tongue.

He must sense my wish to talk, because he gestures to the chair opposite to him. "Go on, sweetheart. I'll let you have some of my fries."

I pat my belly. "I already ate my fill and then some, but thank you." I take the seat across from him. "And... thank you for all the times you took me to the diner. And for helping out. You didn't have to—"

"I did," Asher interrupts. "You're my blood. I should've taken you from Clyde when your mother passed."

"Why didn't you?" I ask quietly. My life would've been drastically different if I'd lived with Asher instead of Clyde. I would have a lot less trauma, but I'd also have less life experience and slower instincts.

"Because he threatened to kill you, and I couldn't find a foolproof way to keep you safe," Asher replies. "I'd already let you down in so many ways, I couldn't live with myself if you died."

"What about earlier?" I ask. "Surely you weren't hooked on drugs my entire childhood." I wince at the words as they leave my lips. I don't mean to shame Asher for his old habit—I can't imagine what he had to go through after his honorable discharge.

"I wasn't a good person for several years. There's a reason your mom broke up with me," Asher says. "I got clean after a few years, but even then, I was directionless. Lost. Unfit to be a father. By the time I got my shit together, it was too late."

"I don't mean to condemn you," I murmur.

"I know. Even if you did, I wouldn't blame you. I didn't take responsibility for you when I should've; I failed you in more ways than I could count."

"I should've realized when I started coming around here," I say, gazing around the living room. "You were always unusually kind to me."

"I did the bare minimum."

"You did a lot more than that," I disagree, shaking my head. "You had my back when no one else did. I never heard about a hospital bill for my leg. I never went hungry when I was here. You taught me skills that saved my life more than once, then sent me off to find a better life. You did everything you could, and for that, I'll be forever grateful."

Asher blinks a few times, a sheen overcoming his grey eyes. Eyes that I inherited.

"I'd like to get to know you more, but I understand if you want to keep your distance," I offer.

He smiles. "I'd like that too, sweetheart. Now, tell me about that school of yours while I gorge myself on carbs."

Chapter Thirty-Eight

Asher finishes his meal just in time for Sergei to show up with a goddamn *entourage*. I watch through the window of the lobby as three black SUV's pull into the parking lot. Dorian stands right beside me, with Seamus and Connor next to him, forming a perfect straight line. Their shoulders are squared, chests puffed out. They look like soldiers awaiting orders, which I suppose they are.

A bell over the front door rings as a goddamn *beast* of a man opens the door, holding it wide. In steps another, slightly leaner man, who's no less imposing. Danger swirls around him like a shroud, suffocating his energy with dark fumes. His expression is blank. His black hair, slicked back from his face; his teal eyes, sharp and watchful. He carries himself with the confidence of a conqueror and quiet calm of an apex predator. Even though I'm reasonably sure he won't hurt me, I can't help but feel disconcerted at his presence.

"Gentlemen," he greets the legionaries. His eyes fix on me, and the hairs on the back of my neck stand on end. "And you must be Mira. I've heard a great deal about you."

I glance at Dorian instinctively. He meets my eyes and gives me a slight nod, silently telling me to be at ease.

"I guess you have me at a disadvantage, then. All I've heard about you is that you own at least half the world."

Sergei shrugs. "I'm an ambitious man." He walks forward, and five beastly men file in behind him, standing in front of the door and windows. Sergei stops two feet away from me and extends his hand. "It's a pleasure to meet you."

I swallow and step forward, taking his hand and giving it a firm shake. "Same to you."

"Thank you for arranging our rendezvous here."

"That's entirely thanks to Asher." I nod at the man in question, who's standing at the bottom of the staircase, arms crossed over his chest. Sergei appraises him with a searching gaze, then also walks over to him and makes introductions. He greets his legion with familiarity and even a hint of fondness.

"Right, then. Shall we find somewhere private to talk?"

Asher motions to the staircase. "Follow me."

He takes us straight to the vault, where Sergei and his men take their time looking at the available weapons.

"I'll compensate you for our use of them," Sergei tells Asher. "Thank you for your help."

"I only want one form of compensation," Asher says seriously. "Allow me to join your mission. I want to kill as many of the wannabee gangster fuckers as I can, but *especially* Clyde. Leave him to me."

Dorian opens his mouth to protest; I elbow him hard in the ribs. Clyde got the love of Asher's life killed and severely abused his daughter. Aside from me, he's the person who most deserves revenge.

"Igor?" Sergei prompts, glancing at the beastly man who opened the door for him.

Igor shrugs. "He's an ex-marine. Spec ops, by the looks of it. He'll be useful."

"Very well. Cross me and die screaming, help me and you'll be rewarded handsomely," Sergei tells Asher. "Now, gentlemen, I'm quite tired and my wife is waiting for my call. Why don't we get our plans and contingencies settled, and then head to our respective hotels for the night?"

We talk with Sergei and his men for about two hours. My unease around him doesn't go away, though I do relax when I confirm he has no ill will toward me. I think he might be a bit intrigued by me, but there's no malice between us.

Dorian lets me drive back to the hotel—it's nice to be behind the wheel again, and I enjoy the rural scenery. Seamus and Connor take the other car.

There's a steakhouse just a few doors down from our hotel, so we go there for dinner, and then back to our room. Dorian wastes absolutely no time in hooking an arm around my waist, pulling me right into his chest, and kissing me. Deeply. Passionately. So thoroughly my toes curl in my shoes. I clutch his broad shoulder with one hand and curl my other arm around his neck. His hands drop to my ass, and he starts kneading the pliable flesh, groaning into my kiss. His groan is so goddamn sexy my nipples pebble in my bra and I press closer to him, desperate to feel him inside me.

"On the bed," Dorian growls, pulling his mouth away from mine. "I'm going to tie you down, spread-eagle, and play with you. Work your body over until you're begging. Then, I'm going to fuck you until we're both screaming. Any objections?"

Feeling a flush course through my entire body, I shake my head. "We don't exactly have any bondage gear."

He smirks. "You brought some scarves. I have ties and belts. I'm sure we'll manage." He jerks his chin. "On the bed, Mira. Now."

"You want me fully clothed?" I tease.

A few quick yanks free me from my clothes. Instead of letting me walk, Dorian picks me up and carries me to the bed, setting me on the center of it. "Stay."

I frown playfully. "I'm not a dog."

"No, but you are my good girl, so you'll do what I tell you. Won't you?"

His voice has deepened into a smoky, dominant, self-assured tone that melts me on the spot. "I'll be your good girl."

He ambles over to our suitcases that lie by the dresser. He retrieves two scarves, two ties, and two belts, then gets to work. The bed is four-poster, ideal for what he has in mind. My hands are tied to the top posters, my ankles to the bottom. By the time he's done, I'm well and truly immobile. I test the bondage, jerking my limbs, feeling a thrill travel through me when there's barely any give.

"Settle in," Dorian murmurs, gazing at me with a mixture of reverence and dark obsession. "I'm taking my time tonight."

He shucks his shirt, showcasing a mouthwatering set of abs and beautifully-honed chest, then climbs between my legs. He drags his fingertips up my thighs, making me shudder with anticipation.

"So beautifully responsive," he murmurs, circling my belly button with his index finger. He leans over me and drags his tongue up my navel. He licks a path around my nipple, then sucks it into his mouth. A scrape of his teeth arches my back, and he sits back with a smirk. "Do you like being my little fuck-toy, Mira? My personal doll that I can use at my leisure?"

The words are degrading, but they set me on *fire*. I nod. "Yes."

"That's my good girl. I can do anything to you right now. Leave you tied up until morning… spend all night fucking you… have you come until the sun is up." An evil grin stretches his lips. "Or not let you come at all while I use you."

I whimper as he drags three fingers up and down my slit. "Don't be mean."

"I'll be as mean or nice as I want, and all you can do is take it." He grins. "But I do like it when you beg, so feel free to."

"You don't *listen* when I beg," I point out breathily.

"True, but I still like the sound of your desperation, of the beautiful pleas that leave these gorgeous lips." He brushes his lips over mine and pinches my clit. My gasp makes him smile. "You're my favorite toy."

"And your favorite person?" I ask meekly. He's quickly becoming my favorite person; I *have* to know that it's reciprocated.

Surprise flashes through his eyes, and they quickly warm. "My absolute favorite person. My best good girl. My *only* woman, now and always."

Fuck. His words undo me, and the way he works me over for the next hour forces me to submit to him completely. He plays with my breasts. Eats my pussy without letting me come. Lightly fucks my mouth, holding my chin in place. Bathes in my pleas to let me come but doesn't respond.

By the time he unties my legs and wraps them around his waist, I'm a mindless mess, desperate for release. Ready to do anything he asks, if only he lets me crest.

"Please, please, *please*," I chant as he slides his cock into my sopping wet channel. "Dorian, I'm *begging*," I mutter. "*Please!*"

"Keep begging and I might eventually listen," he teases, letting out a low grunt as he bottoms out. Even though I'm as wet as I've ever been, his cock stretches me out, igniting a delicious burn in my pussy.

I yank futilely at my hands, wishing I was untied so I could get *myself* off.

"Look at you," he murmurs, tracing a finger over my jaw. "Jerking, struggling, begging. Submitting so fucking prettily. Giving me all the power." He kisses me. "It's well-placed, love. You can trust me with yourself. I'll take care of you. I'll never betray you."

Tears spark in my eyes as we stare at each other, and my submission transcends something physical and delves into the deep end of emotional. I trust him with more than just my body; I trust him with my heart. It'll crush me if he ever breaks it, but that's a chance I'm willing to take.

"Come whenever you're ready," he says. "I think you've suffered enough. Come for me, Mira."

My back bows so intensely it's nearly painful. A cry of sheer abandon leaves my lips as he grinds his pelvis into my clit. I cry, I whine, I struggle, and I come so *fucking* hard it's a miracle I don't break his cock off. He grunts through my release, fucking me harder and faster, wrapping his hand around my neck to keep me in place. His orgasm follows just a few moments after mine, and deep satisfaction sweeps through me as he throws his head back to the ceiling and roars. *I'm* doing that to this man. He's losing his mind because of *me*. The power is invigorating.

I plant kisses everywhere I can reach as he unties me, feeling grateful to have him in my life. His abs, his chest... I leave a gentle bite over his heart, just enough to form a hickey. My arms fall limply over my head when he releases them, and I shudder in the aftermath of my orgasm.

Dorian scoops me up and carries me into the en-suite bathroom.

He runs the bath while we shower, and he takes care to wash me *very* thoroughly, inside and out. My breasts and pussy receive special attention—he makes me come two more times, until my legs turn to jelly, and I can no longer hold my own weight.

Only then does he take us to the bath, where we laze together in warm water until we come back to ourselves. It's there, surrounded by the foam and bubbles, feeling raw and vulnerable, that the words I've been holding back escape.

"I love you," I murmur. The haze in my head makes it easy for me to confess, though I'm sure I'll be embarrassed at myself tomorrow. "I know it's too soon. We've barely known each other for a few weeks. But still, somehow I fell for you between the kidnapping and punishments. You accept me for exactly who I am and don't expect me to change to suit societal norms. You make me feel... whole. Sane. Perfect, when I know I'm none of those things." Dorian's body is completely still behind me; I don't even think he's breathing. I pick up his hand and bring it to my lips. "I love you."

A slow breath shudders out of him. He leans forward to press a kiss to my neck, suckling the skin there.

"It's a damn good thing that you've fallen for me, because I've already fallen for you. I'm obsessed with you. I can't get enough of you. Your charming way of blurting out random things, your determination to survive and thrive despite impossible circumstances, your way of brightening everything around you. You make me think that this fucked up world might actually be a good place. I love you so *fucking* much, Mira, and I am never letting you go."

Chapter Thirty-Nine

I'm up along with the sun the next morning. Though Dorian tired me out last night, knowing that I'll be seeing Clyde today, for the first time in years, makes me nervous. In the past, I would already have dissociated from the situation, but I don't even feel the longing to do so now. I know I'll be protected, surrounded by people who will kill for me—most notably Dorian and Asher. I know both men will die for me. As for Seamus and Connor, I *think* they'll be willing to kill for me, but I can't say for certain.

Dorian's still sound asleep, his bare chest on display and arms splayed beside his impressive body. He gave me free reign over room service, so I quietly order us breakfast and perch on the windowsill. When the food arrives, I pour myself a cup of coffee and return to my perch, taking a few minutes to scroll through my phone.

Valerie and Cara have both texted me several times—I told them I came down with a bad case of the flu this week, so they've been checking on me daily. I don't want to put them in a shitty position by telling them the truth. If the police catch onto what I'm doing, which Dorian insists they won't, I don't want to risk Cara and Valerie incriminating me. They'd never intentionally do so, but Cara has a bit of a loud mouth.

When I'm done with my cup, it's nearly 8am. I pour myself another cup and fix one for Dorian, taking a seat on the bed and placing both coffees on the bed stand. I run my fingers through his hair, gently coaxing him to wake up.

He blinks up at me sleepily, his eyes clouded as he starts to stir. He stretches his arms above his head with a yawn and sits up, leaning forward to kiss my cheek. I smile as I hand him his cup of coffee.

"Morning," I greet. "I got room service. Hope that's okay."

He sips his coffee and releases a contented hum. The sheets have pooled around his waist, giving me a mouthwatering view of the taut muscles comprising his torso. He really does look like he was sculpted by angels. Avenging angels who gave him endless beauty paired with a dangerous skillset.

"Order whatever you want whenever you want," Dorian says. "Here, at home, wherever. You have a credit card—limit is 30k a month. Go crazy."

I shake my head with a quiet laugh. "I don't spend that much in a year."

He reaches out to cup the back of my neck, squeezing lightly. "I admire your dedication and determination, but you don't have to pinch pennies anymore. You don't have to work if you don't want to, either."

"I want to," I say quickly. "Being a vet has been the sum of my dreams for years. I need to get there."

"So you will," Dorian says simply. "I think you'd be sexy as a vet. I'll probably request to fuck you in your white doctor's coat."

I smile, gazing at him fondly. "I'm sure I'll be able to find a way to accommodate you." I inhale a deep breath, focusing on our tasks for the day. On my impending meeting with the man who tried and failed to kill me or get me killed more times than I can count. "What are our plans for the day?"

"We have a rendezvous with Sergei and Asher at 5:30. Before that, our day is our own."

"Carver might've sent men out to crawl the city and keep eyes on us," I speculate. "He's probably smart enough to anticipate that we're already here, and that we won't stay in Silving."

Dorian picks up his phone and scrolls on it. After a moment, he chuckles. "Sergei already has his people tracking Carver's men in the city. If we want to go out, they won't follow us."

"There's not much to do around here," I say honestly. "I mean, there's a movie theater, but it only plays old titles."

Dorian nods. "Cool. Then I propose a naked day. You, me, this bed. And the couch." He looks out into the small living room, brows furrowing. "I think I'll have you on the dining table, too."

"Will you, now?" I tease.

He nods. "Yes. You only came a few times last night—I felt like edging you into oblivion. Today, I'm in the mood to tease out multiple orgasms." He sets his phone and coffee aside, lifting me by the waist and laying me flat on the bed. "I think I'll get started right now..."

Despite his threats disguised as pleasurable promises, Dorian doesn't go too hard on me. Mostly, we spend the day cuddling and talking. We have sex a few times, and Dorian is a *very* generous lover... but neither of us want to be sore for the meeting tonight.

We meet Seamus and Connor at Asher's range. It still feels insane to think of the man as my biological father, but in hindsight, there were many clues. I always attributed his kindness to pity, but now I know he was looking after me in the only way he could. I greet Asher with a hug, following him upstairs where Connor and Seamus are waiting in his small sitting room. Many additional chairs have been added, presumably in anticipation of Sergei's entourage

"You're both rocking the multiple-orgasms look," Seamus quips, waggling his eyebrows playfully.

Asher leaves the room with a grunt. Evidently, discussing my sex life is a step too far for him. Dorian watches him go, then hooks an arm around my waist and pulls me into his chest. His hand drops to cup my ass, and he raises his eyebrows at Seamus. "I have the best piece of ass I've ever seen readily available to me. If there's a single day when Mira *isn't* rocking the glow, you have permission to shoot me in the head."

My cheeks heat and I hide my head in Dorian's chest. "Do you have to announce our private lives to the world?" I squeak.

"They know either way, baby."

Asher steps back into the room. Dorian's hand disappears from my ass, moving to my waist.

"We've got company," Asher says. He disappears downstairs and returns after a few minutes, escorting Sergei Novikov and his men into the room. The men take up positions in the hall and by the door; Sergei descends on one of the chairs like a king taking his throne. He takes his time examining Connor, Seamus, Dorian and me, before turning to Asher. "We leave in one hour. Between now and then, let's talk strategy."

My heart rate speeds as discussions ensue, outlining location, conversation topics, and a gameplan for getting rid of Carver's entire operation. Not all the men will be in attendance of the meeting—apparently, Sergei's gleaned intelligence that suggests Carver plans to have about twenty of his men with him. Five in the room, five in the bar above where we'll meet, and ten scattered around the perimeter of the brewery.

Connor, Seamus, and Asher are instructed to track down and kill Carver's remaining men during the meeting, then work their way from the perimeter of the brewery into the room, exterminating everyone they cross paths with. By the time they arrive, all of Carver's backup will be dead, and it'll just be him and whichever men he deems fit to sit in on the meeting left.

Sergei specifies that he wants Carver alive. The bratva boss suspects that the local gang leader will have valuable information to give, especially under painful duress.

Even though I know I should keep my mouth shut, I can't contain myself. When there's an ebb in the conversation, I speak.

"Why do you care?" I ask.

Sergei's ice-cold eyes shift to me. He's leaned back in his seat, nursing a glass of vodka that one of his men gave him.

"Mira," Dorian says quietly, placing a hand on my knee. We're side by side on the couch, seated across from his boss.

"It's quite alright," Sergei says, dismissing Dorian's worry. His energy always has a steady hum of danger, but now its overlaid with the faintest hint of curiosity. He cocks his head to the side as he stares at me. "Why do I care about what?"

"Dismantling Carver's operation," I clarify. "Blowing up his trafficking business and freeing the women. Forgive me for my forwardness, but why would a man like you give a shit?"

Everyone in the room's staring at me now, giving me looks with varying degrees of threat and indignation. As if I'm a peasant who has the gall to demand answers from the emperor.

"A man like me," Sergei echoes. "What sort of man do you think I am, Miranda?"

I barely hide a wince. I haven't been called that name in a long time—the last person who called me it was my mother, and only when she was lecturing me.

"My name's Mira," I tell him firmly. "As for the sort of man I think you are... you're dangerous. *Extremely* dangerous. The way you hold yourself suggests you've had a level of training that surpasses the most elite military or civilian forces in this world. I think you're the type of person to shoot someone point blank in the forehead, then go home and sleep like a baby. You're ambitious. Determined. Cruel, but only when you need to be. Too level-headed to be a sociopath, but too moral to be a psychopath." I lean forward. "You have morals—I'm sure of it. Lines you won't cross for any reason. My only question is why *this* is one of your lines." My eyes flick to his ring finger, where an onyx-black wedding band sits. "Is it because of your wife?"

"You are as perceptive as my legion has informed me," Sergei says, a slow smile spreading on his lips. "My wife would *love* your company. I expect she'd want to study you." He chuckles, as if enjoying a private joke. "I've never been a fan of sex trafficking. Business is business; killing a man who would kill you if given the chance is just survival. Killing men whose territory you want falls under the same category. Human flesh, however, is not *business*. Humans are not inanimate objects, and each life taken or abused has a cost. I can easily shoulder the cost of the killing that needs to be done in my world, but the killing of innocents incurs a debt that weighs heavily on me. Events in my past have strengthened my commitment to putting an end to trafficking; so much so that I now actively seek out operations rather than destroying any I happen to stumble upon in the course of my dealings." He sips his vodka, appearing completely at ease. "Does that answer your question?"

I nod. "Yes, thank you. Sorry for speaking out of turn."

He examines me for a moment. "No, you're not."

"No, I'm not," I agree. "But since we're in a room full of people who seem to regard you as their king, I feel it's only fair that my lowly self apologizes for her gall to speak."

Sergei grins at Dorian. "You'll have your hands full with this one."

Dorian squeezes my thigh again. "I know. I can't fucking wait."

Chapter Forty

The meeting ends shortly after my exchange with Sergei. Everyone departs in their respective cars. Though Dorian let me drive us here, he insists on driving us into Silving.

The sun is setting on the horizon as we cruise, lighting up the trailer parks and fields beyond the windows. The closer we get to town, the more uncomfortable I start to grow. Memories assault me, some of them good but most of them bad. As we pass the sign that welcomes us into Silving, and farmland is replaced with old brick buildings, my heart speeds, as do my breaths.

I see streets that I had to walk down with crutches after Clyde fucked up my leg. I pass the school where I tried desperately to hide my abuse, the community college where I took advanced classes so that I could leave this shithole as soon as possible.

Dorian doesn't say anything, but he must sense my distress, because he reaches over and puts his big palm on my knee. I can feel the heat of his hand even through my jeans, and the contact settles me. It doesn't make my anxiety disappear, but it does make me feel like I'm not alone.

I've felt alone in this town for as long as I could remember—since my mom died. But not alone anymore. I won't have to fend for myself with Clyde; I have Dorian protecting me.

I direct him down the main avenue, and then past a few winding streets that lead us to the outskirts of the south side of town, where the brewery and bar are located.

"You have your weapons?" Dorian asks me.

I deliberately wore baggy clothes so I could conceal the handgun strapped to my body and the knife in my boot. Dorian and Sergei's men will go in with all their weapons, but it's best if Carver assumes I'm unarmed.

"Yes," I respond.

He squeezes my knee. "Everything will be fine, baby. I won't let anyone hurt you."

"I don't know why Clyde even wants me there," I mutter. "He said that Carver wanted to see me, but I don't understand his motivation. I've only met him a few times."

"It could be that Clyde simply wants to fuck with your head and made up something about Carver wanting you there," Dorian says. "You bested Clyde and got away with it. He's a vile, power-hungry man, and men like him aren't good at letting go of old grievances. He wants to make you hurt in return for the way you hurt his pride."

I sigh. "Yeah, probably."

We pull into the dirt parking lot in front of a one-story brick bar. The weathered building blends seamlessly with the rugged surroundings. Behind it stands a longer, two-story building, bearing a faint resemblance to an old farmhouse with its barn-style rooflines. That's the brewery where the staple beer of the region is created. Beneath it lies a sprawling basement for storage, where Carver is rumored to conduct his shadowy business meetings.

"There are men scattered around the lot," Dorian mutters, his gaze bouncing around the area. "More hidden in those bushes flanking the left side, probably."

I push my fingers through my hair, taking deep breaths in an attempt to steel myself. I don't have much time to get a hold of my nerves before three black SUV's pull up. Igor steps out from the driver's seat of the SUV. Sergei gets out shortly afterwards, his polished shoes and suit looking remarkably out of place in this dusty lot.

"This business should be over with pretty quickly," Dorian says, just as the wooden front door of the bar opens. Half a dozen men file out, wearing ridiculous getups of ratty jeans and old leather jackets, as if they're in a boyband. I only recognize two of them.

Clyde and Carver. Two abominations to this world, men who don't deserve to breathe. Clyde has mud-brown eyes, a balding head of black hair, and a distended belly that makes me question if he's still in the business of killing Carver's enemies. Carver is slightly more put together, though not by much. He's leaner, a bit fitter, and has hazel eyes and dirty-blond, greasy hair.

Sergei looks back at our car with raised eyebrows. Dorian sighs. "Let's get this over with, baby."

He gets out and opens my car door for me, offering me his hand. I take it gratefully, drawing on his strength. I straighten my spine and lift my chin as we start walking toward the brewery. Sergei parked closer, so he's already shaking hands with Carver.

Clyde's eyes sweep the lot, ghosting over Dorian before settling on me. A smirk spreads on his pudgy face; a taunting look that makes my skin crawl. This is the man who abused me for *years*, who got my mother killed. Nearly got me killed, in between the times he almost lost it and put me out of my misery himself. The majority of the trauma I've endured starts and ends with him.

It's a struggle to keep my stride confident. A swirling storm of emotions overtake my chest as I face down the boogeyman who's haunted my dreams for what feels like my entire life.

"Mira," Clyde greets when Dorian and I come to a stop a few steps behind Sergei. When I don't respond, he gives a mock pout. "No hello for your old man?"

"You're not my father," I say tersely. "I owe you nothing."

Anger sparks in his eyes at my dismissal. "Thought I raised you better than that."

"You didn't raise me at all," I correct. "I raised myself in *spite* of having to live with you."

"You ungrateful little *whore*—"

"Enough," Carver cuts in, sounding bored. "We're here for business, not for a family reunion." He looks me up and down, vague disinterest stamped on his expression. "You've grown up, Mira. I remember you when you were just a little girl." He gives me another, slower look, one that makes goosebumps break out over my arms. I feel like a prize show horse he's perusing, deciding if I'm worth a purchase or not.

"As touching as this reunion is, I haven't traveled all this way to hear you reunite with my soldier's woman," Sergei says flatly. "We have business to discuss. You want to join the operation I'm expanding in the states. Your offer and production lineup is interesting enough to garner a few moments of my time. Don't put it to waste."

"Of course not," Carver says promptly. "Come on in—we can talk inside, where it's safe."

The bar is abandoned, shut down for the night. Shitty wooden tables accompanied by bar stools are scattered around the space. Posters of old rock bands hang on the walls. Bare lightbulbs dangle from the ceiling, illuminating the shoddy interior.

Carver leads us through the bar and into the brewery, where metal machinery holds court, accompanied by wooden oak barrels lining the walls, holding aging liquor. He takes us down a wooden staircase and into a basement used as additional storage. The light in the basement is dim, coming from more bare lightbulbs. The walls are cement stained with moisture, the floors covered with a thin film of dust.

Furniture is laid out around the center of the room—three couches, several armchairs, and even a few tables with accompanying stools. It's clear that Carver uses this place often enough to merit furnishing it, even if his choice of décor is abhorrent.

Dorian stands at the bottom of the staircase, keeping hold of my hand, his gaze glued to Sergei. Igor and two other men Sergei brought with him walk around the room, looking for any weapons or traps. Carver's men idle near the walls, postures alert and expressions menacing. Every person here is armed up to the gills, and nobody bothers asking anyone to hand over their weapons. Sergei doesn't trust Carver, and Carver doesn't trust Sergei.

Clyde is the last to descend the staircase. He stops right beside me, turning to gaze down at me, his lips curled into a sneer and eyes darkened with rage. "Are you enjoying being home?" he taunts. "Back where you belong?"

Dorian and I both ignore him. I long to pull out my pistol and shoot him in the forehead, but I can't. Not yet. I'll know the time has come when Seamus, Asher, and Connor make their appearance.

"You really want to ignore me, girl?" he hisses furiously under his breath. "Just because you've turned into an uppity cunt at your hoity-toity school don't mean that I won't teach you a fuckin' lesson."

"Speak to my woman like that again, and your brains will decorate these barrels," Dorian says with eerie calm.

"Clyde," Carver calls out. "Come join us." It seems that Clyde is Carver's right hand—or that Carver wants to keep an eye on Clyde, worried that he's a loose cannon. *He is.*

Clyde stalks away after shooting me one last glare. Dorian and I remain by the staircase since Sergei didn't give us the invite to sit down. He probably wants us vigilant and ready for shots to be fired at any moment. *God*, I wish I didn't have to be here. I wish I was in Vermont, back at Greywood with Dorian.

As if he can read my mind, he strokes his thumb over the small of my back. "Soon," he murmurs in my ear. "Soon, baby. Trust me."

The next half hour passes at an agonizing snail's pace. Sergei and Carver talk about the drug operation Carver runs. Apparently, Carver *does* have an impressive production of illegal substances going on in this town, and he has lots of product he'd like to peddle into Central and South America, where Sergei has many connections. Carver has a chemist in his crew that makes cocktails of meth, heroin, ketamine... you name it, he cooks it. Sergei doesn't give any indication that he doesn't want to go into business with Carver. In fact, he's so genuine, I almost start to believe he's truly considering making a deal here tonight.

Another twenty minutes pass. I start shifting my weight and growing worried. I don't know how long it's supposed to take Connor, Seamus, and Asher to exterminate Carver's men—maybe something went wrong. One of them could've gotten hurt, even *killed*—

"They're fine, baby," Dorian murmurs, covering his words with a kiss on my cheek. "You're doing so well. I'm so fucking proud that you're mine."

A great deal of my concern flees. Warmth at his praise bathes my chest, almost making me forget about our current predicament.

That is, until Dorian backs away, and I lock eyes with Clyde, who's glaring at me from across the room. When Dorian's hand cups my hip, Clyde's jaw flexes, and his glare deepens. I force myself to hold his eyes for several infinitely long moments, until he finally looks away as Sergei addresses him.

"What will your role be if I do business with your boss?" Sergei asks Clyde.

Clyde sits up a bit straighter. "I cook the books and keep the men in line."

A thin smile spreads on Sergei's lips. "Anyone with a fifth-grade education and some muscle can do those jobs."

"Not like me," Clyde promises. "I specialize in sending messages to enemies of our operation."

"He's an excellent enforcer," Carver endorses.

"I see. You gentlemen are, of course, aware of my policies when it comes to business. I have lines that I do not cross, and that I strongly discourage my associates from crossing. Enforce all you like, but women and children are to be kept out of it at all costs."

"Of course," Carver agrees instantly. "We'd never go out of our way to harm innocents. There are unfortunate times when they get caught in the crosshairs, but—"

"Those times are now at an end," Sergei says, his voice deepening. "This is not a negotiation. You cross my lines, you cross *me*. I don't think I need to tell you what happens to those who cross me."

"We'll keep that in mind going forward," Carver replies.

"If I could say a few words, Mr. Novikov?" Clyde questions.

Sergei tilts his head slowly. "As long as you don't waste my time with bullshit."

"I'll make this quick. You see, Mira is my stepdaughter, and we've grown estranged ever since she ran off to that fancy college."

My blood runs cold. My heart stutters and nearly stops. Dorian's grip on me turns to steel as we both try to figure out what the fuck Clyde's angle is here.

"I've tried to reach out and rekindle our relationship several times, but she's never given me the chance," Clyde goes on. "Then, a few months ago, I heard through the grapevine that she'd shacked up with one of your soldiers. I finally managed to get a hold of her, and she indicated that it wasn't of her own free will. In accordance with your own rules about leaving women out of business, I have to bring up my concern about your foot soldier." Clyde turns to stare in my direction, fixing his gaze on Dorian. There's shielded amusement and victory in his eyes, like he really expects his pathetic ploy to work. Like he didn't insult me outside just a few minutes ago, right in front of Sergei.

Clyde managed to do the near-impossible by sounding genuine. Even though I know Sergei won't feed into his bullshit, I feel an old sense of fear overcome me. A remnant from my time living under Clyde's roof.

"Is that so?" Sergei drawls. He looks at Dorian and crooks a finger. "Forward, soldier. Bring your woman."

Dorian takes my hand, enveloping it in his. I feel a fine tremble in my limbs as we walk forward, breaching the space between the staircase and the center of the room where the men are seated. We stop in front of Sergei, with our backs to Clyde and Carver.

"What do you have to say for yourself, Dorian?"

The energy in the room snaps taut, but not just from Dorian's impending words. It takes me a moment to realize the vibes of the building have shifted—something's going on upstairs. I try to focus in, to find a hint of something familiar... and then I feel it. Three very distinct presences belonging to three very distinct people.

"Clyde is lying," Dorian says simply.

Clyde opens his mouth to protest; Sergei holds up a sharp hand, cutting him off before he can speak.

"Are you sure about your answer?" Sergei asks Dorian.

"Categorically."

"Hmm." Sergei shifts his gaze over to me. After a moment, he beckons me to step forward. The energies in the building turn more tumultuous, more dangerous, but that perversely makes me feel better.

"Mira, was it?" Sergei asks, as if he's only seen me in passing.

I nod, playing along.

"You don't have to fear any reproach from me. Tell the truth; are you with my soldier of your own freewill?"

"I am," I tell Sergei firmly. "If I can speak openly?"

"I'd prefer if you did."

"Dorian has never done anything to harm me. He's never raised a hand to me, never made me feel poorly about myself or like I'm a burden in his life. He makes me feel safe, coveted, and protected." I inhale a deep breath. "But there is a person in this room who *has* harmed me. Who enjoyed beating me. Who made a pointed effort to remind me of how much of a burden I was—who nearly killed me at least half a dozen times, and nearly got me killed more times than I could count."

I hear a rustle of fabric behind me as Clyde shifts in his seat, feel the animosity radiating from him double.

"And that man would be?"

"Clyde."

"Lying *bitch*," Clyde snaps. His chair shifts back as he stands from his seat. I gasp as he grabs a fistful of my shirt and spins me around. He truly didn't expect me to speak out—I guess he figured I hadn't changed over the years. That I was the same timid, weak girl who scurried out of his shitty house and ran far away. I am *certainly* not.

His hold on my shirt is firm; if I try to get out of his grip, I'll probably tear the fabric. So, I do the only thing I can think of doing to prove that I am *not* the Mira who ran from him.

I spit in his face.

From there, several things happen at once. Gunfire breaks out from above, the booming echoes of it deafening. Clyde draws out a gun and points it at my head, just as Dorian draws out his own weapon and points it at Clyde.

Every man in the room leaps to his feet and grabs his weapon. Total fucking chaos ensues.

Footsteps sound coming down the stairs just before Seamus and Asher make an appearance. I knock the gun from Clyde's hand with a swift, sharp jab, sending it flying to the ground. He backhands me in the cheek so hard I'm sent stumbling backwards, pain exploding across my jaw. Dorian fires off a shot just as one of Clyde's men crashes into him from behind, fouling his aim.

Everything that happens after that is a blur. Clyde grunts and his leg buckles. He manages to get a hand around my throat and take me to the ground, pinning me beneath him. Before he can get a good enough grip to crush my windpipe, I knee him in the balls, making him release me with a high-pitched cry. I swipe the knife hidden in my boot and take a second to glance around, taking stock of this clusterfuck.

Bullets fly above us, some burying into the cement walls, some ricocheting, others piercing through the barrels and spilling the liquors hidden inside. I glimpse Dorian grappling with two of Carver's men.

Clyde doesn't take long to recover and leap on top of me again, but this time, I'm ready for him. I let him get his hand around my throat again. I look him dead in the eyes, and spit on his face once again. He jerks back, yelling an obscenity at me, and I take his moment of distraction to grip his wrist and slice through the vulnerable underside of it.

This time, Clyde *roars*.

Blood spurts from his hand, staining my face and neck. I lunge forward and bury the knife so deep in the base of his throat, the blade disappears into his skin.

A single trickle of blood runs from the wound. Clyde's eyes meet mine, widened with shock and brightened with fear.

He attempts to reach his injured hand up to his neck. Fails. Opens his mouth to say something, only for a gurgle of blood to rush from his lips, trapping his words.

The gunfire around us is dying down; Carver's men are dropping like flies. I can take a beat to enjoy this moment, revel in it. Bathe in the way I've flipped the tables on Clyde.

Once, I was the vulnerable little girl who gazed at him with fear, hoping that he'd change overnight into a better man. Into a decent stepfather. I hoped he'd leave his abusive ways behind.

Now, he's turned into the helpless child, incapable of caring for himself or keeping himself alive. I leave the blade in his neck, not ready for him to die quite yet. Spotting the gun he dropped a few feet to the left of me, I pick it up.

A single push to Clyde's chest sends him to the ground. His entire body shakes with pain and lack of oxygen. I crouch over him, pressing the barrel of the gun to his forehead, letting him *see* the vengeance in my eyes.

"I don't like the act of killing," I say softly, "but killing *you* is an exception. This is for all the times you hurt me." I swiftly reposition the gun, firing off a shot into his gut. He releases a gurgle that pours more blood from his lips, eyes wide, body seizing. I return the gun to his forehead, pressing it right between his eyes. "And this is for my mother."

I pull the trigger.

Chapter Forty-One

"That was absolutely *wonderful*, love," Seamus praises me, a goofy smile stuck on his face. We're cleaning up at Asher's range, already having taken turns in his shower to get the blood off ourselves and change clothes. We brought extras with us when we met here earlier today, in anticipation of having to switch outfits.

Dorian's in the vault, helping Asher clean our borrowed weapons and properly store them. Connor's also on cleanup duty, getting rid of our sullied clothes in Asher's fireplace. Sergei's crew is cleaning the mess in the brewery and gathering information on all of Carver's operations. Sergei will take over the drug op and dismantle the prostitution ring.

We said our goodbyes to him and his men before leaving.

"You spit in his face *twice*," Seamus says, "stabbed him in the neck, and shot him. Again, *twice*. If you ever want to join us on ops, I would be *most* glad to have you."

"That'll happen when hell freezes over," Dorian says smoothly, strolling into the room. He makes a beeline toward me, wrapping his arms around me from behind and pressing a kiss to the crown of my head. "How are you, baby?"

"Better than I've been in a long while," I sigh. "Killing Clyde was cathartic. I feel like my mother can rest in peace now."

"I only wish I could tell Valerie about what a badass you are," Seamus says, still locked on the way I ended Clyde's life. "She'd eat that right up. Alas, we don't do much talking, and even if we did—"

"I don't want to hear it," I say, holding up a hand. "What you do with her is your business, I don't require details." I've already warned him that I think his involvement with Valerie is a setup for failure, but what he does is none of my concern.

Seamus sighs. "Fair enough, love. Wouldn't want to blister your innocent ears."

"Innocent?" Dorian repeats dubiously.

Seamus tilts his head from side to side. "Yeah, fair point. I've heard the screams late at night—I expect the two of you get up to an exotic array of bed-sport."

"We do," Dorian agrees. "Now, don't you have something better to be doing? You don't need to spend more time with Mira than necessary."

Seamus holds up his hands in a mock gesture of acquiescence. "Very well, I'll leave you two lovebirds to it."

After he's wandered off, Dorian spins me around, cradling me close to his chest. "We're leaving in a few hours," he murmurs. "Anything you want to do before then?"

I bite my lip. "Actually, yes."

The cemetery where my mother's buried is on a beautiful, scenic patch of land about forty minutes outside of Silving. Rolling hills show off masses of headstones, most belonging to former residents of Silving.

There are no pathways to lead people through the winding maze of graves, but I don't need any markers to know where I'm going. Even in the dark, with only the light of the moon as my guide, I'm able to make my way to my mother's resting place without issue.

With Dorian's hand clutched firmly in my own, I find Mom's designated lot. There are patches of wildflowers growing over her grave, pretty dandelions that refuse to wilt beneath the frost. I sink to my knees beside her headstone, running my palm over the cool marble surface. Asher bought Mom's headstone; he held me while I sobbed my way through her funeral.

Even now, years after her death, I can feel her presence. Her energy. I know she's here with me, perhaps peeking through the veil of the afterlife. I can sense her as if she were standing right beside me.

Dorian silently takes a seat next to me, allowing me my space even as he stays close. I rub my thumb over the engraved words, *Beloved Mother, Daughter, and Friend.*

"Hey, Mom," I murmur quietly. I visited her often when I still lived in Silving, though I haven't come here since leaving for college. "I'm sorry it's been a while since I came. I ran away from Silving the first chance I got, but you've been in my thoughts and heart every day."

A cool wisp of wind raises goosebumps on the back of my neck. A gentle weight descends on my shoulder, an invisible pressure that I know in my *soul* is my mom. Keeping one hand on her headstone, I put the other on my shoulder, a wobbly smile spreading on my lips. Her spirit, soul, whatever the essence of a person is, always makes an appearance when I visit. It's often teeming with restlessness and regret, but now, there's just warmth.

"I miss you so much," I say softly. "But I'm happy you're in a better place. At rest." I clear my throat. "I know you were never big on vengeance, and neither am I, but I have to tell you something." I swallow hard. "Clyde is dead. I put two bullets in him; one in his gut for me, and another in his head for you. I know murder is wrong, it's a horrible sin, but I never would have been able to truly live while he roamed this earth. I never would've felt that you were truly, finally at rest. I killed him for us, and for all the other people he's hurt. For the people he would've hurt had he stayed alive."

The pressure on my shoulder becomes a bit firmer, almost as if Mom's giving me a squeeze of encouragement. I don't know if my sense for her presence is all in my head or if it's real, but either way, it brings me soul-soothing comfort.

"I hope you'll forgive me for being vengeful. I hope one day I'll forgive myself for just hiding while you were plugged with a dozen bullets." I exhale a long breath, releasing her headstone to pick up Dorian's hand. "I also want you to meet someone very special to me. Dorian Acheron. We go to school together—we met under pretty uncomfortable circumstances, but we've grown... *extremely* close." Tears start to burn in my eyes. "I love him, the same way you loved Asher." My voice cracks. "I found out that Asher's my father. I wish you told me, or that he'd told me, but I understand why neither of you did. I'm glad I know now, though." I pause as a tear spills down my cheek and my throat tightens, a mixture of grief and lightness warring in my chest. "Asher likes Dorian as much as he'll ever like one of my suitors. I brought him with me tonight so you could meet him, too."

Another squeeze on my shoulder, a warm breeze against my back. A sense of approval shifts the energy in the air, as if Mom's giving her blessing. Relief suffuses me, and I offer a wobbly smile.

"I love you, Mom. *So* much. I—I know you're here with me, that you'll always live on in my heart." A soft laugh escapes me. "And you'll live on in the children I'll bring into this world one day, fathered by the man beside me. They'll grow up hearing about you, knowing what an amazing grandmother they have." I squeeze my own shoulder, imagining that I'm squeezing her hand. "Rest in peace, Mom. Go on with the knowledge that the monster in our past is gone, and my future is bright."

I start to stand, but Dorian pulls me into him, cradling me close.

"I wish I could've met you," he says gently, gazing at the headstone. "I wish I could thank you for the wonderful woman you brought into this world, who I'm lucky to call mine. I swear to you I'll love her the way she deserves to be loved, protect her the way she deserves to be protected, and ensure she goes through life with me by her side." He kisses my cheek; I let out a soft sob.

We sit together in silence, both appreciating the moment. Minutes pass before the weight on my shoulder slowly starts to fade, and my mother's energy recedes from the air.

She's gone now, and I think she'll stay gone. Anything tethering her to the earth, such as the need to know I'm happy and Clyde's dead, has been dispelled. She can truly be at peace now.

Dorian wipes away the tears rolling down my cheeks. "Thank you for bringing me here," he says. "I think... I think I felt her."

I smile, nodding. "So did I. She's moved on."

"And now, it's our turn to do the same," he murmurs. "Move on in life, together."

"Together," I agree.

Afterword

Thank you so much for reading Luminaries and Legionaries! Mira and Dorian live rent-free in my heart.

If you enjoyed this book, please leave a review. Reviews are critical for visibility and growth, and I read every single one of them to get an idea of what readers do and don't enjoy.

Greywood University books and worlds are far from complete! **Next up will be Valerie and Seamus's book, Vixens and Vipers**. Pre-order for Vixens and Vipers will be live very soon!

If you're interested in seeing more stories set in the Greywood University world, check out my Greywood Elites Series!

Book 1 is Muses and Monsters, a spicy MFM dark romance with a psychopath MMC, a golden retriever MMC, and a dancer FMC who has a dark past. https://www.amazon.com/dp/B0D6X14VW1

Book 2 is Primas and Predators, a MF dark second-chance romance with a villain MMC and bold FMC who's unafraid to stand up to him. https://www.amazon.com/dp/B0CW1DWT1P

Book 3 is Starlets and Savages, a MF dark billionaire romance with a morally grey MMC and intelligent yet shy FMC. https://www.am azon.com/dp/B0DG9TW8GD

About the Author

Rose likes to write about complex, oftentimes twisted main characters who grow stronger together on whichever journey they take. Watch out for sexy morally grey heroes and sharp, intelligent heroines within settings ranging from fantasy to academia to the underworld of organized crime.

When Rose isn't writing or listening to the whispers (or shouts) of her characters in her mind, she's drinking coffee, throwing herself at anything nature-related (especially in the winter, when there are no spiders or mosquitos to attack her), and reading.

If you'd like to connect with Rose, join her Facebook group: https://www.facebook.com/share/1AgAcE5efaztPjLq/

To stay updated on her upcoming releases, you can subscribe to her newsletter: https://dashboard.mailerlite.com/forms/892614/13013 6824777541065/share

If you'd like to browse her books and get access to VIP content such as excerpts from upcoming books or deleted scenes, visit her website: https://rosegravestone.com/

If you're interested in reading her works-in-progress (pre-edits and re-writes for publishing) she has a Patreon where she posts chapters of books she's working on: https://patreon.com/rosesreaders